PEOPLE OF ABANDONED CHARACTER

PEOPLE OF ABANDONED CHARACTER

Clare Whitfield

HEAD
of ZEUS

ISBN (HB): 9781838932732
ISBN (XTPB): 9781838932749
ISBN (E): 9781838932800

Typeset by Divaddict Publishing Solutions Ltd

Printed and bound in Great Britain by
CPI Group (UK) Ltd, Croydon CR0 4YY

MIX
Paper from
responsible sources
FSC
www.fsc.org
FSC® C020471

Head of Zeus Ltd
First Floor East
5–8 Hardwick Street
London EC1R 4RG

WWW.HEADOFZEUS.COM

For Team Riley-Whitfield

'Thus also faith by itself, if it does not have works, is dead.'

James 2:17 New King James Version

One More Gone to London

Reading, 1885

I t was a bad day for a funeral: the wind was high, the sun weak and the threat of rain too strong. Impossible to dress for. Impossible. The sun came out and one wilted under all those layers – the woollen greatcoat, the sober waistcoat, the top hat – and then a breeze took up and one's fingers turned blue. Impossible.

Mr Radcliffe noted the sparse congregation. As the deceased's solicitor, he was duty bound to attend, but the vicar's wife had had to practically coerce people from the parish to pay their respects, so she'd said. St Bartholomew's was a crumbling relic of a church, so at least the small pews didn't appear so vacant. Mrs Alma Chapman had insisted on being buried there, in 'the real church', next to her husband. The church proper was now in the main village; a bigger, better church, for a bigger, better England.

For each shovelful of earth the gravedigger attempted to throw on top of the late Mrs Chapman, a gust of wind blew *most of it across the faces of the people standing around the grave willing the whole torturous event to a conclusion. A last laugh, perhaps; an indication of the old woman's feelings towards the congregation. It was not a dignified or elegant spot; the farm was in plain view, the donkey could be heard braying, and as the wind took up the gravedigger's earth once again, the gathering finally gave up and started to move away. Even the vicar retreated.*

Now it was only Mr Radcliffe and the Chapman grand-daughter, a tall column of black, her mourning veil pressed against her cheeks by the wind. Hands clasped in pious, observant grief. She appeared young enough, though according to his records the girl was very much a woman. But then everyone looked young to him these days, and he never had had a firm grasp on how to judge a woman's age. They did things to themselves, with hair, and feathers and hats; it could be most confusing.

Mr Radcliffe knew Susannah Chapman the way he knew most people, through annotations in documents: records of life and death, the stuff of ink and blotting paper. The poor thing, what should a girl-woman do with herself when she had no male relatives to offer protection and no real wealth behind her? Throw herself on the mercy of those that would have her, he supposed. In his head he had already prepared what he would say to her after the funeral. A few short words of solace, inspiration, even. He had been overly preoccupied with this, for what could a man of his age have to say to a young woman? For once he wished he'd brought his wife along.

He would start along the lines of: 'Death, to those left behind, does not mean the end but a new beginning. We must

forge a new path, over muddy tracks and hard ground...'
He was especially fond of the 'muddy tracks' part, but as he
took the first step to deliver his monologue, the girl gathered
her skirts out of the boggy ground and turned to leave, and
he had to almost gallop to catch her. It was not lost on him
that it was now he who was negotiating a muddy track.

'Miss Chapman, won't you wait a minute. I only want
to speak with you a moment.' Mr Radcliffe waved his hat,
quite out of breath by the time he caught up with her.

'Forgive me, I'm sorry to bother you so soon after your
grandmother's passing. I only mean to leave you with a
thought, and that is that, for you, this is a new beginning—'

'Yes, Mr Radcliffe, thank you. I understand. I'm sorry,
I must hurry. I have much to do.' And she turned like a
great black obelisk, the veil making it impossible to see her
features clearly.

'Allow me to walk with you, Miss Chapman. I have news
that could offer you some reassurance, security, even,' he
said, making strenuous efforts to keep up with the young
woman's stride.

He explained how he had been approached by the vicar's
wife with an offer of accommodation and a small salary
in exchange for domestic and educational assistance with
her six girls. Now that both Miss Chapman's grandparents
were dead, the best she could do would be to rent their
house to tenants and find herself a husband, quick smart.

'I would ask you to thank the vicar and his wife for me
formally, but I will have to decline their kind and generous
offer,' she said. 'I'm off to London, on the first train
tomorrow.'

Well, that was quite unexpected.

'Whatever for?' he said, feeling dread at what he anticipated would be the most naive of answers.

What was it about London that turned the heads of silly women? What could a spinster of twenty-seven from a small village know of London and its insatiable appetites? How many girls had floated to the city on clouds of dreams only to fall into bad habits with bad people? The air was yellow, the stink of the river enough to make one choke, and beggars slept in heaps in the open like flea-ridden cats. More than once he had walked a street and not heard a word of his own language. In his own country!

It was certainly no place for an unmarried woman. These young girls, they thought it would be all hats and dresses. That they would go to the races every day, pick flowers in the park and be courted by a line of enamoured dukes waiting on bended knee. If only they knew of the broken-spirited, the hungry and the homeless, they'd never set a foot on the train.

'I am to become a nurse, Mr Radcliffe, at the London Hospital, in Whitechapel. Really, I am grateful for the offer, but I can't stay, not another minute. Not now they are both gone. You must understand.'

'Well then, my dear, I wish you good luck in your endeavours. I was making assumptions, but I can see you are a strategist – no, a pioneer!'

She bid him farewell and left him sinking further into the mud. There was scant hope she would thrive. It was not the way of the city. In a village, a man could make a little money with hard work, be honest, fear God and heave himself up a rung or two. He could call himself a success. London was no place for ascension, despite all the promises. Oh, *there was gold, all right: a fortune could be won and lost, or stolen, on the same day. But only the rich, the criminal or the criminally insane thrived in London.*

1

1888

We married in St Jude's, Whitechapel, a tiny dilapidated church that appeared to have sprouted like
a fungus between two unconcerned buildings in
Commercial Street. The vicar complained that the congregation only ventured inside on Sundays if it rained, and even
then expected dole money, otherwise they'd be skipping
and dipping down Petticoat Lane. I wore a blue travelling
dress and a straw bonnet that Sister Park had insisted on
decorating with a veil and paper orange blossoms, squinting
at it by candlelight in the room we shared above the hospital.
I told her to save her eyes, but she wouldn't hear of it, being
the sort that finds cheer in such pointless rituals.

Thomas's best man was a fellow doctor, Dr Richard
Lovett. I remembered him vaguely from the hospital, our
paths not destined to cross, and only met him properly the
day we were married. They seemed as close as two friends
could be: laughing with each other, elbows into ribs and
sly winks. They even resembled each other, both being

dark and well groomed, tall and slender; they could have been brothers.

As soon as we were married, I told Matron Luckes, and she fired me on the spot, as I knew she would. A married woman could only devote herself to one profession, that of wife. Nursing was too demanding a career to accept anything other than complete devotion. There ended my career, the career I'd gambled my very existence on procuring, in the process rejecting everything my grandmother had wished for me. I had moved willingly to quite possibly the worst part of London and for two years had studied until I was near blind, to attain the coveted position of ward sister. Now I'd thrown that all away with both hands in a fit of cavalier delirium. Nevertheless, I couldn't believe my luck: a plain old maid like me marrying so well, and to a young and beautiful man who adored me. It shouldn't have happened. For a moment I really did believe in miracles.

I was giddy with joy and excited for our future. I felt rubber-stamped and approved by all things proper. Catapulted into another realm. Only weeks before, I had not known how I would carry on or what to do with myself, and now I had an entirely different existence and someone to make this future with. There was only one instance when I played my part badly. In the run-up to our marriage, when he suggested we honeymoon in Brighton, I hesitated. He asked if I'd ever been there before. I lied and said no. It was not a bad lie, but Brighton held memories for me and there would be no easy way to explain it.

My new husband took me to a hotel called the Royal Albion opposite Brighton Pier. It rained constantly, but I barely noticed. Summer had trouble starting in the year of

1888; it coughed and spluttered, trying to clear its lungs of a bitter winter. Only the occasional blast of light was able to break through the ashen clouds. We locked ourselves away in our room with its huge windows up to the ceiling. The murders hadn't started yet. I was just another June bride on her honeymoon, struck with euphoria at my novel world, unaware the newlywed glow would tarnish.

At night, the wind would become trapped inside our hotel room and howl around the ceiling. We lay in bed and listened to its whistling with our limbs wrapped around each other, the skin of our bodies smooth and warm, like paper.

'See how we fit, Chapman,' he said. 'We fit so perfectly together, don't you think? As if we were chiselled from the same piece of rock. Made to match.'

And we did fit. I was happy. It was such sudden relief from the misery I'd nearly drowned in, I almost didn't recognise it. This new excitement at a future with someone else, after I'd given up all hope of ever feeling happiness again. We stayed in bed morning, noon and night in those first days. Thomas was building his private practice and had few patients on his books, which made it the perfect time to take a holiday. Soon he'd be far too busy to take any leave. He had grand ambitions, my wonderful husband. If we did not take a holiday now, when would we next have the chance? Anything was possible. Everything could be ours. That was the feeling I'd missed, the feeling that the future could and would be marvellous. Together we would make it so.

We used to leave our burrow for food, and then, like children, we'd chase each other up the stairs on all fours and disappear under the bedclothes. He showed me how to put drops of laudanum in brandy, which burned my chest and made my head seem as if it would explode, like I was falling down a bottomless black hole. But when he kissed me all over, I burst into fits of laughter. We were living in a barrel of feathers.

Thomas experienced the world through his senses, and he had an appetite for it all: food and music, art and beautiful things, architecture and adventure, liquor and laudanum. We were no angels, but we never professed to be. Thomas was drawn on impulse to whatever would give him pleasure in that moment, and, in those days, pleasing me was one such thing. It was a soft and sensory experience; all lust. As yet I was unaware the same desires would quickly become a burden. I was fascinated by him. After the dark events of the last few months, I felt I was being pushed in a different direction and that this was the right path, the life in the light I craved. This man and my role of wife would be the new terrain I could explore and conquer. I would be damn good at it.

Thomas was often like an excitable child, skipping around, eyes always on me, bleary with a damp glaze as if spellbound. He tried to hold my hand at all times. I would wait as long as I could, then attempt to slip free, only for his fingers to search mine out again. His attention was so intense, it was embarrassing. People stared, although I don't believe he noticed. It was as if he didn't care about anything or anyone but us. This wasn't driven by rudeness or a conscious aim to offend; it was simply a matter of training. Thomas had never been conditioned to consider others or to imagine he might not matter as much as other people.

Thomas thought he mattered very much, and, as his wife, so did I.

I wanted nothing more than to be like him. Now that I was married to an upper-middle-class doctor, I pictured a life free of the exhausting, ever looming fear of poverty, free of the drudgery of hard, physical labour, of never being able to earn enough money to put a bit aside. Now at last I had the opportunity to create wealth rather than merely exist. This was my chance. I only had one job: to stop myself from ruining it.

2

After our honeymoon, we travelled straight to the house in Chelsea. I hadn't had time to think about what it would be like, so when our cab pulled up outside I found my knees trembling with fear that I would be found out for a fraud. I had to keep my hands together to stop the shaking being so obvious. I had never lived with servants or a housekeeper. Growing up with my grandparents, there was a charlady, and a gardener came occasionally after my grandfather died, but no one lived in. I had no clue how to manage the situation and any savvy servants would quickly sniff out my ignorance. They wouldn't think me good enough to be the doctor's wife, and they would be quite right. I hadn't been trained for the role at all. I tried to steady my nerves by asking questions, but mostly I was consumed by how ridiculously unprepared I was. What kind of mistress was frightened of the staff?

'You can rely on old Mrs Wiggs, my housekeeper,' Thomas said, 'above all others, including myself. She's the most reliable, steady hand you'll ever meet. By rights she should have been born a duchess, but fortunately she was gifted to us and she's been with the family since my sister and I were babes-in-arms. Mrs Wiggs comes with the fittings in the Lancaster household. We are lucky to have her.'

I was finally ready to meet Mrs Wiggs in person. After Thomas's glowing description, I had imagined a short, squat woman with blonde curls and a bosom deep enough to suffocate a small child. She would have a warm smile and bovine eyes, always on the cusp of tears, on account of her emotional generosity.

As we walked through the door, Mrs Wiggs was waiting in the hallway to greet us. Emotional generosity was not the immediate impression I had. The air around her was stiff and frozen. The instinctive reaction was to hold your breath, as I did then.

'It truly is wonderful to welcome you to our household, Mrs Lancaster,' she said.

Thomas closed the door behind us and we were plunged into gloom, our eyes too used to the daylight to adjust to our new surroundings. The only illumination was a candle on a cabinet with a mirror above it that made the flame flicker in on itself continually, distracting me, demanding attention. Mrs Wiggs stepped forward into its light and I had to tell myself to loosen my grip on Thomas's arm.

The only part of her that moved were her eyes; they drank me in, up and down. When Thomas introduced us, she mustered a smile I recognised, the sort I used to rustle up as I reassured a patient about to go into theatre that they would not be losing a leg. It was unconvincing at best.

'I said, it's wonderful to welcome you to our household, Mrs Lancaster. Did you have a good journey? You must be tired.'

I realised I hadn't responded, only stared at her like a wide-eyed goldfish.

'Oh, yes. Thank you, Mrs Wiggs. The journey was... bearable, thank you. I'm not too tired, but thank you for asking. Thomas assures me we will be great friends. I very much hope so. He tells me you are indispensable.'

What can I say? I panicked. I went for flattery in the absence of authority. I could cringe at my babbling.

'Of course, madam, if that's what you wish.'

'Are there any other servants I should meet?' I asked. I was sure there had to be other members of staff – weren't they meant to trot out and greet me in a line?

Thomas smiled a close-lipped smile I didn't recognise and looked to Mrs Wiggs.

'We have a cook and a scullery maid, Sarah,' she said. 'Also a gardener, and the odd charlady as and when. But, Mrs Lancaster, please, if you need anything, just come to me and I'll take care of everything.'

'See, Chapman, no need for you to think of a thing,' said Thomas.

By this time he had unpeeled my fingers from his arm and found his place beside her, smiling like a portrait and looking about the house as if reorienting himself with its contents. It was as if the conversation we'd had in the cab had not happened and he was oblivious to my need for reassurance. Mrs Wiggs didn't take her eyes off me.

I would learn that Mrs Wiggs had, like a nun, spent her life in servitude to the Lancasters and that she took her devotion quite as seriously. She had amber eyes with glints of orange and dull hair that bore remnants of when it had been fair, always scraped back into a bun. I could not tell how old she was – no grey around her temples, and her skin was smooth – but she must have been in her forties. Not that I dared ask. I was terrified of her. I was certain she could see right down into the pit of my stomach and would uncover everything I had kept secret. She had this petrifying stare, like an owl, big round eyes with heavy lids, and I was a mouse watched by this bird tethered only by loyalty to her master. Mrs Wiggs was always observing, taking notes and already forming hard opinions.

Those first days were polite but passionate. We danced around each other, and Mrs Wiggs watched from a comfortable distance. We played mummies and daddies in our own house, giggling at the grown-up absurdity of it all, lacking a blueprint for how to be a real man and wife. Then, as if the whole thing had been made of thin glass that was always destined to shatter, we had our first disagreement, if you can call it that. It all unravelled from there, I think. By this one misunderstanding, which I can only describe as an embarrassing encounter in the dark, we poisoned the bones of our marriage, and after that the whole beast had to be abandoned. Or that's how it felt. It was probably poisoned before that point, but that was the starter pistol for its undoing.

We had been in the house less than a week. I was waiting for him to come home, staring at the clock, and rushed to greet him at the door. Mrs Wiggs followed close behind. We had dinner, as had already become usual, and moved upstairs. Our little habit of brandy and drops had continued away from Mrs Wiggs' prying eyes. Thomas liked to relax after work and I joined him. Things developed as you might have expected them to between newlyweds, but then he tried to take them in a bizarre direction and I protested. I was confused, nothing more. I really wasn't sure what he was after, but I hadn't been trying to humiliate him. When I understood what he was asking me to do, I was horrified and said I didn't want to. I told him it wasn't natural, and this offended him. He asked me what I meant by that, and I said I hadn't intended anything and was sorry, but he pushed me down on the bed, stood up, got dressed, and told me I was demanding and selfish and spoiled.

He stormed out of the bedroom and I paced around it, confused, embarrassed and worrying. I waited for him to come back. I was sure once his embarrassment had worn off he would return. Then I heard the slamming of the front door; it bounced on its hinges and shook the whole house.

He didn't come back until the early hours. I know because I waited up and eventually gave up and went to bed around one. The front of the house creaked like old knees whenever the front door opened, and our bedroom was above it. It must have been around four: the sky was still inky, the streets quiet save for the odd cartman or flowergirl on their way to work. I lay waiting for him to come, but he never did. His footsteps passed the bedroom and he must have seen the candlelight from under the door and known I was awake, but he continued along the landing and up the small staircase to the attic. For a man who professed to crave me, he did a good job of not yielding to his addiction. It was my first week in our home.

3

At breakfast the next morning we ignored each other. I was waiting for him to ask me what the matter was, which of course he didn't, which of course drove me insane.

All I could hear was the sound of his teeth grinding on his breakfast. I, on the other hand, could only take measly bites. The gentle clatter of cutlery against china supplied a monotonous rhythm; that and Mrs Wiggs, who kept on swinging in and out like a hurricane with more food. I fought the urge to make conversation because I was still firmly of the mind that it was he who had stormed out on me and therefore I was not the guilty party. I had apologised for my reaction at the time. He wouldn't even look at me and I began to feel quite anxious as this was very unlike him. He adored me. I would have been quite happy to disregard the whole awful event and put it down to a misunderstanding, but he was still carrying a lot of anger, which he appeared to be taking out on his toast. If he was upset, it hadn't disturbed his appetite as it had mine.

It didn't take long for Mrs Wiggs to notice the atmosphere. She kept looking at me, then at Thomas, then back at me. I could feel her eyes, though I refused to meet them. She hovered over Thomas as she poured his tea. She was obviously working herself up to say something.

'What time would you prefer dinner served tonight, Dr Lancaster?' she began. 'Mrs Lancaster, would you like me to have Sarah pick up anything in particular? I wonder if you have any family recipes you would like to introduce to the household. It would make it more familiar for you and it would broaden our horizons. Lord knows we've plundered Cook's finite reservoir of ideas several times over.'

'Oh no, Mrs Wiggs, nothing springs to mind.' I had nothing in the bank on this one. I had always been lazy and unconcerned about food. I felt like a disappointment and imagined a good wife would have memorised a thousand recipes already. 'I'll have to think,' I said.

'Very well,' said Mrs Wiggs. 'We look forward to your contribution.'

'I have no idea what time I'll be home tonight,' said Thomas.

'Oh, are you going somewhere?' I asked.

'Not sure what time I'll be finished,' he said, still looking at his damn plate.

'We will wait for you, Dr Lancaster,' said Mrs Wiggs. 'We won't have you starve after a day of work.'

'No, you carry on. No need to wait for me.'

I was about to take a breath and ask him where he was planning to be, but Mrs Wiggs got there first.

'You were out very late last night, Dr Lancaster,' she said.

Thomas shot her a filthy look and she recoiled. Even I winced, and she quickly corrected herself.

'I'm sorry, sir. Forgive me. I am only concerned that you might tire yourself.' She scooped up the tea and made her way towards me.

'Thank you for your interest, Mrs Wiggs, but in case you hadn't realised, I'm a doctor, therefore I'm quite capable of looking after my own health. I'll be out. Why don't you and Mrs Lancaster study the recipe books and see if you can come up with something.'

Mrs Wiggs skulked out of the room.

I couldn't leave it any longer. I couldn't have him going to work and not coming back without having resolved the atmosphere between us.

'It isn't because of last night, is it?' I said.

He lifted his gaze to meet mine for the first time that morning, eyes dead, cold, flat. 'Last night? What about last night?'

I was confused. It was quite obvious what I was referring to, but I wasn't going to say it, it had been embarrassing enough the first time. I wasn't going to describe the event in words, over breakfast.

'I thought perhaps you were still angry with me,' I said.

'Angry? I do have things on my mind other than you, Chapman. I'm not always obsessing over what you might be thinking. I'll leave that to you.'

He stood up, threw his napkin down, walked over and pecked me on the cheek. I smiled at him and half laughed, thankful he was speaking to me, but to be honest I couldn't tell whether he was trying to make light of it for both our sakes or insinuating I was stupid.

Moments later, I heard him and Mrs Wiggs whispering by the front door, though I couldn't make out what they were saying. Then the front door closed.

Mrs Wiggs came back to start clearing away and I went to leave.

'Mrs Lancaster, has something happened between you and the doctor?' she asked.

I was taken aback that she would be so intrusive. It had been my assumption it was not for housekeepers to broach personal matters with their mistresses, but she had me on the back foot, doubting myself, and for a moment I considered I might have an ally. Then I thought better of it. I would take Thomas's lead on this and forget the whole incident.

'No, Mrs Wiggs, everything is as it should be,' I said.

'Is it?' I think her eyebrows lifted a little as she smiled sweetly. 'Well then, that's good. Only the doctor didn't seem himself this morning and I wondered if something had happened.'

'No, Mrs Wiggs. I don't...' I wanted to tell her to mind her own affairs and get her pointy beak back in the kitchen where it belonged. My friend Aisling would have told her where to stick it in a heartbeat, but I was so unsure of how things should be. 'Everything is fine.'

'Forgive me, Mrs Lancaster. I apologise if I have made you uncomfortable. I only wish to help. Perhaps I have overstepped a little. How clumsy of me. Please accept my apologies.'

'No need to apologise, thank you, Mrs Wiggs. I'll start thinking about those recipes.'

I had almost made the door when she said, 'I'd always assumed a newlywed husband would *want* to come home.

Perhaps we should be thinking about more than recipes for dinner, to make sure the doctor looks forward to returning each night.'

'I beg your pardon?' My head nearly snapped off. Had I understood the insinuation correctly?

'Flowers!' she exclaimed. 'The doctor has always loved fresh flowers, bright colours, strong scents. He has a discerning nose. I'll arrange to have fresh flowers delivered every day and we can rotate the arrangements around the house. It will brighten every room, and he'll never know what to expect. It can get a little gloomy at the front of the house, can't it? We need to put some effort into keeping it inviting.'

She carried a tray of plates past me, beaming. I felt even more unsettled, and confused about every conversation I'd had that morning. Had we really been discussing flowers?

It was my nerves, reading too much into things. It was ridiculous of me to think anything else. If only I could have told Aisling. She would have been bursting with opinions on how I should deal with it all.

I decided to pull myself together. The best way to banish this feeling of inferiority would be to find a useful purpose for myself. I would throw myself into learning the ropes. I spotted Mrs Wiggs walking down the hallway as I was coming down the stairs. A narrow corridor led through the pantry and into the kitchen and I saw her bun disappearing down it.

'Mrs Wiggs!' I called out.

The woman was no more than a few feet away, but

she didn't stop or turn back, just kept walking. I assumed she hadn't heard me and scurried after her down the passageway. She opened the door to the kitchen and I was immediately behind her. She turned around, locked eyes with me, her hand still on the door. I smiled at her and she held my gaze.

'Mrs Wiggs, I'm glad I caught you. I was only wondering if—'

She closed the door on me.

I was stood there, quite the fool, feeling confused and conversing with a door. I knocked on it and waited. There was no answer. I put my hand on the handle. I faltered, regained my courage, thrust the door open and closed it behind me.

Mrs Wiggs was addressing Cook and Sarah and stopped talking as soon as I entered. Neither Sarah nor Cook raised their eyes, and Mrs Wiggs seemed bemused that I was there.

'Mrs Lancaster, I was in the middle of instructing the staff on the requirements for today.'

'Right, well, carry on,' I said, sounding more sergeant major than I intended.

Both servants kept their eyes firmly on the floor, and Mrs Wiggs looked about the room as if a bird had flown in.

'Carry on with what, Mrs Lancaster?' she asked.

'Well, if there are instructions to be given, I should be aware of them so I might contribute to the running of the household. I have been thinking that I would very much like to learn the way things are done here. After all, I am... I have run my own ward and assisted in surgery, so I'm confident that with the right guidance I can lend a hand here.' I finished on a flourish, thinking of Matron's motivating speeches where she would rally us as if we were in the army.

I could almost hear the drilling of the servants' eyes as they bored their way through the kitchen floor, trying to find a place they didn't have to witness this, whatever this was. Mrs Wiggs fixed me with a glacial smile, looked towards the servants, looked at the floor as if she were accessing her reserves of patience, and turned to me.

'Mrs Lancaster, this is a wonderful idea and I think it would be best if we began by discussing how to approach it. Perhaps we could do so in the front dining room. There is a fire in there, you'll be warm. I shall be with you as soon as I can.'

I nodded obediently, damn near curtseyed, and closed the door behind me like a meek little girl.

I waited for Mrs Wiggs for well over an hour and she never did come. When I found her, my blood boiling, she apologised and made some excuse about Sarah not having the hot ashes collected, and then discovered that the potatoes for dinner all had eyes, and how by the time she got to the front dining room I had left. I'm sure she found this little farce hilarious.

I had heard I was to be mistress of the house; however, it seemed it already had one. I felt utterly useless, but I would simply have to try harder. Things were always difficult in the beginning. The hospital had been a lonely and unfamiliar business before I'd met Aisling, and I hadn't won this place in the world to give in so easily. This time I would have to work it out for myself. I was sure I could make my marriage a success, and I was still optimistic that even Mrs Wiggs would come to appreciate my efforts eventually.

4

The conversation about flowers haunted me more than it should have. I couldn't help but think that Mrs Wiggs had been referring to my appearance. I had never been good with fashion and paid little attention to my grooming beyond looking clean and presentable. It held no interest for me until I met Aisling at the hospital. She used to help me with my hair and advise which colours I should wear to suit my complexion and which to avoid. Before her, well, they were simply colours. I picked them because I liked them, even if they didn't like me, as she used to tell me.

Aisling said that if you were feeling small, then the trick was to go out and buy a daring dress, a bigger hat; to take a lesson from the animal kingdom and frighten your opponents with exotic plumage until your courage caught up. I needed only to acquire some exotic plumage. Now that the incident with Thomas seemed to have passed, I wanted to make more of an impression and get things back to the way they'd been when I'd had to constantly slap his hands away. Maybe the front of the house did look a little tired. I would spruce it up.

There was also another conversation I needed to have with Thomas, one I hadn't banked on having so quickly. I thought I might be expecting. I was unsure whether to discuss this with him yet, but I was disquieted at being in this new house and displeasing him, and I sensed his attention waning, so I thought... Well, I thought it might help me win back some favour.

I had the idea that if I asked Mrs Wiggs for her assistance, it would make her feel important and might earn me some approval. I felt a little unctuous, but I was willing to do what was necessary, so I let her style my hair. She had been offering to do this since my first day, but I had brushed her away. I hadn't felt the need for it and I wasn't comfortable with her touching me. It gave me the shivers, echoes of the times my grandmother used to brush my hair, hitting me on the head with the brush and near scratching my eyelashes out with each stroke.

When I asked Mrs Wiggs if she would consider helping me with my hair that night, an evening when Thomas had condescended to confirm that he would be home for dinner, she became the most animated I'd ever seen her.

'Really, Mrs Lancaster? Are you sure? You didn't seem keen when I offered before,' she said.

'It was only that I was overwhelmed at being in a new place, surrounded by new things and new people, but it is a weakness of mine and I thought—'

'I have always helped dress the ladies of the house. I have vast experience. I'm so glad you've finally asked me.'

My hair has a natural curl, which makes it stubborn and difficult to work with. Instead of over-preening, I tend to roll it away from my head, allowing any wayward curls to fall around my face. When it came to Mrs Wiggs touching it, she made faces, which I could see in the mirror. This irritated me, of course, and I had to stop my own eyes from rolling because she could see me in the mirror too. She continually commented on how coarse my hair was and how stubborn the curl. Being the owner of the hair, I was well aware of this.

'Where did you say your family were from?' she asked, brushing and yanking my hair so forcefully I could feel my eyebrows being pulled.

'Scotland,' I said. 'They were from Fife.'

'Scotland!' she scoffed. 'Really? I had no idea you were a Scot.'

'I'm not. I was born in England, my father was… English.' I was anxious not to be drawn further into this and have my story unravel, so I turned the conversation around. 'What about you, Mrs Wiggs? Where do you come from?'

Without thinking, I turned around to look up at her. She took my temples firmly in her hands and swivelled my head back to face the mirror.

'Oh, here and there,' she said, tugging at my hair again, making my eyes water.

'You must have been born in a single place.'

'Bristol,' she said, and that was the end of that particular conversation. I sensed I was not the only one being intentionally vague about her origins.

'Scots! I had no idea!' she said again. 'I should think they were Moors, going by your hair.' She sighed. 'It's going to be very difficult to do anything elegant with this, Mrs Lancaster.'

By the time she'd finished, it was up on the very top of my

head, a great pile of ringlets, but flat at the sides and the back. I looked more ewe than woman. That wasn't the worst: she then took to my wardrobe like a plague of moths. She pulled out each dress in turn, held it aloft with a furrowed brow, as if by examining it more closely it might improve, replaced it, sighed, and went on to the next one. Soon she was uttering unintelligible mutterings. When she finally settled on the dress she found the least offensive, I had to laugh, because it was green – pale pistachio green – the very colour Aisling said made me look like a consumptive on the cusp of death. *The kind that rattles, like they're sucking on an empty bottle through a straw. The ones you wish would hurry up and die.*

I agreed to wear it, purely to put an end to the whole ordeal and to please Mrs Wiggs. I hoped that Thomas would be like most men and not notice what colour did what to my complexion.

I had a headache by the time dinner was served. When I sat down at the table, Thomas gawped at me with a horrified expression.

'What on earth have you done to your hair?' he asked, not taking his eyes off me and putting his napkin on his lap with his mouth open.

'I thought I would try something different. Do you like it?'

'No, Susannah, I do not. It's far too high. I'll look quite the circus freak standing next to you – people will think me a dwarf. And for a person who has a very slim face, it somehow makes yours appear round, as round as a pie.'

I felt ridiculous, and I couldn't help but wonder if Mrs Wiggs had done this on purpose. Or if she was simply clueless and I was stupid for asking.

We carried on with dinner. I was determined to make the evening a good one, even if it had got off to a bad start.

But then he said, 'You look a little off-colour – greenish. Do you feel well?'

'This bloody dress,' I muttered under my breath, throwing my napkin down and sitting back.

'I beg your pardon? What did you say?'

'Nothing, Thomas. I said nothing.'

The greenish tinge to my skin was my cue to embark on the subject the whole evening was balanced on.

'I have been feeling a little off-colour over the last few days.'

'Really? What's wrong? How fortunate that you have married a doctor. How can I be of service, Chapman?'

I had no eloquent way of broaching the delicate subject, so I plunged in and hoped my tongue would stumble across its own plan. 'I think I may be... I have momentarily *ceased to be unwell* of late,' I said, and hoped he understood.

His reaction was not what I expected. It sucked the air right out of his lungs, and his face dropped into a long grey tombstone. He kept blinking his eyelids as if he were a broken puppet.

'Thomas?' I prompted.

The silence went on so long, I bent forward and tried to take his hand, but he snatched it away before I could reach it, which made me jump.

'Shit!' he said, and slammed his palm down on the table.

He sat there with a vein throbbing in his forehead and his fists clenched and for a minute I thought he might throw something. I had never seen him like that before.

'What's wrong?' I asked, in a voice as thin as reeds.

'Nothing!' he snapped. 'Nothing. I need to think.'

He stood up and exited the room, leaving me at the table wondering how a whole day of careful planning had gone so wrong. I felt such a clumsy stranger. Whatever I did or said, it seemed I was cursed to make mistakes.

Thomas didn't say it, but I could tell he blamed me, as if I had conjured up by witchcraft a working womb by which to ruin everything. Then, a few days later, when everything returned, I was in a rush to tell him how it had been a mistake, a miscalculation, the upset to my routine brought on by the disruption of my new circumstances. I thought he would be relieved, but instead he was angry all over again. Albeit not so explosively. This time, his immediate concern was what others would think.

'But I've told people at the hospital I'm going to be a father. Dr Treives even congratulated me when he heard the news! How embarrassing. Well... we shall have to say there was an accident, that you fell down the stairs.'

'I didn't think for a moment you would tell anyone,' I said. I had been under the impression that I could appeal to his reason, but one of the many lessons I would learn is that marriage is often a barren landscape, devoid of logic and reason. As it was in this case, it seemed.

'This is just like you, Susannah!' he shouted. 'You are always so dramatic. In future, you should wait until you are sure before telling me such a thing. Why bother me with these female matters anyway? You know what everyone will think—'

I was entirely unprepared for what came next.

'—that you are too old for me. People will laugh at us. Honestly, Susannah, so much fuss over nothing, all caused by your insatiable need for attention. I could really do without the... the chaos of your imagination.'

I was upset and started crying. He told me I was hysterical. This from the man who'd been upset I might be expecting and then upset that I wasn't. We had been married a matter of weeks and I was already confused by his behaviour. But I would forgive him. In fact I would fawn over him, eager to do anything to make peace between us.

Dr Thomas Lancaster was six foot two and elegant, unlike so many tall men who are a mass of knees and elbows. He would glide into a room, shoulders back, as if he were about to dance with every woman in it. I was five foot nine in bare feet and had spent my entire life hunched over in an effort not to loom over other girls. He was twenty-five, five years younger than me, and I was extremely conscious of this. There had been glimpses of what you might call immaturity before our marriage, but flaws are an expensive habit and Thomas Lancaster could afford them.

I accepted the blows about my age and my imaginary dramatics, the jibes about my deficient grooming, the criticism of my education and lack of feminine instinct in all things, because when Thomas entered a space, everything was drawn to him; even the furniture turned inches. He had this way of making you feel like an exquisite thing, a rarity on earth, that it was you and not him who was mesmerising. When he left, he dragged that sense away with him. Without his attention, I was ordinary and dull again.

Everything was my fault, it had to be, and I would fix it. I'd had to learn how to be a nurse; I could learn how to be a wife. I had come to think of life as a ladder made of silk thread that floated on air, barely visible, and like a spider's web only caught the light in places. I was pulling myself up rung by rung, and yet it would take just one badly placed foot and I would plummet all the way to the bottom, to the workhouse or worse. My world, when I met Thomas, had been without hope, and he had offered me an escape. That fact alone demanded some loyalty, did it not? I'd still be stuck at the hospital if he hadn't picked me.

My mother was an unmarried girl of sixteen when she had me, and for the first few years of my childhood, until she died, she and I lived in Whitechapel in a single room on Dorset Street, within the fetid maze of dark alleyways and courts called the Nichol. This was one of several details about my past that I had declined to furnish Thomas with. As far as I was aware, I was the only person left alive who knew of my insalubrious start.

It would be fair to say that Whitechapel had developed into an embarrassing boil on the backside of London, which had a habit of pulling up its trousers and pretending it wasn't there. England's capital was the richest and most powerful city in the world, but you'd never know it going by neighbourhoods like Whitechapel. Throngs of fortune-seekers poured into London from every corner of the country and from the far reaches of the empire beyond – the Irish in a continuous dribble that ebbed and flowed, the Jews fleeing pogroms, the Chinese, the Indians, the Africans, the merchants – and the undesirables among them drifted east, to Whitechapel, like the waste sent out on the tide at

Crossness. My mother too. The rich tarred us native poor of England as lazy and inept, but regardless of the truth or otherwise in that, we unfortunates had nowhere else to go and so we piled up on top of each other in the East End as if driven into a wall.

If Whitechapel was the worst of London, the thirty lanes and courts of the Nichol were the worst of Whitechapel. The parishes of these parts didn't have shitrakers, because tenants couldn't pay, and nor could we afford lighting, so the streets were deep in foul-smelling rubbish and swilling with blood and urine from the tanneries and abattoirs. At night it was a lawless, pitch-black wilderness. The terraced buildings were dry and brittle on the outside and dank and swollen inside. They were crammed to bursting: a single terrace would have sixty or seventy residents, with every adult paying an extortionate rent as a percentage of their pathetic earnings. Many had more than one family sharing a room, with only a hung sheet to separate them. Adults and children slept naked like fish in a bucket; babies were made and waste was excreted all in the same room. Rotten staircases and ceilings collapsed and the wallpaper rippled with vermin. Some lived in inches of filthy water in the flooded cellars, breathing in bacteria and disease. Everywhere stank, thick with the stench of sweat and shit and whatever odour came with the trade of that court's inhabitants: phosphorus, smoked fish, meat. Windows were either black with coal dust or broken and patched up with sacking or newspaper. Not that anyone ever opened them, as the reek from outside was worse. A few years living like that and our lungs never recovered. Little wonder that reaching thirty years of age was considered an achievement.

Strange to say, but the putrid terraces of the Nichol and the other Whitechapel slums were the most profitable in London. So many tenants, and so few improvements ever made. The better classes bemoaned our depravity and fecklessness and yet the buildings were owned by the very pontificating politicians, clergymen and lawmakers that professed to serve those they so despised. Such was the bleak existence I considered myself fortunate to have escaped. I could never be sure what was a real memory or what my imagination had created, but I knew some things, because my grandfather told me, although I didn't dare utter a single word to a soul about my mother, not until much later. Born a bastard, I was lucky to be taken in by my grandparents.

I have no memory of my father and not a clue what type of man he was. My grandmother said he was a gypsy, or a hawker or a navvy, whatever she felt would shame me into obedience; either way, he was not a good man. If anyone ever asked how I came to live with my grandparents, I was taught to say that my parents had died of scarlet fever. I was trained to repeat it, like a mynah bird, and no polite person ever asked more than that.

When my grandmother died, I was left her modest house in Reading with the perennial rat problem, and a small sum of money. Her solicitor, Mr Radcliffe, did honestly by me, but the legacy was not enough to live on and I needed an income, so I became a nurse. I was after a means to support myself and a skilled profession, which was how I found myself back in Whitechapel once again, this time at the London Hospital. We nurses did not live in the slum terraces of the Nichol, but our patients did. Caring for them was not without its dangers, as I was to discover. It was common to lose nurses during an epidemic, for we spent our lives inches from infection with little protection other than our own good practices in hygiene. Also, our patients could be violent.

I hadn't envisaged for a second being swept up in what I was to find at the London. I met Aisling, and for a while was living a life I had no idea existed let alone dared imagine. I was happy. It is a cruel trick that God made me learn such a lesson and then had it end so quickly. I certainly hadn't intended to find a husband, although many women came to nursing with that in mind, much to Matron's annoyance. She tried to sift out the starry-eyed nymphs on the hunt for wounded officers, but that was not in my plan.

Unless you come from wealth in England, you can only float above the fate of the poor, mere inches away from it yourself. You are on your own in this world; I accept that. It's not to say there isn't money rolling about and lots of it; it just stays in the same old families. The trick is to take some for yourself, and to do that you must be willing to play outside the rules. I have observed that life treats you more fairly if you come from a little money.

You must play the hand you are dealt and take the opportunities that present themselves, and present himself Dr Thomas Lancaster did. Who was I to reject God's plan?

5

I was engaged in teaching paying probationers at the London when I saw the man who would become my husband for the first time. My mood at that point was very low – so low that even Matron had taken note and in an act of mercy had moved me off frontline nursing and sent me to instruct the paying probationers in routine tasks. I missed Aisling. I was alone. I had come to London for freedom and a living and found much more than I had bargained on. But now that was gone. It really was better to be ignorant of something than to be painfully conscious of what I lacked. I was happier when I didn't understand I was lonely; now I was bereft.

I had imagined that nursing would be exciting and rewarding, but I did not feel like a pioneer: it was more hernias and bedpans than adventure. I felt trapped by an invisible straitjacket, choked by thick black fog. I could not see any choices ahead of me, and yet they had to be there. I only knew to walk through my little existence, behaving as expected, while life passed me by. I'd spent most of it being such a good girl, waiting to be rewarded, and now I had the sudden realisation I was waiting for something that would never come.

With Aisling gone, my life felt so hollow and meaningless that ideas of ending it crept in. The thoughts came rapidly and uninvited, crawling up and whispering sweetly in my ear, a gentle oiling to an idea in the absence of any other. I wondered how much it would hurt if I jumped from Tower Bridge, late at night so no one would see me, if the water would be very cold, and how long it would take to die. One afternoon, an open window on one of the wards had sucked the curtain out. I went to pull it back and thought how easy it would be to throw myself out. I could already picture myself on the ground, smashed and broken, a bloody bag of sticks, free of the perpetual fear as to what would become of me.

Teaching a roomful of girls the principles of bandaging and how to pad splints and prepare surgical dressings required minimal physical effort and very little emotional investment, which was perfect as far as I was concerned. Paying probationers were the moonfaced girls from middle- and upper-middle-class families who could afford to shell out for training. They tended to be plain and doughy, with thick middles and nondescript features. When all clustered together and gawping at me, it was much like giving a lecture to a heap of boiled potatoes. They were the odd sisters from affluent families, devoid of obvious charm; they couldn't sing, made clumsy dancers, and were in the habit of excitedly correcting each other. Lonely girls who clumped together, like bristles on a hairbrush. In other times they would have been sent to the convent. They reminded me of myself, which was why I found it hard to be kind to them, but they were a profitable source of income for the hospital. Once qualified, they would become the private nurses of aristocrats or other moneyed patients. The normal girls, like Aisling and myself, had to remain at the hospital for at least four years after training, and I was still in my first year. The thought of another three was overwhelming. The other option, of course, would be to get myself dismissed. I wasn't keen on that idea; the thought of being branded a failure, even voluntarily, was not something my pride could bear.

On this particular morning, I had the potatoes gathered around an empty bed and had started to lecture them on how to give a bedridden patient a bath when I became aware of two men at the back of the group who were chattering away as I tried to give the lesson. Distracted by their low voices rumbling under my own, my temper rose. How rude and typical of doctors to disrupt something they had not been invited to. I kept throwing them stern looks, but they carried on, oblivious. I recognised one as a hospital governor, but the other, younger and taller, I didn't recognise at all. When he burst out laughing and every one of the girls turned to look and started giggling, simply because they were in the proximity of a young man, I was furious.

'Sirs,' I said, 'how fortunate it is that you have joined us. We were about to discuss the principles of bed washing, and as you can see, our bed is empty. Perhaps one of you kind gentlemen will volunteer?' I patted the taut sheets.

There were gasps and twitching shoulders and my own cheeks began to burn. I had felt braver when the words were inside my head. The governor, an older man with an ostentatious waistcoat and a round stomach, flushed a deep purple and shuffled off, but the younger man didn't seem embarrassed at all. He laughed along with the girls, seemingly enjoying the attention, and stood with both hands in his pockets, which I thought incredibly rude. He struck me as obnoxious and arrogant, and his broad smile showed far too many teeth, like a prehistoric exhibit at the museum.

The second time I saw him, and the first time we really met, I was sat reading on a bench in the garden of the crypt behind the hospital. Two well-polished shoes came into view, and when I looked up it was the young man with too many teeth, which he was flashing at me, though at least his hands were out of his pockets.

'I feel I must give my apologies,' he said and offered his hand.

I stood up to take it, caught off-guard, and glanced around, worried it might be meant for someone behind me.

His black whiskers were groomed with surgical precision, but it was his voice that felled me. Something clicked into place when I heard it; the sound of it cleared my vision, or blurred it, perhaps. Low and smooth, it had the resonance and authority of an older man's; I can only describe it as gravel and honey.

'Oh, what you are apologising for?' I gave him my hand briefly, and snatched it back as fast as I could.

'For offending you. That was never my intention. You were commanding a group of probationers as if about to go into battle, and Dr Davenport said that you had a reputation—'

'Oh! A reputation? What reputation?' This worried me. With hindsight I can see I was strolling too easily into his little trap.

'In fact, he said he'd put money on you being the next matron.'

'Really?'

It was like shooting fish in a barrel, and I was a big clumsy stupid fish who'd never held a boy's hand. I was sweating under his flattery, and not just a gentle glow that brought colour to my cheeks – the skin of my face was wet. He must have noticed.

He had the longest black lashes I had ever seen, even on a woman. How wasted they were on a man like that, I thought, curling up and fluttering when by rights they belonged on a baby deer.

Thomas Lancaster came from a village near Bristol, had worked for two years in Edinburgh after completing his studies, and was now a surgeon at the London Hospital. As he was telling me this, I noticed that two young doctors had stopped at the gates to watch us. They were sniggering and whispering to each other and I sensed I was the victim of a cruel trick. Only much later did I realise that one of them was Richard Lovett, who would be Thomas's best man at our wedding.

'Wager, is it?' I said.

'I'm sorry?'

I gestured towards the gentlemen, and he turned to look at them, then back at me, and rolled his eyes.

'Again, let me apologise. I'm afraid they thought me bold for approaching you. Truth be told, I think they are frightened of women, especially nurses. I told them I was going to ask your name.'

'My name is Chapman.'

'Right. My name is—'

'You've told me your name. And you've already apologised, in case you've forgotten that too.'

'Yes, I have, haven't I? Do you know, Chapman, I think you are making me nervous.' He put a palm to his chest. 'It's a pleasure to meet you. May I ask your Christian name?'

The cheek of it. Hands in pockets and asking for Christian names. He tried to make my eyes meet his, and in response mine rolled around like marbles. His were intense, as if they were boring holes in my body out of which my secret thoughts would fly like paper messages that he would catch and read. I was not familiar with men socially. I only knew how to be shy or rude.

'Sister. My name to you will always be "Sister Chapman".' I chose rude. I walked past him with my chin in the air, my book clasped to my chest, and didn't say goodbye. I don't think I exhaled for at least five minutes after our encounter.

After that, he was everywhere. He made a point of seeking me out and talking to me as if we were on familiar terms. I wasn't sure how I had given him this impression. He wouldn't let me walk past him without him saying something, however inane.

'Good morning, Sister Chapman.' Or, 'Good afternoon, Sister Chapman.' Or, 'Weather's a bit gloomy, don't you agree?'

It was hugely embarrassing because the other nurses would watch, open-mouthed, wondering how on earth we knew each other. Everywhere I went, there he was, popping up or leaping into view with those ridiculous lashes.

I had made a few observations, mainly so that I could reason with myself when I found that I kept thinking of the toothy young man. He talked far too loudly and had a habit of making himself the centre of attention, wherever he was. His eyes were too pale and too feline, and they were overly large; he didn't blink often enough, to the point where more than once I worried how dry his eyes must be. Even his walk irked me: he was a strutting peacock of a man, with his chest puffed up and his head tilted. Whenever I saw him with nurses, which was often, I thought him a creep; he stood too close to them, making them blush or act coy, and that in itself caused me to wince. I thought him a tart and expected him to plough through the younger nurses like a donkey at harvest time. I was sure Nurse Mullens and he would seek each other out. She was exceptionally fair and seemed to be in nursing solely to find herself a suitable husband. I overheard girls talking about him in the lounge and couldn't understand why my insides did a loop when I heard his name. They discussed how charming he was, how elegant, how tall, and wasn't he kind and softly spoken. When he asked for assistance, didn't he ask sweetly! Another said she'd heard he was the son of a baronet.

That he had fluttered those lashes in my direction did flatter me, but I was not a girl who was commonly described as fair. I had to assume he was this way with all girls, and I was no girl, for by then I was thirty.

One night at the end of April, a fire broke out in a storeroom behind the hospital pharmacy. Thomas and his friend, Richard Lovett, were still trapped inside when the fire engines arrived. The receiving room had to be evacuated, causing chaos on Whitechapel Road, but the fire itself was put out quickly enough. Dr Lovett had somehow been knocked unconscious – they assumed by a falling object – so Thomas had thrown him over his shoulder and tried to flee. But one of Thomas's trouser legs had caught fire. He was admitted to one of the men's wards and I heard that his leg was swollen and blistered but would recover with some scarring. He was considered quite the hero for carrying his friend out. Dr Lovett suffered no meaningful injuries. He said that one minute he'd been discussing something with Thomas and the next he was unconscious, with no idea of what could have fallen on him.

I struggled to know what I should do. I wanted to go and see Thomas, since ignoring someone who had made such an effort to be friendly seemed indifferent and cruel, but I was too shy. Instead, I took to walking past his ward pretending I was heading somewhere else. It took me three days of these engineered laps to build up the confidence to go and see him. I waited until my evening shift had finished. It was quiet in the ward and dark. I nodded at the ward sister on night duty, who smiled knowingly, nodded back and then carried on working at her desk.

Thomas looked the picture of tranquillity lying there, and with no obnoxious teeth on show. He seemed very young like that, and I felt embarrassed at being there, so I went to sneak away.

'The lengths a man will go to simply to discover a nurse's name,' he said.

When I turned back, his eyes were wide open and he had that broad smile again, the one that said he had rarely been told 'no'.

'That was a joke, of course,' he said, leaning up on one elbow. 'Only a madman would set himself on fire to gain a

woman's attention. You may be intriguing, but you're not
Helen of Troy.'

I found this funny habit he had of insulting me most
charming in the beginning. It made me laugh, and certainly
caught my attention, but he would use this in the months to
come to confuse me and deny that he had been cruel.

'Does it hurt?' I asked.

'Well, you can tell that witches were women! All that fuss
about being burned at the stake – it's really not half as bad
as they made out.'

He was in obvious agony; he was sweating and the ward
was cool.

'At least with your strange idea of humour you can amuse
yourself,' I said.

'My father was a collector: antiques, mementoes, art,
anything he could bring back from his travels. At home
in the main hall there's an old cracked vase from Ancient
Greece, and on it there's a chorus-line of girls, for lack of a
better description. There's a girl at the back, taller than the
rest, with long black hair and dark eyes, and she's carrying
a water jug on her shoulder. The others are smiling, ambling
gaily among the reeds, happy in their mundane work, but
my girl is serious, as if she's annoyed at finding herself stuck
at the back, tripping over the others who are in her way. I
could swear it's you, Sister Chapman – an exact likeness. I
wish I could show you. My father said he would thrash me
if I broke it, but I've always been drawn to it, ever since I
was a boy, and now I know why.'

Not knowing what to say or do, I smiled back, an imbe-
cilic smile, awkward and clumsy, but I needn't have worried, because Thomas knew how to steer an empty vessel.

'Come sit with me, will you, Sister Chapman?' he said. 'I would be most grateful, because I don't think I'll be sleeping any time soon.'

I was beyond caring about anything when Thomas intruded into my life. I had let my heart take the lead in a fit of optimism, and look where that had found me: I was near broken. I had been raised to believe that hard work and good behaviour would be rewarded, but I had learned that being kind, forgiving and well behaved, living in denial of one's desires and impulses so as not to offend came with no reward at all, except for martyrs who subscribed to their pain. I would not wait until I died to find out if blind obedience would earn me a place in heaven. I had wasted enough time, now I would do what I wanted – within reason, of course. This new rule applied to Thomas, and we did what we wanted indecently quickly. I even shocked him with my newfound eagerness.

It all started while he was still in hospital, when I had gone to sit with him again. He pulled me towards him and kissed me and I let him. It might not have happened if he'd chosen a different time or day. I might have screamed or pulled back and run away, but I didn't. I would be lying if I said I felt passion when his wet squirming tongue forced its way into my mouth, but I didn't stop him. Soon, I did everything but lie under him – I had no intention of repeating my mother's mistakes. Not that he didn't try, with the frenzied begging of a spoiled schoolboy who wanted to open his presents on Christmas Eve. He would sneak me into his house in Chelsea and hide me in his bedroom, where we drank brandy. The first time he offered me laudanum I refused, but next time I tried it and made a good friend. It would help me relax, he said. It did more than that. It made me forget, stopped me thinking with such clear edges; it was like breathing in a dream.

I asked him how many nurses he had spirited away to his bedroom before me.

'None,' he replied.

'I don't believe you. You think me a fool.'

'All right... None to this house, from this hospital... Does that answer suit you better?'

'That's more like it,' I said. 'You needn't furnish me with the details, but please don't presume me an idiot. I've seen too much to pretend men are not painfully predictable when it comes to their urges.'

'You shouldn't base your expectations of men on what you've seen at the hospital, Chapman. You're seeing only animals there; animals at their most desperate, injured or dying. Try not to think of them as people – the ones at the London barely are – but as a mass, a means to an end. I do. As far as I'm concerned, they exist purely to help me become an accomplished surgeon. These people actually seem to have purpose when you think of them as an entity of sorts.'

But what motivation did I have to become an accomplished nurse? There would be no additional money or glory, only martyrdom. I could work and hope to take on more responsibility in my future years, receive better accommodation, become more senior but the gains would be immaterial. A nurse could work herself to death, and often did being so close to infection and disease, and she could still die poor. I would have to trust that I would reap my rewards in the next life, but I had trouble believing I would be invited upstairs. It was different for surgeons. They could become rich, be admired, and they were respected, which was a reward in itself. Rare women like Matron Luckes and Florence Nightingale were already upper-middle class when they chose their professions, so they would never have to worry about affording food for the table or coal for the fireplace if their career failed them; they could simply retreat to their family estates.

Thomas was fun, brash, playful and confident – all useful antidotes to the state of gloomy self-punishment that was then consuming me. The old Susannah would have spurned his cocky advances; she would have squealed and run, forever destined to be the prig, and Thomas would have moved on to the next nurse, but I wanted to keep him, like a pet. He adored me. Even when I was his shameful little secret and he'd tug at my clothes with what seemed like so many hands and beg me to let them wander, I didn't give in, much though I wanted to. I never got to meet Mrs Wiggs at that point, though she would pester us by knocking at the door, and I would giggle and wince as he shouted at her to go away.

'What can she think of you, hiding nurses in your bedroom?' I asked him once.

'Nothing! She worships me – I can do no wrong. It will be you who is cast as the temptress,' he replied, laughing. 'You must be a very wicked woman indeed, to seduce a young man so unused to the big city.' He used to say that sort of thing in between trying to get his tongue past the boundaries of my clothes. It was like being attacked by an eel.

Then he would put me in a cab and I'd ride back to the hospital still squirming from the state he'd put me in, desperate to let him in, my blood thick like oil, my veins swollen, my skin hot. Was this the badness my grandmother had claimed to see inside me? Why was it a bad thing to feel pleasure? Why should I be obliged to remain lonely and miserable?

I did worry he would lose patience, but Thomas was from a class of men so unused to rejection that the effect this had was to drive him insane. Even on the wards he would sniff round me like a dog, desperate to crawl up my legs.

The gossip spread like wildfire and I was on borrowed time before it finally got to Matron. The other nurses whispered and I caught sly looks, but I didn't care. I had become a terrible nurse: distracted, indifferent and uncaring, never doing more than the absolute minimum, for what was the point?

Thomas talked a lot about himself, his favourite subject, but I never had much to say, so it worked rather well. I thought him sweet and myself clever. I believed I was letting him do all the talking, which meant I rarely had to disclose anything about myself. He asked about my family, and I told him the old scarlet fever story, that my grandparents had raised me and now everyone was dead. I had no one. Poor, vulnerable little me. I never lied and he didn't ask again.

He told me all about growing up in a house called Abbingdale Hall, a large Georgian mansion in the village of Wraxham, a few miles outside Bristol. To me he may as well have been describing a palace. It had a small farm, an orangery and an aviary. He mentioned once that there were twenty servants and my head almost snapped off. Twenty! I struggled to imagine what on earth these people could be doing all day. There were arable fields where crops were grown, pastures on which cattle grazed, and tenants that maintained hedgerows, so they had to employ a farmer and his family to look after the land. He talked of formal gardens, terraces, rose gardens, ornamental flowerbeds, and there was even an arboretum. I worried he would sense my newfound lust was more than a little influenced by his wealth.

'My father called it paradise,' he said. 'Wild garlic grows under the trees. It's quite beautiful.'

It certainly sounded like paradise to me. Thomas's childhood was a world away from mine.

One evening in his bedroom, he said, 'When we are married and I have established myself as England's greatest surgeon, we can retire and live there. You know, I will inherit the lot once my mother dies. There is Helen, my twin sister, and she'll have to be well looked after, of course. I consider myself a forward-thinking man. I'll give her enough to keep her happy – she does like to order and organise. Little Helen! She has always been such a busy little hen and she's really rather good at it. However, I am the male heir, and nothing can change that.'

He was saying everything I wanted to hear, but I was sure he was teasing me. Of course he had no intention of marrying me. Why would he?

'And we shall have Queen Victoria to tea, and I will grow angel wings. As if someone like you would marry someone like me! It makes no sense. While I'm grateful for your flattery, it doesn't mean I will let you insult me.'

I felt a twinge of guilt when I saw how crushed he was by my reaction. 'I take it you have other plans?' he said.

'You think I am desperate for a husband? That I'm an old maid of thirty? Well, I have ambitions of my own. When I am finally released from the hospital after my mandatory four years are done, I will work in the colonies. You are not the only one who seeks adventure and success. Africa, or India, I think... I have always wanted to live in sunnier climes.'

I had no such plans, of course. It had been Aisling who had talked of these things; these were her ideas I heard coming from my lips.

'Don't go to India, Chapman. It may sound charming, but, trust me, there's nothing romantic about a bout of dysentery. And then there's the malaria.'

'Is that your idea of a proposal? Marry me – it's better than dysentery?'

He burst out laughing, which only made me angry. 'What's so funny?'

'I'm imagining you in a village full of lepers. I'm not sure it's for you, Chapman, considering your feelings on nursing the natives at the London. You know, you should stop getting in your own way and avoiding the inevitable for no good reason other than pride. Marry me! Despite our origins, we are too similar a breed to stay apart.'

'I'm glad you think my ideas amusing. I may look like a desperate spinster to you, Dr Lancaster, but even I would demand a better proposal than that.'

'You do yourself an injustice. You talk as if you are as old as Matron.'

'I'm older than you.'

'Only by a little.'

'How much?'

'I'm twenty-five.'

'You look twelve. Besides, what about your family? They'll never allow it. I'm sure your mother would be overjoyed to hear that her son has asked a lower-class nurse five years his senior to be his wife. I grew up in the Salvation Army, Dr Lancaster, crashing cymbals and having vegetables thrown at my head by drunks, so forgive me for being dubious as to why a surgeon would consider me his belle.'

I got up from his bed in a temper and walked to the mirror to smooth my hair and clothes from where his rummaging had disturbed them.

'I am too old and bitter,' I told him. 'Better to spend your pretty words on a younger girl. You won't have to work so hard.'

'I like to work hard, Chapman.'

I reminded him that I had no family and that there would be no wealthy aunts or uncles leaving an inheritance. He said dead family members were his favourite kind, that it would make Christmas more bearable. I told him there was no money, certainly not a dowry. He said he would have his own income once his practice was established and would inherit Abbingdale Hall one day, along with all that came with it. But what of his mother? Wouldn't she need to consider a match for him; wouldn't she have done this already?

'There are things you need to understand about me also, Chapman. There is my beloved twin Helen, who is small and, like many small creatures, is inclined to think of herself as much bigger than she is. Picture an extremely ferocious Jack Russell. When you meet her, you'll see what I mean. Helen very much prefers me being far away in London so she can play queen of the castle, and for the time being I'm happy to let this continue. My moment will come, and meanwhile she is occupied with the drudgery of running the household and admonishing the staff. Then there's my mother, a fragile old coot who quivers and shakes but still paints her face as if she is a debutante of seventeen, despite the fact that it droops on one side and she can't speak without dribbling. I can do what I like. My father was the one to be wary of, but he's long gone, dropped dead when I was fourteen; his heart stopped, like a watch. You and I are similar in that we are both free birds, Chapman. They won't make a fuss if we marry, and even if they do disapprove, they won't risk the embarrassment of making a scene.'

Thomas had this indestructible belief that life would reward him. Only money brings that kind of confidence. Wealth in England is guarded by a closed conspiracy: you have to be invited in. Someone like me may as well have been a vampire, but Thomas was already on the inside, begging me to join him. What could it be like to sit in a grand house with twenty servants and know you would never fall to the bottom of the ladder? Thomas was impulsive, spoiled, over loud and an attention-seeker. Like his father, he enjoyed collecting things and he loved shopping and spending money – he bought me a shrunken head from South America just to watch me open it and scream. A small part of me worried that I was just another thing he was attempting to collect, but even if that were true, would it matter? I would be living in a house in Chelsea.

The second time he proposed, he told me I had to marry him because he was colour-blind and in danger of leaving the house in badly put-together clothes, so it was my duty to save him from this fate. We both laughed. It was true, he confused green with red and sometimes brown. I stopped laughing when in the next breath he got down on one knee and presented me with a huge diamond solitaire on platinum. I had to put my eyes back in my head. I kept waiting for him to snatch the ring away, but he didn't. I accepted. I couldn't know what I was stepping into: it was more of a mirage that disappeared if you stared at it too long; a concept. Concepts are so easy to fall in love with, and I could only imagine it would be a vast improvement on the life I had come from, with its very troubled start.

6

My grandparents used to take great pleasure in retelling the story of the day they brought me home from the Nichol for the first time. How I burst into tears upon sight of my grandfather, horrified that a person could be so tall. He was as high as Big Ben to me. I burrowed into my grandmother's skirts to get away from him, and no matter how much he tried to coax me out, cajoling me with flowers he picked from the train station and sweets he bought in the village, I refused to look at him even once on our journey to Reading. I stayed stuck to my grandmother's side like a puppy, and, like a puppy, I thought if I couldn't see him, he wouldn't see me. The pair of them loved to relive that day, taking turns to tell each part, finishing each other's sentences, even though I'd heard it a thousand times and could tell it back to them myself. It was a moment of true joy for them, when they found me: a little girl to replace the one that had been lost to them.

I was intrigued by my grandmother at first. Her dark hair and small features made me think of my mother. But where my mother was soft, my grandmother had girders of steel. I don't remember that in my mother. My memories, as fragile and distorted as they are after twenty-five years, are that she was gentle and quiet. I used to think her weak, but given that she left her home at sixteen to be with the man she loved, and then, when abandoned, survived for five years in Whitechapel with a child, she must have had some of that steel. My mother may have been foolish, but she was braver than I have ever been. Yet for many years I judged her, arrogantly wondering how a girl could be so foolish as to risk her life for something as silly as love. I didn't understand at the time.

When my grandfather returned home from work each day, I would hide behind the drapes and refuse to come out. My grandmother took this as disobedience, a lack of respect for my grandfather, and dragged me out.

'Don't do that, Alma,' he would say. 'Leave her.'

'We will have to be firm with this one,' came her reply. 'She's half feral. Do you know, she refuses to wear shoes! Throws them off, she does, runs around the green in her bare feet, comes back with them black as coal. Whatever will people think!'

'Let the poor thing alone,' he'd say. 'She'll come out when she wants to.'

How I hated wearing shoes, and being tied up in ribbons and trussed up in fussy dresses and having my hair pulled about. But I loved the bed I had all to myself, and the warmth, and the house with rooms you could go in and out of, and the food. There were so many rules I didn't understand, and no one explained them. It was like being in a game where no one told you its name or any of its rules, you had to learn for yourself by losing, over and over. My grandmother said I drove her mad, because the only thing I would say when she tried to have me do something was, 'But why?'

It continued like this for some time. I kicked off my shoes, tore the ribbons from my hair, chased the ducks around the green and tormented the nicely turned-out little girls from the village with my wild games, then hid behind the curtain when the big tall man came home because I was petrified.

His footsteps made the earth shake, or at least the floorboards beneath my bottom. When he sat down in his chair, I could hear it groan. The scale of him made me think of a monster, and I'd met monsters before. He started to read books aloud from his chair while I hid behind the drapes. He would find the good stories from the Bible and share them in his booming voice; when he got to the most theatrical parts, the loose glass on the old cabinet would rattle and the fire would spit and I would peer out from behind the curtain to look at him.

'You look daft reading aloud to an empty room,' my grandmother told him.

'It's not empty – you're in it,' he said, flashing me a wink as I crouched on the floor, having emerged from the other side of the drapes.

'Whatever will people think!' said my grandmother.

'No one will think anything, Alma. It's an empty room, remember – you said so yourself.'

I began to sit cross-legged at his feet so as to listen to his operatic flourishes. Soon I was running to meet him when he came home, then crawling up onto his lap so I could see the words on the page. I still didn't say much, and I was mute with all strangers and continued to hide my face in my grandmother's skirts.

We were sat this way one afternoon when there was a tap at the window that startled us both. We looked, but there was nothing there. It sounded like something had been thrown at it, so my grandfather told me to stay inside while he went out to investigate. When he came back, he was carrying a tiny bird in his hands.

'It's a little dunnock, Susannah. He must have got himself confused, or scared, chased by a sparrowhawk maybe, and flown into the glass. He's only stunned himself. We'll find him a box and keep him warm, see if he comes to.'

The bird looked dead to me, but my grandfather lined an old box with straw, placed the tiny bird inside and closed the lid.

'We need to remove him from all the terrors of the world for a while, let his little body recover. You know, it's a very good thing for an animal to hide if he's injured or in danger. All the clever animals do it. He crawls into the tiniest space he can find and makes his world very small. It's a natural thing, when you're very scared, to make your world very small indeed. The trick is to understand when the danger is gone, to be very brave and let the world be big again, or else there may as well be no world at all.'

The next morning, when I came downstairs, my grandfather was peeking inside the box. He ushered me over.

'He's alive, but he's hungry. Susannah, go outside and dig for worms. We'll cut them up and feed him.'

I ran outside in a frenzy and dug for earthworms by the rosebushes with my bare hands. I felt like a hero – we had saved something! I found at least three squirming worms and came running back indoors with them wriggling in my hands.

My grandmother screamed on sight. 'What are you doing with those!'

'Shhh, woman! We're feeding the dunnock,' said my grandfather. 'Well done, Susannah! We'll give him the breakfast of a king and let him have his freedom – off to his new world.'

'Good grief, Andrew! Susannah outside on her hands and knees like a dog, digging through the earth. Whatever will people think!'

'I doubt very much that people will think anything at all.'

Grandmother had a very different view: she was adamant my world should remain small. Which was strange, considering how preoccupied she was with the notion that everyone was watching us. Who even were these people? My initial closeness to my grandmother didn't last. I sensed her disappointment in me and responded with sullen insolence. When she brushed my hair, she'd complain that it was too thick and coarse – quite impossible. I guess I had *his* hair. I swear she would start the brush at my eyebrows on purpose and scrape my forehead with the bristles. The more I complained, the harder she hit me with it. My grandfather turned a blind eye for a peaceful life most of the time.

When I put a foot wrong, which was often – like when I was caught squirrelling bread underneath my bed, an old habit from being hungry, or the time I went missing in the village for hours because I'd found a litter of kittens – she would blame the *otherness* in me.

'There's too much of *him* in her. I see a lot going on behind those black eyes,' she'd say.

'Nonsense! They're eyes – what colour would you have them be? Pink?' my grandfather would say.

Or she'd make innumerable comments on how I needed to be something other than what I was. 'Look how tall she is already! Who will dance with her if she keeps growing like this? Name one boy in the village who looks likely to outgrow her at this pace. Oh, it's a worry.'

'I'll have to dance with her then,' my grandfather countered. 'She gets her height from me. We'll look far and wide to find you a husband – Sweden, Norway, the land of the Vikings. We'll send for a nobleman, Susannah. Someone tall enough and good enough.'

'Stop it, Andrew, you'll give her ideas.'

'How can that be a bad thing?'

'A girl should be humble and modest.'

'This girl should know her worth, at least to me.'

'You'll turn her into a boastful creature, and no one will want her then.'

'Good. Then she'll have to stay with her old granddad for ever. Won't you, Susannah?'

One day I committed the great crime of being the only girl among a group of boys playing blind man's buff, and she had found me falling on top of a boy in my efforts to grab hold of him. We were only playing, but she dragged me home and beat me until the handle of her wooden paddle snapped. Even the old charwoman burst into tears and begged her to stop. When my grandfather came home, he told her she was never to beat me again. She told him that was the day he gave me permission to defy her.

I didn't hate my grandmother; I found her fussy, particular and a slave to silly rules and regulations that had no purpose. She was obsessed with pretence and impressions, even though no one was watching. My grandfather and I were more alike. I don't think my grandmother ever recovered from her second heartbreak: that the child she had rescued and brought home was no replacement for the first. I had turned out very different to her fey little Christabel, my mother. I was tall and clumsy, had an opinion on everything, and was half whatever my father had been, which could only be terrible. This badness, she told me, ran through me like black tar, thickening with age.

I thought my grandfather immortal. I never knew him to be sick or complain of being tired or aching. He was six foot four and always wore a topper. He refused to apologise for his height, but he didn't use it to intimidate. He insisted I go with him on his work for the Salvation Army, so I could bear witness to what happened to women who made bad decisions. On account of being in the Salvation Army, he was opposed to the concept of the workhouse and its method of misery and public shame as a form of social control. He subscribed to the belief that, merely by being unfortunate enough to find themselves poor, people deserved charity and compassion. Several times a month we would stand outside Reading Union workhouse with other Salvationists, playing drums, clashing cymbals and singing. We were only allowed as far as the iron gates, and as the bent frames and sloped shoulders of the inmates dragged past us on their way through, some of the older women among us would cry out as they beat on a drum.

'Are you saved, brother?'

They would shout back, 'God would have saved me long ago if he could be arsed.' Or, 'If I was saved, I wouldn't be here, would I, silly cow.'

My grandfather had his immovable beliefs, and many disagreed with him. Most, even among the poor themselves, considered those beneath them to be wretched and thought that charity bred the wrong behaviour. Nonetheless, he was well loved and influential, whether he was breaking up fights, settling scores between rival shopkeepers, convincing an errant husband to return to his wife or helping a deserted woman avoid the workhouse and thereby keep her children.

'You won't marry an idiot man such as that, will you, Susannah? You wouldn't break my heart, I hope? You'll marry a scholar, a thinker, an educated man, will you not?'

I laughed. The idea of marrying seemed ridiculous and far away. From what I had seen, it didn't look much fun.

I was eighteen and he was sixty-four when he cut his foot on broken glass. He was dead two weeks later from blood poisoning. How was it possible? I thought Almighty God a wicked fool for taking him. Taking him but leaving so many terrible men behind. Men that would set the world on fire from their deathbeds without a second thought. I was told by the vicar that the Lord took the best ones first; I think he meant to give me comfort. If God had asked me, I would have swapped my grandmother for him in a heartbeat. That might be wicked, but it was true.

I spent the next nine years alone with my grandmother. Her spirit faded faster than her body. She would become confused, forget things, and I would find her wandering around the house, lost and aimless. In her attempt to deny this, she tried to make our world so impossibly small that even we couldn't fit inside it. If I was on an errand outside the house, she would sit in my grandfather's chair and count until I came home. If I took too long, she would accuse me of running with boys from the village, and often she would call me Christabel. She became convinced the villagers were conspiring against her, even started an argument with another woman over a plant pot she accused her of stealing. I had walked past that plant pot in the poor woman's garden for as many years as I could remember. People were sympathetic but kept their distance. It's a cruel curse to have, even crueller to watch.

When I took too long to come back after one errand, she struck me about the face with the back of her hand and cut my lip, making it bleed. In the next breath she asked what I had done to make her strike me. A few days before the end, I found her foraging in the garden in the dead of night in her nightgown, the back door wide open and her skin like ice. As I walked her inside, she asked, 'Whatever happened to that little bird you both found, Susannah?'

'He flew away, Nanny, he flew away.'

'Aw, I'm glad. That's good, isn't it?'

She died in the January of 1885 when I was twenty-seven. To say I was relieved would be an understatement.

7

Things improved between Thomas and me for a while, towards the end of July. Then, as we entered the first week of August, the absences started again, for at least three nights running. I no longer strained to stay awake to hear what time he did come in, so it was a surprise when he emerged for breakfast one morning.

I was pretending to read the newspaper, trying to embody righteous indignation, but I kept glancing up at him, waiting for him to look back at me, and it was then that I saw the scratches on his neck: two red lines, fresh, as if from a woman's sharp nails. My stomach lurched. He sat there pushing his breakfast around as they taunted me. I blinked several times and waited for them to disappear, but they insisted on being real. Two months! We had been married for two bloody months!

Whenever I asked where he disappeared to of an evening, he replied that he was working, he was seeing private patients, he was dining with his peers, making important acquaintances... The list of seemingly plausible and reasonable excuses was without end. My first thought was to fly across the table and give him some scratches of my own. I didn't. I blamed myself: I should be more grateful. I was nowhere near the most attractive nurse at the hospital, and yet he had picked me. So I sat there like a resentful idiot with my temperature veering up and down, just like my self-doubt. I'm surprised I didn't whistle. Two months!

'Thomas,' I said, 'how did you come by those scratches on your neck?'

He froze. It was as if every muscle in his body went rigid. He stopped chasing his devilled eggs around his plate and glared at me. I almost apologised. Thomas may have been blessed with long black lashes, but when he was angry his pale blue eyes turned cold as a fish's and held you in a dead man's stare.

'What scratches?' he said, then took a bite of toast and turned back to his breakfast. The sound of metal scraping against china filled the room again.

I couldn't believe it. Here we were dancing about in a pantomime of manners and he sat there with another woman's branding on him, expressing no shame or apology. I should have kept my mouth shut, but I was still finding the required docility difficult. How was one meant to deal with such a blatant denial? I flicked through the newspaper as noisily as I could, waiting for him to ask me what was wrong. It didn't work. My thoughts drifted to the woman who had made the marks on my husband. I hoped she was beautiful, because I would burst into flames if she were plainer than me.

Mrs Wiggs was hovering as usual and came bursting in carrying a tray of tea and devilled kidneys that neither of us would eat and that would instead rise and create a stench between us like the fog on the Thames.

'Mrs Wiggs, do you see the scratches on Dr Lancaster's neck?' I asked.

I knew she would fuss. True to form, she slapped the tray down with a clatter and rushed to him. He attempted to swat her away like a fly.

'Oh, good heavens, Dr Lancaster,' she said.

Thomas shot me a dark look and I had to bite my lip to keep from smiling.

'You must be vigilant or else they will become infected. Was it a patient?'

'It was a cat. I had forgotten – it's only now I remember,' said Thomas.

I had to stop myself from laughing. Thomas hated cats. He hated all animals. Thought them dirty creatures. In no situation would he have allowed himself to come into such close proximity to a cat. Mrs Wiggs stood listening to his amazingly tall tale, lapping up every word. He conjured this fantastic story about a lady losing her cat as he was walking home. He took the time to mention how charming and elegant the young lady had been, while looking in my direction. The beautiful young lady's cat had escaped and got stuck in the mud on the banks of Chelsea creek and he had climbed down to rescue it. Thomas detested dirt; the only mess he would tolerate was the blood and matter of surgery, and that purely because it paved the way to success. When he'd finished, Mrs Wiggs was full of pride, as if he were George fresh from slaying the dragon, when all he'd done was retrieve a mucky cat. An event I very much doubted happened at all.

'Oh, Dr Lancaster, cats are wretched creatures. You should have let it drown, lady or not,' she said.

'One must do the right thing, Mrs Wiggs,' he replied.

If I'd known what he was, I wouldn't have baited him about the blasted scratches. I would have scarpered right then, leapt up and raced out the front door and far away. If I'm truly honest, I already knew something was wrong, but I refused to accept I had made a mistake. I reassured myself by feasting my eyes on my diamond engagement ring. I liked to feel its weight, how it anchored me to that house in Chelsea and warded off any fear of hunger or the English winter. I was learning what money felt like. It felt like space, room to move and breathe, to stretch out my legs in comfort without worrying about falling. Being poor was to be small and cramped, a body bent over and locked up, folded in on itself. Stifled, trapped and unable to breathe. Here, I had room. Quite literally. There were rooms in the Chelsea house that I could roll about in without hitting the furniture for a good few feet. I know, because I'd tried it one aimless day.

Thomas stood up, put on his jacket, paused to admire his reflection in the mirror over the mantel and smoothed down his impeccable black whiskers.

'Is there anything interesting in the news, my dear?' he said, turning his head this way and that to make sure he saw only perfect symmetry.

Thinking it prudent to avoid angering him, I looked down at the newspaper I had been wrestling with all morning. A small paragraph caught my eye.

'Only that a woman has been murdered in Whitechapel.'

'How unusual,' he said. Without looking, he tossed the *Evening News* onto my lap. 'Here, why don't you turn your attention to something more cheerful. There is news of the prince's bad foot.'

He bent down and gave me an aggressive peck on the cheek, said goodbye, spun on his heel like a German count, and left.

I was more than a little bewildered by the denial of the scratches and then the ridiculous cat story. It was as if when a man was within his own household the credibility of his stories was beyond reproach, regardless of their ridiculousness to anyone else with eyes and ears. I put this down to my not knowing anything about being married or being upper-middle class. It was all strange, practically foreign, in truth. We might use the same words, but at times they seemed to mean entirely different things. My earlier passion to carve out an influential position in the house had already dissipated, and for now I could only muster the energy to try and fit in. But at least I wasn't emptying bedpans or nursing men with hernias the size of Wales. It was my fault. I kept putting my great clumsy feet in all the wrong places and had difficulty keeping my mouth shut. I had screamed at him like a fishwife when he'd mentioned my age. That hadn't helped, but it would not be the last time I would fail to grasp what was expected of me.

It was in this reflective sulk that I found my eyes drawn back to the news story Thomas had dismissed so flippantly. It wasn't very large, or by all accounts unusual, but the scant details leapt out, as they always do when there is news about one's home town.

A WHITECHAPEL HORROR

A woman, now lying unidentified at the mortuary, Whitechapel, was viciously stabbed to death between two and four o'clock this morning, her outraged corpse found on the landing of a staircase inside George's Buildings, Whitechapel. George's Buildings are tenements occupied by the labouring classes.

The woman was stabbed in twenty-four places. No weapon was found and the murderer left no trace. She was of middle age and height, with black hair and a round face. It appears she was a woman of the lowest class.

There wasn't much in that first report; a few cursory lines notable only for their sparsity and violence. For some stupid reason I thought of Thomas and his scratches, but he was not the type to loiter in Whitechapel. Twenty-four stab wounds...

A few days later, more pages were given to the murder. One paper stated that the woman had been stabbed thirty or forty times, not twenty-four. Some poor tenant had come down the stairs of his block and stumbled over her body. He wasn't the first to pass by her either; another man had stepped over what he thought was a sleeping vagrant and continued to his bed at three thirty. By quarter to five the next man to pass could see the woman was lying in a swamp of her own clotting blood and ran to find a policeman.

There were reports of two soldiers from the Tower being arrested; then the soldiers were released without charge.

I found myself thinking about the story throughout the days that followed. Finding a dead body on the streets of

Whitechapel or on a landing in a Nichol terrace was not that unusual, and there were murders over mundane things such as tobacco or soap, but this woman had suffered stab wounds all over her chest and to the rest of her body. As a nurse I had tended to many such injuries, inflicted with all manner of sharp objects and sometimes more than once, but the effort and time it would have taken to stab that poor woman some thirty times, over and over again, shocked me. It was dispiritingly common for men to beat their wives to death in a frenzy of rage or passion, using whatever came to hand, either stabbing or strangling them, but this was mutilation for the sport. For a person to have expended such energy and at so much risk, he must have anticipated deriving a huge amount of pleasure from it.

Everything else about this woman was unremarkable: she was of average height, aged between thirty and forty, dressed in dark, dirty and torn clothes and carrying no discernible possessions. Someone who would likely not be missed. The only remarkable thing the poor cow achieved was to have been found on a stairwell, punctured like a sieve, and to have died silently, because none of the seventeen lodgers in that building heard a thing.

I was in the habit of saving news stories and so I saved each one I found on this murder. I had kept stories and articles of memorable events since the day we were wed, hoping to build a scrapbook, moments in time that would document our marriage. A stupid idea, a pathetic attempt at romanticism on my part. I wasn't very good at it, finding myself drawn to the more macabre articles. Thomas found my morbid fascination hilarious, an indication of my naivete, and he would laugh and pat me on the head like a child. Had he learned of my true knowledge of such matters, I doubt he would have found it so amusing. What kind of romantic reflection would my habit inspire twenty years hence, I wondered. *Oh look, do you remember this murder, darling? Wasn't it gruesome!* In truth, my interest came in part from my desperate desire to find something to do. The boredom was torturous and I missed having a purpose, now that I wasn't nursing and had to keep myself occupied. I was intrigued by those stories that were at once familiar and thankfully distant.

Mrs Wiggs attempted to throw my clippings away when she saw them scattered over the table in the dining room. 'The macabre recordings of depravity covered in the fingerprints of a thousand filthy men, and who knows where their hands have been,' she said as I gathered them up.

I filed them away in a sideboard in the back dining room, a space largely forgotten. We were a small household and we could easily accommodate ourselves in the front part of the room, closing off the rear section behind folding wooden doors. The back room had remained cold and dark, its fire and lamps unlit, until I claimed it as my own space.

'Mrs Lancaster, I only ask that you think of the germs on those dirty newspapers, which are now contaminating the house,' Mrs Wiggs would say at regular intervals.

'It is only so I might discuss current affairs with Dr Lancaster, Mrs Wiggs. I must work to keep his attention, for he is so very clever, as you well know.'

★ ★ ★

Mrs Wiggs was the only servant who lived with us. Cook, and Sarah, the scullery maid, came every day. Cook may have sometimes slept in the kitchen, although I never had the need to go out there, and after the last debacle I never wanted to. She could have had her entire family living there for all I knew. Sarah was a frail and thin-lipped girl with wispy hair and sharp features who always appeared to be glowering. I think she found my newspaper collection odd, and I'm sure she had hoped for a real lady once her master married, one who would throw dinner parties and fill the house with ribbons and bonnets – things I had been taught were wasteful and frivolous. I confused her. I confused myself.

Wherever I retreated to in the house, Mrs Wiggs did her best to seek me out, chasing me from room to room, forever dragging Sarah behind her, making statements for my benefit. 'The home is a battleground, Sarah. We feeble women can never rest or declare the enemies of cleanliness conquered.' She would strut about like an officer inspecting the aftermath of a land war, giving Sarah seven tasks to complete at once.

Mrs Wiggs had convinced herself she was dying because of the city air. If the London air itself wasn't trying to assassinate her, then its vermin were. They were plotting a coup and would take over should she rest for a minute. Poor Sarah was the henchwoman of her defence plans. She had her making up flypapers and hanging them all over the house, especially in the passageways and the kitchen, because this was where the flies collected. When she wasn't battling flies, she was making up plates to kill the cockroaches, using red lead, molasses and baking soda. They were in the corner of every room. Thomas put his foot in one once and went mad, hopping all over the house, cursing and shouting. I had to disguise my giggles with a coughing fit and run into another room.

'I have a persistent cough I cannot shift,' Mrs Wiggs would say. 'It must be the fog. It creeps under the doors, along with the soot and filth and the disease that floats this way from that stinking pit they call the Thames. And the smell…! I cannot open a window for fear of inhaling poison and I cannot open the back doors because we will be taken over by flies. I cannot breathe in this city. What if the bad air has given me consumption? I wonder how long I have left.'

'It is not the bad air, Mrs Wiggs. Those are old-fashioned ideas. We have germ theory now. It's the diseases lurking inside other people that will kill you. If they cough or sneeze, you will be done for, so you best not invite anyone in.' I could not help but tease her from behind whatever newspaper I was devouring in search of more news on the murder, pulling faces like a child as I did so.

She kept a detailed account of whenever there was a light mist on the Thames. It was as if she believed the underworld would creep out of the river.

'It is impenetrable! I cannot see more than twelve feet in front of me. No wonder criminals and thieves come to London; it gives them the perfect conditions for their deviancy. The smell sticks to the drapery, the linens, the rugs. I cannot rid my nostrils of this foul odour.'

'I thought your nose was blocked because of the consumption?' I said.

'Unlike you, Mrs Lancaster, I am not a city dweller. I miss the clean air and flowers of the country. I suppose it is

the river's revenge for having all that effluent flushed into
it. One day it will rise up and come back to kill us. I do
wish we could go back to using cesspits. Life seemed much
simpler then.'

'It is much healthier sending the waste into the sewers.'

'I'm not convinced these modern solutions are as good
as we are led to believe,' she replied, covering her mouth
and nose with a scented handkerchief. 'One must take
responsibility for one's output; you cannot simply flush
it away.'

Aside from fretting about the murderous germs, she was
also convinced we were wasteful and would go about the
house turning the gas lamps off, or refusing to put them
on altogether, issuing candles and hiding the rest in her
bedroom. I began to harvest half-burned candles and then
ask for more, although I swear she routinely searched my
room for contraband. I learned to feel my way around the
house soon enough, but in the beginning I was forever
bumping into furniture and stubbing my toes, bruising my
knees, straining my eyes and cursing in the dark. We always
had the drapes closed to keep the filth out, the lights off to
save the gas, and the candles rationed to save money. It was
as if we were in hiding, waiting for some horrible event to
be over before we could start living.

The one time I challenged her on her candle rationing, I
soon came to regret it. She gave me a lecture on the prudent
running of a house for at least half an hour – as if she would
let me have anything to do with it.

'Running a house economically is a virtue unto itself,
Mrs Lancaster. Regardless of income, a thrifty woman is a
morally upright woman. We are using six pounds of candles

in a week! Are we eating them? Whoever heard of burning six pounds of candles in a week in a house as small... as... as this?' She glanced about herself, as if she were standing in a fourpence-a-night doss house. 'At Abbingdale Hall we used twenty pounds of candles and I do not need to tell you – or I suppose I do, as you have never been there – it is a great deal larger than this house.'

I hadn't felt so managed at the hospital, and there I'd had Matron to report to. I was mistress of this house in name only. I felt like an imposter. I had not been to Abbingdale Hall to meet my in-laws. I had not met a single relative and I wondered if they even knew of our marriage. What kind of husband failed to take his wife to meet his family? Mrs Wiggs liked to remind me of this at regular intervals. She saw it hurt me once and kept trying to find the same spot.

8

Chelsea was a confused area: neglected in parts and immaculate in others. It had a small parade of shops and big shady trees along the shore where the boats were moored. When there was a strong wind, I could sometimes catch the scent of tar and oil from the shipyards. Our road was a clutter of tall, shallow-faced houses with iron-railed fronts and flagstone paths, and a pavement lined with lime trees.

The house itself was old, spacious and well built and would doubtless survive long after I was gone. Each storey extended at least forty feet, which felt huge compared to what I was used to. It was almost strange not being cooped up in an attic, as I had been at the hospital, with the water dripping down the walls. Everything had been freshly painted and repaired when Thomas moved in. The hardwood floors gleamed and the hundred-year-old pine panelling of the entrance hall and staircase had been papered over, which I actually thought was a shame, but what did I know of style? Towards the back of the house a narrow staircase led down to the pantry and the kitchen, which had a new range oven and a door to the garden. The cellar also had an outdoor hatch into the garden for hot ashes. We had three bedrooms upstairs and – my favourite luxury of all – a bathroom with a flushing water closet! This was the room I was most excited about. The servants had to use the outside privy – all of them but Mrs Wiggs, of course. Somehow, she was exempt from that irksome rule, although it was she who invented it.

At the very top of the house was the attic, which Thomas claimed as his study. He spent hours up there, isolating himself on the evenings when he did come home. It made no sense to me because there were plenty of other huge, empty rooms he could have used, rooms with windows and natural light. When I raised this with him, he complained that the noise from the street disturbed him, or the neighbour's birds gave him headaches. He needed complete silence to work, he said. The servants were forbidden to go in there, as was I. Thomas kept the key on him at all times.

Not that I didn't try. A little while after the embarrassing incident and him storming out for the first time, I thought I should try and give him some assurances. I crept up to the attic in the middle of the night in a clumsy attempt to seduce him. I had practised being the seductress in the mirror: my robe was unfastened, my hair was down and falling over my shoulders, and my nightgown was loose. Eight weeks earlier he had announced how well we fitted, but when I knocked on the door I heard the turn of the key as he unlocked it. Things that fitted together did not have doors bolted between them.

'What is it, Susannah? Are you well?' He had taken to

asking me that often since we'd married. Was I ill? As if a woman seeking her husband's attention had a disease.

'Will you be coming to bed?' I asked, attempting my best impersonation of Nurse Mullens with my eyes wide and gamine, though I probably looked more like a fish.

His eyes, on the other hand, were glassy, the skin of his face clammy. He must have seen me take this in, because he wiped his upper lip with his sleeve, which struck me as slovenly and not like Thomas at all. Not the man I knew. He stared at me with a vacant expression, flat and lifeless, and I suddenly felt the idiot with my robe dangling open, so I pulled it around myself. I had no need to pinch my cheeks, for they had gone red enough of their own accord. I made a dreadful Jezebel, and it was clear Thomas wasn't remotely tempted.

'I only wondered if you needed company,' I said. 'Or if you are working, perhaps I could help? It can be useful to have someone to talk to.'

He laughed. 'You're a doctor now, are you? Why don't you go to bed.' At which he leaned forward and gave me a brotherly peck.

I glimpsed over his shoulder nothing but dust-covered clutter, as you would expect to see in an old attic. Thomas reeked of alcohol, but another bitter, faintly floral scent crept up my nose. He had been smoking opium. Drops were one thing, but opium was something altogether different. I had seen opium eaters with my grandfather. He had shown me on purpose, made sure I witnessed the hollow shells of gaunt-faced men and women lost in their own fogged-up world and quite prepared to hasten their own death and even sell their children for the sake of a few hours within an impenetrable cloud of nothingness. I was still considering how this could be possible when Thomas closed the door in my face.

Thomas made intimations about having the attic decorated, putting in lamps, plumbing and a laboratory of sorts. None of this came to fruition. Instead, he hid himself away – in part to forget he was married, I feared. I did not complain, for there were enough empty rooms in the house for my own purposes. I had not thought much about his need to keep a private space. I had swallowed the handed-down belief that a man needed to unwind when he came home from work and should not have to subject himself to the demands or even voices of the women in his household until he was ready. Thomas, however, was never ready. Once he was holed up in that room, he was gone. Or he left the house altogether.

Unlike me, Mrs Wiggs had complete freedom to access his sacrosanct space. She had her own key and let herself in whenever it suited her, busying herself on one of his many errands or in duties of her own creation. On occasion, Thomas would shut himself in that room and then open the door and bellow for Mrs Wiggs. She would scurry up to meet him and if I tiptoed up the stairs and listened, I could hear their muffled voices playing together, rising and falling in a duet that often built to a crescendo of laughter. They clearly enjoyed each other's company. Yet when I attempted to extract a sentence from Thomas, word by word, he submitted with a reluctant huff. There was no melody, and certainly no duet. It was the laughter that irritated me most. What on earth were they laughing about? What could be so hilariously funny? I began to think it was me.

I suspected that my attraction had diminished the second I was acquired. When I was beyond his grasp, I had been desirable. Now that I could be easily had, I was just another worn-out toy to abandon. Although I felt hopelessly adrift, I still thought I could learn to swim back to land. I wanted only to win them both over.

On a whim I bought some cheerful yellow and red tulips from a street vendor. Mrs Wiggs' campaign to buy fresh flowers daily had not lasted long, for the flowers hadn't lured Thomas home, so the pleasure they gave the rest of us in the house was deemed irrelevant. Nonetheless, I saw the tulips and bought them. I felt braver and happier for it, and I trimmed the stems, put sugar in the water, and arranged them into a display such that whoever saw them couldn't help but be uplifted. They had not been on show for more than two hours before I walked past and found them gone, replaced with a vase of violets.

Violets were Aisling's favourite flowers. Mrs Wiggs couldn't have known this, but it made me think of her when I didn't want to be reminded, and I was quite unprepared for it. Mrs Wiggs simply laughed when I questioned her, and in the most condescending tone said, 'I'm afraid red and yellow tulips send the wrong message, Mrs Lancaster. One doesn't put such a display in the hall. It was frankly overwhelming, and a little... How do I say this without offending you...? Gauche. We are not French; we have no need to inflict our passions upon everyone who should happen to walk through the door. I thought you might not be aware of the subtlety of such matters, so I replaced them with violets. Violets convey discretion, loyalty and devotion. A more appropriate message.'

Seeing violets, Aisling's violets, in the hall was like being struck about the face with a bat. It upset me more than it should have. I was trying to forget about her, yet she kept sidling in, reminding me how lonely I was. I was hopeless at this. I was no sort of wife at all. I needed Aisling back. I wanted her to come and tell me to pull myself together and make fun of Mrs Wiggs and tell me Thomas was an idiot. Instead, I ran to my room and buried my face in the pillow so that Mrs Wiggs could not gain any satisfaction from my tears. I would not cry in front of people. Not if I could help it. I would rather die.

Living with Mrs Wiggs was like being under permanent attack, only she sliced at you with tiny invisible blades so you didn't know you were being cut until you were nearly drained of blood. It was exhausting. She was never happier than when Thomas needed her, but if I plucked up the courage to request something, it was as if I had asked her to send the tide back in the other direction. She stiffened wherever she found me, as if surprised to find I was still there, disappointed I hadn't been collected with the ashes.

I tried to discover more about her, but she was no more forthcoming regarding her history than I was. All I learned was that she had started with the Lancasters as nanny to Thomas and his twin sister Helen. She had been Helen's governess when Thomas was sent away to school in Winchester, then a lady's maid, and eventually housekeeper of Abbingdale Hall. Now that Helen was in charge there and could cope with a less experienced housekeeper,

Mrs Wiggs was spared to look after Thomas in the wilds of London.

I could only assume that she had shown more deference to her employers at Abbingdale Hall. On one occasion she told me that I did not have the correct number of hairbrushes for a lady. 'What will you do if a lady friend calls and has need to clean the city dust from her hair?' she asked, her eyes wide, as if this were one of life's greatest questions.

'Well, I don't have any lady friends, so it shouldn't cause too much of a problem,' I replied. It was true, I didn't have any lady friends, not a single one, not any more.

She next developed a preoccupation with my usage of the water closet. She was apprehensive of the water closet, being that it was new, and technical, and she worried it would break. I think she perceived it as dark magic. She was petrified of the noise the flush made, and of it exploding. She said she had heard many stories from other households of maids burning to death after lighting a candle and igniting the gases that had leaked back into the bathroom from the pipes. 'The announcement of effluent is at once reprehensible and morally repugnant,' she said. She then attempted to decree that I should only use the water closet between certain hours of the morning and then again for an hour in the afternoon.

I could endure being nagged and marginalised and made to feel irrelevant and stupid, but I would not have anyone take control of my bodily functions. Lord knows, even I couldn't predict those with any surety.

'No, Mrs Wiggs, I will use the water closet as and when I, or nature, dictates, and I shan't be consulting anyone for permission to do so.'

I didn't wait for a response. I walked away, my pathetic sparrow heart fluttering in my chest.

Mrs Wiggs was somehow able to look straight through me and see the peasant, no matter how much I convinced myself she was gone for good. The girl who had hoarded food beneath her bed, raced barefoot across the mud and dug out worms with her fingers was not so far from the surface. Mrs Wiggs had sniffed her out and sought to chase her into the light.

We called a truce on the water closest. But that same week, I went into what was meant to be our private bathroom and found her bent over the bath tub in a cloud of steam. She was scrubbing what appeared to be Thomas's shirts.

'What are you doing, Mrs Wiggs?'

'I should think it terribly obvious what I'm doing. I assume you would like to use the water closet? On this occasion, while I know you have opinions on this, I would ask that you use the privy.'

Her face was wet from the steam, her sleeves were rolled up to her elbows and even her hair was damp. Wiry tendrils had escaped her torturous bun and were making wild springs about her temples. I had never seen her so ruffled.

'What's the matter, Mrs Lancaster?' she continued.

White shirts were swirling in a pink pool of scalding water and there was a bottle of kerosene to the side of the bath.

'Why haven't you sent the laundry out or at the very least had Sarah do it?' I asked. 'Come to think of it, did poor Sarah have to carry all this up the stairs? Why not wash linens in the scullery? What is that smell?'

She stood up, put both hands on the arch of her back and then wiped her forehead with her forearm. 'They are Dr Lancaster's shirts. He asked me to have them cleaned quickly as they had stains. I didn't have the time to send them out.'

'That doesn't make any sense. Why not have Sarah do them downstairs? And why are you using kerosene? Is that blood?'

'It's useful for removing stains.'

She shooed me out of the bathroom and I gave up with the questions. It had never been as bad as this at the hospital. Mrs Wiggs was worse than sharing a bathroom with thirty other nurses.

I retreated downstairs, to take refuge among the newspapers, my collection of clippings, and my unhealthy obsession with the Whitechapel murder.

The story about the stabbed woman had not had the good grace to die as quietly as she did. Inches and inches of newsprint were dedicated to unravelling the mystery of her identity. Several different families came forward to claim the deceased as one of theirs, but it took about a week before she was formally identified. She was called Martha Tabram, she was thirty-five and she'd been living with a hawker on Commercial Road.

The investigation floundered, leaving a gaping space for speculation about the maniac who did it. The doctors believed that three different blades may have been used on poor Martha: a penknife, a long knife and a bayonet. The popular theory was that it had been a group of drunken sailors, though in truth rusty old bayonets could be bought from any number of stalls on Whitechapel Road.

And what of the other missing persons whose families had tried to claim Martha Tabram as theirs? Were there more bodies to be found?

'That I cannot say,' said a detective. 'Whitechapel is not like any other part of London.'

This was a truism that I was only too well aware of, and something the fancier newspapers – the sort Thomas preferred to take his opinions from – spent a vast quantity of words discussing. I didn't need *The Times* to tell me that Whitechapel had a great many more people crammed into its shoddy tenements than most other parts of London – one hundred and ninety per acre, apparently, compared to the average of forty-five per acre in better-off neighbourhoods like Chelsea that I had managed to save myself a place in. Nor was I surprised when the police estimated there were some twelve hundred prostitutes working there. These women had to eat and pay their board, what else had they to sell?

I laughed at my strange fascination with seeing the home of my early years paraded through the papers like this. At other times I wondered why I was so drawn to it, as if I couldn't truly believe I had escaped and I was preparing myself for when I inevitably found myself back there, trying to scrape by and stay alive.

Either way, scouring the papers for updates and new theories on the murder had become the high point of my day. And that morning's report in the *Echo* did not disappoint. It made the blood drain to my feet.

THE WHITECHAPEL MYSTERY: NO TRACE OF THE MURDERER

Observations have been made of the apparent similarity between the outraged corpse of Martha Tabram and another woman, brutally murdered in April.

This woman, a widow aged 45, was also of the lowest class and was brutally assaulted along the Whitechapel Road on bank holiday night. She was taken to the London Hospital, Whitechapel, where she later died of her injuries.

The coroner said the woman had been most barbarously assaulted. Such a despicable deed he had never seen before. A verdict of wilful murder against person unknown was returned by the jury.

The police are now investigating a theory that the killer or killers of Martha Tabram are the same ones that attacked the victim in April.

A paragraph at the bottom and I nearly missed it. The other woman had been savagely raped and beaten. A stick had been forced inside her, tearing her from one end to the other, and she had died from her injuries. The paper didn't state the victim's name or these details, but I knew them. Her name was Emma Smith. I was at the hospital when she was brought in.

9

When I left Reading to begin a new life as a nurse at the London Hospital, I was conscious of the paradox. Returning to the place I'd been rescued from two decades earlier did seem a strange choice. Was it the inevitable pull of fate or an unwitting attempt to help others from a privileged position? I honestly didn't know.

On seeing Whitechapel again as a naive twenty-seven-year-old, I could not believe that a prestigious hospital, famed for its matron and the skill of its surgeons, could exist in such a neglected district. Men and women were wandering the streets with black eyes and missing teeth, many of them drunk, stumbling towards their next gin or the doss house. Everything was bleak and drained of colour. And yet, standing amidst this grey gloom as if it had been lowered from the heavens on winches, was the London Hospital: a white-fronted beacon dumped on a wasteland.

I arrived a day too early for my hospital interview and was dispatched to a boarding house, instructed to go straight there, with no messing about. 'There are no sights worth seeing here,' I was warned. 'Get yourself a room, something to eat, stay inside, and come back tomorrow.' I spent that night listening to freakish, animalistic howls coming from the street outside. I stared at the ceiling that sagged above my head, convinced it would collapse if I shut my eyes. In the morning, the landlady told me, in a voice like a pipe-smoking mariner, that I could not have porridge that morning because a mouse had drowned in it.

The next day at the hospital, when I saw the nurses gliding about like starched icebergs, it was impossible to imagine I could ever be one of them. Matron's portrait hung on the wall outside her office and may as well have been Queen Victoria herself. Nursing positions were hard to come by. There were applications and interviews, and a girl's background had also to be examined. For Matron Luckes' nurses were a new breed, an attempt to professionalise the care of the sick, to employ educated women, and to submit them to a regime of intense and militaristic training. They were to work alongside doctors, and as such would have to demonstrate they could conduct themselves appropriately, behave with discipline and follow instruction to the letter. This was not an easily won opportunity; the support of doctors and governors had to be extracted over years. The wrong recruit could contaminate this brave new experiment, and there were already too many who felt threatened by the concept of a troop of *professional women*, an oxymoron in their view, and wanted it to fail. Despite the obstacles, I was accepted as a sister probationer.

The London Hospital offered care to the working classes of the East End. It was funded by donations, but that was never enough. Surgeons didn't get paid at the hospital; they worked there for the experience and the reputation it earned them, and they made their money by private practice. We took all emergencies and accidents, being so close to the docks and located among the abattoirs, the bell foundry and the factories that crushed bones. A person could get drunk enough to forget their own name on fourpence worth of gin, but could not earn enough to eat, so most patients were malnourished. In Whitechapel, the music halls, the travelling navvies, the sweeps and the sailors were all thrown together. Desperation and lunacy were provoked by starvation, laudanum and alcohol; it was inevitable this would erupt on occasion, and that gave surgeons their opportunity. It was why they all came to the London; it was why Thomas came. Like vultures, to pick over the broken bodies and chase glory.

I soon learned it was best not to think about the scale of human despair or the sheer pointlessness of healing. The destitute were sent to the workhouse, the wealthy rooted out and sent away, but they all came and tried. There were syphilitic women with noses half sloughed off and swollen bellies that carried the same disease. There was the tide of infants brought in already dead, poisoned with opium or gin by their halfwit mothers. These women would cry and beg for help, wail about how they hated their children and couldn't afford to feed or clothe them, but if ever I dared suggest they avoid having more, the abuse would come like a flood. Ceaseless childbearing was an inevitable curse to these women and they accepted their fate without question. When finding food and keeping warm was an all-consuming occupation, it left little appetite to improve one's circumstances. I learned to keep my mouth shut, for no one wanted a priggish nurse lecturing them about abstinence.

I'm sure I was most annoying when I was still trying in earnest.

Soft-cheeked boys would be carried in by old dockers with faces like weasels. The canny older men gave the youngest the most dangerous jobs. I shall never forget the two Polish brothers, one fourteen, the other nine or ten. The older one came in carrying the younger. They had a job of putting in rivets, and the older one had dropped a piece of scalding metal in the eye of his brother, who would now lose it. The next day the older brother was back, having tried to burn his own eye out with a scalding iron. When asked why, he said their mother had told him to do it; to make it fair before God.

By the time Emma Smith was brought into the receiving room in April 1888, I'd seen three years of the futility of Whitechapel at the London. I'd had my fill. Aisling had gone and I was barely eating or speaking. I was thoroughly miserable. Matron gave me the talk: how the resilience of her nurses was of utmost importance and that professionalism must be maintained at all costs. We were not individuals but a single mass working towards the same purpose. There was no time to indulge in personal issues. Her nurses were pioneers, no ordinary women, and all emotions must be suffered in stoic silence. Scared of losing my job, and now alone, I convinced her I could work.

Sister Park had been moved into my room. She was pleasant enough, but no Aisling, and I resented her for that. Having this stranger in what had been our space, singing and forcing her gaiety on me, was torture. I had to fight the urge not to roll her up in the rug and throw her out of the porthole window. She would blather on and I would sit there, saying nothing and staring at the ceiling. I was still finding strands of Aisling's hair about the place and I would take each one and wind it about the handle of her hairbrush until it shone like a band of copper. Sister Park caught me doing this and looked at me strangely. But it made perfect sense to me; it didn't seem such an odd thing when you had loved a person. I would save every trace of her I could.

Sister Park also snored. I used to lie there and listen to her snuffling like a farm pig, dreading what horrors the next day would bring. When morning came, all I wanted to do was sleep. I didn't know how I was going to last each day let alone the rest of my contract at the London. I had years ahead of me.

And then in came Emma Smith.

She was carried into the hospital between two dishevelled women who reeked of old booze, together with the usual fug of the unwashed and general dampness. The enquiry officer assumed they were drunk and tried to send them away. But he stepped aside when he saw the smeared trail of blood behind Emma.

The two women could only give scant details of what had happened to their friend. The older one with the bloated face of a drinker was the deputy at the doss house where Emma had been staying, and the younger girl with white hair had only known Emma for a few weeks but had been sharing her bed for convenience's sake. Emma was in her forties, they thought, but age was hard to gauge in women like her. Her skin was like an old saddle, the bottom half of her face was collapsed and narrow for lack of teeth, and her reddish hair was thin and brittle. She was so bony that when we lifted her onto the bed she flew up in the air as if we were hoisting a sack of oat-chaff.

She'd been beaten. Her face was bruised and swollen and her ear was bleeding. The other two women huddled in the corner, like timid mice.

'They jumped her on the corner of Osborn Street and Brick Lane,' said the white-haired girl. 'She said there was three, maybe four. They took her purse and all of 'em done her and then shoved a broom handle up her, she reckons.'

'A broom handle?'

My cheeks burned as soon as I understood. I turned around to hide my face and saw Nurse Mullens smirking from under her freckles at my ignorance; clearly, I was the only virgin in the room. I told Mullens, who was more junior, to take the women out of the emergency room. She didn't look so smug then. She hated taking instruction from me, but she had no choice.

Left alone with the bleeding woman, I attempted to peel back her clothing, which was rotten and crawling with lice. When I drew back her skirts, I saw a shawl looped around the top of her thighs; it was thick with blood. Once Mullens was back, I tried to pull the shawl away with my fingers while she stood by with clean bandages. We had not worked together much, which was obvious from the way we constantly bumped into one another and tried to do the same task. Aisling and I had been in synchronicity, moving in anticipation of the other, like swans, each instinctively knowing our place. We fitted together perfectly.

Mullens was as pretty as a painted porcelain doll: bright, vivacious and charming, with the small and obvious features of the type that turn men's heads. Aisling had a fresh and open face, far superior to Mullens' in my view, and pink lips that were always in a half-moon curve. By comparison, Mullens was a sugar-coated tart, with her lumps and bumps and bouncing auburn curls. I had never known what it was to be a pretty girl; my features were all in the right place but forgettable. As well as being pretty, Mullens was reliably stupid. She was easily distracted and always found the time to flirt with any man who so much as looked at a scalpel. I always imagined she was destined to have a life easier than mine, but on that I would be proved wrong.

When we had almost finished unwrapping the shawl from between the woman's legs, the blood came flooding out faster. The trays either side of the bed filled and then started dripping onto the floor.

Emma Smith sat up, gasped, and in a last burst of consciousness grabbed my arm, staining the sleeve of my uniform with her bloody fingerprints. 'Please, don't. If it comes off, I will break apart,' she said. She looked at me with wide eyes, then her fingers slipped, her eyeballs rolled back, and she fell back onto the bed.

I could only stare at the bright red marks on my sleeve, but Mullens was beginning to panic.

'Where's the bloody doctor?' she said, desperate for him to come, as was I. 'Sister Chapman, what shall we do?'

There was nothing we could do. Emma Smith had been ripped apart from front to back passage. Her stick-thin legs, yellowed and covered in bruises, hung at a horrifyingly unnatural angle.

Dr Shivershev finally arrived, much to our enormous relief. He was a good doctor, if cold, distant and impersonal.

He wasted no regard on us mere nurses. Behind him, his three dressers stood alert, like trained gundogs, and behind them were his pupils, all smooth-faced, blinking eyes and flat haired. They peered around the one in front.

Dr Shivershev examined Emma Smith for no longer than two minutes and told us to make her comfortable and stem the bleeding as much as we could.

'Aren't we going to theatre?' I asked.

Mullens stared at me. A nurse was meant to wait for instruction from a surgeon and was certainly not expected to challenge him.

Dr Shivershev looked at me with raised eyebrows, then back at Emma Smith. 'You think if I operate on her she will jump off the bed and go home tomorrow? If she's not dead within the next day or so I'll be surprised.' And with that he left, his dressers and pupils scurrying behind him like an entourage of privileged rats.

Emma Smith was translucent, as if all her insides had emptied and now all that was left was an empty grey sack. I felt a strange tingling in my cheeks, and I thought I might be sick. For some reason I laughed, which made no sense. Mullens stared at me in horror, as if I were laughing at the death of the woman on the bed, but the truth was, I had realised the ridiculousness of it all, the waste of effort. It was pointless. Emma Smith was going to die and, if we were honest, we all knew there would be scores more like her. Our pathetic attempt to help her, if we were any help at all, felt as good as holding up a cup to catch a flood.

We were in the laundry room, changing our uniforms, when Mullens said, more to herself than to me, 'Who'd do such a thing as that? Who would put a broom handle inside a woman? What a vicious thing.'

I didn't say a word. I was consumed by the sense that something terrible was about to happen. I should have realised then that I wasn't well, but too conscious of my last conversation with Matron, I waited until Mullens had left and then slapped my own cheek, hard, three times. For what was another dead woman? I had seen hundreds – what was one more?

Emma Smith had further inconvenienced us by leaving her insides all over the receiving room, so when Mullens returned we went to fetch Dykes, one of the ward maids. We called ward maids 'scrubbers', though it was wise not to do so within earshot of Matron. Dykes had been one of the hospital's old, unqualified nurses, the very ones Matron Luckes' radical new scheme had sought to get rid of. Most of the old nurses had duly left to go to the prison service or the workhouse infirmaries, but a few, like Dykes, had stayed and taken roles as ward maids. Dykes was also the woman to go to if you found yourself pregnant.

When we asked her to come, she screwed up her face and reluctantly agreed. She dragged her noisy old bucket behind her and the screech of it was unbearable to my ears. I genuinely could not bear it. I kept telling her to stop it, but she would make it quiet for only a few seconds, then go back to scraping it along the floor.

I began to see flashes: blobs and patches, ghosts of the blood left behind by Emma Smith. Spots and swirls appeared and disappeared. When I saw something from the corner of my eye, I would spin around and it would disappear, but when I closed my eyes and opened them again, more would come. I felt light-headed. I touched the back of my neck and it was wet. I panicked and thought I must be bleeding somehow, but it was only my own perspiration. And yet the hall wasn't hot. There was something wrong with me. My heart thumped and my hands shook. When I closed my eyes, I saw only blood on the back of my eyelids. I slapped my face again as hard as I could.

Mullens gave me another look. This time she had the same expression Sister Park had had when she'd seen me collecting Aisling's hairs. 'Are you well, Sister Chapman?' she asked suspiciously.

'I'm tired, is all.'

The hall had rows of benches much like a church, except I'd never seen these empty. The sound of all the people talking was like a million squawking seagulls. The scraping of Dyke's metal bucket was like the squealing of a pig who knew it was about to be slaughtered. I went to a wall to lean up against it, put a hand to my chest and felt what was like a tiny foot trying to break out.

A girl, fourteen at most, came towards me. 'Nurse, won't you look at my baby? He's not right.' She thrust the newborn in my face. 'Will you tell me what's wrong with him?'

The child was still covered in the white matter from its birth, fixed in a stiff arch and livid. It was dead and horribly malformed. I pushed the girl and her dead baby away from me. Dyke's steel bucket was still screaming and I could only think of making her stop.

'Will you stop! Stop it, Dykes!'

The hall fell quiet and every face turned to look at me, like a sea of china plates. Even Dyke's mouth hung open.

A man on the bench nearest me, a syphilis sufferer with a

false silver nose and bushy whiskers, stood up, took his cap off and said, 'Nurse, won't you take my seat?'

I pushed past him, through the hall, out of the front doors and onto the street.

I ran and ran, past stunned faces like streaks of oil in a blur. I ran all the way to the garden behind the crypt and hid there until my breathing calmed down.

I would not be the one left behind. In that moment, I knew I had to find another path. It would be uncomfortable, but I had to do it, because left to my own instinct, I would be the coward and retreat to the familiar. I would end up three feet from where I started. I would not live out my days around people like Emma Smith until I became one of them. I had to find my way out.

10

So I played the role of obedient wife and waited for my husband to return every day. Quite literally, I waited for the man I married to return. But, instead, it was this other Thomas, the one with the cold eyes and distant nature, who came back home, on occasion, if only to give the house a sense of purpose. The Thomas who adored me, who begged to touch me and lusted after me like a lovestruck hero, had disappeared – probably the minute we boarded the train back from our Brighton honeymoon. This new man was unknown.

When he did come home, he barely spoke, least of all to me. He did converse with Mrs Wiggs, whose ears were conditioned to sense his footsteps on the pavement long before he reached the door, as if she were a loyal dog. I refused to race her for his attention. When he and I found each other in the same room, I would make efforts to start a conversation and be bright and cheerful, but he was always distracted and often ignored me. The black lashes and charming humour, I learned, were reserved for those with whom he was less well acquainted. I became another piece of furniture lying dormant about the house, waiting to be made use of. And use me he did.

We had flown into bed in our first few days as husband and wife, when all our built-up desire was released in a furious passion. Now, though, all that was left was frustration and anger. I wasn't sure if it was his size or the rough texture of his skin that felt so strange, but I explained it away: I was unfamiliar with men and I knew no better. Thomas had an insidious need to control events in the bedroom, quite beyond what I'd anticipated in a dominating male. I can only describe it as an urge that couldn't be satisfied. Rapidly, it went from us pleasuring each other to his entertainment being the only concern. It became a duty that had to be executed; my only one, really. I began to dread hearing his footsteps coming down from the attic study, because that was the only reason he bothered to seek me out. My stomach lurched every time. I became anxious before each performance.

My body stopped responding through sheer nerves. I had to imagine he was somebody else. He spent little time on me, only pushed and pulled me in different directions, paying no heed if I complained I didn't like it. I became very sick of the press of his hand on the back of my head, of me gagging and him laughing. He issued orders as if he were leading an operation. I joined him in the brandy and drops and soon I was taking them alone in anticipation of him coming down the stairs. It was easier to imagine he was someone else when edges were blurred. He liked to make me yelp or wince in pain and then ridicule me. He accused me of being lazy, of being a stuck-up prude, of being no more fun than nailing a plank. He told me what to do and

when, and how to do it. *Make more noise! Not that noise –
it's as if you're a corpse. At least act like you're enjoying it.*
He squeezed my throat until I couldn't breathe. He
enjoyed the sensation of me fighting him, I think. I didn't
know what he liked. I did not try to understand it. When
I told him it hurt, he was dismissive and said that he was
only playing. I was oversensitive. I was dramatic. I was
overreacting, as usual. I assumed this was how all husbands
were.

On a rainy Sunday in the middle of August we attended a
hospital benefit. The weather was strange: dark the whole
day, like dusk on the cusp of a storm, even in the morning.

I had been to an event like this once before with Thomas,
but this would be the last I would attend with him. He may
have gone to others after that, I don't know, but he didn't
take me. I understood why: I was a terrible conversationalist,
had no family to speak about, and no estates in Surrey, trips
to the theatre or friends getting married to discuss. I could
talk about the biggest goitre I had ever seen, what babies
with congenital syphilis looked like, and how every nurse
dreaded assisting an inexperienced surgeon for fear he'd
faint on his first amputation, but these were not deemed
suitable topics for polite conversation. I found myself on the
fringes, forever wondering how to find a way in. Thomas
watched me, shaking his head, as he talked with his peers,
one of whom was Dr Lovett, the man from my wedding,
with whom I'd still not had the pleasure of becoming
familiar. Though I smiled and waved when I saw him, felt
his face friendly compared to the rest, he simply nodded

and continued his conversation. I felt so conspicuously tall; the burning maypole. Parties were things to be endured, like wet weather and stomach aches, and that day I suffered all three.

It was an elaborate house on the edge of Holland Park in Kensington and belonged to one of the governors of the hospital. I would never have been invited as a nurse. The reed-thin hostess with silver hair explained how Kensington used to be a small village but now felt positively part of the city, with the railway so near and the omnibuses flying around like cannonballs. When she asked where I came from, I hesitated and almost said Whitechapel. I opened and closed my mouth like a fish. She looked at Thomas, who told her I came from Reading, then ushered me away.

As he walked past, I heard her whisper to him, 'Can she speak English?'

Thomas smiled and said how absolutely astute of her, how clever she must be, for, yes, my parents were Hungarian and had emigrated; they were merchants. She seemed pleased with this. Something about me had told her as much, she said, although she'd guessed me to be Greek or French.

I was indeed foreign. I came from the invisible class, the non-existent, and she couldn't even see it when presented to her on a platter.

In better weather we could have made use of the garden, but it rained all day, so we were trapped inside, hemmed in like poor people. Gentlemen bumped shoulders with each other, and the beads on ladies' dresses caught as they passed. The rain beat like stones against the windows and a string quartet gallantly played something even I knew was Beethoven. The chaotic rhythm on the glass, the furious way the musicians attacked their instruments, and the continual jostling and bumping as if we were sheep queuing at an abattoir made me hot and nauseous. I tried to concentrate on the conversation of the group next to me and take deep breaths.

A grey-whiskered man was holding court, attended to by a cluster of brightly dressed elderly ladies and gentlemen who had all been leached of the colour of youth: white skin, milky eyes and silver hair. The man spoke his opinions with great confidence, as if they were indisputable facts. 'The people who inhabit that part of London,' he declared, 'acquire a taste for thieving and violence when still in their mothers' arms. You cannot remove criminality any more than you can extract bad breeding from a dog.'

His audience nodded in agreement.

'Well, they are different, are they not? You only have to look at them. They are short and have terrible complexions. They are simply not well bred,' said a woman who appeared to be missing a chin, her lower jaw an apathetic bridge to her neck. All those generations of good breeding had bred out the ability to fold a tablecloth, but then if you never had to fold your own, what use was a chin?

The better classes tended to talk of money as if there was a finite amount of it, as if it were a cake. They had their slice and didn't want to part with it. But they kept adding extra slices to their plate, using their first portion to justify why they were entitled to a second, and a third. Before long, the original cake was twice the size – a celebration cake! what a triumph to be British! – and yet the rest of us were still waiting obediently for a single piece.

I wanted to interrupt, inform them that gentlefolk were

only taller because they were better fed, that bad skin could be fixed with good food, fresh air and decent hygiene. I wanted to talk to them about the children who left the hospital in better condition than when they were admitted but who would certainly get sick and malnourished again, their parents being too poor to cover the rent and feed them. But I didn't. I was a coward. I disliked myself. I had been disgusted by the patients and happy to marry upwards myself, yet here I was, piously offended by the wealthy and their assumptions that their status was due to their innate superiority and nothing at all to do with luck, or greed, or theft. All this as I drank wine and ate creamed sweetbreads and cold boned turkey, served to me by a waiter who heard everything and kept his eyes nailed to the floor.

The group went on to discuss the murder of Martha Tabram.

'Have you heard, my dears, that there were three cases of infanticide and another murder in Whitechapel this week alone!'

'Indeed. But the latter was a straightforward case, was it not? The man beat his wife to death with his fists, I understand. Nothing like as dramatic as that poor unfortunate found cut to pieces in a stairwell.'

The ladies gasped into their silk handkerchiefs and leaned more closely into the conversation. They appeared thrilled, overtaken with a macabre fervour.

There followed theatrical descriptions of the 'howling wilderness' of the East End and the savages that lived in its criminal corners. How the subversive Jews made blood sacrifices and were conspiring to drive down wages and undercut English tradesmen.

'There are far too many foreigners coming in. It's like a flood!' a portly gentleman opined. 'They will overrun us all.'

'And the socialists will drag us into the middle of Trafalgar Square and guillotine us. Let us not forget the poor French.'

'And the whores! What shall we do with all the whores? Why can they not keep their skirts down? Those women are not women at all. They infect married men and send diseases into good, middle-class homes. Someone should stop them. No wonder they end up murdered and disembowelled in stairwells. Why do they not stay at home?'

My stays felt as if they were shrinking, pulling tighter and tighter, and I thought my ribs would crack. The press of the room was preventing me from taking my breaths deep down into the bottom of my lungs. I needed air. I was scared I would have another experience like I had when Emma Smith was brought in. There was a thunderstorm in my chest. I had to get out. I pushed through the crowds, apologising and trying not to look at the disgruntled faces as I shoved past them. I put a hand on the French doors, and the expressionless waiter approached.

'Madam, it's raining.'

'I know,' I said, and pushed open the doors and ran out into the cold blue rain. The chill shocked my skin and calmed me down.

I must have stood there one, maybe two minutes when Thomas called out.

'Susannah! What are you doing? Get back in here at once.'

He was in the doorway, the waiter beside him. One angry face, one bemused. My hair stuck to my cheeks, dripping wet. Pallid faces stared back at me as if I had gone mad.

In the cab on the way home, Thomas lost no time telling me how humiliated he was.

'I told a few choice people who won't be able to stop themselves from gossiping that you have been in despair ever since you... are no longer... You understand. It was an odd display, Susannah. You are growing stranger by the day. I think perhaps you are unwell.'

I said nothing, but there it was again: *unwell*.

After that, Thomas talked incessantly of me seeing a doctor. He kept suggesting there was something wrong with me, that I was depressed and listless. He urged me to make an appointment with his friend, Dr Lovett. When I insisted that there had been no child to lose, for it had been too early to tell and I'd been foolish to speak of it, he told me I was in denial. I countered that I was only being scientific, to which he called me cold and unfeeling, saying it was not natural for a woman to say such things about her own child. I began to doubt myself. His obsession with finding a mechanical error with my body made me responsible for everything, so I stopped arguing; everything I said only seemed to prove his theory anyway. It dawned on me this was the most attention I'd had from Thomas in weeks. He appeared to take pleasure in talking about my insides as if they were defective, as if I was a rusty old machine that could be taken apart, assessed and reassembled, this time with younger parts.

At the end of August, when I could no longer avoid it, I did see a doctor, but I made damn sure to pick my own.

11

The wiry little clerk took too much pleasure in telling me, down the slope of his nose, that the renowned Dr Shivershev wasn't taking on any new patients at the moment, he was already far too busy. Did I have a recommendation, he asked, in the tone of one who thought he already knew the answer. I lied, told him we were friends, that we knew each other very well from the London. This confused the poor boy, since Dr Shivershev was the type who ignored everyone, indiscriminately. So I told him I expected my friend to be outraged when he heard I'd been turned away. The young clerk lost his superior attitude in a cloud of self-doubt and suggested an appointment for the following week, on Monday the twentieth of August.

I hadn't been hell-bent on having Dr Shivershev as my physician. I had trudged up and down Harley Street and found myself baffled by the countless names on gold plates outside every door. The more I read, the more muddled I became. I nearly gave up and resigned myself to consulting Thomas's friend, but then I saw his name: Dr Robert V. Shivershev. How many Shivershevs in London could there be? We had no friendship; I was simply a nurse. I was sure that to him we were all interchangeable and faceless, smoothed over, like ivory pieces on a chessboard. This was not important. I only wanted to have my physician and my husband's newfound obsession with my health in separate jars on a shelf.

'You say you know him from the London?' the elegant housekeeper asked as I followed her up the grand staircase. Old enough to be my mother, but more beautiful than I would ever be, she had a pile of dark hair arranged in an intricate weave, soft eyes and an accent I couldn't place. She wore a lilac silk dress and was the most captivating housekeeper I had ever seen, like a misplaced duchess down on her luck.

'I was a nurse, but then I married.'

'Oh! How wonderful. If I were an adventurous young woman again... Well, never mind.'

She led me to his office door, put one hand on the handle, hesitated, then whispered, 'Knowing that you, a professional woman, would have kept your ward spotlessly clean, I feel I must apologise for the state of his office. The doctor refuses to let me in, he accuses me of moving things, which I never do.' She shook her head. 'There I go with my overexplaining, when you must be aware of how stubborn he can be, yes?'

'He can be a character.' I smiled. I had no clue as to what we were both referring.

'A good way of putting it, my dear,' she said and opened the door.

Once inside, I understood what she meant. The drapes were in a random state – some were closed, others open, and most of them looked as if they'd been strung up in a hurry and forgotten about. It had a disorientating effect on the light, plunging some parts of the room into darkness and highlighting other areas with bright shards that illuminated the floating dust. I sneezed as soon as I entered.

The room looked as if it had been ransacked and abandoned in a great hurry, as if the doctor had been hunted down and had then fled. There was paper everywhere, weighted down with medical utensils and equipment that belonged in trays and cases, not splayed out carelessly. The air was stagnant and, shall we say, laced with the aroma of nervous patients. I doubted the windows had been opened for days. Specimen jars lined one side of the room, where they'd been pushed onto a shelf, no care taken to their arrangement, and were covered in thick dust that all but masked the oddities contained inside. Piles of books sprang up like wild mushrooms from the floor, and I had to weave my way among them to reach his desk. The building had presented itself as the perfect white-fronted townhouse faced with black ironwork; the hallway, the housekeeper and the winding staircase had conveyed a picture of elegance and conformity; but this room was like walking into a hermit's cave.

There was a loud thump at the window to my left. It startled me. I saw the smear of ghostly grease left by a bewildered bird and thought of that little dunnock and my grandfather coming into the room with him cupped in his giant hands.

Dr Shivershev leaned forward on his chair, emerging from the gloom like a spirit at a séance, which startled me all over again.

'It was a pigeon. They fly into the windows here all the time. I don't know why, for the windows are filthy. I try to stop her having them cleaned – I thought that would help the birds understand what they were, but it doesn't. It's a great shame. The city has developed too fast for some species to cope with; it's as if they cannot perceive the building at all. They cannot adapt fast enough to avoid the new obstacles we build that harm them. If only I knew how to stop them from destroying themselves. Won't you sit down, Mrs Lancaster.'

'Are you sure it's not merely stunned? My grandfather saved a bird once. He put it in a box, in the dark, and the next morning it flew away. I'd thought it dead.'

'My clerk has never retrieved a live one.'

'Your clerk retrieves them?'

'Yes. They are always dead, necks broken. But a tragedy for one species often means another thrives. My housekeeper will throw it to the cat that comes by the back. He will be grateful at least.'

The doctor himself looked like a rumpled piece of old cloth. One that had been cleaned and pressed long ago, and had since been dragged over bushes, trodden on repeatedly, wrung out and reused time and again. His hair, eyes and complexion were all dark. I thought he might be French or Spanish, or Italian. He had that ambiguous colour that Englishmen have a passion to classify but out of ignorance grudgingly characterise as 'foreign' or 'exotic'. His accent, on the other hand, screamed English boarding school. His eyes had dark shadows, his black hair, which was long and beginning to curl at the neck, shot out in all directions, like a hedgehog. He needed a shave. He wasn't wearing a jacket and there were spots on his shirt. He looked more like an alcoholic than a reputable surgeon. I began to think I might have made a pig-headed mistake.

'So, you are my dear old friend from the hospital. Forgive me, I have forgotten how we came to be so familiar,' he said, tipping back in his chair and smirking as my cheeks burned. 'I had to laugh when my clerk described you. I thought I knew who it might be, but I wasn't sure. I would never have guessed you'd be the type to talk your way into my diary. I was intrigued. The question is, why didn't you come and speak to me at the hospital?'

I was red as a berry and squirmed at being trapped by my own lie.

'I'm not at the hospital any more, Dr Shivershev. I married.'

'Now why on earth would you do that?' he asked, his face screwed up as if he really couldn't understand.

I picked at the stitching of my gloves and stared at the floor. I'd thought I would be in there ten minutes at most, that I would blather on about my health and be on my way. Now I wasn't sure what to say at all.

'My husband has a practice further down Harley Street. Though I've never been there, as he doesn't like to be disturbed at work. You should know him from the hospital, he's a surgeon at the London too. Thomas Lancaster.'

As soon as I mentioned Thomas's name, Dr Shivershev froze. He seemed to be making every effort not to betray what he was thinking. He looked about his desk and shuffled things around, pushing an inkpot an inch to the side and some papers to the edge of the desk. Then he interlaced his fingers as if he couldn't trust them either.

'I see,' he said after an unnatural pause. 'Well, Sister Chapman, now Mrs Lancaster, there has to be a reason why you have made such efforts to consult me and not... discuss whatever it is with your own husband. I'm curious, if nothing else.'

The hot blood had reached my chest and burned like a furnace. 'My husband has concerns that there may be... My husband is a little younger than myself. Do you think...? Is there an opinion, a modern scientific one, on the ideal age for a woman...? I want to make sure I am in good health. I have been worrying... about my health.' I had made a hole in the finger where I'd pulled at the loose cotton on my glove. I wished I could crawl into it.

He asked the obligatory questions about my age, Thomas's age, my history – which was amusing, since I knew only half of it – and my general health, the answers to which he scribbled down on a piece of paper snatched from one of the piles strewn around his desk. There was already writing on the other side and I was sure his scrawling was all an act, for my benefit. He could have been compiling a shopping list for all I knew.

'Mrs Lancaster, you are well within childbearing age, if that's what you are trying to ascertain.'

'I am older than my husband,' I said. 'What can I tell him that may reassure him?'

I had the idea that if Dr Shivershev said something scientific, then the next time Thomas accused me of having something wrong with me I could quote him and not be held responsible.

'Tell him that there are many women who have children at the age you are now. That my own mother was forty when I was born. I can't honestly think of any scientifically based medical intervention that would help. Although I'm sure I could invent something and charge you for it, but your husband would know better, or should. Unless there is something else? Are there any other irregularities you wish to tell me about?'

I wondered what would happen if I were to ask him in plain English if it was normal for a man to laugh as he caused his wife pain or to choke her until she gasped for air. If there was truly a God-given appetite that men couldn't control and women had to satisfy whether they liked it or not. If the fairy stories, the tales of married bliss, of love, were all a trick to get us under them, so that once trapped we were embarrassed at our gullibility and bound by bitter resentment to keep the conspiracy from younger girls, else suffer the pain of jealousy at their escape. I could ask him if it explained everything; if many women suffered from a simple overexertion of the natural male urge, provoked by an unresponsive wife somewhere. I wondered if the doctor choked his wife when he fucked her, and if she enjoyed it, or if, like me, she played along, making the correct noises, hoping to make it end a little faster.

'Is there something else, Mrs Lancaster?'

'No,' I said. 'I suppose I have too much time on my hands – I spend a lot of my day thinking.'

'Perhaps voluntary work, Mrs Lancaster. You have skills that come highly valued. Not many lady volunteers are experienced surgical nurses. I can think of several charities that would be thrilled to have someone like you. If that doesn't appeal, I do have some clients who find distraction through keeping a journal; a collection of their thoughts and feelings, some say it helps.'

That sounded terrible, but I made a face that suggested I considered it a good idea.

'Other than that, you should try and relax and enjoy being married. You have time, Mrs Lancaster. Lots of it,' he said.

My eyes darted about the room, trying to avoid his. They had adjusted to the light. I picked out large, worn books of illegible writing in a language I didn't recognise. The specimens in jars were now revealed to be real pieces of flesh: organs and skin in formaldehyde. My eyes fixed on the bottom half of a face floating in yellow liquid, the skin peeled from below the person's eyes, the lips intact, the skin covered in lesions.

'I have an interest in diseases of the skin,' said Dr Shivershev.

'Oh.'

Next to the face there was a mouth with a fleshy tongue and long tentacles like fingers surrounding it.

'What is that?' I asked. 'I've never seen such an organ.'

'That's a sea creature. It's for decoration,' he said.

I was still looking at it when he added, 'You were a companion of that nurse...?'

I stopped breathing, pulled my shoulders back like Thomas had taught me, and cut him off before he could continue. 'Sister Barnard,' I said. 'Yes. We shared a room.'

'Would you describe yourselves as close?' he asked.

Why would he be asking about that? 'Sister Barnard was a very good nurse. We worked together well.'

'I recall seeing you together, always a pair, like twins, apart from the height difference of course, bobbing about the hospital like a pair of penguins.'

I knew I must be careful. Others at the hospital had gossiped. I only hoped Thomas never heard this. It would be something else unnatural to accuse me of.

'Yes, but I am married now. I am happy,' I replied.

'Of course you are.'

I was being ushered out of the door, but I had to clear up one last thing.

'Dr Shivershev, can I be sure our discussions will remain private?'

'Why do you ask?' He was obviously offended.

'You know Thomas personally, so I wanted to be sure that our conversations will remain between us. I would not want to be the subject of discussion between men, however professional.'

He laughed, which struck me as odd, and I realised I'd never seen him laugh before.

'Mrs Lancaster, as long as your husband pays the bill, I can't imagine I'll be discussing anything at all with him.'

12

isling started at the London a few weeks after me. She never explained why she arrived so late and was always loath to talk about her background except in the loosest of terms. She would make a joke and steer the conversation in another direction, such was her way. I think she thought she rather got away with this technique, but I never pried because we all had our secrets, so I let her think her little method of throwing me off effective. I knew her father was uneducated in the traditional sense, but well connected; he had status as a landowner with a respected knowledge of horses.

Lectures took place in a classroom, which made our training much like being at school as a young girl. We had to study a great deal of theory before they let us near a real patient, and much of it was banal: bedmaking, washing patients, bandaging, padding splints, preventing the spread of infectious diseases, how to observe and report symptoms. For weeks we were forced to sit and write for hours at a time and then complete test after test; it was torture.

I distinctly remember the moment Aisling arrived. We fresh-faced recruits were dutifully absorbing the wisdom of a ward sister who relished her role and influence rather too much. She was making the most of her captive audience and labouring every point with a flourish worthy of a member of parliament.

'A nurse must be prompt and intelligent, but above all of this, obedience is the distinguishing quality. Trustworthiness is also essential, for one must be relied upon. A nurse must adopt a kindly and pleasant manner; if she doesn't have one naturally, she must conjure one, out of thin air if needs be. She cannot tire, grow bored of her duties or become weary of the unending churn of human suffering that she will toil to alleviate every day of her earthly life. Her reward comes with the satisfaction of pursuing a higher purpose and gaining the camaraderie of her fellow nurses.'

I was about to let my head hit the table with the boredom of it when the back door creaked open and in walked a slight girl with a shock of bright red hair poking out from her cap. Aisling strode into every room as if she improved it merely by arriving – unlike me, who had to fight the instinct to apologise to a door for the inconvenience I had caused it by opening it. She stood at the back of the class and when our eyes met she smiled at me. I was too shy to smile back, so I turned around, immediately regretting my unfriendliness.

'Probationers are warned not to indulge in gossip,' our lecturer continued. 'You will avoid leaning against the furniture or idling on patients' beds as if catching up with an old friend. Nothing gives the impression of slovenliness more than allowing oneself to become over-familiar with a patient or indeed a colleague. We are professionals, and we are on duty. Have I made myself clear?'

There was a chorus of acknowledgement, and Aisling was ushered in and told to take a seat. There were spaces here and there, but she took the one next to me. I edged further away and didn't dare look at her.

We sat next to each other, in those same seats, for three weeks before I managed to summon the courage to say anything beyond the obligatory greeting. Though we exchanged barely any words, I looked forward to those classes with stomach-churning anticipation, hoping she'd speak to me or look at me and throw me that smile again, which had felt like bubbles bursting all over my skin. I could think of nothing to say: words were thick as porridge in my mind. But then one day, when we'd been left to finish taking notes, she spoke to me out of the blue.

'Can I ask your name?' she whispered.

I was so taken aback, I didn't understand the words. I was mesmerised by the pinkness of her lips, how indescribably soft they looked, how the points in the centre formed a defiant bow curving up towards her nose.

'What?'

'Your name?' she whispered again, leaning forward, her eyebrows raised as if she worried she was speaking to an idiot. 'I might save you by calling it, if I should see you about to be crushed by a carriage on the Whitechapel Road.'

'I'm Sister Chapman,' I said, smiling my best smile.

She looked at me a little strangely, and replied, 'I'm Aisling.'

'Oh!' I understood. 'I'm Susannah.'

'I am fond of that name.'

'Thank you.'

'I had a horse called Susannah, when I was a child.'

'Oh.'

'Where are you from, Susannah?'

'I'm sorry?'

'Where are you from?'

'I'm from… places, I think.'

'I see,' she said, then turned back to her notes as if that was the end of it.

I was desperate to continue, and to not come across so foolish. In the absence of anything meaningful, I gabbled away at the first thing that came into my head.

'I was born in these parts. I lived with my parents until they died of scarlet fever.'

'What! The both of them? What a terrible misfortune. Do you have brothers and sisters?'

'No, none. Yes. I mean, no brothers or sisters, and yes, they both died. I was extremely lucky; I was taken in by my mother's parents. They raised me, in Reading. That's where I lived before here.'

'So you're from Reading.'

'I suppose I am. You're Irish.'

'I know.'

'No, I know you know. I meant only to observe the fact.'

'Yes, and you are English.'

'Yes, but we're in London, so that's a very ordinary thing, isn't it?'

'I'm quite sure half of London is Irish, or will be at this rate. I'll wager you can't throw a stone without hitting an Irishman wherever you are in the world these days. We're restless types.'

'Is that because of the potatoes?' I asked.

'I beg your pardon,' said Aisling. It was not a question, and she gasped as she said it. This had gone horribly wrong.

We didn't speak again for at least another three weeks, maybe four. The training schedule was so gruelling, there wasn't much opportunity for recreation. The only places for casual conversation were the nurses' lounge and the dormitory, but we were all so shattered, we craved sleep above all else. Besides, I had never had a close friendship and had no idea how to go about forging one. Other people's friendships seemed to sprout into existence like weeds, without effort, when they weren't looking, whereas I kept staring at them and willing them to grow. Then one day Aisling just came out with another question, picking up where we'd left off.

'What about your grandparents?'

'Pardon?'

'Your grandparents. Your parents died of scarlet fever and you were raised in Reading by your grandparents. Are they very proud of you becoming a nurse?'

'Oh no, my grandmother thought the idea abhorrent! A disgusting concept. They're dead.'

'Who are?'

'My grandparents.'

'Jesus! Both parents dead, and grandparents, and no brothers or sisters! What about cousins?'

'No, none.'

'Shocking! I have a million. That's why I'm over here. You are welcome to a few of mine.'

'Really?'

'No. I was exaggerating.'

'Oh.' I didn't know what to say, so I said nothing.

'I was trying to make a joke,' she said. 'I only meant to ask a question to get to know you, but so far everyone I've asked about is dead, so I wanted to lighten the mood.'

'Oh, I couldn't tell. I'm sorry.'

'No, my family are all still alive, so it's I who should be apologising, in more ways than one.'

'Where are you from?'

'Kildare. It's in Ireland, but then you knew that, as you're so very clever.'

'There's no need to be rude.'

'I was doing it again,' she said.

The sister supervising the class shot us a stern look and held a rigid finger in front of her dry lips. 'Sshhhhhh!'

'Doing what?' I whispered.

'Joking,' Aisling whispered back.

'You shouldn't do that, you know,' I said.

'Do what? I'm sure I haven't done a thing.'

'Make fun of me. It's very confusing.'

'I'll bear that in mind.'

The next lesson I didn't say much, and Aisling didn't either. But the one after that I thought I would be the braver person and ask her about herself. My grandfather had always said it paid dividends to ask questions of a person, that it was important to show an interest, even when they were hostile. He used to say that I was far too inward-looking, which might come across as taking an unhealthy interest in myself.

'What type of place is Kildare?' I asked, holding my pencil in front of my mouth so the sister couldn't see my lips moving.

'Oh, it's awful,' whispered Aisling. 'It's a big bog and it rains constantly. A big wet peat bog. There are horses, and peat bogs, and that's about it.'

'What's peat?'

'You don't know what peat is?'

'I'm sure I don't.'

'It's earth. Red, fluffy earth. You can grow anything in it. You can burn it. And you can bury things in it. My father owns a lot of land and he's forever having men dig up people from the Middle Ages, and then an overexcited aristocratic Englishman who claims he's an archaeologist will turn up and demand we leave it alone so it can be studied and put in a museum.' She looked up at me then and flashed me a smile and then her eyes glazed over until she appeared to be somewhere else together, before she shook herself back to the moment. 'It's a good place for keeping the dead. It preserves them, nothing can get to them there. The bodies, when they find them, look as if they've only lain down and fallen asleep.'

'Well, now that I know so much about bogs, I shall bear that in mind,' I said, hoping to make her laugh again. It worked.

'Well done! That's impressive, Susannah.'

'What?'

'You made a joke of it. In the moment. I feel we've come on leaps and bounds – we're practically best friends.'

'I can't tell if you are being cruel or not,' I said.

'I'm never cruel. I don't have it in me.'

'I still can't tell,' I said. I had a sharp pain in my tongue and I winced.

'What's the matter?' asked Aisling.

'It's my tongue, I think it has lumps on it.'

'Show me. You can trust me – I'm a trustworthy nurse with a pleasant and obedient manner.'

Without thinking, I poked my tongue out, and Aisling squinted and studied it, went almost cross-eyed.

'Sister Chapman!' shouted the ward sister at the front of class, looking straight at me with my tongue still out. 'What do you think you are doing! Outside at once. Such manners!'

I was sent to sit outside Matron's office and had to explain my tongue and show her the ulcers. She waved me away, irritated that I'd been sent to her, and told me that in future I should keep my tongue in my mouth where it belonged, unless specifically instructed otherwise by a doctor, and only within hospital walls, as if I needed the additional clarification.

When I emerged, Aisling was standing in the hallway.

'Are you waiting for me or did you get into trouble too?' I said.

'Did you get a telling-off?' she asked.

'It wasn't so bad.'

'Good. Would you like to come and walk in the garden for some air? It's quite pleasant out. We should make the most of it. It'll be cold again soon.'

Little Lost Polly

At about midnight, someone shouted that the sky was burning, and they all poured out of The Frying Pan and onto Thrawl Street, pints in hand, to see for themselves. They said there looked to be great yellow tongues licking at the heavens on this last night of August 1888. The rain was coming fast and heavy, and the thunder and lightning made the air thick and tense.

Polly was drunk, but she hadn't realised quite how drunk until she was outside and heard herself squealing. The Shadwell docks were on fire and the flames were coming from the South Quay warehouses, full of produce from the colonies; brandy and gin. It made a hellish scene. The ash was showering down on Thrawl Street like snow. The smoky air hit Polly square in her weak chest and made her giddy, but she skipped beneath the falling grey flakes anyway, danced with some other women from the pub, women she barely knew, and giggled as the ash got caught in her new black straw bonnet with the velvet trim. As she hopped about, she slipped, landed on her backside and had to be dragged up between two dockers, her linsey frock now *wet with muck. She laughed but found it harder to stay upright than she should. It was at this moment precisely that the dark mood came.*

She remembered that she'd spent her night's lodging three times over. The money she'd put aside for her bed had gone on gin and beer, and a wave of her own failings came back around for another blow. Stupid Polly. She attempted to berate herself sober. Silly Polly. She retreated back inside the pub to count what was left of her coins but couldn't manage it. Even so, she knew it wasn't enough and she could not ask for help from her friends because she could not trust them.

Polly stumbled outside again and staggered up to Wilmott's Lodging House further up Thrawl Street. She'd paid for a bed there often enough – and given her fair share to others too, when the begging cap came around the kitchen – so she fancied her chances. She hung about, mentioning to whoever would hear her that she was a few pence short, but she was met with glazed eyes, castaway glances and a change in conversation. Bastards. She'd hoped that when the lodgings' deputy came down to collect his fee, the missing penny or two would be supplied by one of her pals, but there was no such luck.

'I'm not in the habit of letting out beds to those that don't have their money. You know that,' he said. 'You're drunk – you should have thought of this when you were spending your money on gin.'

'I'll be back,' she replied. 'See, what a jolly new bonnet I've got.' It was easier to pretend she didn't care or else she'd get upset, or angry, which was much the same thing.

She got as far as the corner of Osborn Street, where she

was grabbed by a passing woman, causing her to stumble and fall against the wall. It was Ellen Holland.

'Polly? Where you off to at this hour?' *said Ellen.* 'Polls? Jesus, how much have you had?'

Ellen knew Polly liked to drink too much, but didn't they all? Ellen sometimes shared a bed with her, was familiar with her bad and good habits, but on this occasion she was a particular mess.

'I've had it, and spent it, three times over, Ellen,' *Polly said and burst into laughter.*

'What? What have you had?'

'My bed! I spent it all. I'll be back, so can you tell him... can you tell him not to let my bed go? I'll be back... Tell him not to give my bed away.'

'Did you not hear the clock?' *said Ellen.* 'It's struck two. What time did you think it was?'

'I don't know. I'm lost, I think.'

'What do you mean, lost? You know where you are.'

'It's all gone to me. I won't have a bed now, will I?'

'Oh, Polly, come back with me.'

Ellen tried to pull her back towards Wilmott's, but Polly yanked herself free and fell against the wall again.

'No, I've done all that. Not a penny from no one. I won't play the idiot again, not tonight.'

'You going to be all right?'

'Course I am.'

Polly peeled herself off the damp brick wall and stumbled off into the sobering rain. She half registered the worry on Ellen's face and it had irritated her. Worry, guilt, sorry, all cheap and all too easily thrown about when it was a few pence that was needed.

She staggered on up Buck's Row, steadying herself on the small fences outside the cottages with their neat little hedges and clean steps. It wasn't that cold. She was searching for a gap between stairs or a yard door where she could nestle down and hide until the morning. There was no one about. It was pitch black. She was so occupied looking for a spot, she'd not heard the footsteps approaching from behind. Maybe this man would be good for a penny or two? Perhaps her luck hadn't run out after all.

13

In the early hours, I was woken by the sound of the front door slamming, the floor creaking and the rapid fire of feet along floorboards. I sat bolt upright, a jolt surging through me, and strained to listen to the furious whispers just outside my bedroom. I thought it had to be burglars and that I was about to be robbed and murdered in my own home. I sprang out of bed and on my toes watched a wavering light coming from under the door, shadows moving amidst it. Then I noted a familiar resonance to the voice, and my body collapsed like a paper bellows with relief.

'Thomas?' I called out.

The murmurings outside fell silent, and I swear that even the light stopped flickering, as if it too was holding its breath.

'Thomas!' I called out again, bolder this time.

Still nothing.

I fumbled for the matches by my bedside, and the footsteps dispersed. We were in a race against each other. I lit the candle and flew across the floor like a banshee, nightgown billowing behind me. My first thought was he had brought another woman home, as he had brought me, that he was secreting his mistress in the freezing attic and somehow sneaking her out when they were done. I wanted to know what she was. Maybe an exotic bird, all orange hair and black feathers. My insides boiled from fear to fury. How dare he bring back his new whore and play with her above my head? He would curse us both with a disease.

When I tore open the door there was nothing but darkness. My candle blinded me. The only sign that someone had been standing there was the unsettled dust now swirling in circles. I stepped out into the corridor and waited for my eyes to adjust. There was a creak to my left and I turned my head and held up my candle. Thomas was standing with his back to me, halfway up the attic stairs.

'Thomas, what are you doing?' This time there would be no denying what I could see with my own eyes.

'Go to bed, Susannah. I must be up for work in the morning. I have to sleep,' he said, and made to continue up the stairs.

'No, you don't! Where is she?'

I ran to him and grabbed the sleeve of his coat, while trying to keep the candle away from my wild hair. The arm of his coat was wet to the touch with what I thought was rain.

'Dr Lancaster was speaking to me, Mrs Lancaster. Only me.' It was Mrs Wiggs at the top of the main staircase behind us.

It was unsettling to see her in her nightgown. She looked much younger with her hair in a long plait over her shoulder, her gown as pale as her skin. She had a candle in one hand

and a water jug in the other. She was staring down at my wet hand, so I glanced at it too. When I turned it over, it was bright red, bloodied. I looked to Thomas, who was facing me now.

'What's this?' I said.

Then I looked at Mrs Wiggs, who had her eyes on the floor. I knew something terrible had happened, and they had already agreed in whispers that it was to be kept from me. I felt frightened of them both then, and backed away, towards my bedroom door.

'I don't know what has happened, but shall we not pretend I don't recognise blood when I see it,' I said, and took another step in the direction of my room.

Mrs Wiggs moved forward to speak, but Thomas rushed down the stairs and stopped her with a raised hand. Then he came slowly towards me with his palms up and his coat open, as if in surrender. His white shirt, undone, was covered in blood. I was reminded of arteries cut at the hospital and how the blood would spurt out with such force, it would hit me, the wall and the ceiling. A streak of scarlet. I felt sick.

'What have you done?' I said, inching away with my back to the wall, a bare foot over the threshold of my bedroom.

'Mrs Lancaster, won't you...?' started Mrs Wiggs, but Thomas stopped her again with a glance. How close they must have been, to communicate with small gestures and looks.

'Susannah, I'm not going to lie to you. It is blood,' he said. 'I didn't want to wake you. The truth is, I was in a fight and I asked Mrs Wiggs to fetch me some water.'

'There is water in our room, and ample in the bathroom next door,' I said.

This Thomas, the one whose eyes were soft and blue, kept trying to make my gaze meet his as he came towards me. I refused.

'I could hardly come and wake you like this. I didn't want to scare you. You look pale, I've clearly given you a fright.'

'Judging by the colour of your shirt, someone else is looking a lot paler than me,' I said. 'What fight? Why would you be fighting? Is the other man dead? What about the police?'

'Mrs Wiggs, take the water to the attic. I'll be up in a minute,' he said. Then he lunged at me, tried to grab the arm of my nightgown, but I was ready and leapt into my bedroom.

'No!' I shouted. 'You're not coming in here. Go with Mrs Wiggs to your attic!'

I tried to close the door on him, but he butted a shoulder against it and thrust it open. I ran to the other side of the room and stood with my arms wrapped about me as he tore off his bloodied shirt and wiped down his arms and chest with it. I shuddered as he threw the bloodied rag on the floor. He looked at me, his torso blue in the moonlight filtering through the curtains. He stood there for an age, staring at me as if considering what he should do. I felt my own blood drain from my body, because I was frightened of him.

It is a strange sensation to be frightened of someone to whom you thought yourself close. Although the clues are there when you look back, it is still a shock. The understanding that I had no idea of who or what I had married came rushing up to meet me all at once. I could only curse myself for having been so stupid. I had good reason to be fearful too, because after this period of cold regard, he exploded.

'I had a fight. A fight – that's it! As my wife, you might be pleased the other fellow came off worse than me.'

'You still haven't told me why you were fighting.'

'He owed me money.'

'Money? For what? Why would someone owe you money?'

'It doesn't matter.'

'It matters to me.'

'You don't need to know!'

'It would seem there are many things I don't need to know. Like where you go to get in such fights.'

'What are you talking about? This is just like you! Making everything about yourself!'

'I am your wife,' I said. 'I am under no illusions that you have your secrets. I don't know where you go, or whose company you keep—'

'I have given you everything you wanted. You wanted out of the hospital; I took you away. You wanted money; now you have it. But still you complain. Is it any wonder I have to escape from the woman who finds fault with everything – because I work or see my friends, because I want to relax without her whining in my ear. You were never happier than when I was lying in a hospital bed in fucking agony!'

He spat the words with such fury and hatred, and as he shouted, his chest hardened and his veins swelled like worms under his skin. I worried that the blood might burst out. I must have done something wrong, but I could not remember how the argument came to be my fault. Hadn't we been stood in the hallway with him covered in blood? I was still blindsided by this turnabout when he flew at me and grabbed me by the shoulders. I dropped the candle and it rolled about the floor in its brass holder, still alight, until it stopped by the bedclothes.

'The candle! The candle!' I shouted.

He shoved me away from him and I stumbled backwards into the chest of drawers with the arch of my back. My head hit the mirror on the wall behind and cracked the glass. Thomas tried to stamp on the candle, missed it several times as it rolled around and taunted him, then trapped it and the light was snuffed out. We were in the dark, with only his laboured breathing for sound.

Mrs Wiggs pushed the door open; she held her own candle, which trembled as much as her voice.

'Dr Lancaster, is everything all right?'

I touched the back of my head; it was wet with blood.

Thomas kicked violently at the brass candlestick. It bounced off the wall and nearly hit both Mrs Wiggs and myself as it ricocheted about the room. We both yelped as it sailed past. His hair was wet and hanging over his face.

'I gave you what you wanted,' he said. 'And what do I get?'

At that moment I found him utterly repugnant and couldn't even look at him.

I didn't dare say a thing. A watery trickle was snaking its way through my hair and down my neck. He shoved his face right up close to mine. I could feel his breath on my cheek and smell the alcohol on him. My nerves screamed and my heart all but stopped; I thought he was going to hit me. I kept my eyes nailed to the floor.

'I get nothing!' he shouted in my face. Then he spat at me.

I flinched and shut my eyes. He stormed out, stomped up the attic stairs and slammed the door behind him.

I burst into tears, and Mrs Wiggs quietly retreated, taking the light of the candle with her. I was left alone to feel my way back to bed. After that, I locked my bedroom door at night.

14

I was woken by Mrs Wiggs rattling my bedroom door. Her thin voice called out to me between huffs of frustration at the new barrier between us. The memories came flooding in, making me shiver. I threw off the bedclothes, sat up and touched the skin at the back of my head. It was pulled taut into a tender, scabby seam. Mrs Wiggs continued pestering the door handle as if it would change its mind about being locked. In a daze, I stomped over and released it. She swooped in like a buzzard circling for rabbits: all grey skirts and pointed features. I sloped back to bed and pulled the blankets over me. It was Saturday and I had decided I would not get up again that day.

'It is gone midday, Mrs Lancaster. I was concerned that something might be wrong. Are you well?'

It appeared my fragile health was a concern for the servants now. 'I am well, Mrs Wiggs. What could possibly be wrong with me?' I gave her my best wide eyes, and was met with a narrowing of hers.

'You haven't eaten since Thursday evening. Neglect of

one's appetite can make a person… hysterical,' she said. 'You've not emerged from this room since—'

'Since the early hours of Friday morning. When my husband dragged himself home.' I lay down and stared at the ceiling. 'Is he here?'

'No, Mrs Lancaster, he went out early this morning. I shall have the mirror replaced today, and take some of these clothes to the laundry. I assume that is why they are on the floor?'

I was not a tidy mistress and left my clothes scattered about my room. Having the privilege to do so was a novelty I still enjoyed.

'You should leave the mirror, if only to remind us to agree on who should get the bad luck, Thomas or myself. It was my head that cracked it, after all.'

'It will do no good to make a catastrophe of a silly accident, Mrs Lancaster. We shouldn't punish ourselves.'

'Not when we have others to punish us,' I replied.

My comment was met with silence as dense as any Embankment mud. Eventually she sighed and said, 'I shall send Sarah up with breakfast.' She walked towards the door with an armful of laundry.

'No need for breakfast. Just send Sarah, please.'

'What for?'

'I have an errand for her.'

'I can tell her.'

'No. Thank you.'

More silence.

'Very well.' Then she departed, and I locked the door behind her.

Two minutes later, Sarah knocked and I gave her my

instructions and sent her away. While I waited for her to return, I worried. My security depended on being sure of Thomas's affection. My position as his novelty had been tenuous, I knew that, but it seemed my day in the sun was over already. I had not even managed a brief spell in the territory of the comfortably familiar, hadn't had the chance to insinuate myself like a pair of worn slippers he would be hesitant to throw away. I had travelled straight to inconvenience; surely exile or death would follow. My young husband had a dreadful temper, and I feared for the person who had been on the receiving end of it the night he returned home wearing their blood. No, I couldn't leave my room that day. I had too much to think over, too many possibilities to consider.

I remembered the shirt, leapt up and scoured the room for it, but it was gone. Of course! I had to laugh. Mrs Wiggs had only come to retrieve Thomas's shirt from where he had thrown it.

Blood didn't pour like that from punches; there must have been a knife, and Thomas's bare chest hadn't had a mark on it. What if the man he had fought with was now dead? The police might even be on their way. What would I say if they should question me?

Finally, Sarah returned.

'Here, Mrs Lancaster,' she said, struggling with the load. 'Mrs Wiggs said you weren't feeling right. She did give me a look when she saw me bringing these up – she doesn't approve, you know, thinks it morbid. Anyway, I told her it would do you good, get the heart beating, because everyone's in such a state over it. See, it's on every front page. It's what you and the rest of London's been waiting for, missus.

I don't know how you read it – gives me the shivers.'

She heaved the bundle onto the top of the dresser and I snatched the top one: *The Daily News* from the first of September.

ANOTHER BRUTAL MURDER IN WHITECHAPEL

Another woman was found brutally slaughtered in Whitechapel yesterday.

Shortly before four o'clock in the morning, Police Constable Neil discovered the woman lying in her own blood in Buck's Row. Her throat had been savagely cut from ear to ear. PC Neil raised the alarm and a doctor was summoned.

Dr Llewellyn of Whitechapel Road inspected the body and pronounced the woman dead. The corpse was swiftly removed to Bethnal Green Police Station and upon further examination the horrifying details of the crime were revealed. The poor woman's lower half had been mutilated by deep gashes.

The body was taken to the mortuary of the parish in Old Montague Street and the police made efforts to identify the woman.

CAST OUT OF LODGING HOUSE

A petticoat worn by the woman was marked with the stamp of Lambeth Workhouse and the only personal effects found in the pockets were a comb and a piece of looking glass.

As news of the crime travelled, it was discovered that she met the description of a regular at a lodging house in Thrawl Street. Women from this particular house were summoned and recognised the deceased as 'Polly', who had frequently taken a bed on the usual terms of the nightly fee of 4d.

IDENTIFICATION OF THE DECEASED

An inmate from the Lambeth Workhouse later identified the deceased as Mary Ann Nichols, 42, commonly known as Polly, who had been in the aforementioned workhouse in April and May of last year.

Mary Ann Nichols left the workhouse in May to take a position as a domestic in Wandsworth Common, but this did not last and soon she was wandering the streets and staying at lodging houses or the workhouse.

Nichols was married but had lived apart from her husband and children for years.

NO ONE HEARD ANYTHING

It is extraordinary that the noise of this brutal slaying seemingly did not arouse the sleeping tenants in the area. Buck's Row being a street tenanted by a respectable class of people, far superior to the surrounding streets.

There was a mark found on the jaw on the right side of the face as though made by a thumb, and another bruise on the left side. There was a cut under the left ear, reaching the centre of the throat, and another from the right ear to the centre. The neck was severed down to the spine. The gashes in the abdomen must also have been inflicted with extreme savagery.

Dr Llewellyn stated that the injuries were the most severe and shocking he had ever seen in his career.

Just like Emma Smith and Martha Tabram, Polly Nichols had been walking those Whitechapel streets in the early hours. The papers reported that the police thought she'd been killed by a person whose company she was keeping, a polite way of saying she was a prostitute, also just like Emma and Martha.

I kept seeing Emma Smith, the bag of broken twigs, lying there bleeding to death on the hospital bed. I thought of her birdlike legs and the little dunnock and how Emma had been put in a box but did not fly away come the morning. I began to wonder how these women must have felt. What was going through their minds when they realised what was about to happen to them? Did they fight? What does a woman feel in the moment she is murdered?

I found the newspaper reporting frustrating. I consumed newspaper after newspaper, in the hope of filling in gaps in the detail, but to no avail, most simply rehashed the same old facts, which were thin on the ground to begin with and some were more like directions as to what opinions we should form of the women. As a way of making sense of it all, and for something to do – I decided I would walk in these women's shoes, and surmise some of this missing detail myself. I was going to try and thread their stories together, like stitching up my own Frankenstein's monster, but instead I would create the victims, these forgotten and

discarded women, and I would bring them back to life in
their last moments. I understand this to be weird, macabre
and a little indulgent in what some might call the perverse.
God knows what Thomas and Mrs Wiggs would think of
it, they would call me twisted, immoral or sick, but my own
physician had advised that I might find some therapy in
writing my thoughts down. I was curious to see where it
would lead me. I only wanted to bring these women back
and spend a little time with them, have them speak and
for me to listen and understand. The moment you realise
you are to be murdered and your life is to end in such a
miserable way must be the loneliest of all. Someone should
have the courage to accompany them in this and I found
myself compelled to do so.

I scoured the million theories and opinions that filled
the papers, I analysed the articles that were fleshed out
from the most meagre of ideas and the ones that had been
fabricated around eyewitness accounts that were nothing at
all. I curated my scrapbook of snippets, and from all that
text and supposition I fashioned my own account of the last
moments of Little Lost Polly. And I felt better for it. Then
I hid these scrawls in the dresser in the back dining room.

It became very difficult to read the information and
maintain a rational thought which wasn't excited by a most
paranoid fear. Commentators variously held that it had been
a case of mistaken identity, the revenge of a jealous lover,
the work of a maniac, an escaped lunatic... The perpetrator
had to be foreign for no Englishman could have done such
a thing. It was a lunatic Jew down on whores. The murderer
was left-handed. It was a gang of body-snatchers... Some
newspapers said Polly lost a tooth during the attack, others

said she lost five and that the murderer had kicked them loose. It turned out she was missing the top five but had lost them years ago.

The only commonality between the reports was an accepted belief that the murderer had to be the same man who'd killed Emma Smith and Martha Tabram. Detective Inspector Abberline, of the Criminal Investigation Department, and Detective Inspector Helson, of J Division, had also stated this. If the murderer had hoped to make an impact, he must have been extremely proud.

But what of Thomas? He had come home the night of Polly's murder covered in blood. I had been reading about the murder of Martha Tabram over breakfast on the morning Thomas had appeared with scratches down his neck. Hadn't he been missing the night before?

It seemed far-fetched, of course, a mere coincidence. Then I read that the doctor at the inquest believed the murderer must have anatomical knowledge; all the vital parts of Polly Nichols' forty-two-year-old body had been targeted with such precision, he said, he suspected that the killer might be a doctor. I read those words and heard the whistle and screech of a train as it pulls into a station. I dropped the paper and stood up but felt so ill and giddy I had to sit back down.

Those scratches, as if from a woman's nails in desperation. Mrs Wiggs washing his bloodstained shirts in the bath. The scurrying and hiding in the attic, the repeated disappearances. Then coming home covered in blood the very same night as the next murder. I clutched my chest.

★ ★ ★

Once I had calmed myself down, I dismissed my conspiracy theories as the product of a bored and lonely mind; my imagination, encouraged to run a riot, had run away with itself. I had no more of my drops, and without those to dull my senses I was close to peeling wallpaper off with my teeth. There was too much room in my head and it was full of fog. I was invested in this marriage; I had no choice but to make it a functional relationship, at the very least. There was no trail of breadcrumbs leading back to my old life.

We slipped back into routine, and no one batted an eyelid. It was as if nothing had ever happened, but things had changed between us now.

The things I had read and the mystery of those two nights were like flea bites; I could ignore them most of the time, but occasionally they drove me mad with itching. At breakfast he would smile at me, at dinner he would ask if I'd had a good day, and I would hear the clock tick or see a fly landing on an apple and be reminded of the scratches, the blood, the crack of the mirror, the dent in the bedroom wall from the candlestick, the fat veins on his chest. There were the other things he said to me within the bedroom on the nights he did come home: that I was as good as fucking a corpse, how strange I was, how old I was beginning to look, how he could have done so much better, how I should be very grateful for my luck. And when daylight came we must pretend as if we were Chelsea's Adam and Eve.

15

My puppyish schoolboy of April had grown into a debonair gentleman in June, but come September he was the middle-aged grump. Everything irritated him and he had little patience. I avoided him whenever I could, and approached with care when I could not, because he would hiss like a snake at any voice in earshot. Even Mrs Wiggs skirted around him.

Since Polly's murder, he had become agitated and restless. He started to bite his fingernails, a habit I would never have associated with him. His jaw clenched and in the mornings he brushed his teeth too hard and spat blood in the basin. He overgroomed his whiskers and asked me, for the first time, if they were symmetrical. 'You know,' he said, 'I've stared at them for so long, I cannot tell any more.'

This was not the Thomas who had made light of his burns and was confident about his place in the world. To see him nervous rattled my own nerves. I had married him for protection, traded my independence and freewill so that I would not have to hold down a job or bear the anxieties of the outside world.

His fermenting anger choked the air out of the house. The walls practically breathed a sigh of relief when he left for work or for one of his mystery night-time jaunts. I know I did. I had assumed that men were warriors, brave and fearless, but now I had experience of one so intimately, I understood them to be as weak as any woman. Weaker, perhaps, because Thomas still clung to the delusion that he was the strong and rational one. It could not be a strength to ignore one's own flaws.

If I asked what was troubling him, he would talk casually of hospital politics or troublesome patients, or tell me it was the burden of his other work. He had been asked to assist a select group of prominent doctors in some pioneering sponsored study. They were all far more experienced than him, the potential for progression was huge, and the business was profitable, but it was undertaken at night. I knew his private practice was still lacking patients, but he seemed to think this other employment more worthy of his attention and energy.

He was further antagonised by some letters he'd received from his twin sister, Helen. She had apparently adopted an altogether inappropriate tone, was showing a distinct lack of respect and really did think herself queen of the castle. He complained that she was unrealistic about the amount of money required to live to a decent standard in London and how long it took to build up a private practice. She had accused him, he said, of not having a strong enough work ethic. That in particular set him ranting for hours.

'As if Helen has ever understood what it is to work! Someone should tell her that barking orders at people is neither difficult nor tiring. How I should like to rub her nose in it, tell her all about my other job and how profitable it will be and who I am socialising with, but I won't. She wouldn't understand, and I certainly will not be explaining myself to *her*,' he said.

His twin sister, once so highly spoken of was now referred to as a 'vicious little bitch' or the 'bat-faced dumpling'.

He would not let me read those letters but rather shouted his commentaries at me. On one occasion I dared share an idea about how he might gain more patients at his private practice. I suggested he consider simply filling his books rather than acquiring prominent names, which I knew was his inclination. The look he gave me was as if I'd just asked him to walk naked through Chelsea and lick the boot of the first shitraker.

'Is that what you think I should do? Fill my diary with the headaches and boils of civil servants, attend to the bellyaches of people of no significance?' He threw down his cutlery with a loud clatter.

At least I no longer jumped at his little tantrums; I was perpetually braced for them. 'Isn't word of mouth a good endorsement?' I replied. 'Civil servants or not. The more people you treat, the more chance you have of receiving a recommendation to someone well connected. I'm sure this other work is enticing, but you cannot expect a quick path to success, Thomas. Look at Dr Shivershev: his books are full. I had to mention our relationship from my time at the hospital to get an appointment.'

As soon as the words left my mouth, I knew I had made a terrible mistake. Men do not like their property to show admiration for other owners. I held my breath and froze. When I looked up at him, he was staring straight at me, still as a statue. Without saying anything, he tossed his plate in the air. It landed on my glass, shattering it and covering me in wine and shards of glass. He stood up, pushed back his chair and walked out as if nothing had happened. The man who continually accused me of being oversensitive and melodramatic disappeared up to his precious attic like a spoiled child retreating to his nursery, chased by the ever faithful Mrs Wiggs, flapping her hands to fan his fragile ego.

On the positive, Mrs Wiggs and I had slipped into an unspoken agreement that we would ignore each other. I no longer tripped about the house, second-guessing myself, feeling anxious that I might be inhaling the wrong way. There would be no more lectures on candles or hairbrushes. I had come to the idea that it was perhaps Mrs Wiggs that was the cause of many of our problems. I dreamed of being able to hire a meek, pock-faced girl to replace her. Thomas and I would get along much better without Mrs Wiggs to squeeze between us like a jealous lapdog. If I could get rid of her, then it would truly become my house.

I still felt the outsider under her feet, so to amuse myself and drive Mrs Wiggs mad with frustration at not knowing where I was, I had taken to spending my days in the city, wandering aimlessly, sitting in the British Library, visiting museums and churches, or walking in the parks when the weather was dry. At least this way she couldn't report back to Thomas that I lounged about the house all day in a laudanum-induced stupor, poisoning him still further with shrewdly selected words that tarnished his impression of me.

★ ★ ★

The papers were now full of the news that the police were hunting a man they called Leather Apron, so it was a relief to learn that my husband was not the Whitechapel murderer after all. For a while it had seemed plausible, especially at night, when I had the most vivid dreams. I took more drops to try and snuff out the visions, but that only made them more surreal. Come daylight it seemed laughable.

Leather Apron was a petty criminal from Whitechapel. He was a well-known bully of prostitutes, and so many local whores had named him freely to the police that everyone was convinced he was the man. He was a Jew of no known trade and rumoured to be so depraved and devoid of human decency that he'd been rejected by his own community. He had also been missing since the night of Polly Nichols' murder. The police had torn apart more than two hundred houses looking for him. It was true that I didn't know where Thomas had been on those nights, but how many wives honestly knew where their husbands were of an evening? That was marriage. This was what I had traded my freedom for. I might as well get on with it.

The police complained of the crowds that continued to gather at the murder spots and outside the mortuaries where the bodies had been taken. I decided I would go to Whitechapel myself. I had this feeling that if I knelt on the ground and sniffed the pavement like a bloodhound, I would be able to dismiss the idea once and for all that my husband with the symmetrical whiskers had ever stood there, let alone stuck a knife in a whore and slit her open.

I took the river taxi all the way from Chelsea to Tower Hill, then the omnibus to Aldgate. I started at St Botolph's, known as 'the prostitutes' church' on account of the constant stream of mangy old trollops who circled it day and night. They sauntered in a slow circuit to avoid being stopped by the police. It was a farcical circus. They pranced openly in their short skirts with their ankles on display, their coloured scarves flowing around them, and their craggy faces smeared with make-up they had made or stolen, which only made them look older and more haggard. They jeered at men, touted for business and conducted entire conversations with each other by shouting to the woman behind or in front, but as long as they kept moving, the police pretended not to notice. I could not imagine what unhygienic horrors lay beneath those skirts; it was a wonder they managed to trap any man for business. Surely only a blind or suicidal drunk would be tempted to part with actual money for their services.

This was the opening act to Whitechapel from the Aldgate end. I walked up Petticoat Lane until it turned into Sandy's Row and the pavements went narrow and the shops too. Space was so expensive there that all things shrank to fit their means. Everything was stacked on top of something else and every crawl space was filled with tatty stock, cracked barrels or piles of old rubbish on broken bits of wood showered with smashed glass like glittering confetti. Shop goods spilled onto the pavement, and around them hovered gangly, grey-faced boys with the sunken chests of the malnourished and the shaved heads of the lice-ridden. Their bodies arced backwards like whittled bone. The boys enjoyed their purpose a little too much, marauding and staring at women. The stuff they guarded like the crown jewels was so laughably useless.

I had not been in Whitechapel since I married in June.

I had thought that looking at the place with fresh eyes and the comfort of knowing I wasn't trapped there would be fun, but it wasn't, it was depressing, and I had more fear than I remembered. I had dressed in my dullest clothes, but being inconspicuous had always been difficult for me due to my height. I was an obvious outsider, felt only hostility and saw muck and filth. God knows what Mrs Wiggs would have made of it.

I walked past the boys and they whispered to each other. The cobblestones were covered in grease, made slippery from the rain, and I lost my footing and nearly fell. I waved my arms around like windmills to stay standing and must have looked a clown. I marched off to the squawking laughter of the boys behind me and did not look back. I passed rows of dismal rag shops filled with stained and torn costumes tossed out from the theatres, along with ripped and mouldy military uniforms, broken bayonets and rusty helmets from old wars. Sullen-faced gangs of Jewesses stood clustered in doorways and sat on kerbs with their elbows on their knees, glowering up at me as I passed them. They blocked the thresholds of their precious shops with their bodies and black looks, disinviting me before I'd even considered entering.

I came out at the entrance to the Nichol, a rabbit warren of alleys and courtyards I didn't dare go down. I often wished I could walk down Dorset Street and see the room I had lived in with my mother, see if it matched my memories, but there was no way I would go there on my own. I stood for a moment or two on the corner and then turned. A flash of eyes and a small pale face peeped up at me through the grate of a basement, then disappeared just as quick. It was a child or maybe a young girl in a sweatshop underground, hidden away, snatching a moment for themselves from the sweaters who run such dens of human misery. Men, women and children are sweated to death if not blindness first, working feverishly in the dark, trapped, they rattle their fingers to the bone for a pittance.

On Commercial Street the busy traffic and shrieking hawkers made me feel more relaxed. It had gas lamps too, whereas the smaller roads would be pitch black at night. It was a feat that Leather Apron had managed to see the women well enough to stab them.

The corner of Osborn Street was where Emma Smith had been attacked by what she'd said was a gang of three or four, though the papers made it clear they thought it was Leather Apron's work. They said she'd been too frightened to name him, even in her last moments. Less than two minutes' walk from there I reached the tenement building where Martha Tabram had been found. Women carrying children stood gossiping with their hair uncovered. I continued on towards the London to see Buck's Row, the place where Polly Nichols died. I passed the stalls along Whitechapel Road hawking celery, comic books, hairbrushes, fish; ribbons and door keys together, cabbages with trousers. The crowds slowed me down, so I chose a quieter road that had once been full of French silk-weavers. They were long gone, their livings stolen by machines and their grand houses neglected and crumbling. The names above the shops were all Jewish now, engaged in artisanal trades: cobblers, tailors and furniture makers. Shops sold books in Hebrew, and Jewish restaurants were run from houses with strange ornaments on the windowsill, the glass covered by heavy muslin drapes to guard against nosy gawkers.

At Buck's Row I cringed when I saw all the other ladies like myself, except they were in pairs. They clung to each other, giggling, and I felt terribly lonely and missed Aisling's arm pulling on mine. I could feel her fingers from where she used to pinch me when she was bored or tired. I only let myself think like that for a minute and then I pushed her away.

The spot where Polly had been murdered was being sold by a young girl of around ten or eleven. She was charging a ha'penny to look. It was her pavement, she told the crowd. She gave a theatrical re-enactment of how Nichols had died, pretending that her guts were being ripped out, and wearing a scarf as a bonnet. She performed with such gusto that I laughed and threw a few pennies for her entrepreneurship. It was very close to the London, only two roads behind it; you could be there in one or two minutes, less with a long stride. All three murder spots were a close and comfortable distance from the hospital. It seemed obvious that the police should make enquiries there, but I had read nothing of this in the papers.

In no rush to get back, I made my way towards Spitalfields. I walked back up Commercial Street, past Christ Church and the Ten Bells pub. The yard at Christ Church was known as Itchy Park because of the vagrants who slept in piled-up heaps like puppies on the benches there, swapping lice with each other. A few lay face down on the wet grass as if killed in battle. There was a spread of ages, but it was mostly men. Very occasionally, there was a family: parents sleeping with their backs against each other and a baby or two in their arms, trying to avoid the workhouse, where they'd be separated. I think most people were so used to the sight, they became blind to it.

I passed the iron railings and looked into the barren yard. There were no flowers or plants, only thick rye grass – the bulbs had been dug up and eaten by the starving years ago – but my eye was caught by a gentleman roaming amongst the vagrants like Jesus at a leper colony. He was upright and open, bumbling almost, his gait quite different from the hunched and angry stoop of the unfortunate and desperate. I approached the railings to look more closely and was taken aback to see that it was none other than my newly appointed physician: Dr Shivershev. He was wearing a black billycock and a long black frock coat at least two sizes too large. His face was still unshaven. He walked from group to group, crouched down and talked to the bobbing heads. He must have felt my eyes on him because he suddenly swivelled in my direction, searching for something among the iron bars. I shrank away, pulled my bonnet down and scurried off in the direction of the Ten Bells.

I took an omnibus to St James's Street and drifted into a milliner's. Seeing Dr Shivershev had reminded me about my glove with the hole in the finger. I pushed past a gaggle of brightly feathered ladies yipping at a shop assistant and found myself overwhelmed by the rows of beads, ribbons, feathers and flowers in all colours. The bleary-eyed ghost I'd glimpsed earlier in her underground prison could very likely have been the one to cut and stitch and piece together some of those pretty fripperies. If the ladies had known the provenance of the pretty feathers and flowers they were posing with so delightedly in front of the mirror, they'd have run screaming.

I made my way to the back of the shop, mostly to get some space, and for the second time that day I saw someone in what I understood to be their wrong place. The scrunched-up figure had her face turned away, but the tiny waist and bouncing red ringlets could only belong to one person: beautiful, pert, little Nurse Mabel Mullens. For some reason I had the urge to rush over, tap her on the shoulder and say hello, as if, being outside the hospital, all our old gripes would be forgotten. But before I reached her, she scurried off.

She glanced over her shoulder at me, and we locked eyes for a second. I smiled at her, but she disappeared around the corner. Of course, it was obvious: we had never been friends, so why would she speak to me now? I exited the shop feeling lonely and rejected. I cursed Aisling. I wanted to blame her for everything at that moment.

I had only walked down the road for a few minutes when I felt a sharp tug on one of the wide sleeves of my dolman. When I turned around, there was Mabel, out of breath, panting on the pavement and wearing neither coat nor bonnet.

'Su-san-nah...' she said, as if trying out the sound of my name for the first time. 'I can call you that now. No need for "Sister" any more, is there?'

We were blocking the pavement and the crowds tutted and brushed past us, but we didn't move. I didn't know what to say. Mabel was still small and pretty, maybe smaller than I remembered. She looked delicate, as if I could scoop her up in my hands. Her apple cheeks were hollow and she had a fading yellow bruise under her left eye.

'Mabel, how are you?'

'Haven't you heard?' she said.

'What am I meant to have heard?'

'It is good to see you. You look well,' she said.

She kept glancing behind her as if something might jump on her back, and shuffling from one foot to the other, her arms crossed over her chest against the cold.

'Are you all right?' I asked.

'I can't talk now. He watches us – the man who owns the shop. I can get away tomorrow, maybe for an hour or two. It would be good to speak properly. Shall I call on you?'

I realised what I had been too stupid to see: that Mabel was working in the milliner's. For a girl to go from a nurse to a shop assistant was a considerable fall. I looked at her dress. It was clean but old and worn. She saw me looking and folded her arms tighter across herself.

'I had to sell most of my clothes,' she said, and I felt my face flush.

'Yes, please come,' I said, not sure I believed the words even as they left my lips. 'If I tell you my address, will you remember it?'

Mabel laughed. 'I only need the number,' she said. 'I know where you live, Susannah. All the nurses know where you live – we all gossip, you know this, we all know you married the handsome young surgeon from Chelsea.'

16

My troubled history with Mabel Mullens had much to do with Aisling's dislike of her. There was one significant spat in particular, which happened during a lesson.

Mabel was sitting in front of me and Aisling. As usual, Aisling was leaning up on her elbows, swinging on her stool and whispering to me. She found it nigh on impossible to concentrate for long periods of time, especially in class. She was better at practical things, but when she was forced to sit, she would wriggle and distract me, which I found irritating. I helped Aisling with her theory and, later on, when our group of new nurses was unleashed on the public, she would teach me how to manage people. We were a good team.

Aisling also had a remarkable knack for never getting caught playing about. She had such an innocent-looking face that no one could believe she would ever do anything wrong. The result was that in any situation it was I who was cast as the Machiavel – such was the curse of being tall, dark but not necessarily handsome, and a girl. People forever assumed my severe frowning was because I was plotting something and not because I was actually concentrating.

Mabel hated our silly antics and would frequently shoot us spiteful looks. This time, she turned around to berate us while the doctor giving the bandaging lecture was facing the board. 'Will you two be quiet! It's so annoying, you whispering all the time while the rest of us are trying to think,' she hissed.

Aisling was having none of it. 'Oh, give it a rest, Mullens,' she spat. 'Like you've ever had a thought that someone else didn't put there. The only reason you're pretending to pay attention is because there's an unmarried man in the room.'

'What's wrong with that? Isn't that the natural thing?' Mabel said, and she smirked. The nurse sitting next to her looked shocked but then started smirking and laughing too.

'No educated man who can string a sentence together is going to be interested in you,' Aisling said.

'I can assure you, when I have a man's attention, the last thing he's thinking about is forming sentences,' said Mullens.

Some of the other nurses started to giggle. The doctor at the front of the class sensed something was going on and looked over, so everyone settled down for a couple of minutes.

But Aisling was getting increasingly worked up.

'You realise she's trying to antagonise you on purpose,' I said.

'Well, it's working,' said Aisling.

'Don't give her the satisfaction.'

'I can't let her have the last word,' said Aisling. She leaned forward and whispered at the back of Mabel's head, 'I'm sure the only thing you've learned in the last ten months is how to kneel and open your mouth. But then I expect you knew how to do that anyway.'

Mabel gave an audible gasp, picked up a roll of bandages from her table and threw it at us. Aisling and I ducked quick enough and the roll flew between us and travelled across the floor. Another nurse bent down and scooped it up, just as the doctor noticed the flurry of movement and gave us a stern look. I waited until he'd turned back to the blackboard.

'Are you happy now?' I whispered to Aisling.

'Why do you let people walk all over you?'

'Wait, are you angry with me now?'

'I'm always the one that sticks up for the both of us.'

'That's not true,' I said.

'Shhh!' A nurse from another table tried to quiet us.

'You shush!' I spat back.

Without thinking it through, I picked up another roll of bandages and threw it straight at the back of Mabel's head. My aim was perfect – I was very proud of that. The bandages bounced off Mabel's head in the only way a tightly wound roll could, sailed across the room and came to a stop at the feet of the doctor. He was young and nervous and clearly felt intimidated at being surrounded by such a large group of female students, with only his moustache for armour.

I still had my hand in the air from where I'd thrown the bandages, so there wasn't even any need to winkle out a confession.

'Chapman? Really?' the doctor said. 'Well, I didn't expect that. I think you'd better go and see Matron, don't you? I don't know what's the matter with everyone today. There must be something in the air.'

Matron Luckes was surprised to find me outside her office yet again. She was most disappointed, she said, to learn that I had engaged in such childish behaviour. I had to work hard to convince her that yes, this behaviour was out of character indeed. Outside, Aisling had waited for me. We walked arm in arm back to our quarters, laughing at how surprised we both were to learn I was such a good shot with a set of bandages.

17

Mrs Wiggs described the visitor as bedraggled and waited for an explanation. I enjoyed being given the opportunity to disappoint her, and told her to show the woman in, however unkempt. She turned to leave but then hesitated at the doorway, waiting for me to ask what the matter was, which I didn't. That, of course, drove her insane. I learned that technique from my husband.

'Is the lady collecting for charity, or a women's refuge?' she asked eventually.

'Please send her in, Mrs Wiggs,' I said.

This was the nature of our conversations at that point. In hindsight, those were the glory days. It would soon get much worse.

Once Mullens was shown into the front dining room and Mrs Wiggs was clear of the door, I found myself performing an anxious monologue of vapid small talk, adopting airs and graces I didn't have and that didn't suit me. I felt such an obvious fraud in my own home; it was horribly uncomfortable. We were overly congenial, as women who dislike each other tend to be when forced to spend time together, only a few badly chosen words from tearing each other's hair out. I knew that neither of us could sustain that level of nauseating sweetness for long, and it was me who broke first.

'I wasn't sure you would come. Yesterday, in the milliner's, I could have sworn you ran when you first got a glimpse of me.'

'How much do you know?' came the blunt reply.

'Mabel, if there is something I'm meant to know, whatever it is, I can assure you I don't.' I was already tired by the mystery.

Mabel went quiet and studied her hands in her lap. When she'd first come in, she'd looked about the room, appraising every ornament and trinket, trying to assess the worth of all that shined. I'd done the very same thing when I first took up residence there. Then she progressed to taking an inventory of me. Her glowing eyes alighted on the brooch at my throat and then examined the silk of my dress. Our knees were close enough as we sat together on the settee to make the clash of fabrics brutal and humiliating. She'd arrived wearing a baggy old duster with brass buttons, and beneath it a green chintz dress with daisies. I knew it had been chosen because the pattern made the wear less obvious; you had to really look hard to see where the holes had been repaired. I used to do these things myself. She had such pretty eyes, large and childlike, that it was hard to ignore them as they kept creeping back to my engagement ring and following my hands as I waved them in theatrical loops while I talked. Again, this was not my habit. Now she was there I couldn't wait for her to leave.

'I did run away at first... I didn't want you to see me, I

was ashamed, thought you'd laugh at me. You must think it odd that I am here. The truth is, I've nowhere else to turn. Laugh if you will, get it out of the way, then please say you will consider what I'm about to ask you.'

I felt the dread of an unknown favour in the pit of my stomach and hoped her request would not be something to further embarrass us both. I tiptoed over to the door, opened it an inch to check Mrs Wiggs wasn't listening, closed it again and sat down.

'What is it? Only don't talk too loudly, my housekeeper has very big ears,' I said.

Without any warning, Mabel started crying and put her face in her hands. I sat stiff as a scarecrow, trapped between her quivering shoulders and the door, imagining Mrs Wiggs and her omnipresent ears pressed to the other side. I kept telling Mabel to be quiet, but she continued to cry and rambled in between breathless sobs.

'I'm sorry. I don't even know why I'm here. Can you even remember why we never became friends, Susannah? Because I can't. I was always envious of how clever you were, I know that. I was right to be. I mean, look at you. You should be proud of how things turned out. I must have known, somehow, that you would get everything I wanted. I was jealous before it happened. It's not your fault, it's mine.'

I had always found it difficult to know how to act when people cried or displayed great emotion like that. It frightened me. I wanted to shake them or hit them. Why should such feeble creatures have the luxury of crumbling while the rest of us had to carry on?

When Mabel had finally calmed herself and wiped her nose on her sleeve, she looked at me with red eyes.

'I got myself a dose of scarlet fever, Susannah,' she said.

I didn't understand at first, but when she explained that she'd met a soldier, I knew what she meant. She had been courting him in secret for months, long before I met Thomas.

'He was an officer and we were to be married – or that was what I thought, anyway. We talked of being married, what type of house we would live in, children... I know that sounds stupid now,' she said.

Mabel had voluntarily left her job at the hospital, not wanting to suffer the humiliation of being fired, as I had been. She was sure her soldier would marry her imminently, on account of the fact she was carrying his child.

'But when I told Walter, he said he couldn't marry me, because he was already bloody married. I thought I'd gone mad, that I'd imagined the whole thing, but he did talk about marrying me, I swear. He let me believe it all along. We argued, of course, and when I asked why he'd said he loved me when it was so clearly a lie, he said, "I did at the time."'

That was the last she heard of Walter, the charmer.

'Why don't you go home to your father's farm?' I asked.

'My father won't have me, unmarried and with child, and nor will my sister's husband. I have to get rid of it, then I can go home.'

'So get rid of it,' I said.

This sent Mabel into another crying fit. I tried not to roll my eyes as I worried about the noise.

She had started to pay nightly bed rent in various doss houses, not being able to afford a decent boarding house. Some of the doss houses had more than forty beds, all of them with soiled straw and crawling with insects. 'It was frightening being so different to the other women in those places,' she said. 'I was afraid to fall asleep for fear of being robbed. All the women were thieves. Thieves and drunks. They drank beer when they had money, gin when they didn't, and they watched for new girls like hawks, working out who they could prey on.' She sniffed into her handkerchief again.

'I can't understand how I've found myself like this. How fast I have fallen – and I am still falling, Susannah. It feels like no more than a minute ago, a blink of an eye, that I was a nurse at the London. I felt safe. Now I don't know how to stop it getting worse. Where will I end up? You hear about those poor women found slaughtered like pigs in the gutter. Who is to say it won't be me one night?'

'Don't be silly, Mabel,' I said. 'Of course that won't happen to you,' I lied.

Obviously, it could happen to Mabel; it could happen to any one of us. Why else had I married Thomas? Why else had I stayed with him? All that talk about ending up like those poor dead women made me nervous. In nurturing my macabre obsession with them, was I inviting the same fate to befall me? With Mabel there, it was all too close; it was as if my destiny was circling above my head like a vulture.

'Will it be me next who is cut and found dead?' she wailed. 'Really, what is to prevent it? Where do I go? What shall I do? I did not think myself a bad person, Susannah. Why has this happened? I have been foolish, yes, but not *bad*. I am desperate, Susannah. You must understand how desperate I am, to have come to you, the woman I was so jealous of, and to be begging you, quite without dignity.

I have no one. The man who runs the shop you saw me in takes my wages to pay for my board. I can never earn enough to save any money. He and his wife, they keep us like billy goats upstairs in a bedroom cold as a barn with water running down the walls. I am always in their debt.'

She glanced up at me. 'You haven't asked how I came by this bruise on my face – I know you can see it.'

'I didn't think it polite to ask.' I took a sip of my by now very cold tea, just to keep my hands occupied.

Mabel had refused to go to bed with the owner, who complained to his wife, who then screamed at her, called her ungrateful and told her that her husband always tried the girls first, so he would know how to price them. If Mabel did not lie with him willingly, she would be strapped to the bed by the woman herself and offered to whichever man came for the cheapest whore.

'When I refused, she hit me, punched me with a closed fist like a man, then told me how she was in with the peelers and would have me fitted for stealing, unless I worked off my debt of £5, the debt I'd accrued for being rude.'

'What about Dykes from the hospital?'

'Dykes? I don't have time for squatting over pots of steam or chewing herbs that will do nothing but give me a headache! There's nothing I haven't tried.'

'How much money do you think you'll need?'

'I was thinking, what about your husband? He's a doctor. He must know how to flush it out. Don't tell me to go to the quacks for this – I'll die, I know I will. I have a feeling, the same way I had a feeling about you.'

'Then it's not my help you are asking for, is it?' I spat this out. I was beginning to tire and my head throbbed. I needed my drops but hadn't taken them that day because I'd known Mabel would be calling.

'Please, Susannah, I am begging you. If I have this baby, I swear I will throw it in the Thames along with myself.' She grabbed my sleeve and her fingers pinched my forearm. It was the same hopeless grasp as Emma Smith's when she'd lain bleeding to death in the hospital. It disgusted me.

'That's your choice, Mabel, not mine,' I said, and pulled my arm free.

She had inched closer to me on the settee and I could smell the mouldy scent of the unwashed. There it was again: Emma Smith, the bag of twigs on the hospital bed. Blood dripping off her and running across the uneven floor.

I told Mabel I would think on it and would get a message to her at the millinery, but I only wanted her out of the house. I gave her five shillings at the door. She went to kiss me, but I flinched away and we were stuck in that excruciating moment. Then she nodded and smiled as if she knew I would not be sending any message, thanked me, and left. Because of the gentle way she managed my indifference, I felt I deserved my marriage after all.

18

As much as I tried to convince myself it wasn't my problem, I kept feeling Mabel's pain, and I cursed her. The next evening, I caught Thomas alone, without the cloying Mrs Wiggs. He was in the bathroom, tending to his precious whiskers, which were becoming sparser by the day, making his face thinner and drawn.

'Thomas, do you remember a red-haired nurse from the hospital, pretty little thing called Mullens?' I asked.

He turned a soapless patch of upper cheek to me, so I might kiss him. I stood with my back against the wall, next to the mirror, and faced him as he continued shaving.

'No, not sure I do,' he said.

'You must remember her. Everybody knew Mabel Mullens: small, pretty, freckles, red curls, the most brilliant green eyes, always flashing them at the handsome doctors. I would be disappointed if she hadn't flashed them at you.'

His pursed lips cracked into a small smile, and I understood he knew exactly who I was talking about. If only I could have suffered the pain of being a creep, my marriage might have been more successful.

'I saw her in a shop on St James's Street. She told me she's left the hospital. I think she's fallen on some hard luck, Thomas, and she asked for my help.'

'What did she say to you?'

'You remember her?'

'I remember hearing about her. I assume she wants money.'

'I thought it might be the charitable thing to do.'

'You are most certainly not to give her any money, Chapman. If you give these people money, they'll only come back for more.'

I smiled and swallowed down the lump of paternal condescension. There, I had tried. Mullens would have to find her own solution. I didn't dare discuss the subject any further.

Thomas walked to where he had hung his jacket, took something out of a pocket, and pulled me by the arm to stand in front of him and face the mirror. He placed a heavy gold necklace around my neck and kissed me below the ear as he clasped it. I was ready; I did not flinch.

'No more silly arguments between us,' he said. 'We are both as bad as each other. Call it a peace offering, if you will. I hope you like it. Look, I'll even ignore your choice of physician, but honestly, only you, Chapman, would choose Shivershev. He's the most arrogant, rude physician, and of debatable talent. Though, paradoxically I might add, he has the most superior attitude I've ever had the displeasure of working with. But if it makes my darling wife happy, I'll suffer it.'

I was so preoccupied by how to play the good wife and what expression I should wear, it took me a while to focus on the necklace. It was a heavy pendant of a gold heart, a solid ball of yellow gold with a small sphere of green peridot in the middle, a bulky object that weighed me down, as if I was wearing an anchor. It was an odd piece of jewellery and I was not the sort to favour shapes like hearts or bows. It had scratches. It struck me as something an older woman would admire for being weighty and therefore of quality, though there were of course far more delicate designs that were just as expensive.

He wrapped an arm across me and pulled me backwards into his chest. I could feel the heat of him behind me.

'You know he has a weakness for whores, don't you?' he whispered into my ear.

The hairs on my neck stood up and I prayed he didn't feel them brush against his lips. 'What?' I said. If my reaction was the wrong one, would he smash my head into the mirror?

'Your Dr Shivershev,' he said. 'He collects them – whores, I mean. He gives them money, so they keep coming back, the way whores do.'

'No, I promise you, I never heard anything of the sort,' I said. Then I remembered how I had seen Dr Shivershev at Itchy Park, walking among the vagrants.

'Surgeons' gossip, most likely. You know there is also a rumour he performs abortions. Not on his own kind, I doubt. Why else would such women come to his office, apart from for the money, of course?' he said. 'I can't imagine they could find him attractive, could they, Susannah?'

'Oh no, absolutely not.'

He let me go, and I could breathe. He picked up a towel and threw it on the floor, as he had with his bloodied shirt the night of Polly Nichols' murder. Then he turned me to face him with both hands on my shoulders and I don't know why but I had thoughts of spitting in his eye.

'Look, Chapman, I want you to know I do think of you. Always. I love you. I hope you like it.'

'I adore it.'

19

'And you say you've been suffering from these headaches since your last appointment?'

Dr Shivershev made a long, laborious effort of moving his chair from behind his desk to face mine. He yanked and pulled at the heavy old thing, which squeaked like an old man's bones and struggled against the pile of the rug. Our knees were nearly touching now, just a sliver of air between us, as good as a steel barricade. He put his cold fingers either side of my jaw and asked me to open and close my mouth like a fish.

'Are you all right?' he asked.

'I bit my tongue,' I said. I hadn't bitten my tongue. We were like the last two children in a game of musical chairs, waiting for the music to start.

'Only the last week or so,' I said.

'Pardon?'

'The headaches. You asked how long I've had the headaches.'

'Ah yes, I did. Any blurred vision?'

'No.'

'Please, look past here.' He pointed to the tip of his ear with a tobacco-stained finger.

I became preoccupied by the size of his earlobes. They were huge compared to Thomas's. My husband's earlobes were small and attached, neat and purposefully arranged, as if Mrs Wiggs had trimmed, pressed and folded them. Dr Shivershev's, by comparison, were fat and bulging, like uncooked mussels. What could be guessed about a man's character from his earlobes? Because these two were as far apart as they could be. More importantly, could a man with fat earlobes be trusted? These were the things I filled my head with to stop the flow of embarrassingly indecent thoughts from intruding as the man's fingers prodded and poked at my jaw.

At least he didn't look as tired this time, and he'd shaved more recently. Less drunk, more doctorly, which was reassuring. No spots on his shirt. His office had been cleaned, and there were no piles of books sprouting from the carpet like forest mushrooms. I could see the pattern of the rug, the specimen jars had been dusted, and light bounced off the windows, all of which were now graced with curtains that had been tied back with rigid conformity.

'My housekeeper found her way in,' he said.

'Ah,' I said. I could only ever think of 'ah' or 'oh' when Dr Shivershev said anything. He gave so little away. I had the suspicion I bored him with my mundane Chelsea gripes. Perhaps Itchy Park vagrants elicited more enthusiasm. Encephalitis or a suffocating goitre might be enough to register a flicker of a response.

'Irina moves things. It is not that I have a problem with her cleaning, but she moves things and I cannot find them, so we play this game of cat and mouse, all in sport, of course. I stole her key one day and she responded, rather ingeniously, I thought, by slipping a sheet of paper under my door, pushing out my key with a hatpin and dragging it back under. I had to ask how she did it. She had such a look of triumph on her face when she finally explained.'

'I met your housekeeper – a very elegant lady.'

'She is a countess by marriage. Before... Well, before. Romanian. Never play cards with her – absolutely ruthless.'

'I saw you,' I blurted out, sounding more than a little like a creep.

'Oh?' His turn for the 'oh'. He picked up some spectacles from his desk and cleaned the lenses with his sleeve. I had never seen him wear spectacles.

'At Itchy Park – I mean, Christ Church, in Spitalfields. The great white church down from the hospital. I was walking past this week and I saw you in the yard, with all the... the people who sleep there. Are you a Methodist, or a Salvationist? My grandparents were Methodists before they converted to Salvationists. I... wasn't spying, Dr Shivershev. I was only walking past and saw you quite by chance.'

'What were you doing in Whitechapel, Mrs Lancaster? I can't imagine Chelsea housewives have much need to visit Spitalfields.'

'I went to see the murder spots,' I said, as if it were obvious. It sounded terrible, made worse by my excitable tone. Made so much worse by his uninterested silence. Still, I felt obligated to fill this by further uninvited explanation.

'You know – the Whitechapel unfortunates, the women stabbed and mutilated. You must have heard. The whole city has heard of the murders. Are you to tell me you haven't read of them at all?'

'I don't read the newspapers, Mrs Lancaster. I find them hysterical at the best of times. I find it impossible to read one without the feeling that someone is trying to make me angry at someone or something, when before the paper I felt ambivalent at best.'

'They think they know the man now anyway. They say he is a Polish Jew, or Russian. Polish or Russian, I can't remember – neither have the reputation of being trustworthy, do they? Anyway, they call him Leather Apron, a monster's name, I think. He is so very vicious that even the other Jews have rejected him.'

'The Russian ones or the Polish ones?'

'I'm not sure. Do they not all mix together?'

'I suppose it depends if the Russians trust the Poles or the Poles trust the Russians. Who knows? Maybe neither are to be trusted.'

'Perhaps.' I suspected he was making fun of me, but I was so taken with my own train of thought, I continued. 'The police have torn apart two hundred houses looking for him. Do you remember Emma Smith?'

He shook his head, eyes down, and continued his polishing.

'I'm sure you will. She had horrific injuries – beneath her skirts. They think she was a victim of this Leather Apron but that she was too frightened to speak the truth, even as she lay bleeding to death. She must have known she was dying... Or perhaps not.'

'Tell me something, Mrs Lancaster. Why be so taken by these murders? It is a subject I have heard other doctors express confusion about, that their wives are also fascinated by these crimes. It seems... perverse.'

'How so?'

'Such gruesome crimes. Why would ladies especially be so enthralled by the macabre? It seems a misguided romanticism.'

'Please, Dr Shivershev! I can think of a million reasons for being interested in the murders, yet it is so typical of men to assume a woman's interest can only be of a romantic nature; about men, in essence. As if in between our busy day of daydreaming of children and wedding dresses we must now make time to swoon over a murderer. For goodness' sakes! What of curiosity? The will to survive? Strategy and intrigue? These are not the sole domain of men.'

It was precisely these concerns that compelled me to keep my scrapbook on the murders, my personal study; it might not make much sense now but maybe at some point it would, wasn't this how all scientific discoveries were made? I did not share with the doctor that I had taken up his suggestion of writing in a journal, but I was not done with making my point yet.

'We are told when we are young to stay indoors, to never venture out at night, and we are raised on fairy tales in which we are in danger of being devoured by beasts at every turn, and yet a woman who dares to think and find ways to defend herself by learning about the very monster who hunts her is somehow an abomination. What do men expect a woman to be, Doctor? I'm sure I don't know.'

'Have you finished, Mrs Lancaster?' he said.

'Have you *heard*, Dr Shivershev?'

'You were an excellent nurse, by the way.'

'Was I? You never said.'

'It was implied by its omission, like "thank you" in Spanish.'

'How so?'

'I always asked for you.'

'Did you? I was not aware you even knew my name.'

'I didn't. I asked for the tall one.'

'Is that why I was always given the worst shifts, at night?'

'Yes. I like to keep my days free for my private patients, and the nights can throw up the real spectrum of the human condition.'

'Yes, the nights could be especially creative in their variety. Well, it all makes sense now. I thought only that Matron wanted to punish me.'

'I'm Jewish,' he said, looking up, peering through the spectacles and checking how clean they were against the light.

'I beg your pardon?'

'You asked if I was a Methodist or a Salvationist. I'm Jewish. My mother was Jewish, my father Russian Orthodox, but it was my mother who made such decisions in the house and it was what she knew. Remove that hat, please.' He put the spectacles back down on his desk and waved a nonchalant hand at my bonnet.

'Oh,' I said. Inside, I had withered, curled in on myself like a burned leaf. I took my bonnet off and set it down on the edge of his desk. I shuddered when I felt his hands at the back of my head. With his thumbs on the corners of my jaw, his fingers searched for something along my neck.

'Any back or neck pain? Have you received any blows or fallen?' he asked.

'No.'

His fingers located the scab hiding in my hair.

'Then how did you get this?'

'I fell against the sideboard and cracked my head on the mirror above it. How stupid of me – I forgot it was there.'

'Were you dizzy when this happened?'

'Oh no, only clumsy.' I laughed.

He walked back to his desk and sat down. The chair groaned under his weight. He was a little shorter than me, stocky even, with broad shoulders and bandy little legs. I imagined he ate like a horse when food was put in front of him yet would happily starve if left to his own devices. He didn't look Jewish to me, though I only knew the Jews from Whitechapel and they were easy to identify by their dress. I had offended him with my ill-conceived attempt at conversation, and I had to fix it.

'The book with the gold writing along the spine, is that Hebrew? I've seen some like it in Whitechapel. What does it say?' I wanted to prove I was no bigot. So I ploughed into the topic with interest.

'That book is a Russian medical text, Mrs Lancaster.'

'The name Robert doesn't sound very Russian.' Or Jewish, I thought.

'The V in my nameplate stands for Vasily, but seeing as I didn't want to be beaten to death at boarding school, I changed it to Robert.'

'Why Robert?'

'Robert the Bruce. I couldn't quite bring myself to take the name of an Englishman, so I made do with him. Do you know, I think, yes I'm sure, you are the first person to ever ask me about that. Are you always this inquisitive?'

'Yes! My grandmother used to find it unbearable. As a small child I would ask her "Why? Why? Why?" about everything. I could never simply accept things as they were. She said it drove her insane.'

'I can imagine. You've been carrying heavy loads with one arm, correct?'

'My grandmother used my arm to keep herself steady when we walked.'

'You are aware you stoop to one side?'

'Yes, because of her very short stature.'

'Do you still walk her?'

'No, she's dead,' I said, and laughed, my second inappropriate reaction so far. This elicited a puzzled flash of his brown eyes, so I explained further. 'That's how I was able to become a nurse. If she were still alive, I would still be rotting in Reading, stooped to one side, bored. She died after a fever. It was quite unexpected. Although she was ill for years, the doctor thought she would outlive us all.' It was mostly the truth.

'You should correct your posture; it will give you back problems later.'

He glanced at my bonnet, a signal that the consultation was over. He looked at it again and then back at me, as if willing it onto my head.

'Is there something else, Mrs Lancaster? I'm not known for my scintillating conversation and I charge by the hour, so for your husband's benefit, you might want to come to the point.'

This was it. I told him about Mabel. He professed not to know who she was, but he was lying – every man noticed Mabel. I explained about the officer, the bruises, the baby, the manager of the shop and his violent wife – a little too theatrically, perhaps, for he seemed bored, and what I described sounded more like a Punch and Judy show. He didn't react at all. I had no sense if this was going well or if, when I finished, he would shout at me.

'What made you come to me about this? You know what you are asking for is illegal,' he said finally.

I had no answer. What could I say? That my husband had told me he had a weakness for whores and abortions?

'I saw you at Itchy Park and you seemed a man of compassion. I thought it worth the risk of asking.' In my panic, I pitched straight for flattery. He said nothing. 'What will you do? Throw me out, refuse to see me as a patient? It seems a small price compared to what Mabel must pay. If not you, then someone else might say yes. I will keep asking.'

'For God's sake, Mrs Lancaster! If you walk up and down Harley Street asking doctors to perform illegal operations, what do you think will happen? You have put us both in a dangerous position, and for what? A noble urge to occupy a bored housewife? I'm going to pretend this conversation never happened. Now, please, take that hat off my desk.'

He began to write notes, ignoring me. I refused to move or pick up my bonnet. I dug my fingers into the underside of my chair and shut my eyes. After what seemed like an age he coughed and I opened my eyes to find him staring at me, his nostrils flared.

'So that we're clear, Mrs Lancaster,' he said, pointing at me with his pen, 'I undertake charitable medical cases, along with a group of my peers: skin diseases, deformities, birth defects, infectious diseases. That's why I was in your churchyard. I was there for charity, yes, but that was secondary to the scientific opportunity those people – unfortunately for them – represent. I'm not Jesus, Mrs Lancaster, despite being Jewish. I am a scientist. You should understand how scientists think – you married one.'

He stood up and began pacing up and down behind his desk, while I still sat lodged in the chair, gripping my seat.

'I can't just leave her,' I said.

'Yes, you can. You can do exactly that.'

'I have an obligation.'

'Please, Mrs Lancaster, spare me the Christian obsession with saving people from themselves. It's nothing more than a narcissistic attempt to inflate the ego in the absence of any real purpose.'

That made me angry. I stood up. 'Do not patronise me, sir. I'm not talking about God – I think he's made it perfectly clear he's not remotely concerned. I'm talking about offering someone a chance to rescue themselves. Didn't you talk about miserable mothers giving birth to miserable children in poverty? Well, here's one asking for help, ready to make a hard decision, live with the consequences and take responsibility, which is more than the father will ever have to do. Where should such a woman go, Dr Shivershev? Please do not say to Itchy Park. Would you help if you found her there?'

He stood still with his back to me, pretended he was organising books, but I knew he heard me. Aisling used to say that the past existed only to remind us to leave it behind. That this was the only way we could be free. Telling him about Mabel had not been enough, so I offered him a torrid little piece of myself. I told him that my parents had not died of scarlet fever and that in fact I had no knowledge of who my father was at all. I was born a bastard and my mother was still a child herself. I told him about how we lived together in a sordid little room in a dank little courtyard in the Nichol and how my mother was a prostitute who was strangled to death by a man whose company she kept. I couldn't believe I was speaking these things aloud. I never had before. My voice shook as if it was trying to choke the words before they came out.

'It is not necessary to leave things to chance, Dr Shivershev, or to God. How will Mabel end if I don't help her? How will I end knowing I could have helped her? Isn't this what science is *for*? So we can save each other when our Holy Father leaves us to suffer?'

The dust stopped floating between us, and after a long while Dr Shivershev dragged a piece of paper towards him as if it were the weight of a rock and started to write. When he'd finished, he folded it and pushed it across the desk towards me.

'There is a woman who takes on this type of business. You are to give this to your friend. She is to go to this address and follow the instructions. This came from you and you alone. Do not mention my name. I will speak to them so they expect a woman with red hair.'

'So you do remember Mabel?'

'There is a cost attached. I assume you will take care of that,' he said.

I took the folded paper, put my bonnet on and made my way to the door. He stayed in his chair. I was at the door when he said, 'You should tell your friend this is not without its risks. And one more thing, Mrs Lancaster. I don't suppose I need to stress that you are not to mention this to your husband. He is not a man I trust. I warn you, if this comes back, I will ruin you with what you've told me.'

'As you can imagine, Dr Shivershev, I am very good at keeping secrets. I only hope you are too. And I do not blame you – I would not trust my husband either.'

I waited for the moment I could pass Mabel the envelope. Inside was the note and money. My own money. There was no way I could explain that amount to Thomas.

Mabel glanced around the interior of the milliner's to see if anyone was watching, then gestured for me to wait. Once she was sure it was clear, she came the other side of the cash register and ushered me to a dark corner at the back of the shop. She stood with her back to the corner so she could see down the aisle.

'Is there anything I can do for you?' she whispered. 'Anything! Name it.'

I could not think of a single thing, and yet there was a multitude of things I did want. I wanted to reverse time and go back to the day before Aisling left me. I wanted to grab her hand and run away. I wanted never to have married and to still be a nurse. I wanted to have taken my chances with Matron Luckes, thrown myself on her mercy and asked for help and guidance. In hindsight, I'm sure she would have given it. I wanted to find others like myself. But what could Mabel do with any of those things? What was I meant to ask for? I supposed I did need new gloves.

'You don't need to do anything for me. I have everything,'

I said. I realised how smug this sounded and hoped Mabel didn't think I was trying to make her feel worse.

'I will pay you back,' she said. 'You'll see. But now I'd better get on.' She moved to leave and instinctively I grabbed her tiny arm. How would someone so fragile and small survive what was to come?

'Mabel… you know, marriage isn't everything, it's more a concept really. The reality is a bit like being a nurse – or a Catholic, so I hear.'

She stared at me, confusion in her eyes.

'That was a joke,' I said.

'Oh, I couldn't tell.'

'Aisling used to say that. I'm not very good at making jokes.'

'No, I… On reflection, it was amusing, I think,' she said. 'I'm sure you must have found it terribly difficult after—'

'Yes. I'm much happier now, thank you. I've been most fortunate.' Now it was me who moved to leave.

'Susannah?'

'Yes?'

'Are you all right? You aren't unwell, are you?'

'No.' I laughed, then remembered I was meant to be discreet, for Mabel's sake. 'Good luck,' I whispered, and then said in a louder voice, 'Your assistance has been excellent, Miss Mullens.'

'Thank you, madam.' Mabel smiled, then whispered back, 'I'll write to you when I get home. I'll pay you back. I will.'

20

The odd heart-shaped pendant was the first of a flurry of gifts. Our Chelsea home had been sparsely and tastefully furnished up to that point, decorated with a restrained awareness of what was proper. I had not added to it myself; it was never my house or my money. But it began to be filled with curiosities and ornaments seemingly purchased by Thomas when drunk or in some kind of excitable fit. The money worries that had been the subject of letters from Helen had clearly disappeared. There were boxes upon boxes of hideous cigars, despite the fact he didn't smoke, and disgustingly expensive cognac that tasted as revolting as it smelled, but the bulk of his purchases were clothes. Thomas adored buying clothes.

Thomas had changed again, from agitated and distant to giddy, manic even, and we had barely finished the first week of September. The household was far from relieved by this; having suffered from his moods before, there was an uneasiness about this new side of him. Something simmered beneath his skin. What remained consistent was that whenever Thomas was forced to spend time with me he was restless, as if waiting to get the husbandly duty over and done with so he could hurry to the real destination. Where that was and with whom, I had no idea. I cared little that he wanted to be away from me, but I did care that he was taking days away from work with cavalier abandon. I may not have known much, but I did know how hospitals worked, and there were many young, ambitious and talented doctors waiting to work for free at somewhere like the London. Failure to show up would not be tolerated for long, no matter the doctor's background or connections. Thomas kept complaining that he barely had any private patients, yet he would cancel them with little notice, saying he was not in the right frame of mind that day or that he needed rest. He would disappear come the evening and return late, only to lock himself away in his attic and sleep well into the next day.

I avoided him for the most part, until one day he announced that he would purchase me a new wardrobe, cover me with the latest fashions. As his wife, I was a reflection on him. It was much like being a doll, a plaything. Even as I obediently followed, I hated myself. Dressed up in clothes I would never have chosen, I would reveal my true self for all to see, the unctuous, creeping whore that I was. We traipsed in and out of dress shops for hours and it was inside one of them that what had been waiting to split his skin almost did. He had driven the shop assistant ragged, demanding dresses and hats and coats in different colours on my behalf while I stood like a dummy.

'What about all the concerns regarding money?' I whispered when the girl was out the back. 'Helen's letters...'

I thought I'd been discreet, but the hysterical grin slipped from his face, and he walked over to me, gripped my arm and purposely dug his fingers into my flesh. I'm ashamed to say I yelped.

'How dare you embarrass me,' he hissed into my ear.

Through a gap in the curtain I saw a sliver of the shopgirl's face. She blushed when she realised I had seen her watching and slipped away into the shadows. There was pity in her expression, which made it difficult not to cry.

I did not argue with my husband, but I was running out of ways I could acquiesce without disappearing altogether. To survive, I would have to adapt. If what I said made him angry, then I would keep my mouth shut. If what I wore displeased him, I would wear what he preferred. If he didn't want to spend time with me, I would be uncomplaining in my solitude. If he griped that I looked miserable, I would wear the vacant smile of an imbecile. If he wanted me to do whatever on the occasions he sought me out in the bedroom, I would be docile and hope it would be over quickly. I accepted my disappointment. I had been an idiot to let myself dream the marriage would be a happy one, but it would do. I couldn't admit it yet, I was still bribing myself with money, space, warmth and comfort, the house in Chelsea.

Immediately after the incident in the shop, he went back to being happy again, at least for the time being. It was not for my benefit, but for the audience Thomas always imagined was watching.

It was Friday the seventh of September when he told me we were to see Richard Mansfield in a new production of *Dr Jekyll and Mr Hyde* at the Lyceum. Afterwards, we would have dinner at the Café Royale. I erupted into giddy excitement, or hoped I did a good impression. In truth, I was dreading spending such a long time in his company. I knew I would find it difficult not to displease him.

Thomas wore his most decadent recent purchase: a dark blue overcoat fashioned from the skin of thirty-two wolves and trimmed with fur at the collar and cuffs. I was trussed up as fussy as a trifle in a rose-coloured silk dress trimmed with satin and embroidered net and pulled tight in the bodice thanks to its many uncomfortable strips of baleen. Thomas had picked it. He had also chosen the dolman I wore over it, a snow-white mantle with sling-like sleeves, half cape, half jacket. It was edged with arctic fox fur at the neck, front, cuffs and hem, decorated with silk chenille like marabou, and lined with cream satin. It was the most outrageous thing I'd ever worn. I'd never imagined owning anything like it. Mrs Wiggs had nearly fainted when she saw it. 'How in the heavens am I ever to keep that clean?' she said, throwing her hands onto her hips. As we were preparing to leave for the theatre, she told us we looked like a pair of Russians.

The play went smoothly enough. The lead actor was English and had returned with this production after finding success in America, so it was a homecoming of sorts. 'It is easier for the common man to be mistaken for a gentleman over there, since there they have no class,' said Thomas. Which was his way of dismissing a working man's success, a concept he could not conceive of.

At the Café Royale, his mood deteriorated. Little clues told me: the one-word answers, the bored expression and wrinkled nose, the twitching of his leg under the table, which made it shake, though not quite enough to rattle the cutlery or the glasses. He kept looking over his shoulder, as if trying to spot someone he was expecting to see.

I knew I had played my part impeccably and could not be responsible for his change of mood. I'd styled my hair in the fashion he said suited me best, and I was wearing the ugly heart-shaped necklace, which felt like a lead weight on my chest. When he started to bounce his leg under the table, I wanted to scream. I kept quiet even though I had the sense he was daring me to say something. I avoided his eyes but saw he kept catching glimpses of his own reflection and pouting into the mirror. I wanted to laugh, to let him know he was vainer than any woman I had ever known, but I didn't. Aisling would have. She would have laughed in his face and walked out of the restaurant. I didn't. I couldn't.

The menu was written in French. Frightened I would order incorrectly and embarrass him, I whispered this to him. I thought it might even amuse him, make him laugh. The old Thomas at the hospital would have made a quip and set me at ease. This Thomas rolled his eyes and snatched the menu away from me, made a comment about me signing my name with a mark and chose for me. In retaliation, I ordered more wine, and he glared at me.

'Why order good wine when you can't tell the difference between that and a glass of witch's piss?' he said as soon as the waiter had disappeared.

'You are beginning to sound like Mrs Wiggs,' I snapped.

Thomas had preached how this restaurant was popular with writers, artists and actors – beautiful, cultured types. Quite what we were doing there, I did not know. The walls were mirrored, the ceiling and walls painted in thick orange gold and decorated with Cupids. The flickering candlelight and endless reflections made the whole room appear as if it were glowing a hedonistic yellow. The chairs were red velvet. It felt opulent and garish, like being trapped inside a Christmas bauble. To be frank, the style was not so dissimilar from what I had seen at Wilton's Music Hall in the East End. I went there on a demonstration once: a group of women, all Methodists and Salvationists, forced our way inside, incensed by rumours that the actresses in the gallery could be hired for a few shillings. The Café Royale had the same tawdry and vulgar décor, only its whores were more expensive. I included myself, an overdressed poodle sat tethered to a wealthy brat by a leash that I had chained around my own neck.

The room buzzed with clinking glasses and other people's conversation, as Thomas and I sat in stony silence. As much as he teased me for my lack of friends, I had seen little of his. He made a great show of discussing people, namedropping, identifying certain individuals as close confidants, but never had any of these so-called friends been to our house. When we attended events or benefits, he would introduce me, but I think now that I did not imagine their discomfort at his over-familiarity. They were polite enough, but confused, as if they had only a vague idea of who he was, and inside I cringed. Thomas was a man of a million acquaintances but no real friends. The more I learned of him, the more disappointing he was.

It was a relief when he announced we were leaving the restaurant, even though he loped off without waiting for me. I emptied the rest of my glass and hurried after him, dragging my fussy skirts. We collected our coats and made our way through the crowded foyer. I was trying to keep up when he stopped abruptly and I barged into his back. He had paused to talk to an older gentleman, a man with a bushy grey beard, cheeks and a red nose from too much brandy, a swollen stomach, and medals on his lapel. The man had a finger pointed in Thomas's chest. I stood in Thomas's shadow; he didn't introduce me and the conversation was rapid and the words didn't travel. I could tell it was about work, and that the other gentleman certainly had the upper hand. Thomas kept nodding at everything he said, almost like a schoolboy trying to absorb all the instruction he was being given by his master.

The gentleman's wife was a dumpy little thing and as she smiled, the thread veins on her cheeks made a mesh-like rouge. She leaned over and put her spectacles to my neck.

'What a charming necklace, my dear. Have you recently had a birthday?'

I shook my head.

'Your necklace, it's a birthstone – isn't peridot for August?' She nodded, confident in her assumption.

'Is it?' My suspicion that the necklace had belonged to someone else came charging back. I put my fingers to my throat to feel it. 'My birthday is in January,' I said.

The lady looked bewildered but smiled anyway. The men stopped talking and we were pulled apart, swept along by the crowds and hustled towards the entrance, Thomas, with a gloved hand on my back, pushing me along. Whatever had been said had put him in an even worse mood. Trapped with him in the confines of the coach was like being strapped to the side of a rumbling volcano. I could feel the heat coming off him and I sat at the very edge. If I asked him what was wrong, it would be like baiting a bear, but if I didn't ask, it might seem neglectful.

'Is something the matter?' I asked.

He gave a forced, operatic laugh. 'It wants to know if something is the matter. Tell me, why bother asking.' It was not a question.

I looked down at my knees. There was nothing I could do or say to avoid being drawn into this argument. I would just have to make myself as unobtrusive as I could. If I gave him nothing to react to, perhaps his temper would burn itself out. We stayed in silence, bobbing with every jerk and lurch as the wheels of the cab rolled over the cobbled streets. I let it roll through my bones, thought about being soft like a rag doll.

'If you must know,' he said, 'that gentleman is on the board of governors, and he said I am making a name for myself as unreliable. I cancelled a friend of his – a whining pain of a man who's constantly self-diagnosing with tropical diseases he has read about and has little chance of acquiring in London. I couldn't care less about him, but the governor is an important member of the group of doctors with whom I have my other work and I cannot have him think badly of me. I shall have to remedy the situation somehow. It's really not fair. I've done everything they've asked me to without question, and to have some whining old boy spread rumours and ruin my chances... I won't have it. He said he told me because he used to know my father. So it would appear that even though the old man is long buried, he still finds ways to judge me.'

I stayed silent, head down.

'Aren't you going to offer any wisdom? No wifely comfort?' he said.

'Do you not think it was kind of him to tell you, so that you might remedy this… false perception?'

'Oh, you think it kind, do you? How kind of him! Susannah thinks he is kind.' He mocked me, his voice high like a little girl's, then said, 'I have been summoned to do more private work for this man already, so I must be sure to go over and above any expectations. It is stressful work, Susannah. The position I play is beneath me, I'm aware, but if I am to be accepted and progress, I have no choice. The money is what keeps us, and these are not the sort of people to let down.'

I had no idea what this 'other work' was, but I was not about to start asking questions. 'That's good, isn't it, if he's well connected? Isn't that what you wanted? And you said yourself, this work is handsomely rewarded.'

'But of course you don't care, as long as I can keep you in furs and dresses.'

'Thomas, it was your idea to buy all these things…' There, the wine had dulled my senses, and I had walked into his trap, baited and hooked.

I was still gawping with my mouth open. I didn't even flinch when he slapped me across the face with his gloved hand; it happened so quickly. The sting spread like fire across my cheek.

'You enjoy humiliating me, don't you?' he said, and when I didn't answer, 'I said, you enjoy humiliating me, don't you? I'm asking you a question.'

I was turned away from him and he was addressing the

back of my head. With one hand he gripped my hair, yanked my face towards him and pulled me closer.

'I won't get drawn into it.'

'Do you have any idea of how you embarrass me? How people laugh because my wife went and picked the fucking Jew as her physician. You did that on purpose! You knew how it would make me look.'

I fell further into the trap of explaining myself, convinced I could reason with him.

'I didn't know he was Jewish when I chose him. I didn't think of it. I only knew him as a good doctor. Why would I care about anything else?'

'You know he hates me with a passion, which is why you selected him, to antagonise me.'

'I didn't, I swear. All I know is… I know he takes charity cases. I've seen him, in Spitalfields, looking for vagrants with skin diseases. I thought he would be a good doctor, that is all.'

He burst out laughing. 'You really are a fucking idiot.' He stopped laughing and leaned close into my face, but he still had hold of my hair so I could not pull away. 'Poor, simple Susannah. So stupid. You know the real reason he goes there, don't you? He pays them, he tests his new little surgeries on them. He pays them, because only the most desperate accept money for operations they don't know whether they'll wake up from. Sometimes they don't need operations at all, he just likes to ferret about inside and have a good look, especially with the women. Everyone knows he likes to open them up and tinker around inside his whores. What do you think of your doctor now?'

I said nothing.

'You know what I think?' he said. 'I think the man loves his whores. And you are a tired old whore, aren't you? Do you enjoy fucking Jews, Susannah? Do you moan underneath him, and then act the dead dog with me?'

He pulled and then pushed me onto the floor by the front of my dress. I lost my breath when my back hit the floor. His hands were everywhere, tearing at the dolman clasp around my neck, trying to rip it off me. His face bulged over mine, his eyes a freezing blue against the livid red of his cheeks. I undid the clasp myself and threw the dolman off my shoulders. It wasn't white any more but brown from the dirt and spotted with my blood on it. My lip had split where he'd hit me.

I sat on the floor with my knees bent up to my chest as the coachman shouted, 'What's going on down there?'

'Drive on!' shouted Thomas, and he thumped the roof of the coach. He pushed me onto my back by my neck and slapped me twice round the face. Now I could taste blood.

The driver shouted again, but Thomas told him to keep driving. I thought he was going to strangle me there, on the floor of the coach, but his hands found what they were looking for: the heart-shaped pendant, and he tore it from my neck. The chain burned my skin where it snapped.

When we arrived home, I got down from the coach by myself and left the door open for him to follow, but he reached forward and slammed it shut. The driver looked down at me. I met his eyes for a moment before he chose to pretend he'd not seen anything. I could tell from his face that I looked a mess. Then the coach pulled away. Thomas had taken my dolman with the white fur and the pendant, the things that had been my gifts. I was naive to think they had ever really been mine. I was left standing in the fussy dress, blood from my mouth dripping down the front. I ran my tongue over my lip; the skin was smooth and taut where it had already begun to swell. When he'd hit me, I knew he was holding back. There was still so much more to come out.

When Mrs Wiggs saw my face, she gasped, then, quick as a flash, collected herself and pretended as if nothing more than another silly accident had occurred. She pestered me to take off the pink silk dress, chasing me as I walked up the stairs.

'Quick, quick, Mrs Lancaster! Blood becomes more difficult to get out the longer it is left.'

The Ghost of Dark Annie

Timothy Donovan, the deputy manager for Crossingham's Lodging House on Dorset Street, was by all accounts a grim-faced and unapproachable man. It was widely known that it was never worth asking him for any kind of favour, as his answer was sure to be no. For his part, Donovan avoided all unnecessary engagement with dossers because no matter how often he reminded them of the rules and terms of business, they would always try their luck by pushing for more or paying less. They had no honour or dignity, and this disgusted him.

It was still fairly light when Dark Annie appeared in the doorway of his office. She was a sloping, apologetic figure and he steeled himself in anticipation of the request that was sure to come. The woman was a regular, a reliable payer for at least three nights a week, but where she got to on the other nights he had no idea; most likely she slept under the night sky like the rest of them.

It wasn't that he didn't like Dark Annie – the woman was notably polite, well-mannered, articulate even. He's heard that her father had been a guardsman and that she'd once *been married to a coachman but he'd died. The woman came with an air of ominous melancholy, as if she were already a long-gone soul somehow still trapped in her earthly body. How the woman was still alive was beyond all reasonable comprehension. She was sick and getting sicker, which was apparent each time he encountered her. She was probably in her forties, but she looked older. Her face was long, with sad, down-turned eyes and slow lumbering footsteps. She was a drinker, but a courteous drunk, and so one of the more tolerable. And here she was, haunting his doorway. He knew the reason for her visit.*

'Good afternoon, Annie,' *he said.*

'Afternoon, Mr Donovan,' *she said, coughing into a yellowing muslin.*

Mr Donovan turned his chair round to face her but would not give her the satisfaction of asking what she wanted.

'Mr Donovan, you know me to be a reliable tenant. I know the terms of business and I always rent a double-bed, but I'm unwell at the moment, Mr Donovan. I've been sick.'

'Have you, Annie?'

'I've been up the infirmary today. I have pills – look.' *She took out a small paper envelope and shoved it in front of Donovan's face, at pains to show him the stamp on the envelope:* Sussex Regiment, London.

'I see. Well, I hope those do the trick.' *Donovan turned back to his desk, but Annie stepped a little further into his cramped office.*

'Would it be all right if I sat in the kitchen awhile, by the fire?'

'Course it would, Annie,' *said Donovan.*

'Thank you,' *she said and turned to leave.*

'You have a few hours yet, before I send the night-watchman to collect. You make the most of that fire, Annie.'

Annie stopped walking but didn't turn around and didn't say anything. After a pause, she slowly dragged herself back down the stairs towards the kitchen. They both knew she hadn't had the courage to ask for what she wanted.

It wasn't long after midnight when Donovan looked out of the window and saw Dark Annie leaving the kitchen with a couple of others. He was surprised at the relief he felt. He was relieved she'd had the dignity and respect for both of them not to grovel.

At about two in the morning, Donovan sent the night-watchman into the kitchen to collect the night's rent. There was the usual groaning and grumbling, and Donovan tutted and shook his head. Every night, it was a great surprise to them. What he hadn't expected was to find Dark Annie blocking his doorway again. He nearly leapt out of his skin when he saw her.

'Jesus Christ, Annie, what you doing there?' he said.

'You know me to be reliable. I always have my bed money, but I've been unwell. I would ask if you could trust me only this once, Mr Donovan.'

'Yet you can find money for your beer, can't you, Annie? How much have you had tonight? Enough for a bed? Enough for your double? You can find money for this, but you can't find money for your bed.'

Donovan waited for her to argue, but instead she sighed and said, 'Keep Number 29 for me, please, if you will, Mr Donovan. I shan't be long.' Then she sloped away again.

★ ★ ★

Annie trudged towards Christ Church in Spitalfields. She knew where she was heading, had thought of the spot earlier in the afternoon when she'd failed to ask Donovan the first time. She'd known then what the answer would be. She made her way to Hanbury Street. She knew it well, even in the darkness. It was full of poorly kept houses, seven or eight rooms in each one and every one of those occupied by at least one family. The communal areas – stairwells, yards, landings and hallways – were open at all hours and the comings and goings of tramps and vagrants did not arouse attention.

Annie had consumption. She grew sicker and achier and more feverish by the day, and by God she wished it would hurry and take her. In the next life she dreamed there would be no fear or loneliness and certainly no rum. John would be there, and so would all her babies, and her brothers and sisters. The urge would leave her in death too, and she would finally be free.

She knew she should have pushed harder for the bed, but, forever the soldier's daughter, she could not bring herself to beg. Not even now when her bones ached and her limbs shivered, but at least the fever kept out the cold. She pushed on the unlocked yard door in Hanbury Street and was pleased to find her spot empty; it would be all hers for a few hours.

21

It was Sarah who woke me from my screaming by banging at my locked bedroom door.

I had been lying on the floor of a coach. I must have fallen asleep there, or maybe Thomas had hit me too hard and I'd passed out. I didn't panic, not like I had that first time when Thomas squeezed my neck until I lost consciousness. I was fairly used to it now. I could feel that the blood had dried on my face. I brushed off the flakes with my fingers and prodded the new scab on my swollen lip.

I was looking at the ceiling of a coach; its walls were black. It was still dark outside. We rolled over a particularly bumpy stretch of road and when I put both hands up against the bottom of the seats to steady myself I realised Thomas wasn't there any more. He had left me in the coach on my own. But where was I going?

I sat up and stared out at the navy-blue skies and black branches like crooked fingers. I was being driven out of London, but to where? I pulled myself on to my knees as the coach picked up speed over the rough ground. These were country roads, not city streets. The coach was being thrown from side to side and I struggled to stay upright. The driver was obviously a reckless fool. I had to make him take me back home to Chelsea. I reached up and thumped the ceiling with my balled fist. There was a thump back.

'Hello!' I shouted, but there was no answer.

Thomas's head appeared, upside down at the open coach window, grinning at me, his face livid, his cheeks slack and his blue eyes bloodshot. His hair was long and ungroomed and he held his hat on his head. When he grinned, there was a gold tooth. I screamed. How could I not have seen that before? How could I have missed it?

I screamed myself awake, and heard Sarah hammering at my bedroom door.

'Missus! Missus! Let me in! What's going on? Are you hurt?' she shouted as she rattled the handle. 'Shall I fetch Mrs Wiggs? Oh, what shall I do?'

She sounded like Mabel. I told her to go away, but she wouldn't. So I let her in.

'I was having a nightmare, that's all. I'm quite all right. What time is it anyway?' I asked.

'It's gone eleven, missus.'

I hadn't had the chance to look at my face yet, although it was tender, but to her credit Sarah didn't give anything away. I wondered if domestics received lessons in such things: how to maintain an expressionless face when confronted by the awkward evidence of violence. They used to tell us nurses that when delivering bad news we should be truthful, brief and gone, but to leave out gruesome detail. For example, when a patient had died on the operating table, we were told not to say, 'He died in agony, half of his leg off,' but rather, 'The end came mercifully quickly.'

I sent Sarah away to get the papers once I'd reassured her I wasn't dying and there was no need for a doctor, and certainly no need for Mrs Wiggs. When she came back and gave me the *Telegraph*, I nearly took to my bed again.

FOURTH WHITECHAPEL WOMAN MUTILATED

Yet another brutal murder was committed in the Whitechapel area this morning. This is the fourth woman to have been stabbed and mutilated, in circumstances strikingly similar to the others. She was attacked in the same way as Polly Nichols and there is little doubt she too was of the unfortunate class.

At six o'clock this morning she was found lying on her back in the yard of 29 Hanbury Street. This is a respectable street, but it is only a short distance from Spitalfields Working Men's Club. Number 29 is let to tenants of the working class.

DISEMBOWELLED

Dr Phillips, the Divisional Surgeon of Police, found that the woman's throat had been cut nearly to the vertebrae and that she had been entirely disembowelled. Her intestines lay next to her. She was removed to the mortuary.

While not yet officially identified, it is thought that she was known as Sievey and that her real name may have been Annie Chapman. She was last seen drinking with a man at the Ten Bells, five minutes' walk from the spot where her corpse was found.

She had lodged at 35 Dorset Street, Spitalfields, on and off for the past eight or nine months, but last night she was unable to pay for her lodging. Recently she was an inmate of the Whitechapel Workhouse, making use of the casual ward.

EXCITEMENT IN WHITECHAPEL

The excitement in Whitechapel is high.

The discovery of this body so soon after the others has paralysed the district with fear. All business in the vicinity of the scene has been stopped and the streets swarmed with people this morning. Many stood about in groups, discussing the murders, and there is a firm opinion that all the murders were committed by the same person. The police have thus far failed to bring anyone to justice and are still hunting for the man they call 'Leather Apron'.

He is clearly a madman with uncontrollable homicidal urges. It is widely accepted that lunatics are often more devious and cunning than any sane man. While this murderer is at large, no one in Whitechapel is safe.

'No Englishman could have done this' was the phrase quoted widely in all the papers. Groups of feral youths were reported to be harassing local Jewish men, trying to bait them into fights, and Jewish families were getting heckled outside their shops and homes. Groups were being followed home from synagogues.

The police found bloodstains and a piece of water-saturated leather apron in the yard. Annie's meagre possessions had been scattered about nearby: a pocket of her underskirt had been cut away; a piece of muslin, a comb and paper case lay near her body; and a brass wedding ring and its keeper had been torn from her fingers but left on the ground. An envelope containing two pills had been carefully placed by her head, as if left intentionally by Leather Apron as his calling card. If only the inept police could find this man, the papers screeched, the murders would stop.

I seemed to be the only person in London who felt differently. When I read the descriptions of how Dark Annie was found, I saw Thomas's face as it hung down above me in a bloody rage while I lay on the coach floor; I saw its twin apparition from my nightmares. Where did he go after he left me and drove off in that cab? Where could he have gone? It was too much of a coincidence now: scratches after Martha, coming home covered in blood after Polly and now this. He would have had ample opportunity to murder Annie. Was he thinking of me when he cut her throat? I took to my drops, if only to steady my nerves.

Witnesses emerged. A woman said she'd been harassed in the Queen's Head in Spitalfields by a man fitting the description of Leather Apron. 'You're about the same style of woman as the ones that have been murdered,' he'd leered at her. Given that the murdered women were all prostitutes, that warranted a slap round the face, but instead she'd merely asked what he meant. To which he'd replied, 'You're beginning to smell a rat. Foxes hunt geese, but they don't always find 'em.' A weird conversation, but the papers loved it, and the woman enjoyed her moment of fame.

Dark Annie stuck with me, and I spent a lot of hours – whole days – thinking about her, imagining her last evening, filling more pages of my scrapbook with my notes. There were things about her that sliced at me, things that were a little too familiar for me to undertake my macabre observation without guilt. For a start there was her name. 'Chapman' was also my mother's name, and Dark Annie's story could easily have been my mother's, if only she'd had the chance to get to forty-two. Like Dark Annie, my mother was a gentle type, quietly spoken, and chose her words carefully. Those were the qualities I remembered.

It seemed all the more tragic the way the papers wrote about Dark Annie as if she was an ailing, listless vagrant. Yet it was clear she wasn't always that way. Little details came through, such as the fact she sometimes sold flowers or crochet, and she was known for her love of rum. She lived with a sieve maker, which gave her the nickname: Dark Annie Sievey. She was stout with a thick nose and missing teeth. By all accounts, none of the woman had been considered attractive, even by the standards of the labouring poor.

More details were released, ever so gradually so as to keep us in a perpetual state of quivering horror. Her uterus, the upper portion of her vagina, and the posterior two thirds of her bladder had been removed. As this was done so quickly, the murderer would need to have had knowledge of pathological or anatomical examinations. According to the coroner, the killer had half strangled her to the ground, rendering her voiceless, and then cut her throat. It was blood loss that caused her death.

At the inquest, the piece of leather apron was dismissed as irrelevant – a bitter disappointment, as it had made such good theatre. It was found to have belonged to the son of a tenant.

If there had been hysteria over the murders before, then after this one it went wild. The murders were headline news as far as New York, Montreal, and all over Europe. When they weren't printing fantastical witness accounts, speculative theories or letters from moralists, the press dedicated column inches to savaging the police. Even the coroner joined in, complaining he had not been given a map to show where or how the last body was found. The general consensus was that the police were stupid, plodding clowns.

At the morgue, Annie's body had been stripped and washed down by inmates of the workhouse and her clothes dumped in the corner, ruining any evidence. The police surgeon protested that he could not work in such terrible conditions, it being an outrage that Whitechapel didn't even have its own morgue. The police were overwhelmed and had few resources. They had to rely on word of mouth, and there were a lot of flapping mouths in the East End. A group of local tradesmen started their own organisation in frustration. The Whitechapel Vigilance Committee duly issued a notice stating they would offer a substantial reward for any information that led to the arrest of the murderer. An MP put up £500. As a result, the police were bombarded with even more witnesses, letters, confessions, hoaxes and ever-helpful theorists.

Moralists and commentators posed some difficult questions. Surely the poverty and depravity suffered by the innocents of the East End were a matter of public responsibility? If the lawless, morally corrupt and dangerous conditions there created killers such as Leather Apron, who would address them?

On Monday the tenth of September, Leather Apron was found, hiding in a house on Mulberry Street. His real name was John Pizer. The police discovered several long blades in the house, which Pizer said were for his work as a boot finisher. He protested his innocence but was taken, along with those who had hidden him, to Leman Street Police Station.

It came as a surprise to find myself deflated, disappointed even. Was that it? If it was Pizer, then that meant I was to be stuck with the man I had married. I think I had rather hoped the police would knock on the door one day and take him away, solving my problems. Still, I had to take comfort that it was my wild imagination making Thomas capable of such horrific acts. Of course that was absurd. It was the drops. I needed to cut down on them; they were sending my thoughts racing, making my dreams surreal. I had to accept the humiliating truth that Thomas's hatred and anger were apparently only for me. But if he wasn't out murdering women, what he was up to?

Even so, I needed to know conclusively that this John Pizer was the murderer. I scoured the countless inches of cheap hearsay and unfounded opinion filling the columns of every newspaper known to womankind, but there were gaping holes all over the place. Often I became so frustrated, I almost tore the papers in pieces. I considered writing my own version of the story of Leather Apron. Putting him into the picture alongside Little Lost Polly and Dark Annie in an attempt to understand more about him, try and fathom his motives but I couldn't find enough about him to conjure up anything worth writing down. I could not understand such a man. What struck me was that I had not felt this lack of understanding when it came to the victims, and that filled me with fear. Why was it so easy for me to imagine their lives, had I not moved far enough away from that fate, was my writing hobby a danger? A way of pulling me back to the fate I had escaped.

The city waited with bated breath for the confession, but then all of a sudden Pizer was released without charge. I couldn't believe it. It wasn't him! Leather Apron was not the Whitechapel murderer, though everyone – the papers, the people, and myself – had assumed his guilt was a certainty. But John Pizer's alibis stood up. He was a rogue; that was not in doubt. He was an altogether nasty person, and a quite horrible and violent bully of women. But they couldn't imprison him for that. If they had, they'd have had to lock up half of London, and most of Westminster.

I had resigned myself to the fact that the monster had been caught and had laughed at my ridiculous suspicions about Thomas, but now that was all possible again. I felt a twinge of satisfaction that my instincts could be correct, but it was difficult to find solace in being right when I was petrified of what I might be right about. I had not seen Thomas since the night of our argument and Annie Chapman's murder, and that was some days ago now.

I found myself back at the beginning, with no answers at all, no clue as to where my husband was or with whom, and dreading him walking through the door.

22

The days passed and I still had no idea where Thomas was hiding. If Mrs Wiggs knew any better, she kept that to herself. I fantasised that he'd killed himself, taken by a fit of guilt after beating his wife and murdering Annie Chapman and the others, or that the police had him, or that he'd tripped, knocked himself out and drowned in the Thames. I rehearsed in my mind the various conversations I would have with the police should they turn up.

The longer Thomas stayed away, the more fearful I was of how things would be should he return. My cheek was bruised and my lip split on my left side. I studied my face in the mirror every day, sometimes every few hours, and convinced myself it was getting better. I wished I could have shown Mabel at least. We could have compared wounds, to measure who was the bigger fool, but I hadn't heard from her, hadn't received any letter. Cloistered in my bedroom, I broke up the hours by taking my drops with brandy, abandoning my self-imposed rule of never doing so during the daytime. I thought of Mabel often, and worried what would happen to me. By the end of the week I had taken all the clothes, feathers and frivolous things that Thomas had bought me, dumped them outside my bedroom door and told Mrs Wiggs to get rid of them.

'Where? What on earth for? What are you going to wear?' I think she had serious concerns I was about to parade naked through the streets of Chelsea.

'Give them to charity for all I care.' I found out later she stored them in an unoccupied bedroom, along with the shrunken head that had made me scream.

From then on I wore my old dresses and hats: dour grey and brown linsey frocks and plain black bonnets. They matched my mood and I felt more comfortable that way.

Bored out of my mind, I decided to go to the one place a woman could walk freely after having suffered a beating. Somewhere no one would care or notice. Whitechapel. As I made my way out the house, with clumps of powder on my face, a dark bonnet pulled down and wearing a nondescript brown dress, Mrs Wiggs chased me down the hallway. She threw her body against the door as I opened it.

'You can't go out like that, Mrs Lancaster. What will people think?'

'Please stand away from the door, Mrs Wiggs.'

'If you are in need of distraction, I can send Sarah out for you. A new book or more of your newspapers, perhaps?'

I pulled the door open and shunted her out of the way. I could feel her eyes boring holes into my back as I walked down the garden path.

My first stop was Hanbury Street, the place Annie Chapman was found, only a couple of streets away from

Itchy Park. There were still crowds there, five days later: bare-headed women holding infants, and gangs of weasel boys with patchy hair and concave chests. Throngs of ladies stood giggling in pairs, thrilled at the thuggery, coarseness and proximity of the labouring poor. It was more than a little embarrassing, but I had to acknowledge I was one of these birds. We were no more than canaries, briefly escaped from our mind-numbing cages. The labouring poor knew they were being gawped at. There was tension, an atmosphere of simmering rage.

This time there was no ten-year-old girl re-enacting the drama of the victim's last moments and asking a fee for the spectacle. For those of us curious about Dark Annie's demise, the tenants of the Hanbury Street property were offering the chance to stare down at the murder spot from their windows, and charging for the privilege, of course. There was a queue of tourists. It was unseemly.

I ended up wandering into the church of St Jude's, where Thomas and I had married. I had been so full of optimism, greedy with expectation. I had been so pleased to make such a miraculous marriage to a boy who, I thought, worshipped me. I'd imagined I was in control, but I was too inexperienced, too easily flattered, too arrogant in my ignorance to question what a man like Thomas could want with a woman like me. Though it was only five days since he'd gone missing, everything had changed for me, and in the city, in that time. It had given me the opportunity to develop a million theories, all of which confused me. One minute I thought him an immature, bad-tempered husband, the next he was the Whitechapel man. How many women in London worried about the same thing, that they were married to the man who ripped whores? Probably hundreds, and we all convinced ourselves otherwise, if only for the peace of mind it gave us.

I stopped to drop coins into the collection box on my way out. I hadn't noticed that the vicar had been watching me, had observed my introspective gloom and the marks on my face. When the noise echoed around the church, he glided over.

'My dear, that's a very generous sound you are making.'

'Good afternoon, Father. I was praying that they'll catch the Whitechapel man soon.'

'Ahhh... Let us hope those poor women didn't die in vain, that the world has at last woken up to the pitiful lives and horrors that exist.' The reverend, likely not as old as his lack of hair suggested, stared at my face. 'The sisters at Providence Row are very welcoming, my dear. I can open the box, if you think you could use the money... to find a safer place?'

For some reason, I burst into laughter. It echoed round the church and I heard myself cackling like a witch. The reverend was nonplussed, and so was I. He had mistaken me for a poor woman, battered and helpless, one who needed saving. How pitiful. How hilarious. But it was in fact deeply humiliating, and I was ashamed. I had looked at such women in the hospital, thought them feeble and pathetic as they held their puffy faces together with swollen hands and broken fingers where their husbands had stamped on them. We had tutted and judged as they trotted back like mindless idiots for their husbands to eventually trample them to death, boots moving from hands and fingers to faces.

'No, thank you, Father,' I said. 'I think I'll go and get pissed.'

I went to the Ten Bells next to Itchy Park for no honourable reason. I had to push my way past the scruffy men standing on the steps between two columns at the door. One of them barely moved, stood stiff, gave me the look up and down, his body rigid, so I had to rub against him. I rolled my eyes so he could see and shouldered past him, pleased with myself for acting bold. It was where I was meant to be, after all. By birth, I belonged to the rough and the common. Perhaps I had escaped what was meant to be my life, and all these freakish twists were fate pulling me back on course. Perhaps by marrying Thomas I had made him cruel and violent and turned him into a murderer. It was me that had ruined his life. I was the badness that had crawled into the yeast, as my grandmother used to say. Bad blood thickened like tar, turning good people into monsters by proximity.

I was not frightened of the men in the pub so much. As always, they either ignored or stared at me, scoring what they saw, but the women were hostile, so desperate to hold onto the scraps of male attention they'd blind a woman with broken glass, give her a scar so she wasn't a threat. The sawdust stuck to the floor and my feet, there was a dense fog of tobacco smoke and a sickly smell of stale beer, and the bar was sticky. I waded through a pack of ruddy, bloated faces; everywhere there were the red eyes and swollen noses of dedicated drinkers. I was glad of my bruises, my Whitechapel rouge, the mark of someone who belonged. I squeezed in between two men at the bar and the barman saw me instantly – the benefit of being tall, or the curse. He asked what I wanted and I didn't know, so I said rum, because it had been Annie Chapman's drink. One thing I learned about rum: it's revolting. I nursed the vile drink, determined to not let the disgust show on my face, until the sweaty barman with forearms like trees slammed another down in front of me.

'But I don't want another,' I told him. I didn't understand what was going on. Did they bring drink after drink in these places until you told them not to? No wonder the poor were always plastered, and poor.

'Think you've caught someone's eye. Aren't you a lucky girl.' The dour barman gestured with a tilt of his head.

My eyes travelled across the bar until they settled on the familiar form of an unkempt Dr Shivershev. He was sat on a stool looking straight at me from the other side. He lifted his drink and gave a nod, a funny little curl on his lips. Next to him stood a ferociously pretty woman with drowsy eyes and wideset cheekbones. She was draped over his arm like a saloon girl from the Wild West. Tendrils of fair hair curled around her face. She didn't wear a bonnet and carried herself in a way that said she didn't need rescuing. To the other side of Dr Shivershev stood a man with gingery whiskers, a flashy waistcoat and jacket, smoking a pipe.

The woman leaned forward to whisper to Dr Shivershev and winked at me as she did so. Dr Shivershev said something to the man with the whiskers, and they all started laughing. I felt incredibly stupid. In a fit of temper, I grabbed the rum and downed it, slammed the empty glass on the bar and shot them all what I hoped was a filthy look, although it may have appeared – quite accurately, as it happened – more like I was about to vomit. The sweaty barman scooped up the glass and I ran out of the pub, trying to contain the

panic at the fire in my chest. My eyes watered. I barged past
the men who'd looked me up and down earlier and they
barely moved, just swayed to the sides like blades of grass
in a breeze and continued their conversation. Meanwhile, I
stood on the pavement and retched.

23

I never touched rum again after that. I hadn't been much of a drinker anyway, but not for want of encouragement, from Aisling, of course. Drink just didn't agree with me, as I discovered on our trip together to Brighton.

We had decided to catch the train to Brighton, all because Aisling wanted to go to the Pavilion. I was entirely willing, but it was she who had all the ideas and made the plans, and I was happy to follow. It was obvious to anyone who cared to notice that Aisling and I had grown close. I hadn't realised how close, of course, I only knew I was in awe of her. I followed her around like her devoted shadow. Aisling had the courage to be all the things I was so frightened of. Bold, fearless and unashamedly herself, she carried this innate belief that everything would be all right, come what may. I even started to feel that way myself. I had never had a sister, or a best friend and so she became all things to me. We were together as much as we could be, and if we were apart, I spent my hours thinking of her. Whenever I dared to dream of the future, Aisling was most definitely in it, leading from the front, me trailing behind her, quite happily as it should happen.

When the day came for Brighton it was bright and sunny, we couldn't believe our luck, but the train was packed, too crowded, and it appeared everyone else in London had had the same idea. We spent the morning walking along the pier, sitting on the beach on pebbles that dug into our behinds, and throwing winkles at the seagulls to see if they would catch them. Eventually we decided not to bother going to the Pavilion after all. It was early afternoon when Aisling suggested we start making our way back, to miss the rush.

'What? After coming all this way? It was you wanted to come,' I said.

'You can't do that,' said Aisling.

'Do what?'

'Let me make all the plans all the time and then criticise.'

'I wasn't.'

'Yes, you were.'

'Not really. I thought you wanted to come here, that's all.'

'I did, but it's too busy, and there's nowhere to sit. It's like being cattle, we have to keep shuffling forwards. Why don't we go home?'

'All right,' I said, although I was confused by her change of heart.

Partway through our journey back, the train pulled into a quiet little station. I was staring out of the window not paying much attention when Aisling stood up, grabbed my arm and dragged me to the door of the carriage.

'Come on, let's get out here.'

'What? Why?'

Before I knew it, we were the only people on the platform and our train had left. I didn't know where we were. The station was positively ghostly. A tiny ticket office with a geriatric stationmaster and a half-dead lurcher were the only souls.

'What's the point of this?' I asked, but she ignored me.

We trudged along a country lane to nothingness, with fields on either side. It was a dry earthen track that stretched for miles and we had no idea what awaited us in either direction.

'Aisling, what are we doing here?'

'Stop worrying. We can catch a later train. Isn't it a lovely day? We don't get to feel the sun on our skin often, we should make the most of it.'

'I thought we were doing that in Brighton.'

'It was too busy – I couldn't breathe. It was as bad as Whitechapel.'

'Honestly...' I stopped and threw my hands in the air. 'I have no idea what pleases you.'

She turned around, walking backwards, laughing, 'Come on! Let's find somewhere to sit down, under a tree, somewhere in the open. I miss having so much space!'

The shouting disturbed the dozing birds and started a ripple of their cries. One after another they shrieked and took to the air, out from under the canopy of the trees.

'In London you can't move for people, and Brighton was the same. I'm disappointed. I should like to go back when I'm rich enough to pay for other people not to be there.'

'Good luck waiting for that day,' I mumbled and tramped along behind.

We ambled along the uneven track for an age until Aisling found a spot under a tree in an open field. There wasn't a soul around, just cows grazing. We sat down and leaned on our elbows, squinting at the haze of the sun as the warm air was shaken off the long grass. Aisling let out a sigh and flopped down onto her back with her hands stretched out to either side.

'Why is it when you get a telling-off it makes you sulk so?' she said. 'Like after you got sent out of that lesson. You must have been told off before.'

'I've been told off plenty. But it means a lot more at the hospital. I only want to get it right. I've pinned all my hopes on being a nurse, I don't want to ruin it. I don't want to be average; I want to be extraordinary. I want to be perfect. To prove it was worth it.'

'What was worth it?'

'Oh, you know. The upheaval.'

'No one is perfect, Susannah. No one. Have you noticed that it's only women who curse ourselves with such a stupid ambition? You don't catch men worrying about being perfect. They go about the world making a great hash of things and don't think much of it. You know what my brother says? "Do what you will, and if no one catches you, it didn't happen."'

'But I did get caught.'

'You threw a bandage, it's hardly a crime. I'm only sorry you didn't throw a brick at Mabel's face – she's such a curious combination of tart and self-righteousness. You know what my brother would say?'

'I don't, but I'm sure you're about to tell me,' I said, lying down beside her, propped up on one elbow.

She slapped me on the arm. 'Well I won't bother imparting my dear brother's wisdom then. He's a wise man, my brother.'

'I thought you told me he shot himself in the foot with his own rifle?'

'He did, but he was drunk. Anyone might do that.'

'That's why I don't drink.'

The sun was shining straight into our eyes. I was relaxed and warm. I could easily have fallen asleep right there. Aisling rolled up onto her elbow so that our faces were now only inches apart. She squinted and picked something out of my hair. I held my breath.

'You have grass in your hair,' she said, but didn't roll away.

I knew she was going to kiss me and I froze. My stomach threw itself in all directions and I didn't know what to do. I was like a frightened rabbit. Aisling didn't look away or move. Only her lips came towards mine.

I was saved by a distant rumble coming along the tracks behind us. I leapt to my feet.

'Come on! It's our train. We might miss it.'

I picked up my skirts and raced towards the station. Aisling came running behind me.

We spent the train journey home in silence. Aisling sat in her seat, stiff as a board, staring out of the window as if she might cry. I didn't know what to say to make it right again, because I wasn't sure what had happened or how to talk about it. We jerked from side to side with the movement of the carriage. Every so often I saw tears welling up in her eyes, but she seemed angry. When we were nearly back at London Bridge, I tried.

'Are you speaking to me?'

'Why wouldn't I be speaking to you?' she snapped.

'Have I upset you?'

'No, of course you haven't.' She still wouldn't look at me.

When the train finally pulled to a stop and we alighted, I had difficulty keeping up, she was striding towards the exit at such a pace.

'Where are you going, Aisling?' I had to run to catch her up.

'For a drink,' she said.

'What, on your own? In the daytime?'

'Yes, in the daytime. Shocking, isn't it? There I am, being outrageous, doing something simply because I want to do it. I guess I must be mad, or sick.'

'I'll come with you,' I said.

'You don't drink, remember?'

'I don't think you should be on your own, drinking alcohol. I'll come with you.'

'You don't think I should be on my own?' Aisling came to an abrupt stop and several people almost barged into the back of her. I cringed, but she didn't even notice. 'I'll be fine. I don't need you looking down your nose at me.' Then she stomped off.

What on earth was she talking about? I had never judged Aisling. I hardly considered myself in a position to judge anyone.

I caught her up as she turned out of the exit and followed her down the road. Where we were going, I had no idea.

'I'm sorry I ran away,' I said.

She stopped walking again, sending more people almost straight into the back of her. They moved around her, grunting and complaining. I was painfully aware of the inconvenience we were causing, but she didn't care.

'What are you sorry for?' she asked.

'I don't know. I was nervous.'

'Do you think me disgusting?'

'God, no! If anything, it's me that's... I... You know... I'm not sure what to say. Can't we go for that drink?' I asked.

'Fine, you're buying.'

'I can do that,' I said.

I don't actually know how we got home. Afterwards, I could barely recall a thing – just vague images of me walking or being all but carried, and streaks of people blurring into one another as I glided down the street. It was like someone had run their fingers down a wet oil painting and sent all the colours into one another. The world was a smear of everybody and everything.

I'd never drunk alcohol before; my grandparents were teetotal. It tasted foul, and for a long while I didn't feel a thing. All that talk of gin making you happy and giddy and gay – to start with, I thought it all a great swindle. But the very next moment I was a stumbling, dribbling wreck. Aisling had to drag me through the hospital and take me upstairs without anyone catching us. In the room we shared, the other nurses were already asleep. We both broke out into fits of giggles because we couldn't see what we were doing or where we were going. I must have grabbed someone's feet in one of the beds as I felt my way along and that set me off laughing again. There were shrieks and gasps and requests to be quiet until someone lit a candle. I remember scrunched-up faces with bedraggled hair squinting at us, like moles, as Aisling set me down on my bed. Even though the walls were made of stone and the draughts blew through without obstacle, it was still a room in the attic, and with six bodies in their beds, breathing and snoring, it was not the most fragrant.

As soon as I lay down, the room started to whirl about, so I sat bolt upright. The other girls were whining, sitting up and rubbing their eyes. Aisling was on the floor trying to pull my boots off, but then she fell back on the floor herself and started giggling. I did not feel well.

'My Lord, you two! Where have you been? Look at you,' said Nora, one of our roommates.

'Oh Susannah, you are going to struggle tomorrow,' said another.

'We'll all struggle tomorrow if we don't get back to sleep.'

'Where have you been?'

'We went drinking.'

'Susannah – drinking? Well now I've seen everything.'

Aisling pulled herself up next to me on the bed. Nora was standing over us, lecturing us in her nightgown. All I could see was her naked feet, toes wriggling, as she was telling us off, saying how selfish and irresponsible we were. Aisling was holding me upright; I couldn't control my eyes.

Then Aisling said, 'Oh, Nora, I would not stand there if I were you.'

'What do you mean?' she replied.

I threw up on her toes. Nora squealed like a pig and hobbled off crying. I spent the next few hours vomiting into my own chamber pot with Aisling holding my hair back in the pitch black. Whoever had said I would struggle the next day was correct.

24

I could not stop thinking about the woman I'd seen with Dr Shivershev. She'd been so confident, so unlike me, an anxious bag of rigid fears. There'd been triumph in his expression, not to mention a distinct lack of embarrassment at being seen in the Ten Bells with such a woman. I was a little disgusted to learn that my physician, who had become the only man I had any faith in, was not above the usual male weaknesses. Thomas was right, he did like whores. He was disappointingly like the others with their rampant, indiscriminate urges, eyes bulging on account of the beast they professed to have no control over. I wanted my men to be just as I'd been taught they would be – dignified, wise and morally upright – but I no longer believed such men existed.

That night, I woke to the sound of pigs snuffling beneath my bed. I rolled over to look, but there were no pigs, only Mabel lying flat on her back, staring straight at me, a white finger drawn across her lips urging me to be quiet. She was sinking into the wet mud the pigs had turned over. Her skin and hair were wet through, as if she'd crawled out of water.

She gestured for me to come and lie down beside her, so I got down on my belly on the floor and crawled to her on my elbows, slithering through the mud, my hair slick with it, dragging me down, my nightgown caked in it.

When I reached Mabel, she whispered, 'I told you I'd write.'

'But this isn't writing, Mabel. Where are the pigs?'

'They were brutes, I sent them away. Look, Susannah, it's gone.'

She lifted her head and gazed down at her abdomen; it was completely open, with a flap to one side through which she pulled out her own intestines. Blood was everywhere, and I saw it hadn't been mud I had crawled through but Mabel's blood. Her dress was scarlet, but her hands were black and wet.

'Mabel, stop it! We must close you up,' I told her.

'He cut it out. That's good, isn't it?' she said. 'See how it's gone?'

A noise came from something on top of the bed, a choking sound.

'Is that my mother?' I asked Mabel.

'No,' she said. 'It's your grandmother. She still isn't dead. Quick!'

The bed had lowered over both of us, as if its legs had shrunk. I had to slide out on my back, leaving Mabel behind, and climb up onto the bed again.

Mabel was right: there was my grandmother lying in my bed in Chelsea. Her anguished squirming had twisted the bedsheets into a sweaty knot, and she had soiled herself. How I hated looking after her. I sighed, started to pull the bedclothes from under her. I would have to scrape off her mess and wash them – again. I began to cry because I thought she was already dead, but I must have been mistaken and it didn't feel fair. Her wiry white hair was a tangled mess from all her rolling around. She had eyes like a spooked horse, and the skin of her wrinkled face was almost purple. She was still writhing in agony, like a woman trying to birth a child too big, and clawing at her mouth. I stopped with the sheets, sat down on the corner of the bed, held onto the brass finial, closed my eyes and waited for the noise to stop.

When she was finally still, I was desperate to tell Mabel the good news. I crawled back below the bed to find her, but Mabel was facing the other way, so I pulled on her hair to get her attention. Her hair wasn't wet any more; it was dry and the colour of dark copper. When she turned around, it was Aisling and she was smiling. The skin on her face was smooth and luminous, still peppered with freckles, and the small scar on her chin was there. I touched it and she giggled. I remembered her neck and searched for where that scar should be, but I couldn't find it. She kept laughing, then slapped my hands away, kissed my face and pulled my head onto her bony chest.

'How did you get yourself in such a mess?' she asked.

'Because you left me all alone. I didn't know what to do. I still don't. Are you back now?'

'No, I came to tell you one thing: you must trust only yourself. Have you not heard me shouting? I scream and scream, but you never seem to listen.'

We lay underneath the bed together. It was the most beautiful feeling of freedom I'd had in such a long time. My nightdress was covered with mud and blood; Aisling's was clean and stark white. I ran my lips against the skin of her cheek, to remember how soft she was, and how she smelled of violets. She loved violets.

'I should have told you about my grandmother, then this might not have happened,' I said.

'I left my boy in Kildare,' she replied. 'I filled his mouth with peat from my father's bog. I covered him in it like a blanket, left him there, quiet, it's as if he fell asleep. I left him and ran away.'

A slow, drawn-out rhythm struck the floor – heel, toe, heel, toe – and a pair of man's legs made their way around the edge of the bed. I pulled Aisling close and we both lay stiff as twigs; only our eyes moved as they followed the man's boots. He sat down on the edge of the bed and it sagged with his weight, close to our faces. Aisling stroked my wet hair, her skinny fingers catching in the knots and tangles. Then she disappeared, and I was alone again, and now I was frightened. The man's weight on the bed shifted. He bent down and looked underneath and saw me, and I screamed. His head was upside down, the blood in his face draining the wrong way; it was Thomas, grinning and wide-eyed, his whiskers grown out and unkempt, and there was blood on his face and in his teeth. His eyes were that bright, freezing blue; soulless.

I woke up at that point.

I lost the dignity of a normal routine and began to keep odd hours. It felt like my eyes were disappearing further and further into the back of my head and as if my face was a blank, wax-like ball that had been pushed in on one side. My features were bloated and puffy, my cheeks had red blotches; I was taking too many drops. The bruises faded to brown, to yellow and finally to a dull grey shadow, much like my complexion. I was possessed of a quiet dullness, as if my overworked nerves were padded with cotton wool. I could see things from a distance, form an opinion if I tried, yet I didn't care.

It was a pleasant feeling to be dazed and indifferent when the whole of the city was living in perpetual fear. Perhaps I had less fear because I knew what a monster looked like. I opened my bedroom door only for Sarah to pass me the daily newspapers and more drops when I sent her out for them; otherwise I kept it locked. They sent up meals on a tray, but I worried they might be poisoned. I nibbled at the edges, assuming any poison would be administered in the middle, then left the tray on the floor outside my room.

I continued to devour the papers. At Annie Chapman's inquest doubts were raised about the time of her actual murder. If it had taken place at the exact time the witnesses stated they had found her, the murderer would have been walking around in broad daylight covered in blood. The crowd burst out laughing at this. It was explained to the better classes, who remained without a clue as to what was so funny, that due to the hundreds if not thousands of small private slaughterhouses in the maze that made up the Nichol, it was not uncommon to have to leap out of the way of a stampede of sheep or oxen as they were driven through the narrow streets to their slaughter. Those who worked in such places often wandered the streets dripping in blood. The murderer would walk unnoticed.

One journalist observed that after the laughter subsided, an uneasy silence descended on the courtroom. He found himself wondering whether everyone in that room inhabited the same small island-nation or not. When men had such vastly different experiences of the same few square miles, especially when one considered the size and breadth of the empire, let alone the world, could they really call themselves countrymen?

Annie Chapman was buried on Saturday the fifteenth of September. Thomas had not come home for a week.

25

Not long after we graduated, Aisling dragged me upstairs to the oldest part of the hospital. She wouldn't tell me why, only that it was a surprise. We came to the door of one of the smaller rooms in what used to be an attic; it was shared by two senior ward sisters.

'Go on in, have a look.'

'What about the sisters?'

'Just open it, you coward,' she said.

I pushed the door open and crept inside. It was empty. The beds had been stripped and pushed against the walls. There was nothing on the nightstand. The walls were bare brick, there was one small porthole window and a wardrobe built into the eaves. I could hear the pigeons on the roof. The place was tiny. The roof in that part of the building was very narrow and there was just a little strip in the middle where we could both stand up full height. It was a room for miniature people, barely big enough for one Aisling, let alone a gangly Susannah as well.

'Sister Chase is transferring to a hospital in Leicester to be nearer her mother, and Sister Eccleston has been promoted and has a room in the new block, nearer Matron. It's ours, Susannah! Just us! I arranged it with both of them weeks ago – got in there before anyone else.'

'Did you have to fight some elves for it?'

'I'm going to ignore that comment because I know you only said it for the craic. Yes, it's small – but it's all ours. What do you think?'

I was exhilarated by the prospect of having so much freedom. There would be no intrusive eyes on us, watching us too closely; there would be privacy and space. At the same time, I was petrified because now, in an altogether different way, I had nowhere to hide.

'What is it? What's wrong? Don't you want to be with me?' she asked.

'Yes, I do want to be with you, but...'

'Let's simply concentrate on getting on.'

'Agreed.'

Aisling was so untidy, it always looked as if there'd just been an explosion, as if one of those elves had managed to get into the wardrobe and throw everything about. We began to fantasise about running away – always to somewhere with pirates and jungles and, oddly, a British regiment. Aisling's brother had been a soldier in India and had returned with the wildest tales, which she would recount to me. We didn't want to stay within our four walls and wait for a man to come home and describe the world to us – we wanted to touch it and feel it ourselves. We would finish our contractual obligation at the hospital, then take jobs in India. I liked the sound of that.

'We can go anywhere,' said Aisling, leaping onto the bed with her legs crossed, wild eyed like a child. 'Anywhere but rainy old England, which is no better than Ireland, only it has more buildings and more people, and less peat and less Church. We can go somewhere where no one knows who we are or where we're from, where they've never heard of Ireland or Reading and don't care what class we are. We'll be the exotic ones, instead of just the plain old boring poor. And the freaks.'

She lay down next to me and rolled over like she had that day in the field. I held my breath again.

'Wait a minute,' she said. 'I know...' She pulled her blanket over our heads so it was dark underneath, then whispered, 'Now shut your eyes. What you can't see coming, you can't be guilty of.'

During those few months we had together in our little attic room, we fell into a rhythm, and I forgot to be shy. We used to have to remind ourselves that we were not a usual couple; it was easy to forget and not be as vigilant as we should about the little nuances that might give us away, but we were not the only pair, there were more than a few among us at the hospital. We made efforts to be discreet, and everyone else made efforts not to see. In the evening we would push the beds together, and in the morning we'd knock them apart as naturally as making them. My only regret is that the time we had was made so brief, and I wasted a huge sum of it, being full of self-doubt, so frightened of being wrong.

I managed to keep a few things that belonged to Aisling in an old sewing box. Personal items that wouldn't be missed. I had her textbook, *Matron's Lectures on Nursing*, with her exotic winged loops in the margins. She'd written her name inside the cover. I used to tease her for her flamboyant writing with all its extravagant flourishes. It was my decision, she told me, if I chose to leave a dull mark on the world. My own handwriting was a rigid apology.

When I moved into the Chelsea house, I wrapped the sewing box in a shawl and put it at the bottom of the wardrobe in my bedroom. I hadn't sought it out for a while, but one morning I woke with a jolt from another dream about Aisling and had a desperate urge to go through the box and hold its treasured contents. The dream had upset me. I had felt her skin against my dry lips. I could smell her and, if I'd wanted to, I could have rolled over and kissed her shoulder, but when I woke I found I had forgotten her scent; the memory was missing. I was gripped by a terror that I had lost another part of her.

I dashed out of bed and scoured my wardrobe for the box, but it wasn't there. I found the shawl, which had been folded and was exactly where I expected it to be, but the box was gone. There was no possibility I could have mislaid it. I never lost or misplaced anything, and especially not that. I had intentionally, purposefully, put that box there, wrapped in the shawl. It contained my most precious mementoes, little pieces of Aisling.

After what happened, most of Aisling's things were scooped up and taken away, but I did manage to salvage her silver crucifix and her dark green kid gloves, both presents from me for the birthday and Christmas we had together. The thing I cared about most, though, was Aisling's hairbrush, the one that still had her hair on it, the one I'd wound the strands of her hair around. I had not lost that sewing box. I did not lose things. It had been taken.

I tore apart my room, but I couldn't find it anywhere. It

had to be Mrs Wiggs. She was always nosing through my things, tampering, looking for any conceivable way to judge me. A second punch to the gut came when I remembered there was also the photograph of our graduation: Aisling in the row in front of me, Matron at the centre. Even Mabel was in there. I was devastated to think I'd lost these things for ever. I pored over every inch of that room, ripped out every item in every drawer, until I could no longer deny what was obvious: Mrs Wiggs had taken it.

I flew downstairs. Trembling, barefoot, and still in my nightdress – the same one I'd been wearing for the last week – I shot into every room, opening and slamming every door, shaking the house like thunder. Eventually I found her on the narrow staircase that led to the pantry with the china cupboard. Sarah and Cook were at the large table in the kitchen behind her.

'Where is it?' I shouted.

Mrs Wiggs looked startled. Then, as if she knew what was coming, she folded her arms across herself. Sarah, and Cook, whom I had very little to do with, both stared up at me open-mouthed, then when I glared straight at them, dropped their eyes to the table and carried on preparing dinner.

'Mrs Lancaster, you are not making sense,' said Mrs Wiggs.

She peered at me as if I were filthy: a rat she had been ordered to keep alive. She cast a knowing glance at Sarah and Cook, as if seeking validation regarding a previous conversation. No doubt they all gossiped about me. I thought about hitting her. I wondered if she'd ever been slapped across the face. Instead, I demanded she come with me to my bedroom. Again, she looked at Cook and Sarah, wanting them to share in her ridiculing of this inconvenience. I marched up the stairs. She followed behind at a glacial pace, I'm sure to antagonise me, just as Dykes had when she'd dragged her screaming bucket through the hospital on the day Emma Smith bled out.

When we entered my bedroom, she stood and gasped in shock at the horrific mess.

'Good Lord, Mrs Lancaster, what have you done?'

'There is a box missing from my wardrobe. It's a small wooden sewing box – where is it?'

She didn't answer, only stood with her hands pressed to her cheeks, looking about and shaking her head, as if it were a battlefield strewn with dead bodies and bloodied limbs.

'Mrs Wiggs!' I shouted. 'Answer me! It was here, in my wardrobe! Why would you steal it?'

My hands shook, my whole body trembled with rage and I wanted to tear the hair from her head, wrench each strand out of that tightly wound bun and make her squeal. She just stood there, staring at me as if I were mad, while I shrieked at her, tossing aside clothes I'd already thrown onto the bed, hurling them now onto the floor and trampling on them, screeching that she'd done it all on purpose, that she was trying to trick me into thinking myself mad. She denied ever taking anything, denied it over and over. Her reaction made me doubt myself. She begged me to see what I had done to the room. I did look. I saw the mess and heard myself screaming. Then I became overcome with a paralysing fear: what if we did find the box and what if she saw that inside was a collection of worthless things, strands of hair collected in memory of a dead woman? I would seem deranged, and she would tell Thomas.

'I'm going to send for a doctor,' she said, and moved to leave.

I chased her as she made for the door. Her face turned back towards me as I pulled on her shoulder. Then she fractured into a million little mosaic pieces that broke apart and fell away, and everything went black.

When I woke up, I was still in my bedroom, in bed. The room had been tidied and everything was cleared away. I couldn't remember if the episode had really happened or if it had been another one of my bizarre dreams. I looked under the bed to see if Mabel was there, or the pigs, or Aisling, but there was only the floor.

'It's not under the bed, Mrs Lancaster. I've looked,' said Mrs Wiggs.

Her voice gave me a start. I hadn't even realised she was in the room.

'I'm afraid I do not know where this box is. It is obviously very precious to you, so I shall have the house turned upside down to find it, rest assured. I've asked Sarah to draw you a bath.'

As she came into focus, I began to understand what she was talking about.

'Perhaps after that we should call a doctor,' she said.

I shook my head. 'No, I'm fine.'

'Mrs Lancaster, you fainted, do you remember? In the middle of attacking me.'

'I did not attack you, Mrs Wiggs. I was trying to stop you

from leaving, that is all, and there's no need for a doctor, I am not ill. I merely fainted.'

The windows had been opened. It was freezing. I pulled the bedclothes around me. Mrs Wiggs came and sat on the edge of the bed, trapping my legs under the covers. I'd never been in such close proximity to her before. I could smell her: a sickly combination of vinegar and cloves. If a nurse had been caught sitting on a patient's bed like that, they'd have been fired. I could see delicate little thread veins on the white skin of her face; the lines around her eyes were like marks made on clay. She had the smallest ears: round with no earlobes at all. Everything about the woman was definite and sharpened to a point, as if she'd been whittled away by so much. But she must have been quite attractive once.

'Mrs Lancaster, I hope you understand. I know I am not... I don't set out to offend you, Mrs Lancaster, I really don't... May I ask a question? And of course, please do not feel obliged to answer it.'

'Go on.'

'When you fainted, I thought... Could it be what I think it could be?'

'Please don't tell Thomas, Mrs Wiggs – you know how disappointed he was last time.'

I hadn't planned to lie, but I was interested to see if she would act differently towards me. I didn't think I was pregnant. I doubted anything could survive in my body the way I'd been treating it.

'I thought so,' she said.

Though she smiled, it was hard to glean anything from her expression. She didn't appear happy or excited, but then why would she? She was just a servant. A baby would only mean more work for Mrs Wiggs. She remained quiet, gazed past the walls of the room. A dark thought appeared to cast a shadow over her face before she swiftly whipped back on her servant's mask.

'Of course, I won't say a word to Dr Lancaster. It is not my place, after all, and he will return shortly.'

'You know where he is?'

'I only know he was called away on business.'

'He's been called away?'

'Yes. He has these other interests he pursues. I'm sure he'll be home shortly.'

'Mrs Wiggs, I must ask you something, and I want you to tell me the truth. I will not be angry.'

'Of course.'

'Did you take the wooden sewing box from my wardrobe?'

I fixed her dead in the eyes. If I could discern the tiniest flicker across her owl-like glare, I would know she was lying.

'Mrs Lancaster, I promise you, I would never remove anything without your permission.'

I didn't discern a thing.

26

'Susannah, let me in.'

Pale light lined the gaps around the curtains.

'Susannah!'

It was early morning. A yellow flash bounced off the brass door handle and came into focus. Someone was trying to turn it from the other side.

I sat up in bed and stared at the glinting metal, wondering if I'd imagined the voice. A child appeared to be whimpering outside the door.

'Susannah! I'm sorry…'

It was Thomas.

My stomach sank. He hadn't fallen in the Thames and drowned, nor had he been murdered in a fight. He had in fact come back safe and sound and was now scratching at my bedroom door like a mangy old cat. Was he trying to trick me with his sobbing? If he thought I would feel sympathy for him, he was very much mistaken.

I crept over and put my ear to the door. The sound came from low down; he was sitting on the floor on the landing.

I crouched down so only inches of wood separated us. He was talking to himself, muttering. He sounded drunk and God knows what else. I considered ignoring him but knew that would only sustain the bad blood between us. Ultimately, he would win whatever fight I started.

He fell through the door as soon as I opened it. Tumbled through in a sweaty mess and wearing neither a jacket nor a coat. Perhaps he'd part undressed on his way up the stairs – entirely possible in his state. As I stood looking down on him, he rolled onto his back like a beetle and tried to focus his glassy eyes on me. He grabbed the hem of my nightdress, balled the fabric into a tight fist, and with his other hand flailed around as if to steady himself.

'Chapman... will you...? You have to help me...' he said.

I pulled him up onto his knees. I could smell as well as feel the cold sweat from his damp body. It was disgusting. I struggled to assist him onto the bed. His usually angular face was swollen and puffy, eyes red from crying. He clearly hadn't shaved, and his whiskers looked as if they'd broken out of their meticulous borders days ago. When I asked him where he'd been for the past week and more, he wouldn't say.

I sat next to him on the edge of the bed and sighed. I would have to suffer his stupefied presence for the night, and no doubt his pig-like snoring too. I could smell urine. I touched his trousers and he'd wet himself. I yanked my hand away and then shook him by the shoulders, but it did nothing, he only stirred a little. I was reminded of my grandmother, how she used to soil herself near the very end. I would clean up after her and change the bedclothes only for her to do it all over again. Now I'd be doing the same for my young husband. Aisling would have found the humour in this somehow.

'The woman in the attic,' he mumbled. 'She won't leave me. Help me! Tell her to stop talking! It's the talking... All the time...' he said, or at least that's what it sounded like.

'What woman, Thomas?' I whispered close to his ear. I put my hand, still wet with his urine, on his bare chest and shook him. 'Tell me about the woman. Who is she?'

For a moment I thought he might confess to the Whitechapel murders, if I could only get him to talk.

He repeated those same words – and other words, equally unintelligible.

'I don't understand,' I said. 'Do you mean *women*, Thomas? Do you mean the *women*? What happened to them? What did you do?'

I gripped his head between my hands, but it still flopped about. His eyes were a sliver of white and his mouth was loose and dribbling. I tapped his cheek to stir him, but he just rolled over and started to snore.

I pulled his legs straight, took his shoes off and deliberately dropped first one then the other to the floor, noisily, from a height, to try and wake him, but he was dead to the world. I thought about smothering him. I really did. Surely God had sent him to me in this state for me to do something? I could blame it on the alcohol, or whatever else he'd taken. He could have just stopped breathing, couldn't he? Like so many people.

But I didn't. I simply unbuckled his damp, stinking trousers and tugged them off. As I folded them, a gold key fell out of the pocket and bounced across the floor. By the time it had settled flat, I knew what room it was for and what I was going to do with it.

I made my way up the narrow steps to the attic, clutching the key so tight it hurt my hand. At the door I turned back and held up my candle, but all I could see was a few feet behind me. Anything could have been there in the dark watching me. The only noise was the sound of my breathing. The lock made a click and turned first time. I wrapped the key in the palm of my hand again and pushed open the door.

I didn't know what I was looking for. I imagined a knife, a stained bayonet, something incriminating and dripping with blood. I had never been in his precious attic and didn't know where any of the furniture was. It was windowless and pitch black except for me, hovering in a yellow bubble with my candle. I could see bare floorboards beneath my blue feet – the temperature was arctic. I had no idea how Thomas could have spent so many hours holed up there without freezing to death. The air was thick and musty with dust and mouse droppings. From the little I could see, one half of the room was a huddled mass of old furniture: tables and chairs pushed together, the finials of a brass headboard, a scratched chest of drawers with missing handles, armchairs with broken backs and threadbare, moth-eaten upholstery.

I inched towards a slightly better desk and chair, which was where, I assumed, he spent his hours 'working'. I was only a few feet inside the door when I heard a rustle above my head. Something hit the floor beside me and I froze. My heart raced as I peered down. Fresh bird droppings! I looked up and listened. Pigeons were roosting in the rafters and I could now see splatters of bird faeces all over the floor. Were there rats too? My bare feet curled at the thought and I shivered.

I searched the desk, but all I found were a few metal instruments and some medical texts lying open. One page was plastered with dried bird droppings and another showed drawings of the female anatomy. None of this was remarkable or sinister for a doctor to have in his possession. My eyes drifted up again and this time I very nearly screamed. A pair of shining eyes were staring back at me – from the face of a stuffed owl on a wooden stand. I had to laugh, because the owl wore the exact same supercilious expression as Mrs Wiggs.

I blew on it and as years of dust flew out of its feathers and back in my face I sneezed and waved the cloud away. Which was when I caught sight of the glass specimen jar on Thomas's desk. It was clearly a recent arrival, because it was the only thing that was clean.

The specimen was cream and pink in places, and solid, as if it had been carved out of yellow limestone. It was the size of a man's fist and looked much like a peach that had been halved and had the stone removed. In the hollow, encircled by sediment and other matter, was what looked like a tiny foetus. It had an oversized head, barely formed arms that shone white like marble, unformed hands crossed over the front of its body, the faintest shape of a nose and ear, and a dark line where the eye would have been. A human foetus in a womb. I shuddered. I'd never seen anything like it before.

There was nothing to find, no bloodied knife, no evidence. As I turned to leave, I held the candle up one last time, not expecting to see anything. But what did catch my eye scared me half to death. A woman was standing in front of me, stiff and staring. I thought it was Mrs Wiggs and let out a yelp and pinched my mouth closed. The woman didn't flinch or move.

After a moment I realised it was only a tailor's dummy, dressed in ratty old torn clothes. I put a hand on my heart and felt it thump. I was shaking.

The dummy was wearing dark burgundy skirts and a blue velvet jacket with a high collar and black brocade buttons. Balanced wonkily on its head was a cheap black straw bonnet adorned with paper flowers and berries – poor, sweatshop stuff, similar to the fripperies sold at Mabel's milliner's. There were dark, stiff patches on the skirt, as if the woman who'd worn them had spilled a drink, and the velvet jacket had lots of rips and random slashes as well as some crusty dark brown stains.

Why on earth would Thomas dress it up and have it loom over him like that?

At the foot of the dummy there was a pile of clothes. I bent down and pulled a white petticoat out, also torn and slashed. When I held it up, I saw more stains, the familiar brown-red I knew to be blood. I threw it back down and stood up, and then I saw the heart-shaped pendant. The one that Thomas had ripped from my neck, the one I knew had belonged to someone else. Now it hung around the dummy's neck. My stomach lurched and my knees went weak. Hadn't Little Lost Polly been wearing a fancy black bonnet when she was knifed? I wracked my brains, tried to remember other details, things about Dark Annie and the other women too. Had I mentioned Dark Annie's clothes in my writing? Could the blue velvet belong to her?

I was feverish with fear, quivering uncontrollably. Could this mannequin be the 'woman' Thomas had muttered about earlier, the one who whispered to him non-stop? Was she an amalgamation of his victims, twisted into a single vengeful spirit he'd dressed up in the dark to relive the memory of each kill? Was this some depraved arrangement of his clever crimes, so he could congratulate himself daily?

I inhaled the fuggy attic air, tried to calm my thoughts, stop my mind from running away with itself. I had no proof these were the clothes of the Whitechapel women – and there weren't that many items here anyway. Besides, the newspapers had said nothing about the murderer having taken clothes from his victims as well.

I hurried out, locked the door and stole back down to the landing. When I reached it, I saw that something had been placed at the top of the main stairs. My heart thumped as I tiptoed over. Aisling's hairbrush! There was no mistaking it – the sterling silver, the yellowing boar bristles splayed out, the shining copper hair still wound about the handle.

Tears came to my eyes and I had just crouched down to pick it up when I felt a sudden push in the middle of my back. Next thing I knew, I was rolling headfirst down the stairs. I instinctively pulled my arms about my head and dropped the candle. The flame was snuffed out. I landed in a heap at the bottom, winded and in agony.

A dim morning light was coming through the glass either side of the front door. My eyes returned to the stairs, where I saw the amber haze of another candle as it hovered across the landing, like a fairy. I swear I caught the swish of a long plait and the white of a nightgown. It had to be Mrs Wiggs. I struggled to focus. Everything hurt, but I knew I could not be caught with the key. I managed to slide it away from me, across the floor, and it came to a halt underneath the sideboard by the front door. Then I passed out.

27

'I want her gone,' I said. I didn't shout. I sat in the armchair in the front dining room while Thomas wore down the carpet in front of me like a Prussian soldier stomping across Europe. He was still wearing those piss-stained trousers he'd dragged himself home in.

I was bruised and sore from my fall down the stairs but not badly injured. No doubt Mrs Wiggs was bitterly disappointed about that. Of course, I had been fortuitously found by her resourceful self. How could we ever survive without her! I'd come round as I was being dragged by my arms along the floor into the front dining room. I saw my own white feet poking up at the heavens and couldn't understand why the rest of the world was moving away from me. I thought I was dead. Mrs Wiggs groaned with the strain of heaving me into the armchair as I struggled against her. It must have been seven or eight o'clock, because it was as light as it was going to get on a dreary London day now we were nearly in October.

Mrs Wiggs left me there while she went to rouse Thomas, which she attempted to achieve by slapping his face and then applying smelling salts, but it was another hour before she was successful.

My only injury was a green, egg-shaped lump on my forehead that shone like a beacon and throbbed like I'd drunk a bottle of brandy. After Mrs Wiggs had dealt with Thomas, she came at me with a cold compress.

'Get away from me,' I hissed. 'I saw you! It was you who pushed me. You put the hairbrush there to trick me and it was you who pushed me down the stairs.'

Still holding a wet washcloth in one hand, she had the audacity to look at me like I was the lunatic. She had only two expressions in her repertoire: the haughty owl and the startled horse. Both made me want to smack her. She wore the startled horse now; her head began to wobble and she looked as if she might cry. She said I must have either dreamed it or imagined it altogether and then walked in my sleep and fallen down the stairs. After all, I had fainted before. That was how she tried to brush the whole incident away.

I told her plainly that I knew it was her, that she had done it on purpose because of the secret I'd shared. The shock on her face enraged me. It was as if I'd taken a shit on the rug and was now asking her to eat it. She ran up the stairs clutching her nightgown like a little girl. I sat back in the chair and felt the familiar cramps. When I pulled up my nightgown and saw prints of bright red stuck on either side of my thighs, I knew the blood had started to come. Perhaps something had been alive inside me after all and been damaged by the fall, but I couldn't be sure, for, since I'd married, my routine was not to be relied upon. Mrs Wiggs would now have the reassurance she craved: there would be no new intruders in her house.

When she emerged again, the owl was back – dark grey dress, hair swept back into a bun – and she entered the room two feet behind Thomas with a rather smug expression. Thomas looked bloody awful, far worse than me. I barked at Mrs Wiggs to leave us so I could talk to him alone, and I told him without hesitation that I wanted Mrs Wiggs gone, fired, sent back to Abbingdale Hall, whatever, I didn't care, but she was to leave our house.

It was more than Thomas was able to bear. He collapsed into a chair and held his head in his hands, his long fingers tangled in his greasy black hair like crooked spikes. When I told him what had happened, he guffawed. I was sure he was still drunk.

When he'd finally stopped laughing, he said, 'Why on earth would Mrs Wiggs feel the need to push you down the stairs?'

'She hates me, always has. She doesn't think me good enough.'

He laughed again, then stopped. His face grew dark and he slunk down lower in the chair. 'If only you knew...' he began, rubbing at his jawline, dragging the skin down so I could see the red of his bottom eyelids. 'If only you knew how difficult things are... at the moment. I have a lot going on at the minute, Chapman. I'm going to need you to be a good and patient wife for the time being. Do you think you could do that? The truth is, I can't afford to spend time on such petty concerns as the perennial bickering between my housekeeper and my wife. I'm going to have to ask that you get along – it's essential. If you knew the... intricacies of what I've been having to deal with, you would understand.'

'Then tell me, Thomas. You can start by telling me where you disappear to.'

'I can't.'

'Then I want her gone.'

'For the love of God!' he shouted, and jumped up out of his chair. He paced up and down some more and then stopped and pointed a hostile, shaking finger in my face. 'You seriously believe that Mrs Wiggs would steal a fucking hairbrush and... place this... hairbrush at the top of the fucking stairs, just so she could push you down them? There are easier ways of killing someone, Chapman.'

'Oh, how so?'

'You are aware of how ridiculous you sound, Susannah?'

'I don't care how you think it sounds; it's true.'

He wouldn't have it. He kept going on about this other work, how he was under such immense pressure, that this was not what he needed right now – again: distraction, dismissal, disbelief. When I asked him to tell me what was weighing so heavily on him, he said I wouldn't understand.

'It's better if you don't know – trust me. Sometimes I wish I bloody didn't.'

'Is it something to do with the woman in the attic?'

I couldn't help myself, but I knew I'd pushed him as soon as I said it. The nerves fluttered in my stomach. It was as if I'd thrown a bucket of cold water in his face.

'What?'

I smiled. 'You don't remember what you told me last night, do you?'

'What... what did I say?'

'No matter. I'm sure it's nothing. Are you going to fire her or not?'

He patted down his trousers and looked about the room in a pink-cheeked panic, which, given his sweaty pallor, made his face somewhat blotchy. His eyes darted about, trying to remember what he'd done with the attic key, but it was not in his trouser pocket and I doubted he remembered wetting himself.

'Where is it?' He glared at me.

'I don't know,' I lied.

He came at me, loomed over me with his disgusting breath in my face. I shifted away, but he grabbed my chin and pinched my cheek and turned it back towards him. He looked at the lump on my head and laughed.

'That's quite a bump you've got there, Susannah. Now, where is the key?'

I thrust my nose close to his and whispered, 'I. Don't. Bloody. Know.'

'Stupid bitch.' With the palm of his hand across my face, he shoved me backwards.

As he walked towards the door, I called after him. 'Well? Are you going to fire her or not?'

'I'll see you gone first,' he said, then he swung the door open so hard, it bounced off the wall and hit him on the back as he tried to walk through it. I tried to hide my sniggering, but he turned round and saw me. This made him so angry, he punched the door and made a crack in it. He must have near broken his hand, but he only swore and stomped off.

★ ★ ★

Later that week, on the last day of September, I approached the front door and, like my dungeon gaoler, Mrs Wiggs appeared.

'Mrs Lancaster, Dr Lancaster asked that you stay inside the house at all times following your fall.'

'I'm going to see my physician,' I told her.

'I can send for a doctor; you only have to ask.'

'I wish to see my own physician. Please move.'

I pulled the door open, and she hopped out of the way. She knew from past experience I was willing to shunt her if necessary.

'And the er... baby?' she said, as I put a foot into the outside world.

I stopped. That was as close to an admission that she'd pushed me down those bloody stairs not in order to kill me or even hurt me but because she feared what might be growing in my belly.

'It won't be a concern any more,' I answered, still with my back to her, and stepped onto the path.

'Not everyone can be a mother,' she said. 'It demands enormous self-sacrifice. Some women don't have it in them.'

I did turn around then, to see her grinning at me. I had never seen that face before: a smug grin, the superior cat, to join the horse and the owl. A triumphant smile, as if she'd won this particular battle, and would always win.

Dr Shivershev's elegant housekeeper was walking too fast for me up the staircase.

'You're lucky he lives here,' she said, not even remotely out of breath.

I had to rush to keep up with her. It was me that was huffing and puffing, yet she must have been twice my age.

'He lives here?'

'He owns the building, lets out the other rooms. He has several properties actually, but he lives on the top floor. I know it seems unlikely, but the doctor is quite the speculator. He talks of investing in manufacturing. He's always lecturing me about how the English rely too much on imports and neglect their own industry. Have you not heard him ranting about inadequate technical education systems or the English obsession with excessive overseas investment?'

I shook my head, unable to get a word in edgeways.

'Then you are one of the lucky ones, my dear. Yes, he lives frugally and isn't the sort to spend. If it was left to him, this entire house would be unfurnished, only filled with instruments and those morbid specimens he insists on collecting. You've seen his office. He is not a believer in this new fashion for travelling to and from work, thinks it a pointless waste of precious time.'

She turned back to look at me now, flashed me her most charming smile.

'Here I am, babbling on at you! Now, he told me he must see you, so I arranged his diary to accommodate this appointment. But please understand, Mrs Lancaster, he does not have long.'

I nodded. I was too conscious of catching my breath and noting how she'd expended comparatively little effort while I felt as if I'd run a hundred-yard sprint. I saw her take in the sweat on my upper lip and her expression changed. She seemed suddenly uncomfortable in my presence. I had the feeling that something about me had struck her as odd. I'd checked my reflection that morning and noticed that I was dull around the eyes, that my skin was dry and grey, and my egg-shaped lump still green. I began to worry I'd been spending too much time in my own company, unaware that my lips moved during my imaginary conversations, arguments I always won, with no one to point out my bizarre habits.

She opened the door to reveal Dr Shivershev behind his desk, spinning around on the spot, his head moving in all directions as if he were trying to swat a fly but first needed to find it.

'Come in and sit down, Mrs Lancaster.'

His housekeeper shook her head, irritated by him instantly, showing that over-familiar fatigue one gets from close proximity. She closed the door behind her and I approached his desk.

'I had both gloves in my hand only a second ago, how on earth could I lose one? It makes no sense, no sense at all,' he said, still looking as if the missing glove could be found floating in mid-air.

I spotted it on the floor, picked it up and handed it to him.

'Ah! Thank you. Please, sit down. Now, I suppose Irina told you...'

'That you don't have long, I understand,' I said.

We locked eyes as I handed him the glove and he looked at me with the same expression as his housekeeper. I pretended not to notice. It felt strange enough being somewhere other than my bedroom, let alone out in the world beyond. It was most unsettling. We both stood there holding the black glove, until I realised I was the one who was supposed to let go. I think perhaps we were both recalling the moment we had last laid eyes on each other, in the Ten Bells. Of course, this would not be mentioned, neither of us could have a good explanation for being in there, so we would ignore it. This was an important part of our culture, after all: to understand when it was expected of us to ignore the glaringly obvious and politely pretend things were as they should be.

He asked how I had come about the lump on my head and sat forward, eager to listen, taking in all the bruises I wore in various states of healing.

'My housekeeper pushed me down the stairs.' I wasted no time. 'I'll come straight to it, Doctor. I am sorry if I appear out of sorts, but I fear for my life. It is not my intention to burden you, but I suppose it is your bad luck I have no one else. You're the only person I've really had any conversation with outside of that house since I married, so I'm afraid I'm forced to confide in you. Please, this needs to be written down; otherwise, if anything does happen to me, no one will ever know. This way, there'll be a record of this conversation and you can be a witness.'

I had his attention. He nodded, then took out fresh paper and a pen and gestured for me to continue.

I explained all that had led to my being seated in his office at that moment. How Thomas had changed after we married. How the scab on the back of my head had really come about and how I'd lied to protect him and not embarrass myself. I even confided in him that Thomas had come home with blood all up his arms and all over his coat and shirt.

'Did he tell you what happened?'

'No, only that he'd been in a fight with a man who owed him money.'

I blurted out this rambling, garbled mess and he tried to scrawl as fast as I spoke. I told him about our violent argument after the Café Royal, about Thomas's subsequent disappearance and about how when he did eventually return home, he cried like a child begging for comfort and talked gibberish about a woman in the attic.

'I'm sorry, what woman? I don't understand – there is a woman in your attic?' said Dr Shivershev.

'No, of course not.' I explained again, in more detail, about the attic and the dummy and the heart-shaped pendant. 'And I'm now convinced that the necklace had belonged to someone before me. It had scratches, and it was also inlaid with a piece of peridot, which the woman at the Café Royale commented on, because—'

'I'm sorry, I'm lost. What woman? The woman in the attic or the Café Royale?'

'When we were leaving the restaurant, Thomas bumped into a gentleman – tall, grey whiskers, medals on his lapel – and that gentleman irritated Thomas by telling him that he was getting a reputation for... Well, it doesn't matter. Anyway, the gentleman's wife noticed my necklace and asked me if I'd just had a birthday because peridot is the birthstone for August.'

'I'll take your word for it – I have no understanding of such things. You said Dr Lancaster seemed agitated after speaking to this gentleman, the man with the medals. What did he say?'

'That he'd heard bad things about Thomas, and Thomas was worried about how this would affect this other work he has, for a group of doctors – sponsored work. He tells me it is more profitable, but I don't know much about it. This is what he blames for having to spend so much time away, but I don't believe him. Oh, I am frightened, Dr Shivershev. I have married a dangerous man, one who may have done terrible things to the women who owned those clothes.'

'It's all right, Mrs Lancaster, I am listening. You are safe here. Please go on.'

I explained how I had come down the stairs and found the hairbrush and what that meant to me, but I kept getting events and explanations in the wrong order so they didn't make sense. He frequently told me to slow down and to repeat myself. I was aware I was excitable, maybe a little hysterical, but I never got the sense he didn't believe me. I felt I was doing the right thing by telling him absolutely everything.

'She put the hairbrush there so I would pick it up, then she pushed me.'

'You believe this... Mrs Wiggs, the housekeeper, tried to kill you?'

'Yes! Who else could it be? But that's not all, Dr Shivershev. There's more, much, much more. I think the necklace he took from me that night belonged to one of the women whose clothes are in the attic.'

'Why would your husband be stealing women's clothes, Mrs Lancaster?'

'I think he kills them.'

'You think he murders women for their clothes?'

'No! Well, not exactly, but yes, perhaps! Not for their clothes, but for something. He keeps their clothes for some reason. I... He goes missing sometimes. Often. He doesn't come home for days at a time. When he does come home, he is bad-tempered and cruel... He is not...'

'Not what?'

I just couldn't bring myself to talk of Thomas's urges in the bedroom. Dr Shivershev was taking everything down, and I didn't want that part to be written down and made permanent with ink.

I changed the subject. 'Have you heard anything of Mabel? It's just I haven't—'

Out of nowhere, he stood up and banged his hands down on the desk. I nearly leapt out of the chair. His eyes were wild as he stared down at me. I was so shocked, my cheeks tingled.

'No, Mrs Lancaster. We had an agreement – you are not to mention that again.'

I shrank like a child. 'I'm sorry.' I sat with my hands bunched together and felt small and drained. I was stiff and sore from falling down the stairs and had lost my train of thought.

Dr Shivershev composed himself in seconds and was calm again, as if the eruption had never happened. He picked up his pen and calmly continued.

'You believe your husband harbours violent impulses towards women?'

'Yes, that's correct.' I nodded. 'He has a vicious streak. I think him quite capable of terrible things.'

'And this, er, hairbrush you talk about, can I ask its significance? It is an object of... importance to you?'

'It belonged to a friend. Mrs Wiggs stole it from me to hurt me, to make me think myself mad.'

'Nurse Barnard?'

'Yes.' I wasn't sure if I should have said that. I should have lied and said it was my mother's.

He nodded, as if confirming something he had long suspected, and then he was furiously writing again. I tried to see what he wrote, but it was illegible.

His office had descended into a state of neglect again, with dust on the glass jars and books on the floor. Worried I had lost a little of my currency with my indiscretion over Mabel and then with talk of Aisling, I felt I ought to win his loyalty back. I needed to have at least one person planted firmly on my side.

'There's more, Dr Shivershev,' I said.

'Go on.'

'When we argued in the coach, the subject of the argument was you.'

He stopped, put down his pen and looked up. 'Oh? How so?'

'My husband didn't approve of my choice of physician. He'd picked one for me himself, but I disobeyed him and found you. He doesn't appear to like you very much.'

'What exactly did he say?'

I had him now; his eyes were fixed on me. He sat back in his chair and folded his arms, as if creating a barrier to the words he already knew I would unleash.

'He disapproves of you because you are Jewish, and, he said, because you are known to seek out the company of women of... immoral earnings.'

To his credit, Dr Shivershev remained expressionless, but I knew this had rattled him, for how could it not?

'Why do I get the feeling I'm being drawn into something, Mrs Lancaster?'

'He tore the necklace from my throat and hit me – you would have seen the bruises on my face that day in the Ten Bells. You must have seen them, surely?'

He said nothing, of course. I was not meant to mention the Ten Bells.

'He does other things too. He is unpredictable. I will tell you one last thing, but you must promise not to write it down.'

He nodded again, so I continued. 'On every occasion there has been a Whitechapel murder, I could not tell you where my husband was at the time. He was not at home. More significantly, each time he reappeared, he came with injuries.'

Dr Shivershev appeared particularly interested in this. He seemed to write down every word as I described Thomas's various wounds.

'Don't you think it odd, Dr Shivershev?' I asked by way of conclusion. 'I know he's involved in something troubling because he's told me as much. Do you think it possible, Doctor, that my husband could be the Whitechapel murderer?'

'There are murderers, Mrs Lancaster. I suppose at least some of them might be married.'

'Then it's fair to assume that any woman could be married to the Whitechapel man, and it is logical to assume that it could be a man of a medical education. In which case, could it be me? Could I have married the Whitechapel murderer?'

'I think,' he said, after a long intake of breath, 'that, given all the things you've told me, you have genuine cause for concern. But apart from these strange bloodstained clothes in your attic, is there anything else? This other work, for instance... You've said that it is more profitable, and that he is secretive about it, and that this gentleman at the restaurant with the medals may also have some involvement. What is this work exactly?'

'I don't know. He won't tell me.'

'Have you told anyone else about anything? What about the police?'

'Oh no.' I shook my head.

'Why not?'

'Think of the scandal! What if I were wrong? Thomas is a gentleman and I'm just... the daughter of a whore. It wouldn't be hard for people to find that out, if they were to look, if I were to cause trouble. Who would believe me? The wealthy stick together – you know that. The rest of us are always set apart. Even if the only thing we have in common is our supposed inferiority to the rich, Dr Shivershev, we must be careful not to cause trouble for each other.'

'I do understand your hesitancy. Thank you for telling me all of this, Mrs Lancaster. I think perhaps a holiday would be a good idea. Is there somewhere you can go, even for a few days, to be safe from your husband and this housekeeper?'

'A holiday? Good grief, this is no time for a holiday.'

'I mean somewhere you can go to be safe and out of the way while I... think about this. How do you know this other work is legal, Mrs Lancaster? Have you considered your husband might be involved in something he shouldn't?'

'No, no, I didn't think of that.'

'And you are sure you don't know anything about it, or what it is? There have been no clues or indications? He hasn't said anything?'

'No, nothing, not a word, and I have asked him.'

'Right, right.'

'I have a house in Reading, but there are tenants who live there. Thomas knows of that, so there's no point running there.'

'I understand. But *you* must understand that I now have a duty to your care. I am concerned for you, Mrs Lancaster.'

'You won't tell anyone, will you? I must make a plan, but please wait, please promise me you won't tell the police, or anyone.'

'I promise. But for now, why don't you come back in a few days and we'll discuss things further then. Let's see how that lump is doing and make sure there aren't any new ones. I will need time to digest what you have told me. Perhaps we can make this plan together, Mrs Lancaster.'

I exhaled air that felt as if it had been trapped in my lungs for a lifetime, a poisonous mess of sulphur and lead. It felt so good to tell someone who didn't react as if I were delusional. If I were to be lost or killed, or if something else were to happen to me, at least I had Dr Shivershev, and he would ask questions, I was sure of it. It was a desperate kind of insurance, but it was a comfort.

'There is one thing you can do for me, Mrs Lancaster.'

'Yes?'

'I would like you to reduce your consumption of laudanum.'

'Pardon?'

'Your eyes are not responding to the light the way they should, and you've been scratching at your arms the entire time you've been here.'

'Have I?' I pulled up my sleeves and saw that my forearms

were covered in red scratches and there were scabs on the backs of my hands I hadn't even noticed. I was still staring at them, bewildered by the sight, when Dr Shivershev almost lifted me out of the chair by my arm.

'Now, if you don't mind, I really have to leave. I have an important meeting to attend. Very wealthy clients – you know how they can be.'

As he hustled me to the door, we passed the shelves crammed full of specimens. My attention was drawn to the sole dust-free cloche, and I recognised it immediately: it was the specimen from Thomas's attic, the baby inside the womb.

All the blood ran to my feet and I thought my knees would give way. Luckily, Dr Shivershev still had hold of my arm.

'Are you well enough to get home?' he said. He must have felt my trembling.

'I'm fine. I'm only tired. I think I shall go home and rest.'

'Of course. It can't have been easy speaking about all this. Try to be calm, please. Everything will work out, you'll see.' He glanced at my face and saw that my eyes were fixed on the new specimen. 'Ah, I forget that you are a fellow medic! So of course you have noticed my latest addition.'

With my arm still in his grip, he guided me over to examine it.

'This is an amazing piece, quite artfully removed. What we are looking at here is a uterus during pregnancy. The foetus is perfectly intact and, I think, between fourteen to sixteen weeks. Isn't it spectacular?' He pointed a stubby finger. 'That part there is the placenta. It's beautiful, really, don't you think? Women truly are creators – look what they can grow inside them. No one can replicate their gift. It's fascinating.'

He stared at it as if it were a piece of art. He really did believe it was beautiful – his eyes glistened and I'd never seen him so in awe. For my part, I felt nauseous. Sicker than sick. Mabel had been around that stage in her pregnancy when I'd passed her on to her abortionist. Was it possible that we were admiring the baby that had been cut from Mabel? My whole body quivered at this horrific thought. Was my grip on reality so weak that I had delivered Mabel into the hands of someone who had then carved her insides out? Had I done this? My mind was so thick with fog, I simply couldn't think straight or sensibly.

'Where did you get it?' I said.

'From a dealer in a coffee house. You'd be surprised what you can buy in such places.'

'I doubt I'd be surprised, Doctor, not by that,' I said. I looked along the rest of the shelves, filled with organs split in half, body parts, veins and arteries filled with wax. The shelves were cluttered with every part that could have been extracted; still, sombre and silent, like my women were now. Yet they had all belonged to living creatures with aspirations and fears. 'What is it about these specimens that fascinates you so? You must have seen many cadavers opened up, why keep collecting?'

'Didn't you ever find the carcass of an animal and poke it with a stick as a child?' asked Dr Shivershev, almost before I'd finished talking. He turned to look at me and smiled. 'I am willing to wager that you did, Mrs Lancaster.'

'Yes, I'm sure I did.'

'Well, you tell me, what compelled you to keep poking,

to keep looking, to roll the carcass over and see what was on the inside?'

'Curiosity, intrigue, I wanted to understand...'

'So you have it,' he interrupted. 'You wanted to understand. And understanding is knowledge. Knowledge is progress, it doesn't always make sense in the beginning, Mrs Lancaster. It can appear grotesque, amoral, perverse. It is difficult to imagine where the curiosity and intrigue will take you, but still, you want to see what's on the inside because you wish to understand, you wish to know something.'

I thought of my macabre scrawling of the dead women's last moments, and wondered if somehow, Dr Shivershev was talking about the same compulsion I had found in myself. The execution may be different, but the urges sounded as if they came from a similar place. He continued,

'And why do we wish to understand, Mrs Lancaster?'

'I don't know, I... it is ultimately a selfish pursuit, I think. Perhaps to make ourselves feel better about ... something.'

'I think it is a way of fighting back?'

'Against what?'

'Not sure myself, you?'

'I'm sure I don't know.'

'Well, if you find out, please let me know, I'll spread the word, we can all move straight to confirming what this is all about and leave all the mess and blood and suffering that God seems compelled to throw at us and live in blissful rapture,' he said.

'Is she dead?' I asked.

'Who?'

Mabel, I nearly said. 'The mother.'

'Yes, of course.' He laughed. 'That's the entire uterus.' He tapped the glass. 'And the cervix is that part there, it stretches out like the branch of a tree.'

'How did the mother die?'

'I have no idea. It was removed at autopsy. Besides, it's not the mother I feel sympathy for.'

'Why ever not?' I looked at him, shocked by his lack of feeling.

'There's likely a man somewhere who lost a wife and child in one day. Now, I really must leave, Mrs Lancaster.'

28

After I was hustled out onto the street by Dr Shivershev, I felt more terrified and confused than ever. My head hurt. I wanted to be at home in my locked bedroom. I wanted my drops and my bed, but when I looked at my arms, I was ashamed at how I had lost myself, scratched my own arms red raw and not even noticed.

I walked. My brain was a bursting mess, all the threads tangled with each other. I couldn't identify an end to pick up and follow. How could that specimen have found its way from Thomas's attic to Dr Shivershev's office without the two of them having some sort of relationship?

I walked until I found myself outside Thomas's rented office on Harley Street, further up from Dr Shivershev's. I rang the doorbell and when a bespectacled young clerk answered, I asked if Dr Lancaster was at work today.

'No, I'm afraid not. Are you a patient?' he asked.

I shook my head.

'Would you like to make an appointment with one of our doctors?'

'Where is Dr Lancaster?'

'I'm sorry, but he doesn't work here any more. If it's him you really must see, you might try the London. I hear he still works there – on occasion.'

All that fantastical talk of becoming the finest surgeon in England, and he couldn't even master the discipline of turning up to work every day. I wanted to laugh out loud at my idiocy. I had believed every yarn Thomas had spun for me, taken everything at face value. He'd made sure to persuade me that he was ambitious and driven, but it was all an illusion, words crafted to impress. Thomas had neither the talent nor the work ethic to succeed. Putting in the hard graft required to become a surgeon was just too expensive an investment for him. Too dirty, too boring and too painful. The only sustainable advantage he had was family money, doled out in careful rations by his sister, Helen. Only now did I realise that this too was suspicious. Why would a sister play banker to her brother? The answer was obvious: because he could not be trusted. I began to wonder if he might be the black sheep, kept at a distance in London with his old nanny sent to keep an eye on him – or me. But Mrs Wiggs was too loyal to Thomas to be a spy; she worshipped him.

An hour later, I was standing opposite the London Hospital. The weather was mild but grey; it threatened to rain but was not cold. Whitechapel Road was heaving and groaning like an endless sea; heads were bobbing, and carts were jostling for space with omnibuses and cabs, none of them proceeding at a notable speed. I leaned against a lamppost and stared at the archways of the entrance to the hospital and the clock on its facade. Apart from the occasional scream from a hawker in my ear, and children trying to access the contents of my pockets, I was largely ignored.

I had stood there for what seemed like hours and had almost given up when I finally saw Thomas's slim frame spring from the shadows like a gazelle. He danced down the steps with one hand on his hat, the other holding an umbrella under his arm. He skipped, carefree and gay. Men like him fished for idiots like me. What a desperate stench I must have given off.

He strode through the streets like a fucking dandy, and I followed him. We went down Whitechapel Road, Montague Street and Wentworth Street and came out on Commercial Street, whereupon he walked into the Princess Alice pub. The sight of the Alice made me unsteady. It was well known for trouble, and the Thomas I was familiar with was far too much the snob to rub shoulders with the dockers who drank there. Of much more significance, though, was that the man who took Aisling from me had been drinking in the Princess Alice before he landed in our emergency room. His name was Henry White. Merely thinking his name brings me a gloom I find difficult to shift.

Henry White had got into a huge fight that night in the Princess Alice. One of the men got stabbed in the thigh with some glass, another was beaten about the head with a chair leg, and Henry had his head cut open when a glass was smashed on it. They were all brought into the emergency room at the London, where Aisling and I were on shift.

I was wary as soon as I laid eyes on him. He had that hostile rage hopeless men at the bottom always have simmering inside them. He was loud, cursed endlessly and kept demanding attention, even though the minute he got it, he was abusive. His face was a reddened bloated mess, with blood running into his eyes and teeth. The duty manager had told him once already that if he didn't stop his troublemaking, he'd be thrown out and left to bleed to death on the pavement.

Aisling knew how to talk to men like Henry White. She could withstand their vulgar language and intrusive hands, could flash a smile and with a quick tongue disarm them, charm them into docility, however rough. I, however, was always distant and aloof, and my priggish reserve antagonised brutes like him. I was more useful standing back and assessing the situation. Aisling didn't mind being more involved, and she was a better nurse, cooing at the trickiest, dirtiest men that I cringed from. She was undoubtedly the braver one. I always feared one of them might lash out and hurt me, especially when the room was drenched in blood, noisy with patients writhing in discomfort and screaming obscenities, and frantic with doctors and dressers shouting instructions at each other. Patients could be unpredictable and, like any animal, when in pain, they tended to bite. Aisling said I could see danger where there was none. That makes me laugh now, because Thomas said the same, and I wanted to believe them both. But it turned out I was right.

We were told to tidy him up quickly and get rid of him, because the duty manager didn't like the look of him and wanted him out. When I tried to examine him, he waved his filthy hands around and knocked my cap off. He pushed a dresser away more than once, until he was threatened again, after which he sat mumbling to himself with blood streaming down his forehead and into his eyes.

Aisling could see I was afraid of him. 'Why don't you stay the other side,' she whispered to me.

White managed to remain quiet for a minute or so, then began to rant that his wife was a 'bitch', that he'd been to the Americas and was sorry he'd come back to this shithole of a country now it was full of 'coons, cunts and peelers'. He griped about someone having stolen his money, which was what had caused the fight, but it was safe to assume he had drunk it. It seemed a pity to waste good bandages and carbolic on him.

I had dipped the utensils in the carbolic and put them on the tray when White smacked it upwards on purpose, sending the instruments clattering to the floor and bouncing around the emergency room. The two dressers rushed to gather them up while I retreated to a corner.

Aisling, meanwhile, tried to subdue White and make him lie back. She put an arm across his chest. 'Hey now, they'll kick you out if you keep that up,' she told him.

His head wobbled on his neck and he glared at her in a vile rage. His ugly, unfocused eyes tried to make sense of her defenceless face and then I saw a silver streak flash and rip Aisling on the underside of her chin. The metal sliced into her like a nail through paper.

She didn't scream – it was more of a gasp and a yelp at the shock of it. She didn't understand what had happened and she looked to me in disbelief as she stood there fumbling at her neck with her fingers. The look on her face, her hands at the wound, the blood gushing out... It was me who screamed at the desperate sight of her.

The dressers dragged Henry White to the floor and sat on him. Aisling collapsed to the ground, like a delicate marionette with its strings cut. On my knees, I tried to examine her neck with my hands, but she was bleeding so fast. The duty manager ran in, followed by doctors, porters, nurses. The other nurses pulled me away, and the last thing I saw was her body slumped against the wall, her head at an awkward angle, her uniform soaked in blood and a lake of it creeping across the floor. Her eyes were open and her arms were by her side, palms up. *We can't leave her head like that*, I thought. *Her neck will hurt.*

The Princess Alice was wrapped around a corner and had windows on all sides. I inched my way along Commercial Street until I found a spot outside a window at the far end through which I could see the bar. Though the pub was busy, I had a clear view of Thomas as he weaved his way to a table in the corner. He sat down with a man who had his back to the window. The man wore a black billycock and the sight of it made my hair stand on end. They both got up, walked to the bar, leaned up against it and faced each other. I had yet to see the other man properly, but I already knew who it was.

It was Dr Shivershev, the man to whom only a few hours ago I had confessed all my fears. I flopped against the pub wall and felt the air leave my lungs. The betrayal stung, probably more so than my stupidity. I was lost. I had no one. The man I'd thought could be my last hope was drinking with my murderous husband. I now had to believe that the baby in the jar had come from Mabel and that my husband had given it to Dr Shivershev, who had likely reported back to him after each one of my consultations with him. They were in it together – whatever 'it' was.

I hurried on down Commercial Street and had walked only ten feet when I saw Dr Shivershev's pretty whore from the Ten Bells and the man with the ginger whiskers coming towards me. In a panic, I dipped my head; it had started to rain and the wind was up. I pulled the edges of my bonnet down about my face and bowled straight between them – they even parted to let me through. I glanced back to see them push through the doors of the Princess Alice.

It must have been half past six by the time I arrived home, in a great rush, hurtled into the hallway, ignored Mrs Wiggs and nearly barged into Sarah on the stairs. Once inside my bedroom, I locked myself in.

The vow I had made earlier in the day to abstain from taking further drops was forgotten. I waited for the edges to blur and the angels to come. At any moment, Thomas would arrive like a hurricane, breaking down the door and storming into my room once he'd learned of everything I'd said to Dr Shivershev. Would Dr Shivershev come too? Would I be dragged down into the cellar, past Sarah and Mrs Wiggs, who would watch open-mouthed and blameless as I was murdered, my blood poured down the drains and my clothes burned and left out with the hot ashes. My husband and his friend would know all too well how to dissect me into convenient pieces small enough to smuggle out and drop into the Thames along the Chelsea Embankment.

I could run, but where would I go? I had the urge to go somewhere, but at the same time it was too tempting to remain. What would Aisling have done? She'd have left

Thomas long ago. Better to be free and poor than a wealthy captive, she used to say. But I dithered on that still. I had memories of being cold and hungry and sometimes I was not sure which was better.

Elizabeth the Melody

Aperson can be many things, can they not? Most people are merely acting the parts they've been given anyway. Life is an instrument thrust into the hands of a small child; they play the violin because it's the only one they've been shown how. She had been an Elizabeth before and would be again, soon, but for now she must make do with being this Liz. She didn't much like it: Liz sounded hard, like a hiss or a grunt. The English had a million ways to reduce a person to nothing. 'Eliz-a-beth' had a melody. It rose and fell. It had a beginning, a middle and an end. The name was a story, and how Elizabeth loved stories. She would keep going until hers was a good one.

Elizabeth took care to avoid the mirror, a pointless square of blackened glass that hung from a nail driven into the wall made fat with damp. She had whitewashed the wall that morning and now she'd moved on to cleaning the men's rooms. This being Elizabeth's regular haunt, she had the benefit of the odd piece of casual work thrown her way.

Despite her best efforts, she caught her own eye in a small portion of the mirror and studied her complexion;

the skin was dry, the bones appeared a little too close to the surface and the line of her jaw had become slack. Her eyes had shrunk, and her lashes, which always used to be long, looked as if they'd been filed down. She slapped her cheeks hard to bring the life back into them, then yanked at her bodice and thrust her shoulders back.

'I can always be another,' said Elizabeth.

'What was that?' shouted Ann from the next room.

'What?' said Elizabeth.

'You said something,' Ann said as she marched into the room, wiping her hands on a cloth, shiny-eyed and half laughing. 'You're doing it again, Liz. Gabbling away to yourself. First sign of madness, that is.' She tapped a finger to her temples, then waddled back to where she'd come from.

Elizabeth bristled at the joke. She did not find it funny. She hadn't been able to rely upon her mind of late. It was the strain of remembering all the details. If she wasn't the tragic sailor's widow from the Princess Alice, or Long Liz, she might be the farmer's daughter, the musician's maid, or any number of other parts she'd played. The one thing she did know was that she was not English, even if it had been two decades since she'd come from Sweden, hounded out for whoring, which did not bother this part of London so much. All these stories were jumbled up in her mind and tended to leapfrog each other. It was the thoughts that raced too fast and tried to escape her lips; she must take care to keep her lips still, else people think her mad.

It was gone six when she returned to Flower and Dean Street and paid for her bed. She stopped by Catherine and asked her to take care of some green velvet as she was going

288

out. Then Elizabeth brushed down her clothes, taking care to pull the velveteen bodice of her black dress this way and that before donning the jacket with the fur trim. She discreetly slipped a packet of cachous to freshen her breath into her pocket.

'You're a bit quiet. Nervy, even – that's not like you,' said Catherine. 'Where you off to? Or rather, who you off to see all dressed up like that?'

For her age, Liz was quite attractive. Considering the way she lived and how much she drank, this made her something of an enigma. She wasn't in the habit of wearing a bonnet, and yet here she was stuffing newspaper into the back of one – newly acquired, it would appear.

'Never you mind,' Liz snapped, taking off the bonnet again and then fussing first with her nosegay and then with the red rose on her lapel.

Catherine didn't mind the snapping; they were all getting on a bit. Life was a little easier if one had a fella to partner with and since Liz was faring better than others her age, why shouldn't she try and fix herself up with a better type. Catherine would have done the same herself if she'd had the teeth or the inclination.

There was no point asking Liz what she was up to. One thing Catherine had learned about her was that you couldn't trust a word that fell out of the woman's mouth, and she often forgot the finer detail of her own lies. They weren't bad lies. Not really. Catherine had known girls like Liz before. Sometimes a little embellishment made life easier to bear. Liz wasn't a bad sort. Unlucky maybe, and not the wisest, but not bad. Whatever she was up to, Catherine hoped she would get away with it.

* * *

Israel kept his head down, careful not to catch anyone's eye on his way home from the synagogue. He had stayed too long, he knew that. With each minute spent in the familiar company and comfort of his own kind, he was at greater risk on his walk home. But it was a wrench to leave the friendly faces, the warmth, the conversation that came so easily, all so welcome after having given oneself a headache trying to understand the strange sounds from the strange mouths. London was a desolate place, considering it was so crowded.

It was well beyond midnight when he took himself off down Commercial Street. A wide, clear road, and with that the relative safety of other people, but also the likelihood that they were not his own. It was not easy to blend in. His curls, his features, his clothes... All signposts, clues to those who hated his kind. They had never met him, they could not know that Israel was anything but a threat, but the hostility and anger he felt from them as he struggled to understand their words always felt so personal, so specific to him, that he often questioned whether he might have been mistaken for someone who had done something terrible. These days he avoided such interactions. The language was odd, and the words changed from one person to the next.

His breath quickened; lungs left behind because of the pace his nervous legs insisted on keeping. He hustled with his hands in his pockets and his eyes on the pavement. He turned into Berner Street in the pitch black. It was really too late; he should have left a lot earlier. He would be stricter with himself in future. This was too dark, too dangerous.

Up ahead, he could see the black shapes of what he thought were a man and woman. His chest loosened when he saw it was a couple; the presence of a woman made the pair less threatening. As he approached, the man suddenly lunged at the woman, grabbed her by the arm and threw her across what would be his path and down onto the pavement. The woman screamed, three times in all. A shrill, piercing sound. No one else came. It was only them and Israel and he was stuck to the spot. His pulse started to thump between his ears, everything screamed inside his head that he should run, but his legs would not move. When eventually he managed to cross the road, he felt bad. He should be going to the aid of the woman, but he'd always been told never to become involved in such disputes because invariably he would find himself the outsider.

Israel quickened his pace as the woman struggled to her feet. All his senses were trained on the two of them. When another man appeared from the shadows, his heart nearly burst and he leapt off the pavement and onto the road. The man had emerged from the darkness to light his pipe and Israel was sure he was looking at him. Israel was half running now, and when he turned to check, his stomach lurched. The man was chasing him now, shouting something. Israel couldn't be sure, but he thought it sounded like 'Lipski'. The name of the alien Jew they hung for murder only last year. That was all he needed to hear. He fired up his legs, and he ran and ran. He didn't stop running, even when his lungs seemed about to burst into flames and his legs grew too tired to carry his body. He tripped and he stumbled, but he kept running until he fell upon the door of his home.

Kate of All or Nothing

'What's your name?' the man at the desk asked the swaying woman.

She was like a badly stuffed scarecrow, held up between two officers. PC Robinson had struggled to get her to her feet. She'd already slipped through his arms once, landed in a heap on the pavement and burst out laughing. He'd had to enlist the help of PC Simmons and they'd half dragged her back to Bishopsgate Police Station.

A haggard old sparrow, the woman must have been in her forties. She was skinny, and her face had a misshapen slant to it, as if one too many beatings had shifted the bone structure. The shadows under her eyes were dark, but her features were small and fair. She'd probably been pretty once. A shame, really, what these women did to themselves through drink and bad choices, thought the teetotal PC Robinson.

'I said, what's your name?' the man asked again, a little louder.

This time it looked like the woman had at least tried to focus on him. She bent her wobbling head forward, fixed him with an intense stare and narrowed her eyes as if trying to make them work. Either that or she was going to be sick.

'Nothing,' she said.

PC Simmons and PC Robinson rolled their eyes.

'Did no one out there know who she is? Do either of you recognise her?'

'No one said a word, but that doesn't mean they didn't know her. I don't recognise her. There's thousands of them – we can't remember them all. They all look the same,' said PC Robinson.

'Can we put her in the cells, she ain't 'arf kicking up,' said PC Simmons.

'Suit yourself. Go on then.'

The slight woman hiccupped and giggled her way along the echoing passageway. Bishopsgate Police Station wasn't that busy tonight. Just a few drunks, all men, taking up the other cells.

Of course she knew her own name! Her name was Catherine Eddowes. Kate for short. Other names came and went, like the men they were attached to, or the reasons they were needed. Kate had lived a life of contradictions, of highs and lows, but never in the middle. Consistency had not been a gift bestowed on Kate, same as money, same as work and love. It had either been a barren land of want or flooding over with plenty, but never in between; never steady.

She was already feeling a little more sober, but the prospect of a kip in a nice, warm, dry cell didn't seem such a bad way to spend a few hours. She wasn't sure what had happened earlier that had made her so drunk. She was tired – she'd had to spend the night before in a shed on Thrawl

Street. Truth was, she slept better under the stars, but not at the moment, not with the way they'd all been banging on about the murderer. That had got into her head.

She lay down on her back in the cell and was soon snoring. In a couple of hours she'd get fidgety anyway. Being hemmed in by solid walls always made her feel bad. It brought back memories, the worst kind of memories, from her time at the tinworks in Black Country hell, where the vats of acid had made her eyes burn and her throat itch. Even now, she could still hear the clank and grind of the chain makers, still felt herself choking on the poisonous smoke that billowed out of the brickmakers' chimneys, still remembered the hammering as the men dragged the sheets of steel across the ground, the continuous churn of the pit wheels. No question she'd been right to take her chances in the freezing London outdoors, with its freedom and its music and its dancing. Anything was preferable to spending one more night trapped in the belly of the empire's hell pit, however warm. No thank you.

At ten, Mr Hull, the gaoler of Bishopsgate, had checked on 'Mrs Nothing' and seen her flat on her back, her feet pointing straight up to the ceiling, snoring like a pig. He glanced through the door flap at regular intervals until, much later, he heard her singing to herself in her cell. She didn't have a bad voice, he was surprised to note. He consulted the clock: it was quarter past midnight.

He pulled the hatch down and peered at Kate, who was now sitting up with her back to the wall, her legs dangling to the floor, feet swinging.

'Are you going to let me out yet?' she asked, rubbing her eyes. The gesture made her seem like a little girl, though the cracks in her face said differently.

'I'll let you out when you are capable of taking care of yourself,' said Mr Hull.

'I promise I'm capable of taking care of myself now,' she said in a girlish voice.

He snapped the hatch shut. He would give it another fifteen minutes or so and then speak to Byfield on the desk.

When eventually she was led out of the cell to the station office to be discharged, she asked Mr Hull what the time was.

'Too late for you to get another drink, if that's what you're after,' he said.

'I must get myself home. My husband will give me a good hiding – he must be going spare worrying.'

'Rightly so,' he said.

'What's the time then?'

'Gone one.'

As if John would give a rat's arse where she'd got to. He'd doubtless already spent any money he'd come by on himself and got his bed at Cooney's Lodging House. But Kate was well in the habit of giving a certain impression to those she needed on her side – a habit she'd learned during her days selling ballads, singing on the street. If you presented yourself in a particular way, people warmed to you a little faster, treated you a little kinder, and you could sell them pretty much anything once they liked you. It was important to understand your audience, and the police had very traditional expectations of what a woman should be: respectable, demure, obedient, an ordinary wife and mother, *just like her sisters. Certainly not a wandering balladeer with her husband's initials tattooed on her arm.*

'Can you recall your name now, Mrs Nothing?' asked Mr Byfield.

'Mary Ann Kelly,' said Kate.

'Address?'

'6 Fashion Street.'

They returned her belongings: six small pieces of soap, a comb, a table knife, a spoon, tin boxes of tea and sugar, an empty matchbox, needles and pins, a thimble, a red leather cigarette case and her black clay pipes. She secreted each of them away in her skirts like a squirrel, taking pleasure in every one, smiling and poking her tongue out as she hid them in different places on her person.

Mr Byfield ignored the fact that she had clearly given a false address. She was obviously of no fixed abode, for to carry such items was the habit of a dosser with no place to store tin pots or spoons. He very much doubted her name was Mary Ann Kelly either, but she seemed such a harmless little bird, burrowing her possessions away in her skirts.

Mr Hull opened the big swing door onto the passageway out and held it as she tottered through. 'That's the door out, Mrs Kelly. Mind you take yourself straight home now,' he said. 'Be sure to pull that door to when you leave,' he shouted after her, 'or else it won't shut properly!'

'I will. Goodnight, old cock,' said Kate, *making sure not to close the door behind her.*

29

My bedroom door never was kicked in that Sunday night on the last day of September. Neither my husband nor Dr Shivershev came thundering into the house baying for my blood. And so, eventually, I fell asleep.

But, next morning, there was news.

YET MORE WHITECHAPEL ATROCITIES
WOMAN MURDERED NEAR
COMMERCIAL ROAD
WOMAN MURDERED IN ALDGATE
THROATS CUT AND FACE SLASHED
1 OCTOBER 1888

Two more women were found slain in London yesterday morning. The corpse of Elizabeth Stride was discovered in Berner Street, Whitechapel, with her head nearly severed from her body. Catherine Eddowes was found in Mitre Square in Aldgate, in the City. Her throat had been cut and her body mutilated in the most hideous way.

The gruesome injuries found on the past victims in this tragic series were almost exactly played out with these two new unfortunates. Both victims were known to be night wanderers and of a certain class.

The murderer, who it seems is the same, lone lunatic, grows bolder with each crime. With unnerving precision, he slaughtered two in the same hour, under the night sky, his chosen charnel-house.

No more is known at this time, and there is every likelihood no more will ever be known. It is impossible to avoid the depressing conclusion that the police will fail to find the murderer of Elizabeth Stride and Catherine Eddowes, as they have failed for Annie Chapman, Mary Ann Nichols, Martha Tabram and Emma Smith.

The most agonising of the East End mysteries is the incompetent paralysis of the police, who flounder while the most vulnerable inhabitants of the East End must continue to live in fear.

I could not deny that this 'double event', as the newspapers were calling it, had me enthralled, just as its gruesome precedents had. Reading the stories that Monday was a welcome distraction from my own troubles – or at least I allowed myself to see it as a distraction, despite the concerns about the increasingly bizarre situation I found myself in. I sent Sarah out at two-hourly intervals, bidding her come back with the new editions, and I took up residence in the back dining room, devouring the reports, clipping out the columns and pasting them into my scrapbook.

Sarah also returned with snippets of gossip overheard at the newsstands. Ladies who had, like me, enjoyed their perverse slumming tours were now feeling rather differently, since the killer had moved beyond the East End and into the City. What an outrage! Sympathy for Long Liz and Kate appeared to be muted: to the comfortable of the west, these two latest victims morphed into a single composite image of a wretched, self-destructive, alcoholic whore, defined only by her fecklessness, poverty and diseases. This 'other' woman, this creature who must live at the bottom and stay there so they could keep their rightful place above, had begun to encroach into their territory.

To return some dignity to Long Liz – or 'Elizabeth the Melody', as I came to see her – and to my sparrow-like Kate of want and plenty, I took up my notebook again. I had plenty of material. There were acres of newsprint on the poor women, and out of them I fashioned my own dramas, as I had with Little Lost Polly and Dark Annie. I wanted in my own way to accompany them through their last evening on this earth, grimy and lacking though it surely must have been. Who knew how long it would be before I joined their ranks.

On the Berner Street yard where Elizabeth Stride's body was found there was a club that was popular with socialists, political radicals and Jews. The evening of her murder, there'd been a debate on why all Jews should be socialists, and afterwards people had stayed on, singing and dancing late into the night. It was they who'd found Liz, flat on her back with her throat cut, lying in a slimy pool of congealing blood. The police treated every male among them as a suspect. They tore the club apart, even had the men stand in line so their hands could be examined for bloodstains. They banged on every nearby door, woke the sweatshop workers, cigarette makers and tailors and searched their houses too, accusing them of harbouring the murderer. This went on until five in the morning, by which time news had spread that a second body had been found a mile away.

It was as if the killer had been disturbed on the first kill, and was so enraged, he determined to find another at all costs. Poor Kate Eddowes took full force; he slashed her throat, made a huge gash across her right cheek which severed the tip of her nose and part of her right earlobe – these tumbled out of her clothes when they were removed at the morgue – sliced her open from rectum to breastbone, and disembowelled her in a frenzy, pulling her entrails from her, tossing them over her shoulder and leaving them in a jellied heap on the pavement.

By late evening, Sarah was bringing back tales of a surge in the heckling and goading of Jews on the streets, and even some attacks. Mobs had been heard chanting 'Down with the Jews'. I wondered how Dr Shivershev would feel about that, if a privileged and educated Jewish man like him would feel the same fear as the sweated Jew on the street must, or if like us women, Jews relied on there being a lesser kind of themselves to play the scapegoat. The police were clearly no closer to finding the perpetrator and one of the letters pages printed a solution that had me in fits of giggles: *The police should be given noiseless boots so they can sneak up on the Whitechapel fellow.*

The real breakthrough came when an eyewitness emerged. Israel Schwartz, a Hungarian Jew, had been walking down Berner Street at around the time Liz Stride was presumed to have been murdered. I pored over the descriptions, read them again and again, pictured Israel Schwartz in all his terror and wrote him into my little drama to try and fathom it better. Though Schwartz reported what he saw the police, the public called him a 'hen-hearted coward', for not intervening. I thought that a harsh judgement, what men stopped other men from beating their wives? No one called them cowards. Schwartz said he'd seen a man and a woman having an argument – the man being of medium height and broad shouldered and with dark hair, a full face and a small moustache. And there was a second man too – tall, at around five foot eleven, with brown hair, a moustache and a dark overcoat. There was no getting away from it: when I read these words, I saw Thomas and Dr Shivershev.

When Thomas eventually came home that evening, I waited for the truth to come out, but there was nothing. No explosion of outrage from him about the details of all that I'd shared, in confidence, with Dr Shivershev. No admission, even, that he'd met with Dr Shivershev. The uncertainty and disingenuousness was driving me insane. I was convinced I had seen the two of them together in the Princess Alice and yet now I doubted myself. I wondered why I continued with my inaction, when everything, every clue and warning, was telling me to run. What was I waiting for?

The reality was, I still thought my fate unchangeable, as I always had. I had made plays at a career as a nurse, and then as a wife, but I carried the fear that I had no real place as either. I had to assume this was why I had found both so difficult to make successful. I had whipped up an ambition that didn't belong to me, forced my way into a profession I didn't suit and found a husband that shouldn't be mine. I had set out consciously to trap someone I thought I could manage and now I was the fool who was trapped. All I could do was wait, resigned to the inevitable end.

This was a story with an ending that had been written long ago. I had merely managed to defer it the first time. I somehow knew all along that I would meet my end at the hands of a violent man. Why else would the man with the gold tooth keep visiting me in my dreams? There was no point running, because wherever I went, I carried him with me.

The man with the gold tooth had at one point merely been one of the many men in my mother's bed. I would hide under the bed in our room in the Nichol when he came to visit, as I did with all of them.

That night, I'd kept quiet as a mouse, as I'd been taught, even as the bed shook with my mother and the man above me. At first the noises had made sense – the rhythm, the business of fucking – but then my mother started to make strange gaspings and gurglings, and the bed jumped and bowed, almost touching my face. I lay there willing the floor to swallow me up.

My mother's white foot twitched in the way I'd seen a chicken twitch when its neck was broken. I was five years old and more scared than I'd ever been. I wet myself. The piss began trickling down my leg, but, young as I was, I knew I mustn't let it pool on the floor and betray me. The man must not find out that I was there. I stuffed my fingers under my skirt, tried to stem the flow. But it came out anyway, hit the heel of the man's boot and flowed around it like syrup.

I was frozen, stiff as a board, when the man bent down

to see where the water was coming from. His head was as big as a bear's and the skin of his face was all jowly, like an upside-down bloodhound. There was a black beard and a pair of red, swollen eyes with bright blue circles. He grinned at me, showed me his gold tooth, and left.

My mother's foot hung over the side of the bed. For two days I watched as it turned from white to purple as the blood settled. I was meant to die in that room, but I didn't because the landlord came to collect his rent. Pure chance.

30

There were now just three of us in the house, three souls living in purgatory, no more connected than floating pieces of driftwood. I could feel something coming; an oppressive cloud suffocated the house, filling every room, like the odorous fog that crept under the door. Cook had found another position in Kensington, and Sarah followed a week later. The gardener, who used to work for us on the second and fourth weekend of every month, simply stopped turning up. My house was shutting down from the inside, and those who were not in the eye of the storm could see it approaching and jumped. Autumn became winter, the house grew dark and cold, and everything inside it turned a listless shade of blue. Now that Mrs Wiggs had no one to bark orders at, the house fell silent.

One evening, Thomas and I had an encounter on the landing. We stopped on sight of each other. I hesitated, I wasn't sure why, and he took this as an invitation. He smiled at me, and I felt immediately guilty.

'How are you, Susannah?' he said.

I ignored him. Even then, I feared that if I were to

sympathise with him, I would be underneath him within the hour, if only for the sense of normality it might offer. I hurried into my bedroom, pressed my ear to the door and heard him come closer. I could sense him outside, knew his face was inches from my own. I put a hand over the handle and it turned a fraction. I held it still, felt him try to turn it the other side. I held my breath until he gave up and went away. I never knew if it was a performance; trick or truth.

Another time we met in the hallway. He was about to leave and was wearing his long blue coat with the skin of thirty-two wolves. The sun was just rising and light was streaming through the glass either side of the front door. He made a thin silhouette, a slender black shape in a top hat with a black bag, and in this featureless shadow I could perceive the devil the papers wrote of. He tipped his hat, wished me a good morning, and left.

I could not stop thinking about my grandmother's words. They were like a generational curse to me now, the notion that my father's badness – whatever that was – ran through me like black tar. I had begun to believe that the bad blood she spoke of had sought out my devilish husband, so that I had not acquired him consciously but in a prehistoric, animalistic way. I had found the husband I deserved. If we were both cut open, the badness would run from the both of us.

One day in early November I heard voices near my bedroom door again. I crept over and took the key out of the lock, knelt down and squinted through the keyhole. I could see Mrs Wiggs' head and shoulders. She was standing on the stairs. Thomas was on a higher step and I could make out his torso but not his head. Mrs Wiggs' face was turned up to him in blind adulation, as if he were the son of God; a religious rapture. She reached up an open palm, and in a gesture of tenderness extended it lovingly towards his face – or so I had to assume. Thomas put up an arm, I supposed to cover her hand with his own, also in affection.

I fell back in shock. My first reaction was disgust, but when I looked again, I understood that the gesture was not passionate but maternal. Even so, this was not normal, surely, between nannies and their adult charges?

The intensity of their mutual devotion bothered me. I made it my new vocation to study them and drew up mental notes of their physical attributes. They were both tall and slim, with loping strides and a swift gait, but it was their ears I became obsessed by. Thomas had such small and feminine ears, with barely any lobes at all, and so did Mrs Wiggs. I had a suspicion that somehow they shared blood. That was the epiphany I needed.

The next day I wrote a letter to Mr Radcliffe, my solicitor. I told him I would need to return to Reading imminently and I would be taking ownership of my house so the tenants would need evicting. I would find work as a private nurse or in the hospital, even the workhouse infirmary if I had to. I could forge a reference, but maybe I wouldn't need to. Matron might provide one now that several months had passed since she'd fired me. I would take in lodgers in the upstairs rooms and live downstairs as landlady. I posted the letter.

Some days later, I returned home from an outing to the shops to discover an envelope addressed to me on the sideboard. I tore it open in a frenzy. I thought it was from Mabel and took that to be a good omen, but when I saw it was from Dr Shivershev my heart sank. I had missed our last appointment. It had been a long while already since I had told him everything like a babbling child. In the letter he asked if I was well, said he had concerns for my safety, and requested that I come in to confirm my good health. I threw the letter into the fire and made sure it burned down to nothing.

All of them were wicked tormentors and schemers, liars and murderers. Perhaps when I was free, I would find the courage to write a letter to the police, anonymously of course, and tell them everything. I would give names and dates.

There was a real possibility that Thomas would hunt me down in Reading, harass me and demand I return to him. I was his property after all. I needed to protect myself from this dire eventuality. Thomas could only be hurt in two ways: financially or by reputation. I had no money or way of disinheriting him or damaging his income, and besides, he was doing a fine job of that by himself. I would have to target his reputation. I needed something compelling with which I could threaten to shame him publicly, something to keep him on the back foot and far away from me, something that neither he nor Mrs Wiggs would want to risk drawing attention to.

31

Not long after the clock struck nine, the front door slammed, and sent its thunderous crack through the house, making the legs of my bed shake. I was ready. I looked outside and saw Thomas striding down the garden path. Mrs Wiggs had retired to her bedroom just after eight.

I hurried out onto the landing. I was wearing one of Thomas's hats, a long black overcoat, a white shirt without a collar and a pair of trousers I'd had to fasten around my waist with a scarf. I tried my best to tiptoe down the stairs to stop them from creaking. I had on my own boots with a small heel, but the trousers were long enough and covered them. I convinced myself no one would notice.

I considered going out the front door, but if I was attuned to the noise of it, then it was certain that so was Mrs Wiggs. Instead, I snuck towards the back of the house, down the narrow staircase, past the pantry and into the kitchen. It was dark and empty now that Cook and Sarah were gone. Mrs Wiggs was struggling to keep up with the housework; dust had gathered and a conspiracy of spiders' webs had sprung up everywhere. The moonlight pouring through the kitchen's large windows illuminated the web over the back door and I had to clear it away to get out. I left the door unlocked for my return.

I ran around to the front of the house just in time to catch Thomas's receding silhouette. Tonight he looked like a stickman drawn in charcoal, bobbing across the watery grey flagstones, elbows jutting out at right angles.

I followed him along Chelsea Embankment and then onto Pimlico Road. I hoped he wasn't about to jump into a cab or go to a station as I had no plan for that – I didn't even know if trains ran at night. I almost never went out that late and when I did, it was always with Thomas and we always took a cab. I felt exposed being alone on the streets of London. It was dark and gloomy, the rain had turned the black pavement into shiny mirrors, and the yellow moon was reflected in the puddles. It was a relief to be a man. Even so, I could not but think of all the stories in the newspapers, and I walked in exhausted anticipation of being attacked at any second: stabbed, raped, murdered. My only comfort was the presence of my own murderous husband, albeit at a distance.

After twenty minutes, he turned left onto Buckingham Palace Road. The streets were deserted save for a few men who hurried along, huddled in pairs or alone, all of them walking with purpose. I watched the way they bowled along the pavement and attempted to adopt the same gait. I wrapped the lapels of Thomas's coat around my face and pulled my hat down. I was the same shape and height as any slim young man; only should someone study me with a lamp in my face would they discern that I was a woman in baggy trousers and women's shoes.

Not long after we'd both passed under the shadow of Westminster Cathedral, Thomas entered a pub called the Duke of Wellington on Victoria Road. I did not know this part of London at all. Because of the cathedral I'd assumed it would be populated by scholarly types, but I have come to realise that such men only existed in my imagination.

The pub was on a corner with a big double door in the middle. There were a few scattered drinkers outside, all men, smoking and drinking in pairs and groups. I approached the entrance but dithered, and instead leaned against an exterior wall with my hands in my pockets. I seemed to be making a habit of this these last few weeks – spying on my husband in one seedy drinking den or another. I couldn't see much through the window, it was steamed up, so I used my sleeve to rub a space and then felt foolish since it was clear the moisture was on the inside. Mostly what I could make out was a haze rippling with swirls of thick smoke above dark heads like the rooftops of houses, and a low chorus of voices like the rumble of a distant train. Hats, whiskers, smoke and dreary clothes.

Thomas's head stuck up above all the others. He inched his way to the bar, leaned on it, then turned towards the window as if he'd sensed me there. I ducked, petrified, and stayed low, my back against the cold wet bricks. I watched for the plainclothes policemen, who, according to the politicians, were supposedly enjoying the mild winter too much and drinking with the labouring poor instead of hunting the Whitechapel man.

For some minutes, I was so scared my legs went wobbly, but then I began to relax. Had the papers painted the streets as wilder than they really were? The best thing about London, I reminded myself, was that everyone was so preoccupied with their own narcissistic pursuits that they rarely noticed much about anyone else.

I felt a tug at my sleeve. A doe-eyed, dark-haired girl, short and pretty, had sidled up to me and was now attempting to hang off the arm of my coat.

'Go away,' I said, and wrenched my arm free. I was careful to keep my voice a whisper, so I might make it sound a little lower.

The big-eyed girl wouldn't budge, only gazed up at me and tried to take hold of my fingers, cooing at me in her thin little voice. 'Come with me! Come!' she said, and she pulled me towards a dark alleyway down the side of the tavern. 'Come! Have me.'

'I don't want to,' I told her. 'I don't have any money.'

'That don't matter,' she said and began to rub herself against my left leg.

I didn't know what to do. 'No! Leave me alone! Please.' I pushed her off and she took a step back but wouldn't go.

'What a fine young man you are, to turn it down. I can give you pleasure. If anyone can, I can.'

She made to rub herself against me again and her hands were everywhere. It was ridiculous. The girl was worse than my husband had been. I didn't know whether to break out laughing at the absurdity of it or scream for her to leave me alone. I repelled her again and fumbled in the pockets of Thomas's coat. By chance I found a shilling and threw it at her. It landed on the pavement and as she bent to pick it up, I studied her. She was young, fourteen or fifteen perhaps, a sickly-looking creature with dirty clothes.

When she stood up, she stared at me with a funny

expression. 'You ain't no boy,' she said with a wry smile. 'Look at your skin, soft as a baby's arse.' She rubbed a dirty hand against my cheek. I slapped it away. 'Well, takes all types of fancy I s'pose. Why wait outside a mollies' den? You's lost, I reckon.' Then she burst out laughing, exposing her teeth, which were yellow and black, like the keys on an old piano.

'Why are you on the game?' I asked her. 'You should be at home with your mother.' Susannah the prig hadn't disappeared quite yet.

'I ain't no whore. My mother keeps me. I look after the others all day, and at night I do what I want. I do it for the coins – I spend 'em all on meat pies. I do it for the pies!' She burst out laughing again, cackling like an old woman.

'What do you mean, a mollies' den?' I asked.

She rolled her eyes, laughed some more and ran her tongue over her piano-key teeth. 'Is your man in there? I say let him – a girl can always do it one way or the other, can't she? No need to be lonely.'

She moved to touch my face again, but I caught her wrist. I felt her other hand rifle through the other pocket of Thomas's coat.

'There's nothing in there, you little trollop,' I said, shoving her hand away and wrapping Thomas's coat tight around me. I pushed past her and walked to the main doors of the pub.

'You will come back, won't you?' she said. She seemed genuinely disappointed as I disappeared into the Duke of Wellington.

I shouldered my way through the press of drinkers, just as I imagined a man would. I was glad for my experience of the Ten Bells, though it hardly made me an expert. The place stank to high heaven of smoke and I worried about Mrs Wiggs smelling the tobacco on Thomas's clothes. The stale beer on the floor stuck to my boots and I dragged dirty straw along with me. I tried not to gag as the stench of sweaty men hit the back of my throat.

I looked for Thomas at the bar, but he wasn't there any more. I searched for him and caught what I thought was the back of his head as he disappeared through a door in the far corner. I squeezed through the crowds and followed him. I had come too far to go home without seeing for myself what he'd been getting up to all this time. My heart pounded and my knees shook, but by now I was too involved to turn back. Going through that door was my one chance to garner the leverage that might win me my freedom.

On the other side was a long corridor, very dimly lit with just one or two flickering wall lamps that threatened to snuff themselves out at any moment. I let my eyes adjust for a minute. The muffled voices from the bar had quietened. There was no sign of Thomas, though I was certain he'd gone that way, and nor was there anyone else around.

I put my hands on the naked brick walls to either side to work my way along. All I could hear was my own rapid breathing and the sound of water running or dripping somewhere. The walls were damp, covered in slime.

The corridor ended in another door that opened onto a room so light and bright, all oranges and yellows, that it was blinding after the gloom. It smelled of bitter flowers and I could taste the white smoke of opium, acrid and fragrant. The room was busy with men and women standing around, talking. I assumed it was another bar, but everyone was facing the same direction, watching something in the corner. I tried to walk among them as I searched for Thomas, but I couldn't see him. I worried I'd lost him or missed him somehow.

When I reached the other side of the room, I doubted my eyes at first, thought it impossible that people could be watching something like that. It took me a while to understand what was happening. A couple were having sex on a bed in the corner, in the presence of an older man who was standing by the mantelpiece alongside. He was perhaps fifty or more, with big grey whiskers and wearing a red jacket with medals. I was scared he might be a general or someone of authority, but there was something about his uniform that didn't look right; it was tatty and worn, like the ones for sale in Whitechapel.

When I looked more closely at the couple on the bed, I realised that the one I'd thought was a woman was actually a man, with whiskers, and clownish rouge smeared across his face. He was on all fours and a man with reddish brown hair and a beard was buggering him from behind. The man dressed as a soldier was watching, along with all the others in the room.

I felt as if I were glowing, that I'd be found out at any second. I was not in a crowd of men and women as I had thought, but only men, some of whom were dressed as women, in old-fashioned crinolines, bad hairpieces, and make-up clumsily applied around facial hair. I was now desperate to get out and moved towards the nearest door as fast as I could. I assumed Thomas had gone that way too.

It took a while to steer through the strange clutter in the room, past the tables covered in cheap jewellery, old fans and tatty bonnets, and the screens hung with wigs and torn and dirty dresses. To the left of the door, a man was sitting on a chair with his trousers round his knees, moaning and sighing as he pleasured himself. The man next to him wore a fair wig with ringlets and was smoking a long pipe. His face seemed familiar, but I couldn't place it. As I passed, I dipped my hat and realised it was Dr Richard Lovett – Thomas's best man! The man he'd wanted me to have as my physician. Good God. I had to move quickly before he recognised me.

As I reached the door, the crowd behind me erupted in cheers. I did not bother to look back and find out why but took the chance to exit. I was sweating and my heart was thumping. The next room was less busy, and still no Thomas. It had beds, sofas, a chaise longue and more people puffing white clouds at the ceiling. I nearly died when a chubby man in rouge and black eye make-up brushed past me and whispered 'Hello' into my ear. I tucked my chin into my neck as far as it would go and quickly headed out the room and up the flight of dilapidated stairs beyond.

Thomas had to be upstairs somewhere. Now that I knew what the place was, what company he was keeping and what he must have been getting up to, I felt even more compelled to find him, to discover exactly why he was there, and with my own eyes. I still had difficulty believing it. My husband, secretly hiding away in a mollies' house! Was this where he disappeared to when he wasn't slaughtering women?

A series of doors, each set back in a small recess, opened off both sides of the landing. From behind the peeling green and blue paintwork came the rustling of busy vermin and the gentle groaning of humans. I listened at the first keyhole, heard nothing, moved on, tried again and was nearly exposed when the second door was suddenly wrenched open. I retreated to the shadows, and prayed.

Thomas stepped out onto the landing! I thought he would catch me, but he was focused on other things. He strode to the far end of the landing, walked through another door and shut it. I was about to scarper – I had come too close to my luck running out – but as I stepped towards the stairs I noticed that the door he'd come out of was ajar.

I probably only had seconds before he returned. I peered through the gap in the door, saw a wooden chair in the corner next to a nightstand and what looked like a belt on it. The decrepit walls were grottier still in the lamplight. Somehow I found the courage to push the door open. I pulled my lapel across my face and took in the scene: a bed, and a young man lying on his back, wearing stays held together with pink ribbon, pearl earrings and red lipstick. I gasped, I couldn't help it, and the boy looked at me. He was curly headed, fair, and more of a boy, probably the same age as the doe-eyed girl outside. His body was soft and hairless, except for his genitals.

He lifted his head, looked at me and smiled, seemingly not at all startled, and continued to lie there unabashed. 'Well, aren't you the nosy one,' he said. 'You've got the wrong room, sweetheart – mine doesn't like to share his toys... You'd best clear off – he does have a temper.' He drew on a long, narrow pipe and lay back on the bed.

I pulled the door to, the way it had been left, and shot off as fast as I could. I flew down the rotten stairs, through both rooms and into the pub. My insides screamed and my ears whistled. I pushed and shoved my way through the bar.

I heard swearing and tutting, but it didn't matter. I had to get out.

I thrust open the doors to the street and in my haste stumbled on something and went flying into the back of a huge man. It felt like I'd been thrown face first into a brick wall. I hit the ground in front of him, scraped my hands and landed on my backside. The man had a shiny bald head like a cannonball and piggy eyes. 'Watch it, you little ponce,' he said, and before I could stand or apologise, he knocked me back to the ground.

I fell back, hard, yelped, very much like a girl, and my hat fell off. A group of men gathered round to watch the fight. I was sure I was about to receive a good thrashing, but then my newly acquired doe-eyed girl arrived. She elbowed her way through and knelt at my side with her arms around my shoulders, holding me tight as if I were her sweetheart.

'Lay off, you bastards! Can't you see it's a girl,' she shouted.

There was laughter and whooping, a 'Fucking 'ell!' and the group dispersed. My bald-headed foe appeared most confused, shrugged and walked off.

The girl pulled me to my feet and gave me back my hat. She walked me as far as the cathedral and then left, saying she had to get back to her mother's, that only whores stayed out later, whores miserable enough to risk getting cut by the Whitechapel murderer. That wasn't her, she told me; she only went with strange men for the little extras – meat pies, like she'd told me.

'You're lucky – you nearly got a black eye for your troubles. Tell me, what man is worth that?' she said.

'I'm grateful, I really am.' I rummaged through Thomas's inside pockets for what coins I could find.

'It's all right. To save you the bother, I already took what you had.' She grinned and showed me the coins she'd lifted from my pockets.

I laughed. I hadn't noticed this time.

'They may be soft and queer in St James's,' she said, 'but you'll get yourself cut to pieces and tossed in the Thames messing with those boys.'

She took my cheeks in both hands and kissed me. Her plump lips were dry, and she squished them into mine. 'Goodbye, my love. Come see me again. I'll wait for you,' she said.

As she walked away, I noticed she had bare feet. I had no clue how she wasn't dead from the cold.

It took an age for me to get back home. I half staggered and half ran, my feet sore and blistered. A cartman nodded as I passed – I'd forgotten I was dressed as a man. I needed the journey; I had so much going through my head, it was fit to burst with all that I'd seen. All this time, I had wondered what sort of man I had married, but never in my imagination had I anticipated this. To think how my husband and I were the same in some ways. I felt by turns revulsion, and shock, and disbelief, and, believe it or not, sympathy, and then I found the whole thing bloody hilarious. We really did fit together, but not in the way I'd expected.

When I reached the house, I crept round the back and let myself in through the kitchen door. To be met by Mrs Wiggs, who screamed at the sight of me. 'Murderer!' she shrieked, standing there in her nightgown, pale as a ghost and brandishing a shovel in her shaking arms.

I screamed back, which brought her to her senses. She let out a huge sigh, lowered the shovel and put a hand to her chest.

'Thank God Almighty,' she said. 'I heard the scraping of the gate and thought the Whitechapel beast had commuted to Chelsea.'

As she looked me up and down, she stiffened. 'Why are you dressed in Thomas's clothes? Mrs Lancaster, you stink of... Where have you been?'

'It's a long story and I can't explain. I must go to bed, Mrs Wiggs. I suggest you do the same.' I walked past her, conscious that I'd need to come up with something, however incredible, by morning.

I must have taken two, maybe three steps when I realised that she'd just referred to my husband as Thomas. I stopped and was about to challenge her when I was struck on the back of the head. There was blinding pain, my knees buckled, and everything went black.

32

'Good morning, Susannah. How are we feeling today?' Mrs Wiggs sailed into the room, as she had done every morning since my return from the Duke of Wellington. She was always radiant and cheery these days.

I tended to wake happy enough, being sunny and clear-skied by nature, but then the rainclouds would rush up to meet me and drag me back down. It had been days, perhaps even weeks, since I'd lost my liberty. I'd lost track of time altogether and had long since given up struggling against the restraints that tied me to the bedposts. I remembered being hit on the head and falling to my knees in the kitchen. I remembered the men dressed as women at the back of the pub, remembered being kissed by the big-eyed girl with bare feet, remembered seeing my husband and the boy with pearl earrings and stays. I just wasn't sure quite when that was.

When I woke on the first day, I screamed, as anyone would have, at the discovery that my wrists and ankles were bound by leather straps. I was trapped, tethered to the bed like a lunatic at the asylum. Hearing my shrieks, Mrs Wiggs and Thomas both marched in, one behind the other, like stoic little guards at Buckingham Palace. They stood at the foot of my bed, side by side, and when I begged to be told what was going on, it was Mrs Wiggs who spoke. Thomas just stared at me with flat, dead eyes, a raised eyebrow, and both hands in his pockets.

'You were dressed as a man and you attacked me,' she said. 'I feared for my life.'

'You have made a habit of hurting yourself,' said Thomas. 'It is only a matter of time before this escalates. It looks like we caught this just in time. This type of condition is... progressive.'

Mrs Wiggs looked at him and he looked at her, and she left the room. Thomas and I were alone. I stared at him, I don't think I even blinked, while his eyes moved over the floorboards and his hands stayed buried in his pockets. He didn't meet my gaze once, not without Mrs Wiggs there to protect him. When she came back, she was carrying a silver tray. In my enduring stupidity, I assumed it was my breakfast.

'Where did you go last night, Susannah?' asked Thomas.

'I could ask you the same thing,' I said. 'Your turn first.'

Mrs Wiggs cleared her throat, nervously and needlessly. She walked to the dresser and tinkered with something metallic. It made a clattering noise.

Thomas drew breath and started a monologue; I had the feeling he'd been rehearsing this for some time.

'Mrs Wiggs has informed me of your bizarre adventures. Those who love you are very concerned, Susannah, and have been for some while, but it is time to face the fact that your condition is getting worse. I had hoped you would settle into marriage. I can only imagine it's the combination of traumas you have endured – the adjustment to your new surroundings, and your upbringing – and that this has expressed itself in unhealthy behaviours, obsessions with murders and such. You are very sick indeed.'

'Just because you say the words aloud doesn't make them true. I'm no sicker than you.'

'Oh, but you are, Susannah. You are very sick – so much so that we can't look after you any more. You have become a danger to yourself and others.'

'Oh God, go on, how on earth am I a danger to you, Thomas? Please, I'm dying to hear.'

'I'm referring to your relationship with Nurse Barnard, Susannah. There, I've said it. There's no ignoring it any more. You are... morally defective. It was an unhealthy interest and the hospital proved the perfect breeding ground for it. Women like Matron Luckes don't understand the degree to which they encourage such unnatural friendships between women with their adoption of masculine ambitions. They don't see the damage they cause with their careers and pursuits outside of the home.'

'Where did you gather your opinions on all of this – from the surgeons' lounge?'

'Oh, please, it was common gossip at the hospital. There are always the odd ones who prefer the company of their own gender. "Susannah is in love with me," I said. But I was naive. I was unable to see; being besotted, I failed to identify such a clear case of moral insanity – and myself a doctor!'

'One of several ironies!' I threw him a cold, sarcastic smile. 'What treatment do you recommend? Are you going to tie me up for ever like a prisoner? Are you going to lock me away in your attic?'

'Mrs Wiggs said she would look after you, and we had hoped we could care for you at home, which is certainly a lot less expensive, but you've made that impossible. Your illness is much worse than we anticipated.'

'There is nothing wrong with me – any doctor worth his salt will see this. You can't just have me locked away. There are laws.'

He sat down beside me and brushed the hair from my face. I shrank from him, but the restraints held me rigid. I could only turn my head.

'Do you remember when you smashed your head in the looking glass and scared Mrs Wiggs to death? She thought you were possessed. Then you threw yourself down the stairs. And what about your wanderings around Whitechapel in searching of the murderer? Dr Shivershev even saw you in the Ten Bells, of all places. Do you know how embarrassed I was when he told me that? This macabre determination to loiter on streets with whores and murderers, the hysterical behaviour that drove the household staff away, your tearing your room apart and accusing Mrs Wiggs of stealing a bloody hairbrush. In front of the servants too. For crying out loud, Susannah, how can you not see that you are very ill? And the finale of last night, dressing up in men's clothes. I must accept that I cannot treat you myself.'

I wanted to scream and shout and call him a liar, tell him that I knew exactly where he'd been the night before and had seen his own debauchery myself, but I knew to keep my mouth shut. There was nothing I could say that wouldn't be twisted to suit his story.

'You know, I thought you avoided intimacy because you were naive, but now I understand you had... other preferences. I couldn't help but blame myself when I learned that you threw yourself down the stairs because you thought you might be carrying my child.'

'That's a lie!'

'I try and tell myself it isn't your fault, that it's the disease.'

I didn't answer. I was afraid I wouldn't be able to stop myself from screaming at him, so I shut my eyes. But he carried on.

'Of course, knowing what we know about your mother, how you were born a bastard, without a father, and her still a child, it's clear that this is hereditary feeblemindedness. We should be thankful that there will be no more children to inherit your defective inclinations.'

I couldn't help myself: I opened my eyes, and saw that he was laughing at me. There was only one person who could have told him about my mother – Dr Shivershev. It was the biggest betrayal of all. I was such a fool for trusting him. I felt my cheeks turn purple and my body tremble at the thought of his name. I'd kept my mouth shut about Mabel, just as he'd requested. *All in it together.* Not bloody likely. All the time I'd wasted in not running away, because I was worried about being poor again, that was my own fault. Men would always stick together. I'd been an idiot to think any different.

'You were naughty not to tell me, Susannah.'

He winked at me. I could have ripped the skin from his cheeks with my nails. It was the self-assured gloating of a winner, of a man who would always win. I spat in his face, a token act well worth whatever consequence it prompted;

anything to dislodge his smug expression. He stood up, disgusted, and wiped my saliva from his jaw.

'We will try our best, to manage your... aggression.'

Mrs Wiggs came towards me carrying the tray from the dresser. On it was a large metal syringe and a rubber tube. They were going to inject me.

'Thomas, for God's sake, you can't really intend to let her use that on me?' I kicked up the bedclothes and struggled, but Thomas pinned me down. I screamed and called for Sarah.

'All the servants are gone, Susannah. Remember how you frightened them? Please calm down...' His face hung down over me – saggy-skinned, like a bloodhound, just as it had been that night in the coach, the night of Annie Chapman's murder, just like the man with the gold tooth. I tried to recall all the details, all the dates: the nights he'd gone missing; each murder. I would need to recount all the facts when I found someone who would listen.

The rubber was pulled tight against the skin of my arm. Thomas barked instructions at Mrs Wiggs as he sat on me and held me down while the fluid forced its way into my blood. When it hit me, a pressure at the back of my skull, I thought my eyeballs would burst. A rush swirled about my head, and a smothering darkness like a wet sackcloth was draped across my face. All the lines and edges softened, and everything fell together into one soft cloud.

'It's the best way of getting it into you, Susannah. Relax and enjoy it.'

Their faces went lumpy and misshapen. Their outlines leaked into the air around them, liquefying. I fell, backwards, deeper, into the bed and into the floor. My limbs became heavy, melted.

My last memory was of Mrs Wiggs as she said to Thomas, 'Is this really necessary?'

Mrs Wiggs drugged me several times a day after that and was terrible at it. Her hands shook, and she was both brutal and hesitant at the same time. I was bruised up and down both arms. I kept offering fresh pieces of flesh for her to mutilate. She didn't trust me at first, was suspicious that with my nursing background I was trying to fool her in some way. But after a few days she realised I was genuinely trying to save myself the pain and her the bother. The process was painful for her to administer as well as for me on the receiving end.

When I offered to do it myself, under her supervision, she hesitated for a moment, then untied my restraints and observed me as I injected the muscle in my thigh. After that, she didn't restrain my wrists at all, just left the ankle binds in place. I was still very much tied to the bed, couldn't reach far or escape. I had to kneel on the edge of the bed to use the chamber pot on the floor. Mrs Wiggs struggled with the indignity of that more than I did. I'd been treated little better than an animal in that bedroom many times before, so why would taking a shit over a pot bother me?

The laudanum delivered under the muscle had an intense, stupefying effect at first, but quickly faded. My secret little habit had rewarded me with tolerance. I looked forward to my injections; they broke up the boredom and the tyranny of my own punishing thoughts. I was docile, quiet and obedient, which I'm sure Mrs Wiggs attributed to the drugs, but after the first few days I was a lot more coherent and lucid than she realised. It was the only advantage I had. I did think about throwing a shit at Thomas, should he come through the door, but knew that it wouldn't do me any good in the long run.

I was saving my energy for when I'd be put in front of someone who wasn't under his influence. I would need to choose my words very carefully, so that anything I said could not be used in the argument against me. There could be no mention of my husband being the Whitechapel murderer, or talk of Mabel and her baby being cut out and put into glass jars, or accounts of fighting with Mrs Wiggs over a bloody hairbrush. I had an interest in the murders, but, I would say to the doctor who interviewed me, did not his own wife read the newspapers? Had not his own daughters been to visit the murder spots? If they were to lock me away for having a macabre interest in the slaughter of prostitutes, they would have to put half of the ladies of London away too. Thomas did have connections, though; he was a physician at the hospital, after all. And Mrs Wiggs had been with the Lancasters for years. Who was I? Who knew anything of me?

I didn't see Thomas for many days after that first morning, until one day much later he came and spoke to Mrs Wiggs through a gap in the door. He told her she would need to reduce the dosage, as I was to be awake when Dr Shivershev came to assess me.

'He won't sign if he thinks we're drugging her,' I heard him say. 'He's being difficult, argumentative. He is one of God's chosen people, after all; he can be a pious little bastard. I can manage him, just make sure she's awake.'

As the dosage got lower and lower, the syrup sludge in my brain cleared. I was kept company at all times by Mrs Wiggs, who sat on a chair at the foot of my bed. I ignored her at first, and she ignored me, concentrated on the needlework on her lap. She squinted as she sewed, her face pinched and screwed together, the lines across her forehead deeper than I had seen. She was anxious, worried.

'You need spectacles,' I said. The light was clear and bright, the weather cold and brittle. The pale light leached the colour from the room and turned everything black and white, like a photograph, but it was she who was in shadow. I was a ghostly white, translucent; only my bruises gave me colour.

She looked up at me, caught me with those heavy lids. 'You know, Susannah, I think you're right.'

'Whatever happened to "Mrs Lancaster"?'

She sighed. 'It was never a name for you, my dear,' she said, and returned to her sewing.

We started to exchange words, little more than two cats that hissed at each other, but it was better than silence. It was dull, routine conversation, about the weather and how cold it was getting, or how she was struggling to keep the house clean without any help. I asked if there was any news on the Whitechapel murders, but she said she wasn't following the reports. To my surprise, later that afternoon, she came back with the day's newspapers. I struggled to focus, my eyes danced about and I couldn't see the words properly because of the drugs, so she read them to me. She read very well, putting energy and feeling into it as if she were reading a story. She raised her eyebrows in shock and wrinkled her nose as she became involved. She explained how a series of letters had been written by the killer himself – exciting, but I was sure it was a hoax. There had been three all in all, and now the Whitechapel man had a new name: Jack the Ripper.

'Jack the Ripper? Much better than Leather Apron, I think. Like Spring-Heeled Jack, but it is not very… sophisticated. I wonder what the real killer thinks of it.'

'Sophisticated? What a strange mind you have, Susannah. I cannot think how a man who goes about the business of ripping street walking women is concerned about whether or not he is deemed sophisticated. I should imagine such a monster is not capable of lucid thought at all. But it has caught on, all the papers now refer to him as "the Ripper",' she said.

She told me how Kate Eddowes was found to have been missing a kidney. Half a kidney had been sent to the head of the Whitechapel Vigilance Committee, and the other half, the letter said, Jack had fried and ate. Mrs Wiggs didn't like that bit.

There was still no clue as to who the murderer really was, just a lot of suspects, and theories, all of them barking mad or desperate. Not once did Mrs Wiggs intimate that she knew of the things I'd told Dr Shivershev about Thomas. Had Dr Shivershev kept those details to himself? But why would he tell Thomas about my mother and then hold back from that?

'They will catch him eventually,' she said.

'I doubt that very much. He'll have died of old age before they get round to working it out.'

'I wouldn't mention these theories too much where you're going,' she said.

'Where am I going?' I asked.

She put her newspaper down on her lap in a crumpled mess, gave a heavy sigh and stood up. With the key to my bedroom, which she kept tied to her wrist with a red ribbon, she unlocked the door and went out. A few minutes later she returned with a pamphlet and handed it to me. It had a drawing of a grand house in parkland, and bonneted ladies with their hands in muffs walking in pairs on the grass in front of a lake. It was called Aphra House and it was in Surrey.

'It's only for ladies. I had to press quite hard for Thomas to consider this place – it's not the cheapest. You'll be well cared for, if you behave and don't babble on about this Jack the Ripper or silly hairbrushes. It will be just like the hospital, except this time you will be the one being cared for. Now, doesn't that sound lovely?'

'What did Thomas want to do with me?' I asked, but she was looking at the leaflet, pleased with her selection.

Her eyes flicked towards me, back to the leaflet. I knew she'd heard.

'Mrs Wiggs, what did my husband propose to do with me?'

Still she didn't answer.

'I'm going to leave you for a while. Here, look at the pamphlet, you might be happy there. Didn't you marry him to be looked after? Can you not think of this as a different answer to the same question?' She locked the door behind her.

This was how it went for days. We would talk and she would bring me food, though I barely ate. But as soon as I started with the questions, she would make her excuses and leave, locking the door behind her.

'Why?' I asked many times. 'Why me? What did I do?'

I begged her to tell me, sometimes I shouted at her, but she never reacted, only pretended not to hear. One day, when she came to tie the rubber tube around my arm, instead of being docile, I knocked the tray and sent it crashing to the ground.

She glared at me, exasperated but silent, and stooped to pick up everything off the floor. 'Don't be like this, Susannah. I shall have to get Thomas to help me bind your hands again, and he will be less patient than me. Is that what you want?'

'I want to know why. Thomas chased *me*, he begged *me* to marry him – three times. There were other nurses, lots of them, so why *me*?'

'What does it matter?' she said.

'I'm begging you!'

She inhaled deeply and brushed down her skirts before sitting herself in the chair at the foot of my bed.

'Very well, if it means you'll stop asking. Thomas was engaged to a very beautiful, charming, talented and well-connected young woman. It was a passionate affair – too passionate, as they were both of a fiery nature. Her father is the 1st Earl of Halsbury, a judge and a government minister, among other things. There was an understanding between the families that there would be a marriage, but Thomas didn't want to wed. The whole affair had gone too far, however, and there was a great risk of embarrassment for both families if the union didn't go ahead.

'His sister Helen is a strategist, a very shrewd young woman, and politically she had to insist the marriage go ahead. Thomas begged her to help un-arrange the arrangement, so to speak. If he married that girl, he knew he would be under the command of her father, he would be reduced to a mere whipping boy in a family much wealthier than his. Thomas needs to be free – oh, Susannah, he would have been miserable as the henpecked husband in the house of an earl – but Helen wouldn't hear of it. There was no elegant way to exit such a partnership without causing scandal and animosity, not that Thomas ever cared about the fragility of such relationships. So, you understand, he married you in a somewhat prolonged fit of temper. Helen was livid of course, and humiliated, but it was the only way to put an end to the matter. That is why you have never met Thomas's family, and why there was never going to be a visit here or to Abbingdale Hall.'

'I still don't understand – why me?'

'Because you are no one, Susannah. You have no immediate family, no relatives, no benefactor, no one to cause inconvenience or ask questions. Thomas had affection for you, he spoke fondly of you, but he's so special, you understand, his attention could never be engaged by an ordinary woman. If it could not be kept by a great beauty – the daughter of an earl, no less – it was never going to be kept by you. I knew it wouldn't work. He bores easily. It's a sign of great intellect, some say. I did try and tell him it wouldn't end well, but when he gets an idea into his head, as you well know...'

She bent down to pick up the remaining contents of the tray. When she stood up again, I was staring past the wall.

'See?' she said. 'This has upset you. Sometimes it's best not to ask, in case you receive an answer.' She gazed down at me, tethered as I was to my bed, with such pity, I felt a torrent of rage.

'I saw you together,' I told her. 'I saw you on the stairs. You called him "Thomas" and stroked his face.'

The look of pity disappeared, and her face assumed its stony-faced owl expression.

'You have a monstrous mind,' she said. Her hands trembled and she threw the tray to the floor with a crash, scattering those things she'd already picked up. She stalked out, slammed the door and locked it shut behind her.

33

By November, Mrs Wiggs had taken off my ankle restraints. It was not an act of kindness, but to give the marks on my skin time to recover ahead of my visit from Dr Shivershev. I assumed he was needed to co-sign the lunacy order that would have me confined. I was still locked in my bedroom, but I made no attempt to escape. What would be the point? The outside world was as inhospitable as a snow-covered mountain. I had neither the money nor the resources to survive by myself. Locked in my bedroom was where I was most comfortable, and the laudanum numbed me. I was not frightened of my captors, though I should have been. It was my cowardice that kept me trapped. I could have opened a window and screamed for help; that would have brought the police. I could have climbed down, but I didn't. What would the police have done? Most likely hand-deliver me back to my husband.

Thomas himself looked remarkably different the next time I saw him. His black whiskers were back to perfect symmetry, the silver sparkle in his eye had returned, and Mrs Wiggs was behind him, his eager shadow.

'You don't think she looks too thin?' He addressed Mrs Wiggs as if I wasn't in the room.

'Well, what would you have me do?'

'Pale, she looks pale.'

'Isn't that the point? She's not meant to look well, is she?'

'You don't understand!' he shouted suddenly, making both of us start. 'He won't sign if... He won't sign if he thinks she's being mistreated.'

He peered at me as if I were a specimen, hands clasped behind his back like a doddering old lord inspecting his rose bushes.

'How are her arms?' He grabbed one of my hands and pulled up the sleeve of my nightdress to see where Mrs Wiggs had been injecting me. Both arms were a riot of bruises, albeit fading ones.

'No! What have I told you!' he shouted.

'I'm trying my best, Thomas,' she said, on the brink of tears.

'She looks as if she's been bloody tortured!' He dropped my hand. 'No more injections! Tincture only. We have to let the bruising go down. Dr Shivershev wants to see her this week and when he comes, make sure she has her sleeves rolled down.'

'Tincture? Which bottle is that?'

I had never seen them like this: fractured, bickering. They were like a pair of old seagulls snapping at each other.

As I stared at the two of them, in silhouette, free to observe them uninterrupted, I had a startling revelation. A realisation that should have been plain as day but had taken my confinement to see what was right in front of me. Thomas's hairline had a lopsided widow's peak. I knew that, of course. It was quite distinctive. Now that I was looking at Mrs Wiggs right alongside him, I saw immediately that her hairline followed the same shape. It was the same hairline exactly, a bizarre coincidence, or inherited... How blind must I have been to only see this now.

'The green bottle,' he spat.

'What good is that to me! You know this!' she shouted back.

'The green bastard bottle, the one with the cork in it! For God's sake!' He stomped out of the room. Minutes later, the front door slammed.

Mrs Wiggs was once again left alone with me, shaking her head and muttering under her breath.

'Very well,' she said to herself. She picked up the green glass bottle on the dresser and set it down again next to me on my nightstand.

I waited until she'd left, then fetched my own drops from the drawer in the same nightstand. My own bottle, a brown glass one, was exactly the same as theirs, with a cork in it, only the colour was different. I knew that Thomas struggled with distinguishing between reds, greens and browns sometimes. And now I wondered whether Mrs Wiggs had the same problem.

I left the two bottles side by side and waited for her to come back. When she returned and spotted them next to each other, she stopped, her confused eyes darted from one to the other.

'What is this?' she asked.

'I had my own bottle. I wanted to see how similar it was, that's all. It's the green one, he said. Mine is brown.'

She hesitated. As hard as she looked, she could not tell

the difference. That was the proof I needed. Mrs Wiggs was colour-blind, just like Thomas. Colour-blindness, I had learned at the hospital, was an inherited condition, passed along the maternal line, as it had been in this instance too, from mother to son. I had no understanding of how, but the science spoke for itself.

'He's your son, isn't he?' I said. I had butterflies in my stomach and only dared to whisper it.

Mrs Wiggs' mouth hung open at words which, I guessed, had never before been said aloud.

'What are you gibbering about? You are a lunatic, nothing but a sick lunatic. You don't know anything!'

'Thomas is colour-blind too. You're his mother, aren't you? You are both tall, you have the same hairline, practically the same ears, you stroked his face on the stairs, and now you call him "Thomas". When you pushed me down the stairs, it was because you didn't want a child dragged into this mess, not now, not your own grandchild born in an asylum. Was that why? I don't know how, but you *are* his mother. I know it, and so will a doctor. What will you do if someone should put this to the test?'

She glared at the bottles, unsure of how they had betrayed her. To me it made perfect sense – all her adoration and fawning, the unnatural closeness between them – but then something else struck me, something I hadn't even considered.

'What happened to the real Lancaster boy? What happened? You didn't kill him, did you? You killed him! Oh my God. You murdered a child and replaced him with your own.'

'Shut up!' She had both balled fists up by her temples and

her eyes were screwed up as if she couldn't stand to hear anything I was saying.

'Let me go!' I said. 'Let me go now, this minute, and I won't tell a soul.'

She flew at me from across the room, her arms flailing, her voice wailing. She started to beat me about the head and face. I tried to protect myself with my arms over my head, my head down. She kept on screaming and pummelling me.

'Shut up! Shut up! Shut up!' she shrieked, over and over again.

'You are bruising me again!' I shouted. 'What will your son say when he sees!'

At that, she stopped, as abruptly as she'd started. Her eyes were vicious and round, her chest was rising and falling at pace, and her shaking hands were clenched by her side. I thought she was going to kill me; instead, she hastened out of the room and locked me in again.

If Thomas were to discover that I knew the truth, the sordid details of his own background, his fabricated family history, I would never get out of that house alive, I was sure of it. I lay in bed and turned over the new information in my mind. All those years he'd been a cuckoo in the Lancaster house. He was no better than me – no wonder we found each other. We did fit, after all.

I needed to act. I went over to the door, hoping for inspiration, some way to make my escape. The keyhole was blocked; Mrs Wiggs had left the key inside the lock. When I put my little finger in it, I could feel the metal stump.

I had to find a way to get to Reading. I needed to talk to

my solicitor, not the police, who would only speak to my husband, and it would be my word against his. My solicitor could help me to raise hellfire at the Lancaster estate; he could send a letter to Helen, telling her what I knew for certain and promising that I would share my explosive information with the world. The threat of such a scandal, along with all the other details I had learned, would surely call Thomas off. Even if nothing came of it, it might be enough to keep him away from me. I knew that even if he convinced Dr Shivershev to sign the lunacy order, the order would only last for seven days. I only had to get out of the house and hide until the order expired.

Having Dr Shivershev in my head put me in mind of his housekeeper and the trick she'd used to break into his office. Might that work for me too?

I dressed, slipped a silk scarf under the door, took a rolled-up piece of paper, poked it into the keyhole and pushed the key out. When it fell, I very carefully tugged the scarf to where the gap under the door was biggest, and retrieved the key!

I didn't know where Mrs Wiggs was, she could have been anywhere in the house, so I opted for the fastest exit: the front door was mere feet away from the bottom of the stairs, and from there it would only take a minute to reach the end of the road.

As I ran down the stairs, I made the mistake of glancing into the front dining room. Thomas's black medical bag was on the table. He might come home at any second, but the pragmatist in me said there could be money in his bag. I had no plan for how I would get to Reading, and no money for the train. I would rummage through his bag and give myself to the count of five; if nothing came of it, I would go.

I reached into his bag and straightaway put my hand on something damp in the bottom corner. When I withdrew my fingers, they were wet and red with blood. I delved back in, disgusted but curious, and pulled out a parcel wrapped in bleeding wet newspaper. Inside it was a white cloth, seeping blood. I unwrapped it and into the palm of my hand fell what looked like a soft muscle. It seemed to me very much like a human organ. Was there more in the bag? I felt inside it once again, and nearly sliced my thumb on the thin, sharp blade of a long knife. I laid the knife on the table alongside the bloody package and looked up towards the door. Standing there was Mrs Wiggs. I had forgotten to count to five.

She had blocked the doorway with her body, and her hands were resting on either side of the doorframe. 'Susannah,' she said, 'I'm sorry I lost my temper. We'd been getting on so much better, but you really should be in bed.'

'You have to let me leave,' I said. There might have been the ticking of a clock, or it might have been inside my head; it might have been an alarm that was telling me to run and push past her now, because I knew, as she did, she would never let me go.

'Thomas will be home shortly with your physician. Dr Shivershev wants to see you for himself, he wants to see how ill you are. You have to go back to bed. Upstairs, now!'

'I'm not going back up there.'

'Thomas gave clear instructions—'

'Oh, stop it! I can't bear it any more. I know what you are. You are a murderer, and Thomas is nothing but a fraud and a criminal. You have lied for long enough. It is you who are his mother, not Lady Lancaster. You let me go now, and I will keep your dirty little secrets. That is the deal I will make with you.'

She held me in her owl stare. There was a drumming, a dull thud. I could not tell if it was my own heart I could hear beating, or hers. I looked at the organ in the bloodstained cloth on the table and picked up the silver knife lying beside it.

'I could ask what your son is doing with human organs, and no doubt the police will have their own theories on that. I will keep this to myself as well, only let me go.'

'Oh, you're wrong!' She rushed forward, and I backed away.

I held the knife up with the point towards her. She came to a stop with her hands on the back of a chair.

'Thomas is not a criminal! He is a loving boy. You don't know anything!' She stepped forward again and I moved back, the knife in front of me, pointed at her chest, inches between us.

'Let me go,' I said.

She shook her head and I knew we were both prepared to hurt the other. Mrs Wiggs would never let me go; she could never let Thomas down.

She rushed at me and I waved the knife; she tried to block it with her hand and I slashed her with it. It was a strange thing to find myself instinctively behaving as a criminal would. A second's action, a quick flash, a little swipe and the willingness to do anything, and I was changed for ever.

We both gasped. She stared at the blood dripping down from her palm and onto the carpet, held it with her other hand and turned to me, seemingly not in any pain.

'You know, this behaviour of yours will only further strengthen Thomas's plan,' she said. 'Dr Shivershev will be sure to agree now. You are only proving that you really are dangerous.'

'And when I tell whoever will listen that you murdered the Lancaster boy and replaced him with your own? You can't hide being colour-blind – what will you do if they test you both? I can't be the only one to have had doubts, to have noticed things. What if Helen has had the same suspicions all these years? Imagine. I'm sure she'll be keen to inherit everything.'

I was close to the door to the hallway and I had only the front door to get to.

'If you were a mother, you would understand,' she said, creeping towards me.

'No, I would never hurt a baby.'

'I have never harmed a child in my life!' she shouted, tears filling her eyes.

'But you must have.'

'I never could! The little boy was ailing – they are not robust people, the Lancasters, you only have to look at them to see that money doesn't buy strength. Helen, the little girl, was well enough, but the boy was sickly from birth. I found him in his crib one morning, blue, already dead. I was so frightened. I was twenty-two years old – a girl! I had left my own boy with the baby farmer. I couldn't feed both of us any other way. My child's father was in the navy, left on a ship and I never heard from him again, so what was I to do? What good could have come from telling the truth? I did what any mother would have done. I took the Lancaster boy and I buried him that night in the place they call paradise. I fetched my own baby and placed him in the nursery; he was older by four weeks, but I knew Lady Lancaster would never notice, she barely held her own children.'

She looked me full in the face now, a little smile playing on her lips. 'So now that you know the truth, we can find a way to be in this together. Wouldn't life be better with no secrets, Susannah? No shame. We can make our own family, can't we? Even if it is lies that bind us, and not blood. I'll live with it.'

'I'm leaving.' I was getting closer to the front door, still holding the knife in front of me.

'Let me talk to Thomas,' she called after me. It looked as though she would let me go. 'Think of Abbingdale, Susannah. I know you haven't seen it, but it's worth waiting for, and one day it will all be his. Think of the money – isn't that what you wanted?'

'Your son is a monster. I want nothing to do with either of you.'

I ran to the front door and snatched at the handle. Of course it was locked, but the key was still in it. I did not have time to turn it and Mrs Wiggs was coming for me, so I carried on running. I missed her grasping hands and slipped past her down the hallway, down the pantry steps and into the kitchen. I was almost at the back door when she grabbed my hair and pulled me backwards.

I whipped around, bent over, tried to free my hair with one hand and with the other brandished the knife blindly. I felt it slide into her soft belly, under her stays. She made a noise as if she'd been punched in the stomach. She let go of my hair and stepped backwards. We both pulled away from each other, like boxers at the sound of the bell. I saw the handle sticking out of her abdomen. The blood spread like ink into her dress, slowly at first, and then it surged in all directions as it flooded down her skirts. What had I done? Her owl eyes were large and amber. I saw my grandmother in her face: shock, betrayal and resentment.

'Oh no, Susannah! No, no, no! Now you will never be free,' she said, as tears fell down her cheeks.

She dropped to the floor and lay on her back, groaning, clutching her abdomen. I sat on my knees beside her and waited as she bled to death. I heard a buzzing noise and looked about to find where it was coming from. A fly was dancing at the window, trying to find a route out. As Mrs Wiggs lay dying, I stood up and opened the window so it could go free. It seemed like the right thing to do.

34

S eeing the fly like that struck me as significant. It was a sign, I was being watched, the things I had done would not go unnoticed even if only by the divine. Back in Reading when my grandmother was still alive and I was entirely under her influence, she and I had been at church on a Sunday, as we always were. It was January and bitterly cold, and I was sitting in the pew next to her, enduring the sermon and staring up at the windows.

The stiff taffeta of our dresses rubbed against each other and my thoughts roiled. For the past year I had been trying to speak to my grandmother about my leaving Reading and taking up nursing in London. I was twenty-seven years old and desperate to seize some of the adventure I'd read that other women savoured. I was desperate not to die an old maid, never having left that house in Reading, never having done anything but be a companion to an old woman. Would I never know the touch of a man, get married or have children? But my grandmother never listened to my concerns and hopes; she had stopped listening after my grandfather died.

I itched and crawled with frustration. For some weeks I had carried this oily feeling at the top of my stomach and a burning sensation when I swallowed. I thought I was falling ill, then I convinced myself that it was because my chance to escape was fast disappearing. If I didn't do something soon, I would never leave.

Every window in St Bartholomew's was broken and the missing parts had been blocked up with sacking. It made the patchwork Bible scenes harder to place. As I sat there that January Sunday, trying to decipher the story of one particular window, I caught sight of a fly beating itself against a coloured pane. It was thrashing the glass in a panic, straining to get out. I knew exactly how it felt.

My grandmother forbade me from talking to the others in the church congregation, and so they had long stopped bothering to offer us anything more than a polite greeting. I so lacked practice with people and conversation that on the occasions I did talk to someone, such as the chemist or the lady at the post office, I went as red as a strawberry and couldn't think what to say. People must have thought me either dumb or an imbecile.

As always, we waited in our pew until the rest of the congregation had dribbled out. The frail and unwashed tended to loiter towards the back, the better dressed righteously possessed the front. It took forever for them all to shuffle out of the door though there weren't many of them. Grandmother stared straight ahead at the large crucifix and rolled the beads of her own mother's rosary through her fingers. I imagined ripping them from her hands and throwing them down the aisle.

I looked up to the fly and saw it find an unblocked pane

and escape. Speak now, I urged myself. I drew in breath, but I didn't need it.

'Are you going to talk again of leaving me?' The tension in Grandmother's chin made the knot of her bonnet twitch.

'I wish you wouldn't think of it like that,' I replied. 'It's not about leaving you, it's about finding a life of my own.'

'We have discussed this time and time again, as I recall – and I do recall, as much as you think my mind is feeble these days. Each time, the subject cuts as deep as it did the first, my dear.'

I opened my mouth to speak but was interrupted. 'Drunks, vagrants and defiled women gather like rats in London. They take people apart in hospitals there, you know! They tear limbs from bodies, cut them open – is that what you want?'

'Then what? Am I to spend my life here? I am twenty-seven. If I am able to become a nurse, I can earn a good wage, for the both of us.'

Grandmother fixed her pale blue eyes on me. 'Pah, it's not about money. It's about that part of you that wants to wriggle free of the guidance it requires. I shudder to think what you'd get up to. You don't have the will. Sin seeps through you, but while you are here, I can frighten it away; we can stop it. I'm glad your grandfather isn't here; he would be heartbroken to know you want to abandon me.'

Her paper-white fingers worked her rosary faster and faster, her thin veins like blue and green cotton. I looked towards the hole in the stained-glass window and wished I could fly out too. The sound of her sobbing echoed around the church. This was her trick; she cried so as to sabotage the conversation.

'Please… please don't cry,' I said, and placed my hand on hers, though I had no feeling for it. I didn't like to touch her but knew it was the thing to do.

Her hand felt cold and small, and she snatched it from me anyway. 'Stupid little fool! You don't know anything,' she said.

'Then let me go!' I growled.

Contempt flashed across her face.

I glanced around. No one had seen me struggle to contain my resentment. 'How can I know anything when you refuse to let me leave the house?' I said through gritted teeth.

'You will take me home now.'

In my gut I had made the decision already, but my gut had yet to persuade my head. With her continued resistance to my desires and ambitions she had sealed her own fate. She hadn't always been like this, not when my grandfather was alive. He was more liberal in relation to me and she had respected his male authority. I had learned that girls should fear the jealousy of the women who raised them, for they sought companions in confinement.

My grandmother's health had deteriorated in recent months. She tired easily and complained of feeling ill and feverish all the time, for attention mainly. The village doctor was used to being called and would send me to the chemist for a tonic I could have purchased without his direction, if only she'd asked. She was an irritant. I knew he thought I had the patience of a saint. Often she forgot herself and called me Christabel, which had been my mother's name. When she realised I wasn't Christabel, she became listless and sad. She would pace the house at night, looking for my grandfather, and I would take her back to her bedroom and lock the door – just like Mrs Wiggs now did to me. What was the distance between locking an old woman in her room for her own safety and helping her on her way back to God? It didn't seem so great to me.

I prayed to Him many times, but I think the Devil answered. I prayed for the chance to fly and it came three days later. I was in the potting shed, looking for a trowel to fill in a hole some animal had dug in the garden, and as I sifted through the rusted tools, a box fell from an old shelf – my grandfather never was much of a carpenter – and dropped on my head. It was a box of flypapers with arsenic.

That night she said she would take her supper in bed. I generally served her some broth and bread, and a little mutton if she could manage it. I soaked the flypaper in water and used it to make the broth. As I walked up the stairs carrying that tray, there was excitement, I admit, at the prospect of a huge event about to occur. With each step I took, I thought I wouldn't do it, she might not eat it, it might not work. God could still intervene.

But she became ill after the first night and never left her bed again. I continued to make the broth each day until the end.

On the last night, when she was very weak, I heard her cough from the landing. I hurried to her door but did not go inside, just listened to the rasping for a while. Then I ran down the stairs, out the back door and all the way to the bottom of the garden. From the potting shed I took a spade and dug a hole of my own. I dug and dug and dug. The earth was hard, but I didn't care. It started to rain and I carried on digging a hole right in the middle of the garden. I prayed for someone to help me, vowed that I was sorry for being wicked. I promised that if it didn't work, I would never do anything like it again. I sat on the ground, wet through and with mud under my fingernails from where I had tired of the shovel and had clawed with my hands. It wasn't deep. I wasn't much good for digging holes.

When I finally dared to enter the bedroom, she was dead. Her white face had turned grey, her eyes were open and she was staring at the ceiling. Her silvery white hair was wild and knotted from where she'd struggled. Her mouth was stuck wide open in a silent scream. It was misshapen, as if something, maybe my conspirator, the Devil, had blown a great wind into her, forced it open and reached inside with an arm to take her soul. I took the rest of the box of flypapers, threw them in the hole I'd dug and filled it, because I was the fly and that was my broken window.

35

I stuffed Mrs Wiggs and her lead-heavy limbs and big skirts into a cupboard. I was in a complete panic; any lucid thoughts I'd clung to were crumbling away. I was filled with anger at her. If she'd let me leave, she wouldn't be dead. I refused to feel guilty. It was her own fault. It was self-defence. If she'd only let me leave, she'd be alive now; cursing me, yes, but alive and with her precious monster of a son.

Her skirts kept billowing back in my face as if they were laughing at me, too voluminous to fit in the cupboard. Her old-fashioned habits still fought me, even in death. My thinking became haphazard, desperate and littered with unrealistic peaks of optimism. If I could get to my solicitor, if I could get some money, he would help me. I would go abroad, run to France, walk to Spain if necessary. I would keep running until I fell off the edge of the Earth.

I'd pulled out pudding bowls and crockery, shoved them onto other shelves and heaved her bleeding body, hips first and folded over, into the bottom cupboard. I had no idea when Thomas would return with Dr Shivershev, but if the two of them walked in and found her dead on the floor, they would call the police. By doing this, I might still escape, if I were clever.

I saw myself in court, in a prison cell, trying to explain how I'd been imprisoned against my will, raging from the dock that my husband was Jack the Ripper, the typical hysterical shrew. There would be rows of pale and pompous bewigged men, grey faces puckered in disapproval, and when they heard I was the daughter of a prostitute and had lied my way to becoming the wife of a gentleman, I would be done for. I had wandered across London dressed as a man and mourned a dead woman lover. I would not stay to see how any trial played out. It would end with me imprisoned, or with my feet swinging clear of the ground, or in the asylum, though without any perambulating around a Surrey lake.

A steady flow of blood dripped from between the cupboard doors. Without proper soap and water, I was smearing it everywhere and covering clean linens in blood. I was creating more evidence out of thin air. I couldn't breathe, my chest snatched shallow gasps. I had to wipe up what I could and hope Thomas would not enter the kitchen, at least not immediately. He would think I had escaped and that Mrs Wiggs had pursued me. He would wait for her to return and would not find her body until much later; that was my hope. My dress had blood on it, my hands were red with it. I pushed my hair out of my face and smeared blood across my cheeks. It was hopeless.

A knock at the front door cracked through the house like thunder. I thought my bones would crumble into dust. I tried to open the back door, but it was locked and there was no key. If I'd had any sense, I'd have realised the key must be on Mrs Wiggs, but I didn't think of it. I crept back up the stairs towards the hallway, towards the knock at the door. I heard men's voices and saw dark shadows shuffled through the mottled glass. It was Thomas, and he'd brought Dr Shivershev to diagnose the lunatic. As I neared the door, they knocked again, so loud it made me tremble.

They were waiting for Mrs Wiggs to come to the door. I remembered now that I had thrown the attic key under the sideboard when I fell down the stairs. Thomas had commandeered Mrs Wiggs' key, and she had then had another cut to make up for the missing one, routine had returned and I had forgotten all about that missing key. I knelt down and found it in the same place, covered in dust. I raced up the main stairs and had got as far as the attic staircase when they gave up waiting. I could only be grateful for Thomas's dependency on Mrs Wiggs: he was so pampered by his mother that it took three knocks before he could be bothered to reach all the way into his pocket for his front door key and open it himself.

I locked the attic door behind me as they clattered into the hallway downstairs. Inside the attic, I was in darkness. There were no windows, but streaks of light beamed like torches across the roof where the pigeons came and went in holes in the side of the roof. I was sure there had been a candle on the desk, but I didn't dare try to find it for fear of knocking it over and making a noise. I moved across the floor on my hands and knees to the roar of my rapid heartbeat. It was freezing, but I didn't feel it because of the terror that kept my blood surging. The floor reeked of mouse piss and mothballs. I dragged thick dust along with me and it flew up in my face. The pigeons were roosting and the scurrying and creeping of all the little creatures hiding in the dark with me was as loud as an orchestra. Then I heard Thomas shout for Mrs Wiggs and I shuddered.

I found the edge of the skirts on the tailor's dummy and crawled underneath. A broken crinoline cage had been tied onto it, and I was able to fit underneath it in a ball and pull the skirts over me. I buried my face into my knees and realised I'd left the knife in Mrs Wiggs. I thought of the keys she'd have had on her waistband. Such an idiot. I was trapped in the attic with two men blocking my escape and the dead body of my housekeeper stuffed in a cupboard in the kitchen.

My heart thumped as their voices got ever louder. The attic stairs creaked under their weight. Then came silence, followed by the metallic clank of a key in a lock and everything – heartbeat, breathing, sweating – stopped. My hand gripped the key so tight, I could have made another from the mould it left in my palm. I twisted my lips together with my other hand and tried to breathe steadily and silently.

'What? No gaslight?' said Dr Shivershev. He sounded agitated; I was glad to have inconvenienced him.

'Wait here,' said Thomas.

When he came back with a candle, I realised the skirt I was hiding under had a tear in it. There was a sheer petticoat beneath it. I could see vague outlines through it, but I was pretty sure the petticoat would mask my eyes from the other side. Thomas came towards the dummy. I couldn't see his face, but I knew it was him. He held the candle high and swept it from left to right. Dr Shivershev trudged behind him in his black coat and billycock; he was carrying his medical bag.

'Robert, if she's escaped, we're all going to be done for. I'm telling you now,' said Thomas.

'What exactly did you tell her?' said Dr Shivershev.

'Nothing, specifically, but believe it or not, she's not stupid.'

'Why say anything at all? You've put everyone in this house in danger.'

'You try living with her! I had to tell her something – she was on my back constantly.'

'One might have acquired an imagination – or simply come home on occasion,' said Dr Shivershev drily. 'Who else lives here?'

'No one. The servants are all gone, there is only Mrs Wiggs, and I don't know where she is either. Oh God, it's such a mess. What shall we do? What shall we do, Robert? She's a nightmare.'

'First things first, Thomas, why don't you put that candle down on that desk. We must remain calm. The most important thing is, of course, not to panic.' Dr Shivershev sounded the same as he did when he examined my tongue.

He set down his bag, opened it with black-gloved hands, pulled out what looked like a length of rope or thick cord, then lunged forward. It was an explosion of energy. I heard a frantic struggle, the scrape of boot heels against the floor, energy spending itself to the point of exhaustion. I tried to look through the tear, but the fight came too close and the dummy wobbled. I had to hold it steady. At one point, Thomas's feet reached under the skirts and he nearly kicked me.

There was a hissing sound, and then choking. After an age of this came complete silence, then Dr Shivershev let

Thomas drop to the floor with a dull thud. Just like that, my troublesome monster of a husband was dead. I was shaking so violently, I was sure the whole dummy must be quivering.

Dr Shivershev fumbled in his bag. Next thing I saw was Thomas being hoisted up like a flag in clumsy jerks, until his feet were dangling in the air. His polished black shoes swung side to side mere feet from my face. Dr Shivershev was panting like an old dog. He dragged one of the attic chairs to a spot on the floor in front of Thomas, sat down on it, leaned forward over his knees, let out a huge sigh and wiped his forehead. He stayed like that for a few minutes until his breathing had calmed.

'It would be best if you were to come out now, Mrs Lancaster.'

'You left footprints,' he said, as if I should remember my mistake for next time. 'Like deer prints, leading all the way up here. Are you hurt?'

He glanced around the attic. The pigeons cooed, unperturbed by their new housemate swinging from the rafters. One of them dropped faeces on a redundant chest of drawers and we both watched them land with an undignified splat.

'Charming place you have,' said Dr Shivershev.

His breathing had steadied, and he leaned forward and reached into his bag again. There was no one else in the house, so whatever came out of the bag was going to be for me. He pulled out a long silver knife and cleaned it, although it already gleamed in the candlelight.

I sat on the floor with my knees up to my chest and my

arms wrapped around them. Dr Shivershev remained on the chair, his eyes shining like Vauxhall glass. I knew I had the time it took for him to compose himself to bargain for my life. I had to maintain this focus. Meanwhile, my dead husband's feet swung between us like a metronome, a useful reminder that my time was finite.

'Are you here to kill me?' I asked.

He nodded, and said in a sympathetic voice, as if he were informing me of the death of a beloved pet, 'I can do it quickly. It won't hurt.'

I fell apart. I shook and trembled. I couldn't breathe. I cried without pride or dignity. I begged him not to do it as he looked over my head and into the distance. I had never professed to be brave.

'You could let me go. You know I can keep secrets. I never informed a soul about Mabel, though you told Thomas about my mother.' I surprised myself at how quickly I moved to anger when it appeared my crying had no effect.

'I never said a word to him about you.' His voice echoed across the attic. It was a little strange that the man who had just murdered my husband should be offended at an accusation that he was a gossip. 'I kept my word,' he said. 'I always do...'

Now that his knife was clean to his satisfaction, he pointed it at me as he spoke. 'Your husband – badly chosen, I might add – knew everything. He had that housekeeper of his track down a woman from the Nichol and the woman told the housekeeper all about the little brown-eyed girl who had to be dragged out screaming, by her feet, from under a bed in a puddle of her own piss. As I said before, your Dr Lancaster and I weren't drinking partners until recently, and even then it was business.'

He glanced up at Thomas, who was still swaying between us. I'd been trying not to look, but when I did, I saw that his eyes bulged like a frog's and his tongue protruded from his mouth. How humiliating Thomas would have found this; a man so precious of his appearance was now so ugly in death.

'What of the specimen then, the baby in the jar? I saw that here, in this attic, the night I was pushed down the stairs, and yet when I came to see you, it was in your office, on the shelf in your collection.'

'Is that why you missed the appointment?'

'I had no one left to trust.'

'I rescheduled other patients for that. Who else have you told about your theories?'

'Who else have I to tell?' I said, shaking my head at the bizarre situation I now found myself in. 'I thought the specimen had been cut from Mabel and that was why she hadn't written, because she'd died and that's how you came by it, and I had sent her to you.'

'She was treated by a friend of mine, a Romanian, as qualified as myself – more so, in the practice of such procedures. You've met her: my housekeeper, Irina. She informed me that your friend left that place alive, and that there were no problems.'

'And yet she hasn't written,' I said.

'The girl got what she wanted, why would she write? You have been causing me headaches, Susannah, with your wild theories and indiscreet husband. You aren't mad – a little off the mark, but not mad. I was sent here to deal with the issue at hand and dispatch whoever I found in the house with him. You know, I haven't been sleeping, Susannah.'

Thomas's body had finally stopped moving. I had a fear that Dr Shivershev was only telling me all this, explaining things to me, to alleviate whatever guilt he would suffer by killing me, as if I would skip to my death so long as I had an understanding of his motive, so long as it had been explained to me. I was still thinking on what I could do to change the inevitable outcome, so I let him speak and didn't interrupt.

Dr Shivershev and Thomas worked for the same organisation, unbeknownst to each other at first. Dr Shivershev had been recruited many years ago, but Thomas had only recently been invited to join the secret brotherhood of scientists; he was very much on probation, a foot soldier in a hierarchical organisation. The brotherhood operated as a selective band of brothers; they helped each other in all things and swore loyalty to one another and their cause. At its core, their cause was about true freedom. A man could be who he wanted: the rules that applied to ordinary people were not for them, and no religious or moralising theories were assumed. But this camaraderie was not to be abused. Rules may not have applied in the normal sense, but a man was expected to keep his own house in order and remain discreet. Both edicts Thomas would come to find impossible to uphold.

The foetus specimen, found by Thomas, was an attempt to ingratiate himself with Dr Shivershev. He wanted a favour.

Thomas had complained to anyone who would listen of the difficulties he was having with his 'common' wife.

He'd been seduced by a temptress, so he told his colleagues, who had her sights set on bettering herself. He needed to be free, and so he foolishly complained to his fraternity of brothers long before he had earned the currency to do so, establishing himself as a whining pain. He asked that they order Dr Shivershev, as his wife's physician, to help him have her certified a lunatic, so she could be interned in an asylum.

The brotherhood did indeed assign Dr Shivershev to assist, but his real task was to deal with Thomas. Thomas had become a liability: unpredictable, unreliable, and most of all a risk. A squawking parrot of a man-child. He had been overheard speaking about the brotherhood socially, and his work was sloppy and lacking in the professionalism and rigour expected of a loyal brother. It was therefore agreed that he would have to be dispatched, and his troublesome wife along with him. The removal of the servants in his household was an absolute requirement to ensure that the evidence matched the motive. It must be clear that Thomas had gone on a murderous spree before hanging himself due to humiliating financial and professional difficulties.

Dr Shivershev said that this was to be his last assignment for the brotherhood in London. He would be removing himself to America. He wished to create a distance and had obtained special permission to leave. As a Jew, he had never felt truly accepted into the heart of the circle. His work was commended, admired, and he was respected, but he could never truly become one of them. In a way this worked to his advantage, and he obtained permission to leave as a reward for his loyalty and discreet service.

What Dr Shivershev had kept to himself was that he could

no longer align himself with the direction the brotherhood had taken. It had become far removed from its original purpose; the brotherhood had lost its way. It had turned into a perverted enterprise whose main function was the harvesting and selling of organs for private sale to rich old men. Their principal customers, Dr Shivershev said, were a certain breed of English gent with a fetish for collecting things, the more novel and outlandish the better. The sort of man who had everything already but who would always want more, especially when it came at the expense of another.

I thought of Thomas and his own mania for collecting things; of that shrunken head from South America that he obtained just for the pleasure of hearing me shriek, how he acquired me and clothes and the cigars he didn't smoke.

'What was the purpose of this brotherhood in the beginning?' I asked.

'It was about knowledge! We wanted to understand how the body worked, so we could fix it when it went wrong. Why leave it to God, when he was doing such a shoddy job of it,' Dr Shivershev said, his eyes glistening, his voice rich with passion. 'Nearly fifty years ago, the first collective was a group of outcast scientists, enlightened scholars and astronomers, supported by free-thinking members of the aristocracy who invested money in secret. They all wanted to see what could be achieved with medicine, how far it could go. They wanted to explore the human body without interference from the Church, without religious or cultural morality defining what could or could not be done.'

My mind flitted back to my grandmother's church in Reading, to the stultifying hours I'd spent there, and to my grandmother herself. She loathed the idea of humans 'playing God' with a person's body. One of the many reasons she took against my ever becoming a nurse.

'Medical experimentation is not something everyone approves of,' continued Dr Shivershev, as if he could read my thoughts. He was all but lost in his enthusiasm for his topic. 'We understood that. Innocent people died and we made some difficult decisions, but we believed it was for the progression of humanity.'

What did he mean by 'innocent people', I wondered. Did the brotherhood really go about committing murder and digging around inside people under the guise that it would save lives in the future? It seemed it might not have been so wild a theory that my husband the surgeon was the Whitechapel killer. If not Thomas, what of Dr Shivershev himself? My pulse began to race again. It was imperative that I try to find a way out. I could never physically overpower Dr Shivershev, I must talk my way to freedom. But how?

'Hospitals are wonderful places, Susannah, but they are administrative nightmares run by meddling bureaucrats who want nothing more than to push paper around their desks and feather their nests and who don't give a damn about real science. They go home and sleep in their beds without imagining what could be possible. There were things we achieved in those early years that would never have been permitted in a hospital, and now they are common practice.'

He sighed now, and glared disparagingly at the dangling corpse of my husband. His neck had begun to stretch, the tongue swollen. I had to look away.

'The problem, as so often, was money. Once certain

members of our brotherhood realised the obscene profit that could be made from private collectors, nothing else mattered. There was a sudden mania among the rich for everything from shrivelled hearts to kidneys in wine and virgins' breasts, and medical science was forgotten. This suited your husband very well. He wasn't faring too happily at the hospital, and barely had any private patients, but he did at least know the rudiments of surgery. He had quite serious money concerns, I believe?'

I nodded, thought of Abbingdale Hall and the inheritance Thomas was no longer eligible for, being dead. Mrs Wiggs had counselled me about that. After all my efforts to remain in his house, to remain married for my own security, it didn't seem as if I would achieve this after all.

'The problem was that he would go to his clubs and houses and boast, tell people, in that obsessive need he had to talk of himself. But he didn't realise who was listening, which is why he had to be silenced. The man at the Café Royale you mentioned, with the medals, I knew who he was instantly, and I'm afraid he is rather high up in the brotherhood. So when you told me about their conversation, I knew you were in danger. Why do you think I told you to find a safe place to go?'

'Then, as it's not about me at all, but my husband, why not let me go? I will keep my mouth shut – you know I can.'

'The missing wife of a gentleman who has killed himself… The brotherhood can influence the investigation, they have links to the Home Office and there will be no problem with the police, but a missing wife from Chelsea is a story worthy of the news, and these journalists, you see, they have not been… adequately penetrated, as of yet, shall we say. The brotherhood will be left feeling exposed and they will blame me for attracting attention. There would be the potential for scrutiny, and scientists do not like scrutiny...'

The beginning of his explanation gave me some hope; my grandfather used to tell me it never mattered how desperate a man's situation was, he will always cling to the faintest sliver of hope, as I did now, though I made sure to keep my face expressionless. Dr Shivershev was taking the time to make me understand, so I would sit and listen.

'I also have another problem,' he continued. 'Namely my friends you saw me with in the Ten Bells. The man, Walter, a common man, my driver, will leave the country with me, but the woman, Mary, they will never let her go. Her role is to procure the live specimens. She started as a whore – she has a varied past, as we all do – but she deserves better and I want her to come with me. Once the brotherhood realises that she is gone, they will know she's with me. They will not be happy, though I suspect they will not be surprised. I will need to use all the currency I have earned during my service if we are to survive. They will never let a common prostitute leave. There is hypocrisy there, of course. The brotherhood prides itself on being free of cultural tyranny, but when it comes to women, I'm afraid you are still very much considered to be men's property. There is theory, and then there is practice...'

He inhaled and came to a stop.

I didn't need a lecture on hypocrisy but I let him give it. I was livid now, furious at myself for having got into this mess, worse than the one I had found myself in before, but how simple that seemed now. 'I courted him in hospital and I simpered over him as he lay like the martyr in his bed...'

Dr Shivershev started and glanced at me with interest. 'Ah, so that's how you grew close, was it?' He gave a little laugh. 'You know Thomas was suspected of starting that fire at the hospital?'

'What? Why would he do that? That doesn't sound like Thomas at all, why would he want to burn himself?'

'There was another doctor, a man called Dr Lovett.'

'Yes, I know him. I mean rather I met him, Richard Lovett was best man at our wedding. Thomas carried him out from that fire.'

'Well... he was Thomas's best man in a variety of ways, for a while at least. You understand, of course?'

I coloured at this; I couldn't help it. It made sense as I'd seen Lovett at the mollies' house.

'The night of the fire, Thomas and Lovett had argued – a lovers' quarrel, I assume. Later, Lovett came to believe that Thomas had hit him over the head before the fire started. One minute he was awake and the next...'

'How do you know this?'

'Lovett is the nephew of the man with the medals you and Thomas bumped into at the Café Royale. After their affair had ended, the spurned Lovett didn't waste any time reporting back to his uncle on Thomas's indiscretions. The final straw was when an article appeared in the newspapers about a man who'd been making enquiries about the purchase of a fresh uterus on behalf of a client. The information came from Thomas, who'd apparently been talking while under the influence at a mollies' house. And the person who witnessed this—'

'—was Dr Richard Lovett.'

'Exactly.'

It was time to change direction, I had had enough of being done to. As Dr Shivershev had been talking, I had been thinking and I had an idea, that sliver of hope had made me somewhat creative. 'I know you don't want to kill me—' I said.

'You deserve better.'

'—and, besides, there is a way I think I can help.' I looked him straight in the eye, made sure I had his attention.

'What if the newspapers had a bigger distraction than that of a missing Chelsea housewife? What if Mary were believed to have been murdered? And if there was a body, no one would know she'd run away with you.'

My obsession with the Whitechapel murders might be put to practical use. I knew all the gory details, every last one of them. 'You say Mary was a… well, that makes her ripe for being murdered by Jack the Ripper, does it not?'

I saw Dr Shivershev's eye shift towards me and I knew immediately that he got it, understood there could be value in this.

'What if we were to swap Mary's body for another's?'

His mouth twitched. 'I take it you aren't offering yourself as the substitute body, Susannah? Are you suggesting I wait for Mrs Wiggs and kill her instead?'

'No,' I said, 'because she is dead already.'

'Ah,' he said, shifting in his chair. His face broadened into a smile. 'I see.'

Marie Jeanette: la Grande Blonde

Mary's heart leapt and fluttered. She wasn't frightened, but she was desperate, and she knew her time was running out. She had caused many of her own troubles, but she only had a temper when she drank, and she would defy any woman to spend her youth as she had, underneath men flopping on her like pigs snuffling for truffles, and not take what they could to lighten the load, alcohol or otherwise. She was trapped between the impossible, between the men who had owned her and those who owned her now, dangerous men who would not be humiliated by a defiant piece of cargo.

At five foot seven and with long fair hair, Mary had been compared to all the famous beauties – Venus, Salome, Cleopatra. The name that stuck was Marie Jeanette, La Grande Blonde: the clientele in Paris had bestowed that on her. It was a testament to the shit men let tumble from their lips in the pursuit of fucking. The one man who hadn't drooled over her or even said she was beautiful, had barely seemed to notice her at first, was the doctor, Robert. Meeting him had been her only solace. If everything went as Robert *had planned, both of them would be gone by tomorrow. For the first time in her life, Mary would be really, truly free.*

There was a rustle of skirts and a familiar bout of coughing, and through the door barged Lizzie Albrook, come down from upstairs to Mary's room to hear about Sally's flit. Mary was irritated by the intrusion, but it would be a useful sighting, once Mary had disappeared. All those who had spoken to her on this day would be asked to give an evaluation of her demeanour, so she mustn't give a clue that anything other than business as usual was on her mind.

As luck would have it, she had another interruption, even while Lizzie was still visiting. Today of all days! Joseph knocked on the door, which annoyed her even more, for he well knew the door could easily be opened from the outside, since it was he who had lost the bloody key.

'Hello, Mary, how are you keeping?' he said, sidling round the door like a lost puppy.

Those earnest eyes, and that fair hair, sticking out in all directions and giving him an impish charm. He was handsome, even if he was starting to wrinkle a bit. His skin had darkened from working outdoors, and he had lost some fat from lack of nourishment. Joe could not keep a penny in his pocket when there was beer to be had.

'I'm well, thank you, Joe. I wasn't expecting to see you. Did you lose something?'

Mary said this to slice at the man. Joseph had lost her because of his inability to provide as he had promised, but she was no longer his and he could forget creeping round her, the bright-eyed sprite.

Lizzie Albrook sucked her teeth and pulled her shawl around her as if Joseph Barnett had dragged in the cold air with him. 'Right, I'll be off then,' she said. She heaved her creaking bones up on her fists and pursed her lips at Joseph, like a cat's arse.

Joe, for his part, stood on the threshold of what had once been his own home, holding his cap in his hands like a virgin holding his cock.

Mary ushered him in and he remained standing as Mary sat back on the bed, an ageing fossil of brass and screaming springs that threatened to sink to the floor. She let her legs fall apart and arched her back, held herself up by her locked elbows, head to one side, no bonnet, all blonde tendrils, round cheeks and open lips.

'What is it you want, Joseph? If you have come to see what I've done with the place, it will be a short conversation.'

'Don't be like that, Mary, I only came to see how you've been getting on.'

'Well, how have you been getting on?'

'I wanted to see you. Can I sit? I see Sally's coat came in useful.' He nodded at the black coat that was now acting as a curtain over the window.

Mary sighed and walked over to the single wooden chair and set it down in the middle of the floor for Joe to sit on. He had meant for her to invite him to sit beside her, but she knew he would look for the moment to lean in and kiss her. He was obviously missing some comfort and regretting the firmness of his principles. He'd broken it off when Mary refused to disassociate from other prostitutes, women like Sally, who'd done a runner anyway.

This was what men did, she had found. Women tolerated so much, waiting for their menfolk to keep their promises, then when they'd suffered enough, their feelings expired.

Men, on the other hand, acted the cavalier, fled too fast from any complaining, then remembered what life was like looking after themselves and crawled back. To men like Joe, women were home. It was the reason she held so much esteem for Robert. To him she was a person, not a useful implement or a comforting concept.

She patted the seat of the wooden chair and Joe sat in it while she returned to the saggy bed.

'Like that, is it? I didn't realise we weren't friends, Mary.'

'Friends don't sit on beds together, else they end up as bedfellows.'

'Why do you save such a tone for me? We were good once.'

She sighed again. This was an inconvenient obstacle. She had her instructions and didn't have time to waste on Joseph. It was clear he was hankering for a reunion. She would have to be swift.

'I'm sorry, Joe, it's only that I'm very tired. Won't you come back another time? Perhaps you might have found some work and I won't be so weary. Real friends should take care to give each other their best. I simply don't have it in me today.'

'Right,' said Joe. 'I can come back tomorrow?'

'Yes, tomorrow, when I've had a good night's rest,' she said, knowing only too well she wouldn't be there.

He stood and took the two or three steps to reach the door. It was a poky little room, Number 13 Miller's Court, with barely the space for one, yet they had lived together in those squalid surroundings, on top of each other, for some happy months. This was the Nichol, after all, where privacy was a luxury no one enjoyed.

'Tomorrow then.' Joe put his cap on and looked at the broken pane of glass in the window. 'You should get that fixed, get another key for the door. It's not safe like this – there's a murderer.'

Mary laughed. It wasn't the murderer that frightened her. But not wanting to seem flippant, she said, 'He cuts them up on the streets – I'll be safe inside here.'

'Still, better to have it fixed,' said Joe as he pulled the door to.

36

D r Shivershev left me in the Chelsea house with two dead bodies – my husband's and my housekeeper's. I considered it fortunate that I had my time as a nurse and had been among the dead before. He came back in the evening with his assistant, Walter, the man with the ginger whiskers. They brought with them a private coach, a rickety old thing that did not inspire confidence and looked as if it might fall apart if run too rigorously over the cobbled streets.

We had packed Mrs Wiggs into an old trunk together with the bloodstained linen and the by now shrivelling organ I'd found in Thomas's bag. It was her own trunk – she would have liked that, for at least she could have verified its cleanliness. Dr Shivershev showed me how to make corks from cloth to stop the leaking from her body as it stiffened and changed colour. Then he told me to change into her clothes, and he and Walter carried her out. I followed behind. The pretence was it should appear as if Mrs Wiggs were taking her luggage onto a coach and disappearing, never to return. If anyone were to have a casual glance, that's what they would see. My story would be that she abandoned us, along with all the other servants, because of Thomas's volatile behaviour. Only my survival would require an explanation.

I had winced when putting on Mrs Wiggs' clothes. The feel of her dress on my skin made me cringe, and her bonnet carried her smell: vinegar and cloves. Strands of her hair that had caught in the straw brushed against my face. I wobbled a little when I watched the two men lift the trunk between them and put it onto the coach. I was scared it would fall and that the lid would fly open, sending Mrs Wiggs tumbling onto the pavement. I must have looked ill, because Dr Shivershev slapped me on the back, the way a sailor would another. I stumbled forward into the road.

'Made of sterner stuff, aren't we? Remember we're British,' he said.

I nodded my agreement but wasn't sure. I wanted to ask him about the British part because I understood him to be of Russian descent, but I didn't have the energy.

He must have heard my question in his head because he answered it anyway. 'I've always liked the way that sounds.'

Walter drove us to Dorset Street in Whitechapel, where he and Dr Shivershev took the trunk from the coach and set it down on the pavement. I couldn't take my eyes away from it, scared to blink, petrified if I should shut my eyes that something would happen.

A skinny little boy ran up to Walter, who passed him some coins. They exchanged words, then the boy led the horse and coach away.

'Where is he going?' I asked.

'We'll walk the rest of the way,' said Dr Shivershev.

They picked up the trunk. It was night-time, maybe ten
o'clock, eleven even. Fear of the Ripper had left most streets
dark and empty. They bumped and jostled Mrs Wiggs
between them as I blindly followed along a cobblestoned
road made smooth by gutter mud and horse muck that had
dried and then been made wet again with fresh rain. My
feet kept getting sucked into it. The houses were tall and
shallow to the pavement, with bitter little bricks and large,
broken windows boarded up with newspaper and sacking.
We came to a stop. In between two wooden doors there
was a small archway – I would have missed it myself. We
walked under it and into the dark. We were in the heart
of the Nichol. The hairs on my neck stood to attention at
the familiarity of it. I had come all the way back to my
beginnings, as I feared I would. My circle was closing.

We felt our way along the narrow alley and came out
to a cramped and overlooked courtyard. There was the
sound of damp, running water, muck underfoot and the
smell of rotting rubbish. We passed dark stairs on the right
and I heard the scurry of rats as we disturbed them and
they reassembled behind us. A single lamp emitted a weak,
quivering glow. There were seven little rooms around the
perimeter. I doubted good things went on in any of them.

We entered the door of 13 Miller's Court, the dwelling
of Dr Shivershev's friend, Mary Kelly. Her dingy little room
was cramped and sparsely furnished and the door would
not open all the way because it hit something on the other
side. This was intentional, a little trick to alert the occupant
should a stranger intrude. I remembered that my mother
used to do a similar thing.

We had to wait outside while Dr Shivershev slipped

through the gap like an eel and removed the blockage – a nightstand – so the trunk could be carried through. Once inside, he replaced the nightstand by the door, lit an oil lamp and set it down. There were half a dozen half-burned candles on the nightstand and I wondered if Mary had stolen them from the houses she charred in, though from what I'd seen of her in the Ten Bells, she didn't appear the charring kind.

Dr Shivershev sat on a wooden chair in the corner and gestured for me to sit on the brass bed butted up against the wall. I lowered myself onto it. It had layers of blankets and some of them looked to be quite fine, not the sort of quilts I would expect to see in a whore's dwelling. Maybe they were gifts from Dr Shivershev, or other men. Perhaps Mary had purchased them herself with the money she earned from luring innocents to their deaths, unwitting suppliers of harvested organs to gentlemen's collections. What if they had lured me here for the same reason? It would be one way of getting rid of me.

Walter stood by the window with his back to the wall. Every so often he would peer through it, though it was opaque. I guessed he did this to calm his nerves. There was a small fireplace in the corner of the room. I had started to feel the November temperature in my toes and hoped that when Dr Shivershev's Mary came, she would light the fire, though I didn't dare ask. Even so, I removed Mrs Wiggs' tight bonnet from my head. That whiff of vinegar and cloves again.

There were footsteps the other side of the door and we all sat up, rigid. I looked at Dr Shivershev and he raised a finger to silence me.

'Goodnight,' called a woman outside. 'I'm going to sing.' The others visibly relaxed. It was Mary.

The door opened and in she came, her slender frame slipping easily through the gap.

'Who were you speaking to?' Dr Shivershev asked her.

'Only Margaret from the last house, the one in front of the privies.' Mary had an accent, it could have been Welsh or Irish, with London coarseness, I couldn't be sure.

I stood up as she came in, embarrassed to be sitting on her bed, and conscious of what might have taken place on it, likely with my own physician. The movement made everyone turn towards me, as if I were about to make a toast. I blushed.

Mary looked me up and down and gave a small smile, the type a woman reserves for a competitor. She kept her pretty eyes on me as she walked over to where Dr Shivershev was sitting, bent down and held his grizzly head in both hands to plant a lingering kiss in a display of affection for my benefit. I fought the compulsion to tell her there would be no threat from me. I could only imagine she thought my status as a middle-class lady might usurp her looks. Dr Shivershev, for his part, had that smug expression men adopt on such occasions. I wasn't sure which one made me feel more nauseous. I had the horrible shivers of opium withdrawal, not to mention I had stabbed my housekeeper that afternoon and seen my husband murdered. I was hardly in the mood to jostle for male attention.

'What are we to do now?' I asked, eager to get on with the next part of the plan.

Mary started to sing 'A Violet from Mother's Grave' and set about making sure the only window in the room, which faced the courtyard, was covered. She used a scrappy old cloth nailed to the wall above it, and, bizarrely, a black coat.

No one answered me, so I let out an exasperated sigh and sat down on the bed again. It creaked and squeaked like the string section of an orchestra. If Mary was a whore, I pitied her poor neighbours.

'Mary, would you light the fire, and one or two of those candles,' said Dr Shivershev.

She did as she was asked. She wore a bright white apron, spotlessly clean, and a linsey frock with a red shawl about her shoulders. She didn't have a bonnet. Come to think of it, on none of the three occasions I saw her had she worn one. Her fair hair hung a long way down her back and bobbed up and down as she moved. It made me think of Mabel. Mary had a similar charm, her open, wide-eyed face seemingly stuck in perennial girlhood. I didn't doubt men found her attractive. They would surely describe her as 'sweet' or 'fair', but girls like Mary and Mabel had no need of words, they had adoration enough and no sense of what it was to be plain. They could remain oblivious as long as they still had their looks to fall back on. For the rest of us, it made no sense to build a world around something as fleeting as beauty anyway.

It was obvious by the dwelling, her attractiveness, and the state of her clothes and furniture that Mary made a better than average living, and she didn't look like she spent much time on her knees charring to me. On her knees maybe, but certainly not scrubbing.

'Mary, what time do you have to meet our man?' asked Dr Shivershev.

'Oh, not till two, Robbie. We have plenty of time. Are you ready enough?'

Robbie? Urghhh.

'Right, I'll be off, I'll see you later,' said Walter. He gave a wink to Mary, a nod to Dr Shivershev and a wary blank-eyed stare to me before he slipped out of the door. I was definitely the spare wheel in this arrangement.

Mary moved the nightstand in front of the door and started singing again. In between phrases, she looked me over once more and said, 'Sorry, it is my habit.'

'I beg your pardon?'

'To sing... When I'm nervous. It's a habit of mine.'

She stood over the trunk and Dr Shivershev joined her.

'Right, are we ready, Susannah?' he asked.

'Ready for what?' I said.

'For surgery.'

At first I didn't understand what he meant.

The plan was to put Mrs Wiggs in Mary's bed and forge a Ripper murder. I had assumed it would be arranged when I was out of the room. That was as much thought as I'd allowed myself. But now I understood that they meant me to take part in it. I actually laughed when I realised that.

'Do we have long enough?' asked Mary.

'Yes. It's not as if we're trying to keep the woman alive. We can work quickly,' Dr Shivershev said.

'Good.' Mary threw an anxious glance at me, then turned to him. 'Will she be all right?'

'She will.' Addressing me, he said, 'Pretend we're in theatre again, albeit in even worse conditions than at the

London. Now, Susannah, help me move the body to the bed.'

'I thought we were using Mrs Wiggs to replace Mary? Are we to take organs from her too... here?' I said.

Mary had dragged out a large wooden box from underneath her bed. She opened it, and inside was a full kit of surgeon's knives, tools and apparatus.

'We can't leave Mrs Wiggs as she is, Susannah. It's very clear she is not Mary. Even our inept Metropolitan Police Force will see that. We will make adjustments so that it is impossible to recognise her as Mary or anyone else. We are to set the scene for the next Whitechapel murder. This was your idea, Susannah – remember?'

'I was defending myself,' I said.

'Ha! Good luck telling that to the peelers,' said Mary.

I glared at her, but she turned her back and moved to the window. She kept checking it, over and over, as Walter had, and then she started to sing again. Her voice wobbled, reed thin and high, like a warbling child. It grated on my nerves.

'Same height, same build. Hair? Similar enough,' said Dr Shivershev. 'By the time we're finished, those will be the only features by which to identify her. I will ask you again, Susannah, open the fucking trunk.'

Mary let out a whimper and we both looked at her. She had sat in a chair and was staring off into the distance, beyond the tiny confines of the squalid room. For someone in the business of luring innocents to their death, she was a nervous thing.

'Mary, check the window is covered. We don't want any prying eyes,' said Dr Shivershev.

'I have done it several times already,' she said.

'Then you won't mind doing it again!'

I opened the trunk and unpacked all the linens we had stuffed around Mrs Wiggs. Mary had the job of burning these in the fire. She had to do this slowly, or else the flames crept too high and burned the mantel. She sat staring into the flames, singing that bastard song.

Dr Shivershev and I lifted Mrs Wiggs onto the bed. He took a knife and sliced through her dress, running up her body as if it were an autopsy. He left her chemise underneath, which was a great relief because I did not want to look on her naked. Call me strange, but it would have felt an additional indignity for her. I hated her, but I didn't want to humiliate her. I passed the clothes to Mary, who took them and burned them, piece by piece.

Mrs Wiggs was a lot stiffer than when we'd packed her, which made the job of taking her out a little easier. Earlier she'd been a ragdoll, but now the blood had sunk to the bottom and settled, making purple and burgundy spots on one side. It was not so hard to reposition a body like that, only a little manipulation was necessary; in all honesty, it was just like removing a dead patient at the hospital, an inanimate object. I made a silent promise that I would reward myself with the luxury of remorse if I survived.

We placed her in the middle of the bed, her shoulders flat, but we had to leave her body inclined to the left, because of how she'd got twisted up inside the trunk. Her head lay on her left cheek.

'You're the expert, Susannah,' said Dr Shivershev, 'given your extensive *interest* in the Whitechapel murders. What do you suggest?'

'It must be vicious, and you must cut the throat first, left to right. That is something he always does,' I said.

He knelt on the bed and lifted Mrs Wiggs' upper body so that her back was resting on his legs. He held her face and chin in his left hand, and with his right he slit her throat. Her gaze remained fixed on the wooden partition dividing that room from next door. She had retained her flat-eyed expression and bloated face, but the blood only dribbled out of her neck.

'The cut needs to be deep, all the way down to her spine,' I said. 'There should be more blood.'

'We will collect blood and spread it by hand. If she were alive, it would spurt out and drain down the side of the bed. We will need to re-create that,' he said.

He opened her up, ripped her from the stomach upwards. I saw no point being sickened or coming over all faint, it would not help me. I imagined myself back in the hospital, assisting a doctor, as I had many times. I watched as he removed the surface of the abdomen and thighs and emptied the abdominal cavity, adhering carefully to the descriptions I provided of the previous victims as detailed at length in the newspapers.

'Stop,' I said. 'It's too neat, too much like an operation. The Ripper cuts with venom. He tears, he is in a hurry and he has rage. You must make it… messy and take less care.'

He nodded. 'Right, then let us really give them something to write about in your precious newspapers.'

When he hacked off the breasts as if he were sawing through meat, my cheeks watered, and I considered singing too. When he dumped them on the nightstand, I recited the Lord's Prayer in my head, or so I thought.

Dr Shivershev looked up at me, his forearms slathered in blood. 'What did you say?'

'Nothing. I'm only praying.'

'It's a bit late for that.'

He made jagged wounds in the arms. I described the shapes that I had read about in the papers and felt dizzy. I thought of my grandfather, and wondered if the dizziness was my soul leaving my body along with any goodness that was left from him or if it was just the awful stench of burning clothes as Mary fed the fire.

Dr Shivershev was still too skilful, the work should be rougher, I said. He tutted, then severed the tissues of the neck all the way down to the bone. The blood seeped out, a leak as opposed to a flow. All the while, Mary sat facing the fire, rocking backwards and forwards. The flames jumped and spat and threatened to burn the wall above them. He removed the uterus and kidneys and left these, with one of the breasts, under the head. He threw the other breast by the right foot and placed the liver between the feet, removed the intestines and threw them down on the right side, and the spleen on the left. Mary continued to sing, her weak voice running through me.

'Do you really have to keep singing that? Surely it will irritate your neighbours, as it irritates me,' I said.

'I don't know what else to do,' she said.

Dr Shivershev flicked blood so it made lines up the right side of the wall, to imitate the spurt of the artery. He sat down and stared at his bloody hands and forearms, wiped his forehead with a clean patch of arm. There was blood on his shirt. He threw his knife down on the nightstand, then took the long silver one, the one he'd pointed at me in the attic. This time, he held it by the blade with the handle towards me.

'It's your turn now,' he said.

I shook my head. 'I cannot do it. I was a nurse not a surgeon.'

'Take the knife. I wish to change instruments, I need you to assist me,' he said.

'Why am I to do it? If it's Mary who's escaping, why not let her assist you?'

Mary tutted, turned her face to the fire again, and whispered, 'I told you, she will get us all killed.'

'Mary is not of the profession,' said Dr Shivershev. 'I said I would let you go in exchange for assistance. Well, this is the assistance I need. I need to know I can trust you and for that you must be more than complicit. We must be in this together. Do not play the defenceless little maid, Susannah. I'm afraid the part doesn't suit you. Now, take the knife,' he said, 'and, Mary, keep singing.'

I looked at the knife. I thought of all the things I could do, other than take it: scream, flee, even dive through the window and run down the passageway of broken glass. It was a simple thing, was it not, to take a knife from someone's grasp? Mrs Wiggs was not the first to die by my hand. Perhaps that was why I was able to do what I did. My grandmother was right: there was a badness in me, the vermin in the yeast, the tar in the blood.

I stared at Dr Shivershev's wet hands, slick with the blood and matter from the open carcass that had once been Mrs Wiggs. I took a cloth from his bag and, holding it across my open palms, let him place the knife on top, then I cleaned it of Mrs Wiggs' blood.

He pointed at the knife he wanted to swap it for and I passed it to him. I moved to stand beside him as he discussed what should be done next, and between us we agreed that it would be prudent to cut away Mrs Wiggs' nose, cheeks, eyebrows and ears. He sliced the lips with incisions down to the chin and I suggested he make some nicks like the ones found on Catherine Eddowes and written about in the newspapers.

I had always thought of myself as an inherently good person, but I assumed now that this was how all monsters felt. I watched as my physician cut into the woman who had brushed my hair and fussed about my not having any calling cards, and knew I could not be good. I was a different kind. There was something innately bad inside me, because I was willing to do absolutely anything to save my own skin. Whether it was to remain silent under a bed, poison an old woman, or stab another and allow them to be mutilated after death. I did not feel the weight of this yet, and I wondered when and if the gravity of the things I had done would touch me.

I accepted this and then we agreed that Dr Shivershev should reduce the right thigh down to the bone. He also stripped the left thigh of the skin and the muscles as far as the knee. There was an age difference of what we guessed might be some twenty years; we needed her body to be so damaged that it would be indistinguishable from that of a twenty-seven-year-old. Dr Shivershev finished by hacking and slashing indiscriminately at any uncut flesh. Together, we made a very good Ripper.

When we had finished, he removed her heart and handed it to Mary, who, with shaking hands, wrapped it in a cloth and made a package covered in newspaper.

'It is for Mary's appointment, by request,' Dr Shivershev said. 'Someone wants the heart of a young virgin. I'm afraid Mrs Wiggs will have to do.'

By the time we'd finished, what was left of Mrs Wiggs looked to have been torn through a machine. We stepped away, blood on the both of us, but since she was dead when we began cutting, the majority had pooled and collected in a congealed swamp under the bed.

'Wait,' I said, and rearranged her legs to fit with what I assumed to be a natural position for a prostitute to be found in. I splayed them wide apart at an angle befitting a whore of the lowest order. I did not mean to offend anyone or upset them, I certainly didn't wish to slight any more of Mrs Wiggs' dignity, I was merely posing her in what I thought would make the scene impressive, in the most dramatic sense. To make up for this slur against her remains, I arranged her arms the way my mother's had been in death: left arm bent at an angle and lying across her body, right arm on the mattress; delicate, peaceful. Restful.

I was told to strip down to my chemise so Mary could cut my dress into pieces and burn it in the fire. I had brought a frock of my own, as instructed. He must have known all along how this would play out, from the moment I offered him my idea in the attic. Mary chattered as I undressed. Her vocabulary was wide and varied, she was fragile, soft, and had none of the hardness the other Ripper women appeared to have, from what I'd read. She told me she had lived in Paris and spoke a little French but didn't like the world there and had returned and struggled to find her footing.

We washed our hands as best we could with a little water,

the rest of which Dr Shivershev poured over the body. It leaked through to form a pool below. Then he took a bottle, the same kind used for my medicine, and for a reason I did not understand, filled it with the blood and put it in his coat pocket. I thought it strange, but it seemed stupid to point this out. Considering the oddity of everything that had occurred, what was a bottle of watery blood?

Mary left to meet the man with the package containing Mrs Wiggs' miraculously virginal heart, and Dr Shivershev looked about the room.

'Make sure the stuff is burned, and put the fire out. Then we go.'

'What about the trunk?' I asked.

'We'll take it with us, to Boston. We'll dispose of it there, but for now it will come in quite useful. Now let's get you back to Chelsea.'

37

D r Shivershev was to take me back to the house and bruise me, put marks on me, he said, to make it look like Thomas had beaten me more recently than my old bruises would account for.

Walter drove us back to Chelsea in the deep darkness of the very early hours. We stood at the end of the road to watch for the lamp of the policeman, waited for him to pass, and made our way to the house. Inside, Dr Shivershev hovered in the hallway as I lit a candle. Then I remembered how my husband's dead body still hung in the attic. The thought of being left alone with it up there, in a dark house, affected me in a way that cutting Mrs Wiggs had not.

'Take me as well! I can't stay here – they will catch me and I'll hang, I know I will.' My resolve had gone. Everything that had happened in that house overwhelmed me all at once and I feared I would never survive. I started to cry.

'Susannah, you will be fine. You have strong nerves. You would have made a brilliant surgeon, far superior to your husband. I've seen men faint in much less torturous conditions than you endured tonight. Keep going a little longer, remember the plan and do not give up. You are nearly there.'

'I can't! I can't do it. I don't know what I'll do if I'm alone. I might forget my story – I'll be weak. What if they question me over and over and I make mistakes?'

He pulled me close and I buried my face in his coat to the point where I could barely breathe. It was wonderful for a brief moment to be enveloped; I had forgotten how it felt to depend on someone else, even if only for a few seconds.

'Now, remember,' he said, as his rough, unshaven chin scratched the side of my face, 'the most important thing of all is not to panic.'

'What?' My heart raced at those words. He had said those same words to Thomas moments before he strung him up. What did that mean?

I struggled against him, but I could not free myself.

He let go, then shoved me with a hand on my chest against the wall of the hallway. It was enough to take my breath away. I saw a flash of silver, but my eyes travelled too slowly to do anything but anticipate the pain, which was of insane heat, a burning sensation of metal across the thin skin of my neck.

My mouth hung open but silent. My hands flew to my neck. I felt the warmth of my own blood running away from me. Tears spilled. But I did not panic. He had used me, taken my idea as his own to free Mary, and now I would die.

He held me by the shoulders as my back slid down the wall until I was on the ground. It was the way I imagined the Ripper lowered his victims before he tore them apart. His hand was cradling the back of my head as he lay me on the floor.

He took his knife and wiped it clean on my skirt, then put it back in his waistband. Then he took the bottle he had filled with the watery blood and poured it around me. I lay in a puddle of that and my own blood. Then he held my cheeks in both hands and kissed me full on the lips.

'Good luck,' he said, and left by the front door.

38

I was surrounded by arms coming to bury me: my grandmother, Mabel, Mrs Wiggs, Aisling, and all of Jack's girls, from Martha Tabram to Catherine Eddowes. In reality, the arms belonged to the nurses who were pinning me down, telling me to be calm. A swath of black fabric with a white cap entered the room. It was Matron Luckes. On seeing her, I felt as if I had earned permission to surrender and I passed out, or perhaps I was sedated.

When I woke, it was as if everything on the inside of my body was paper thin and bone dry. When I tried to use my voice, I could not avoid coughing and it hurt like hell. Any movement or tension in my neck pulled at my stitches and irritated my tender skin. I slid my fingers underneath the bandages and felt the ugly raised lumps that ran across my throat. That in itself made me panic. Now I was also a monster, inside and out.

What stirred me from this purgatory? I heard a woman whisper to me.

'He must have loved you very much... to want to take you with him.'

Those words hovered above me. I wasn't entirely sure if I heard or dreamed them. Looking back, they must have been whispered by a nurse who thought she was talking to herself. I inhaled them. Each word scuttled up my nose and choked me, got stuck in my throat and made me cough, pulled at my stitches, threatening to tear my neck open again. I was enraged. How could even my own kind see this supposed act of my husband's, his slitting of my throat, as an expression of love? How was it that the intangible phoenix of a man's ego was prized over the mutilation of a woman's real flesh?

The last thing I remembered was crawling out through my front door and onto the pavement as it was getting light. The bright flash of the policeman's torch as it found my face, and the scream of his whistle. The next time I woke, Matron Luckes was at my bedside, reading her copy of *The Nursing Record*.

'This rag used to be quite dreadful, you know, but it has vastly improved this past year,' she said. And then, 'Any surgeon worth his salt would have cut much deeper, had he meant it, Susannah.'

Even Matron was at pains to protect me from the possibility that my husband had tried to kill me out of hatred. She too was giving the dead man the benefit of the doubt. I said nothing because it didn't matter. No one would ever learn the truth from me. The odd thing was that now Thomas was gone, I didn't spare much of a thought for him at all; out of sight really was out of mind. Yet when I was married, I had felt hopelessly trapped. There was a void where he had once been, and it felt strange. I think it was peace.

In hospital I mostly spent my days recovering and worrying about being interviewed by the police. I rehearsed what I would say over and over and hoped the scar on my neck would elicit pity. Then Matron came and told me that I would not be questioned at all. One of the governors had taken it upon himself to intervene on my behalf and had spoken to his friends at the Home Office. He insisted it would be a gross injustice if I were to be harassed by the police, after everything I'd been through. After all, it was quite obvious to even the dullest policeman what had happened: my abusive husband, gripped by the madness of drink and debt, had driven away the servants and in a fit of desperation tried to murder his wife, then hanged himself. May God have mercy on his soul.

At no point was there a single question regarding Dr Shivershev. Nor did anyone seek to consult my physician. It was as if he had never existed. And Dr Shivershev had been correct about one other thing: no one gave a second thought to Mrs Wiggs. There had been sightings of a woman leaving the house with a man and a trunk. The assumption was that she, like the other servants, had abandoned an unsettled household.

I had barely any visitors in the hospital. A few nurses stopped by – mainly, I think, to see the spectacle for themselves. My solicitor from Reading, Mr Radcliffe, also came. He was full of dread, burdened with his news that my generous sister-in-law, Helen, had written to express her sympathy and had agreed to pay six months' rent on the house in Chelsea, to give me time to make other arrangements. I laughed when he read out her letter. I think he thought me disturbed, especially when I told him that once I had spoken to my sister-in-law in person, I was quite sure she would change her mind.

400

39

Helen finally agreed to a meeting after a long-winded process of letter tennis between our solicitors. It was a manipulative attempt to see which of my resources would run out first: money or motivation. I kept at it. I had a better chance of extracting a settlement if the fear of shame was fresh. I would only have to poke a finger in the open wound and tease the pain to the surface.

My solicitor tried to explain to me, as old men who know better always do, that any grounds I felt I had for improving my financial position as Thomas's widow would be best pursued via the proper legal process, through the courts. As Thomas had yet to inherit anything and we had been married for a mere five months, it was expected that the courts would say I was only entitled to inherit from his earned income, which everyone knew was a collection of debts. The Lancasters had gallantly settled all outstanding debts before the private inquest was held. I would have no real claim, Mr Radcliffe said, but perhaps the courts would feel sorry for me and encourage the Lancasters to help with a small pension. If I wasn't careful, they would humiliate me and ruin me publicly. I didn't listen.

I went to Abbingdale Hall alone. Helen would have her lawyers present. Mr Radcliffe, ever the concerned worrier for my nerves, wanted to accompany me should her team of vultures attempt to pick at my flesh.

'I'm made of sterner stuff than that,' I assured him, though I had my doubts. My newfound bravery was actually desperation. I now, quite literally, had nothing to lose.

Thomas had described his home as poetically grand, beautiful, but then he was given to embellishment. However, in this instance, I believe he underplayed it. The estate was vast. There were ornamental gardens, fountains in front of a dramatic Gothic mansion, and well-tended grounds surrounding it. The looming spire of the family church punctured the horizon. That one family could live in such splendid isolation, cut off from the misery and hopelessness, not to mention the stink, of Whitechapel, and be so arrogant as to think that a few months' rent on a shabby house in London would be all that was needed to get rid of me gave me confidence. This was my only advantage. They thought me a gold-digger, I knew that, a guttersnipe come to demand crumbs from their table. It was not a conversation I looked forward to, but I had need of security. Wasn't that how wealth worked? It was grabbed at, stolen, extorted, taken by force or any other means necessary, and protestations after the fact were dismissed and ignored. I would simply play by the same rules.

I was left waiting in a foyer so large, our voices and footsteps echoed around it. As I stood there, I spotted the vase, the one with three Greek girls carrying water. There *was* a tall girl at the back with a dour face; he had told the truth about that. I felt a pang of pity for the small boy that Thomas once was. It must have been a lonely existence for him, knowing himself to be the cuckoo, petrified he would be discovered at any moment.

I was led into a large, dark study with carved mahogany furniture and red walls. Helen was positioned like the matriarch behind a vast desk, which only exaggerated her diminutive frame. A chorus-line of white-haired and spectacled lawyers was ranged behind her, ready to bend and scrape and give outraged looks on command.

Thomas's twin sister was nothing like I'd expected; she was squat and plump. How had anybody ever thought those two were twins? I understood what Mrs Wiggs had meant when she said the Lancasters were not strong. Helen was a piggish girl in a silk lilac dress; she had a weak chin, eyes set too close together and dark rings beneath them. She was used to conversing with intelligent people, but all in her employ.

'You are not as I imagined,' said Helen as I sat down.

'Neither are you,' I replied. 'Did Thomas resemble your father?'

'See for yourself – his portrait is up there.' She gestured towards a large oil painting over the grand mantel. It was of a round, short-waisted man with the same pug face and small eyes, a set of bristling whiskers and a severe lack of hair.

'I can see the resemblance,' I said.

'You can? You would be the first.'

'I meant to you; you are certainly your father's daughter.'

Her eyes narrowed and she waved one of her lawyers forward. He presented me with papers as Helen talked.

'We understand you find yourself unexpectedly widowed. We assumed you might return to your family, but, as your solicitor has explained, you don't have one. Therefore, as a gesture of goodwill and a token of our sympathy, we would like to offer you the sum of fifty pounds. This is in addition to the rent we have paid in advance on the property in Chelsea. I should imagine you are in need of some immediate funds—'

'Not good enough,' I said, and pushed the piece of paper away without looking at it.

Her gaggle of penguins coughed and balked.

Helen stared at me, her nostrils flared. She tried not to bite her bottom lip. 'Let me be clear...' She struggled to know what to call me. 'There is nothing in this house that will ever belong to you. You may think you have some claim on my brother's estate, but you do not. I'm sure you are bitterly disappointed that your marriage was, to all intents and purposes, a disaster, but perhaps if you'd known him a little better, you might have declined his impulsive offer to wed. However, I'm guessing the decision wasn't entirely based on his charms. At your age, you should have known better, but then I suppose money brings out the worst in all of us.'

'You haven't addressed me directly once, Helen, not as "Susannah", as a sister would, nor as "Mrs Lancaster". Why is that?'

'Because I cannot bring myself to. We are not sisters, and you have not earned the right to be called "Lancaster", not as far as I am concerned.'

'Tell me then, what did I do to earn *this*?' I pulled down the neck of my dress to show my red scar.

All of them flinched, except Helen, who would doubtless have suffered a hot poker in a dark crevice rather than give me a reaction.

'I would like to speak to you privately, Helen, just once, so that I may explain why you might prefer to work with me on a quiet resolution regarding our mutual issues.'

Her solicitors tried to interrupt, but Helen silenced them all with a raised hand. They stopped like a pack of well-trained gundogs. It reminded me of how Thomas would quiet Mrs Wiggs.

Once they had left, I gave her my proposal. I would accept a lump sum and they would purchase for me and make a gift to me of the house in Chelsea. On receipt of the deeds and the money, I would never bother them again.

Helen laughed, which was as expected. 'What on earth makes you think I would agree to such... extortion?' she asked.

'If you don't, I will be forced to sell my pitiful story, which will run along the following themes: your brother was a sadistic, perverted pig who abused his wife, sexually and physically. Of course, I will be obliged to reveal intimate details of the bedchamber, and I will also need to disclose that he was rather workshy and, quite frankly, not very good at his job. I will make public the embarrassing truth that he was an active and not at all clandestine homosexual who frequented mollies' houses – a practice that has been illegal these past three years, as you will know – which will do nothing to enhance the reputation of the Lancaster family. And lastly, I will make it widely known that he was not in reality your brother at all.'

The blood visibly drained from Helen's face. She tried to steady her rapid breathing. This woman had shared a nursery with Thomas and, deep down, as ridiculous as it seemed, there was something in her that knew this to be the truth. I was probably the first person in the world to articulate the instincts she'd kept contained since childhood.

I explained what Mrs Wiggs had told me about finding Helen's real baby brother dead in his crib and swapping the real Lancaster boy with her own. Hadn't she ever noticed that Mrs Wiggs was colour-blind, like her brother?

'The thing I struggle with most, I think, even though I have no children of my own, is how your mother could fail to recognise her own child. But then Thomas said she only ever came downstairs for dinner or to go to parties. I imagine the newspapers will speculate along the same themes,' I said.

I also told a lie. I claimed that Mrs Wiggs had revealed to me the exact spot where she'd buried the Lancaster baby. If Helen preferred to keep this scandal between us, she could agree to my terms and pay me promptly. Otherwise, in order to keep my fire burning and food in my belly, I would tell the first journalist who would listen.

'Where is Mrs Wiggs?' asked Helen. Her face was a picture, the smugness gone. Her mind was clearly desperate to fathom how she could dominate again. Testing her tongue on those in her employ had not been good exercise.

'I honestly don't know. She was seen leaving with a man and a trunk,' I said. 'Perhaps she is making up for lost time.'

'You would be willing to shame yourself to extort a

pension from a family who have done nothing to deserve it? You are not the only one who has endured my brother's temper. He was a cruel child: spoiled, explosive. My mother was petrified of him, as was I.'

'I don't want a pension; I want a chance. What I'm asking for is nothing to you but will change my life for ever. If you think I'm going to go away quietly after putting up with your brother and being left with such a pretty necklace, you're wrong. Give me what I want and you'll never hear of me again.'

It was small change to the Lancasters and Helen was a sensible girl. It frustrated the hell out of her that she would never know if I was bluffing, but she had her lawyers draw up the settlement.

As I left the study, she remained seated.

'I don't want my mother to know about this, but tell me where my brother is, my real brother. I want to give him a proper burial – privately of course.'

'Ask me again in ten years,' I said. It was a trick, of course. That woman was no more interested in her brother than she was in me.

'Funny, don't you think?' she said. 'Look at us, both dressed up in mourning for a man we feel nothing but bitterness towards.'

By the end of the month, I was the legal owner of the house in Chelsea and had £2000 in the bank.

40

There I was, back in Chelsea, rattling around an empty house, when the visitor I least expected knocked on the door: one Miss Mabel Mullens.

Looking a lot plumper and apple-cheeked again, she was back to being beautiful, which, I discovered, was how I preferred her. She was smirking on the doorstep, arms akimbo. It was hard to believe we'd hated each other for no other reason than the belief that there could not be enough good fortune for the both of us. We had moved past that terrain somehow and come straight to a rather abrasive affection.

'Come on, let's see this scar I've heard so much about,' was the first thing she said. Our relationship continued in this vein for many years after.

I pulled down my bandages and stuck my chin up, showed her my scar, still ugly, scabbed and bruised.

'I can barely see it! What a huge fuss about nothing,' she said.

My one solace, I told her, was that Dr Haslip hadn't been on duty, or else I would have woken up with my hand sewn to my forehead and my neck still open. I noticed little lines around her eyes when she laughed; they hadn't been there before, but they suited her. She wasted no time in telling me she was still 'off' men.

'I haven't the stomach for the troubles they bring. You may not believe it, but I'm ward sister at a hospital. The probationers think I'm a dragon – I take my inspiration from you.'

'I assume you mean the Reading Union? Only a workhouse could have you as ward sister,' I said.

She laughed again. But no, she said, she'd found a job at the East London Hospital for Children, where it had spread like a whisky fire that a nurse from the London had been nearly murdered by her surgeon husband.

When I asked why she'd not kept in touch as she'd said she would, she swore blind she'd written twice. The second because she'd not received an answer to the first, which she'd sent as soon as she reached her father's farm. She'd assumed I didn't want anything further to do with her and didn't write again. I would eventually find her letters, along with Aisling's hairbrush and the wooden box with all her things in it, under the floorboards in Mrs Wiggs' bedroom.

We talked for hours. Mabel had come to apologise, said she'd wept for nights, realising that she'd burdened me with her problems when I'd had my own and not said a word.

'I assumed you had struck gold, Susannah. I'm so sorry.'

I didn't dare tell her the truth. I'd told no one, although at times I was bursting. That wasn't strictly true: sometimes I talked to Aisling, and I believed she heard me.

Our conversation eventually drifted towards what happened after I gave her the address from Dr Shivershev.

It was for Princelet Street, in Whitechapel. When Mabel went there, she saw it was a cobbler's shop: small and dingy and full of cobblers' clutter. A tall Jew with a dark beard and his shirt open to his chest emerged from the back and asked her what her business was. On the piece of paper it had said to introduce herself as a woman suffering from chronic headaches. She felt a fool saying the words, but the man nodded then told her to go and stand on the corner of Fashion Street.

As she waited under a lamppost, heart skipping beats, twin girls came towards her, giggling, one carrying a skipping rope and the other a scarf. They skipped around her in circles and she thought they would pick her pockets and she'd be left penniless and still pregnant.

'Won't you play with us?' asked one of the girls.

They were about ten or so, she said, with big brown eyes and long dark hair, beautiful girls, identically dressed in clean blue dresses with black brocade, polished shoes, and blue ribbons in their hair that had been artfully tied by someone who cared.

'Small versions of you, Susannah. I took that as a good omen, so, believe it or not, I let them blindfold me.'

Still giggling, they held a hand each and led her down the road and into a house. She feared she was going to be robbed or killed, but they had such soft little hands, she said, that she half didn't care what happened. There was no going back. They steered her through a building and into a courtyard, laughed when she slipped down a step outside, then tugged her into another house, and through room after room, until finally they sat her down in an armchair. One of them jumped on the arm of the chair and kissed her on the cheek as the other untied the scarf from her eyes, still laughing. Then they ran off.

As Mabel's eyes adjusted to the darkness, she saw there was an old lady sitting in a chair in the corner. She nearly screamed.

'She must have been a hundred at least! Her eyes were milky, her skin yellow; I thought she was dead.'

The room was dark and sparsely furnished, but every surface was covered with lace, ornaments and trinkets. The windows were draped with heavy muslins and fussy scalloped curtains; barely any natural light was allowed in.

'Don't mind my mother,' said a woman who appeared in the doorway. 'She can't see you.'

She was dressed head to toe in black, with a black lace veil covering her face. Mabel said she had an accent that might have been French but could have been Russian, she wasn't sure. I knew, of course, that it was Irina, Dr Shivershev's housekeeper, but I didn't say anything. Questions were not to be encouraged.

'Could have been anything. I only saw her hands, which had no spots or marks. I could see the shine of her eyes through the lace. I had the sense she was older than us, but still attractive, even underneath that veil.'

Mabel followed Irina upstairs to a room that had been set up for a specific purpose. The windows were blocked with heavy drapes, and there were many lamps to see by, even though it was the middle of the day with the sun at its brightest. It was here that Mabel began to think she might die.

In the corner of the room there was an old birthing chair, a heavy mahogany monster tilted back, with leather arm-straps, and wooden planks for the legs to be splayed apart, and more leather straps to keep them still. The chair had half a seat, like an arch with the middle missing. A steel bucket was on the floor under the missing part.

'Don't be afraid,' Irina said. 'The chair frightens everyone, but it works well. It is better for you and you will not feel much.'

Mabel stripped down to her chemise and sat in the chair. She let herself be strapped in by Irina and prayed that if she was to die it would happen quickly.

She survived. Irina told her she must go straight home and lock herself away with her chamber pot.

'Make sure to be as discreet as you can. Say nothing to anyone,' Irina told her. 'There are many who need my assistance. If I am arrested, who will help them?'

For this, Mabel paid Irina two pounds. It was my own money, a sum I would not have been able to get from Thomas without questions.

'The girls will take you to a place you can find a cab.' Irina returned Mabel to the room with the old woman. There was a cuckoo clock on the mantelpiece that chimed on the hour. The two little girls blindfolded her again and led her to the top of Commercial Street.

'Is the lady all better now?' one of them asked her.

'Yes, I think so,' Mabel replied, still dull from the ether, and they ran off.

'That's the thing about London – you can walk around in a blindfold and no one bats an eyelid,' she said. 'No wonder this Ripper hasn't been caught. He's probably been running about with a knife in one hand and a kidney in the other, and people simply haven't noticed.'

Desperate not to spend money, Mabel ignored Irina's advice and took the omnibus. She'd planned to leave the milliner's the next day but decided she couldn't bear another minute, so fled in the middle of the night, preferring to wait at the station for the morning train rather than spend another hour there. The night-watchman came towards her on the platform and asked if she was all right. Thinking him another pervert, she gave him short shrift. He disappeared but came back five minutes later with a blanket, and she burst into tears. He told her she was welcome to wait in his office if she liked, it had a small fire, until the trains started in the morning.

'I don't mean anything improper; you needn't worry. I'm too old for all that, but there's a murderer on the loose, and it don't bear thinking about,' he said.

'So there are decent men, but apparently they're all old enough to be my grandad,' said Mabel.

The experience had left its mark on her face. She may not have had a scar as crude as mine, but it was in the lines around her eyes and the new sharpness in her features. She enjoyed being back at work, she said, especially with the children, but sharing the nurses' accommodation was a bore.

'Have you ever thought about renting a room in Chelsea?' I asked her.

I decided that I would fill my house in Chelsea, and Mabel would be my first tenant. The rent was cheap of course. I was not in it to make money.

41

The murder of Mary Kelly was an opera. It was the climax of a wonderful piece of theatre and had been partly of my creation. The newspapers fed off it for months. The gruesome details flew around the world, bounced off every wall in England, and Whitechapel was forever cast as the epitome of grotesque London.

I spent a lot of time with my notebooks and clippings in the ensuing days and weeks. There was no need to squirrel them away in the back dining room now that Mrs Wiggs was no longer there to pry, and I found that it was not only interesting, and absorbing, to read through all my old accounts, but useful too. It helped me reflect on what I had done, what I had become, and why. I tried not to punish myself for my hobby too much, and to think of Dr Shivershev's words when he'd explained why he collected those specimens. It was about understanding, and knowledge. He was correct, it was not always obvious in the beginning where our curiosity will take us, we wish to learn something but we are not sure what. I understood that my curiosity was driven out of a need to understand in some small way what my mother had been through, to assuage the guilt I felt over her demise. I understood enough now, I only wanted to close the remaining chapters, to tidy up the ends. Then I would close this experience down, file it away for what it was, and move on.

First, I described the last evening of Mary Kelly – or Marie Jeanette, as I called her, although of course neither was the real identity of the mutilated corpse, it being that of Mrs Wiggs.

Next, I sent my imagination back into the past, to the day three years prior when I had finally found myself free to leave Reading and begin my career as a nurse, at the London. I wanted to look at the person I was before I met Thomas, before I met Aisling, to try and see myself through these other, distant eyes I had now. Was I already of abandoned character, like my grandmother had insisted? Had my father's blood, and my first five years in the Nichol, tainted me?

Over time, the Nichol went the same way as Whitechapel's other degenerate and labyrinthine slums. It was built through, built on, and rendered invisible beneath new roads and shiny new tenement blocks laid on top. Some of the old roads remained, but Dorset Street and Miller's Court were gone.

After Mary Kelly, the Ripper murders stopped. Vulnerable women were still beaten and killed in Whitechapel, but they were back to being murdered by their menfolk, behind closed doors, dying quietly without attention. The papers said the Ripper had perhaps succumbed to syphilis, infected by the whores he sought revenge on, or maybe he'd killed himself through madness, or been imprisoned for something else. Or perhaps he'd emigrated?

It was in the summer of 1889 that I received a package marked from California, the United States of America. A brown box, battered and thrown about on its travels. Intrigued, I took it into the front dining room and tore it open.

Inside the package was a small wooden box, and inside this, two envelopes, one addressed to me and the other to Detective Inspector Abberline. The box was full of sawdust, and nestled in the top was something wrapped in red velvet. It had a piece of brocade attached to it and the edges were jagged, as if it had been torn or hacked at. I ripped open the envelope addressed to me and read the letter inside:

Dear Susannah,

I could not be more pleased to hear that you have decided to join our illustrious ranks. I wish you all the best and think of you often.

I'm afraid our friends in London require one more task to be completed. I ask you to take a fresh envelope and from a different spot in London post the enclosed letter to Detective Inspector Abberline of the Metropolitan Police. Do not touch it. Wear gloves, and be aware of a new science they call fingerprinting.

Your husband frequented many places to meet likeminded individuals; one of these is to be found in Cleveland Street. Our friends and sponsors wish to assist the police and give them some gentle encouragement so that they might seek adventure in this new direction and occupy themselves with the 'criminal' behaviour therein. The letter is a present of information about these premises and the activities taking place there. Hopefully, it will give poor old Abberline something more fruitful to focus on. Who knows, our business might go back to running smoothly again.

I enclose a gift. I hope you appreciate the humour with which it is intended. I did deliberate, but I am sure that even if it does not amuse you, you will find it useful in your work one day. Forgive me for the shock.

Your trustworthy Russian,

V

I unwrapped the velvet and out fell a long, thin, silver knife. It was the one he had used on Mrs Wiggs in the dark of Mary Kelly's room, and the one I had taken and cleaned for him. It was also the knife Dr Shivershev had used to cut my throat.

I had no idea how to feel. I burst out laughing and picked it up. The light bounced off the blade and I recalled the flash of silver before I'd felt its blade being dragged across my neck.

There was no one around to hear me. Mabel was at work and the others somewhere out of sight. Sarah, our old scullery maid, was now housekeeper. She came back when I placed an advertisement in *The Times*. She told me she hadn't left of her own accord but that Mrs Wiggs had fired them all. I employed both her and Cook again. Sarah now spends her days barking at a clumsy young girl called Florence. I have three lodgers: a rather strange Russian, an aloof Indian lady and an annoyingly over-friendly woman from Edinburgh. They are students at the London School of Medicine for Women. As am I.

You see, I enrolled to become a doctor. Someone once suggested I'd make a good one.

About the Author

Clare Whitfield is a UK based writer living in a suburb where the main cultural landmark is a home store / Starbucks combo. She is the wife of a tattoo artist, mother of a small benign dictator and relies on a black Labrador for emotional stability. She has been a dancer, copywriter, amateur fire breather, buyer and mediocre weightlifter. This is her first novel.